P9-EFI-622

PRAISE FOR MARY JO PUTNEY, HAILED BY *ROMANTIC TIMES* AS "A DREAMSPINNER OF THE HIGHEST ORDER."

Silk and Secrets

"No other romance author today writes with more exquisite perception of the human heart and spirit than the extraordinarily gifted Ms. Putney . . . this remarkable novel of high adventure and unquenchable love is a stunning reading experience, one you will remember and cherish forever. 4 + !"
—*Romantic Times*

Silk and Shadows

"Dynamite! [This is] Mary Jo Putney's absolutely best yet." —Laura Kinsale

"This one has everything . . . revenge . . . obsession . . . love. I couldn't put it down, and I don't think readers will, either." —Amanda Quick

"A story twisted with passion, violence, and redemption. Ms. Putney just gets better and better!" —Nora Roberts

Uncommon Vows

"A wondrous tale brimming with adventure, intrigue, and memorable romance." —*Romantic Times*

Dearly Beloved

"Sets a new standard of excellence . . . one of the best books of this or any year!" —*Romantic Times*

◆ TOPAZ   (0451)

EXPERIENCE A NEW WORLD
OF ROMANCE

☐ **SWEET EVERLASTING by Patricia Gaffney.** Chance brings sophisticated Tyler Wilkes, M.D. and fawnlike mountain girl Carrie Wiggins together. But something as strong as fate breaks through the barriers of birth and breeding, pride and fear, which has kept them apart ... as each seeks to heal the other's wounds with a passion neither can deny and all the odds against them cannot defeat.   (403754—$4.99)

☐ **BY LOVE UNVEILED by Deborah Martin.** Lady Marianne trusted no one—especially not Garett, the Earl of Falkham, the man who seemed to be her most dangerous enemy. Somehow, in a world of treachery and passion each would have to learn to trust one another, as a desire that could not be disguised turned into a passionate love that all the powers of the world could not defeat.   (403622—$4.99)

☐ **THUNDER AND ROSES by Mary Jo Putney.** Paying a price for his aid, Clare Morgan agrees to live with the Demon Earl for three months, letting the world think the worst. As allies, they fight to save her community. As adversaries, they explore the terrains of power and sensuality. And as lovers, they surrender to a passion that threatens the very foundation of their lives.
(403673—$4.99)

☐ **WILD EMBRACE by Cassie Edwards.** Exquisite Elizabeth Easton discovers the real wilderness when the noble Indian brave, Strong Heart, forces her to go with him in a flight back to his Suquamish people. Here both of them are free of all the pride and prejudice that kept them apart in the white world ... as this superbly handsome, strong and sensitive man becomes her guide on passion' path to unfettered joy and love.   (403614—$4.99)

☐ **WHITE LILY by Linda Ladd.** Ravishing Lily Courtland has the extraordinary gift of second sight. Harte Delaney has never met a woman as magically mysterious as this beauty for whom he risks all to rescue and possess. Amid the flames of war and the heat of passion, these two people find themselves lost in a heart-stopping adventure with their own destiny and the fate of a nation hanging in a breathless balance.   (403630—$4.99)

☐ **NO SWEETER HEAVEN by Katherine Kingsley.** Pascal LaMartine and Elizabeth Bowes had nothing in common until the day she accidentally landed at his feet, and looked up into the face of a fallen angel. Drawn in to a dangerous battle of intrigue and wits, each discovered how strong passion was ... and how perilous it can be.   (403665—$4.99)

Prices slightly higher in Canada

Buy them at your local bookstore or use this convenient coupon for ordering.

NEW AMERICAN LIBRARY
P.O. Box 999 – Dept. #17109
Bergenfield, New Jersey 07621

Please send me the books I have checked above.
I am enclosing $_____ (please add $2.00 to cover postage and handling).
Send check or money order (no cash or C.O.D.'s) or charge by Mastercard or
VISA (with a $15.00 minimum). Prices and numbers are subject to change without
notice.

Card #_____ Exp. Date _____
Signature_____
Name_____
Address_____
City _____ State _____ Zip Code _____

For faster service when ordering by credit card call **1-800-253-6476**

Allow a minimum of 4-6 weeks for delivery. This offer is subject to change without notice.

THUNDER AND ROSES

by

Mary Jo Putney

A TOPAZ BOOK

TOPAZ
Published by the Penguin Group
Penguin Books USA Inc., 375 Hudson Street,
New York, New York 10014, U.S.A.
Penguin Books Ltd, 27 Wrights Lane,
London W8 5TZ, England
Penguin Books Australia Ltd, Ringwood,
Victoria, Australia
Penguin Books Canada Ltd, 10 Alcorn Avenue,
Toronto, Ontario, Canada M4V 3B2
Penguin Books (N.Z.) Ltd, 182–190 Wairau Road,
Auckland 10, New Zealand

Penguin Books Ltd, Registered Offices:
Harmondsworth, Middlesex, England

First published by Topaz,
an imprint of New American Library,
a division of Penguin Books USA Inc.

First Printing, May, 1993
10 9 8 7 6 5 4 3 2 1
Copyright © Mary Jo Putney, 1993
All rights reserved

Topaz is a trademark of New American Library,
a division of Penguin Books USA Inc.

Printed in the United States of America

Without limiting the rights under copyright reserved above, no part of this publication
may be reproduced, stored in or introduced into a retrieval system, or transmitted, in
any form, or by any means (electronic, mechanical, photocopying, recording, or
otherwise), without the prior written permission of both the copyright owner and the
above publisher of this book.

BOOKS ARE AVAILABLE AT QUANTITY DISCOUNTS WHEN USED TO PROMOTE PRODUCTS
OR SERVICES. FOR INFORMATION PLEASE WRITE TO PREMIUM MARKETING DIVISION,
PENGUIN BOOKS USA INC., 375 HUDSON STREET, NEW YORK, NEW YORK 10014.

If you purchased this book without a cover you should be aware that this book is
stolen property. It was reported as "unsold and destroyed" to the publisher and
neither the author nor the publisher has received any payment for this "stripped
book."

To Marianne and Karen,
two of my favorite females

Prologue

WINTER MISTS swirled about as they scaled the wall that enclosed the estate. The ghostly landscape proved empty of human life, and no one saw the intruders drop from the wall and make their way across the carefully tended grounds.

Softly Nikki asked, "Will we steal a chicken here, Mama?"

His mother, Marta, shook her head. "Our business is more important than chickens."

The effort of speaking triggered a coughing spell, and she bent over, thin body shaking. Uneasy and distressed, Nikki touched her arm. Sleeping under hedges was making the cough worse, and there had been little to eat. He hoped that soon they would return to the Romany *kumpania*, where there would be food and fire and fellowship.

She straightened, face pale but determined, and they continued walking. The only color in the winter scene was the garish purple of her skirt.

Eventually they emerged from the trees onto a swath of grassy turf that surrounded a sprawling stone mansion. Awed, Nikki said, "A great lord lives here?"

"Aye. Look well, for someday this will be yours."

He stared at the house, feeling an odd mixture of emotions. Surprise, excitement, doubt, finally disdain. "The Rom do not live in stone houses that kill the sky."

"But you are *didikois*, half-blood. It is right that you live in such a place."

Shocked, he turned to stare at her. "No! I am *tacho rat*, true blood, not Gorgio."

"Your blood is true for both Rom and Gorgio." She

sighed, her beautiful face drawn. "Though you have been raised as a Rom, your future lies with the Gorgios."

He started to protest, but she shushed him with a quick hand motion as hoofbeats sounded. They withdrew into the shrubbery and watched two riders canter up the driveway and halt in front of the house. The taller man dismounted and briskly climbed the wide stone steps, leaving his mount to the care of his companion.

"Fine horses," Nikki whispered enviously.

"Aye. That must be the Earl of Aberdare," Marta murmured. "He looks just as Kenrick said."

They waited until the tall man had gone inside and the groom had taken the horses away. Then Marta beckoned to Nikki and they hastened across the grass and up the steps. The shiny brass doorknocker was shaped like a dragon. He would have liked to touch it, but it was too high.

Instead of knocking, his mother tried the doorknob. It turned easily and she stepped inside, Nikki right on her heels. His eyes widened when he saw that they were in a marble-floored hall large enough to hold an entire Romany kumpania.

The only man in sight wore the elaborate livery of a footman. An expression of comical shock on his long face, he gasped, "Gypsies!" He grabbed a bellpull and rang for assistance. "Get out this instant! If you aren't off the estate in five minutes, you'll be turned over to the magistrate."

Marta took Nikki's hand in hers. "We're here to see the earl. I have something of his."

"Something you stole?" the footman sneered. "You've never been that close to him. Be gone with you."

"No! I must see him."

"Not bloody likely," the footman snarled as he advanced.

Marta waited until he was close, then darted to one side.

Swearing, the servant swerved and made a futile grab at the interlopers. At the same time, three more servants appeared, summoned by the bellpull.

Fixing a fierce gaze on the men, Marta hissed with practiced menace, "I must see the earl! My curse will be on any man who tries to stop me."

The servants stopped dead in their tracks. Nikki almost laughed aloud at their expressions. Though she was only a woman, Marta easily baffled and frightened the Gorgios. Nikki was proud of her. Who but a Rom could wield such power with mere words?

His mother's hand tightened on his and they backed away, deeper into the house. Before the servants could shake off their fear, a deep voice boomed, "What the devil is going on?"

Tall and utterly arrogant, the earl strode into the hall. "Gypsies," he said with disgust. "Who allowed these filthy creatures to come inside?"

Marta said baldly, "I have brought your grandson, Lord Aberdare. Kenrick's son—the only grandchild you will ever have."

The room went dead silent as the earl's shocked gaze moved to Nikki's face. Marta continued, "If you doubt me . . ."

After a shaken moment, the earl said, "Oh, I'm willing to believe this revolting brat might be Kenrick's—his parentage is written on his face." He gave Marta the hot, hungry look that Gorgio men often gave women of the Rom. "It's easy to see why my son would bed you, but a Gypsy bastard is of no interest to me."

"My son is no bastard." Marta fished into her bodice and brought out two grubby folded papers. "Since Gorgios set great store on papers, I kept the proof—my marriage lines and the record of Nikki's birth."

Lord Aberdare glanced impatiently at the documents, then stiffened. "My son *married* you?"

"Aye, he did," she said proudly. "In a Gorgio church as well as in the way of the Rom. And you should be glad he did, old man, for now you have an heir. With your other sons dead, you will have no other."

Expression savage, the earl said, "Very well. How much do you want for him? Will fifty pounds do?"

For an instant, Nikki saw rage in his mother's eyes. Then her expression changed, becoming cunning. "A hundred gold guineas."

The lord took a key from his waistcoat pocket and handed it to the oldest servant. "Get it from my strongbox."

Nikki laughed aloud. Speaking in Romany, he said, "This is the finest scheme ever, Mama. Not only have you convinced this stupid old Gorgio that I am of his blood, but he is willing to give you gold! We will feast for the next year. When I escape tonight, where shall I meet you—maybe by the old oak tree that we used to get over the wall?"

Marta shook her head and replied in the same language. "You must not run away, Nikki. The Gorgio truly is your grandfather, and this is your home now." Briefly her fingers fluttered through Nikki's hair. For a moment he thought she would say more, for she could not possibly mean what she had said.

The servant returned and handed Marta a jingling leather purse. After expertly evaluating the contents, she raised her outer skirt and tucked the purse into a pocket in her petticoat. Nikki was shocked at her action—didn't these Gorgios know that she had contaminated them, made them *marhime*, by raising her skirt in their presence? But they were oblivious to the insult.

She gave Nikki one last stare, and there was wildness in her eyes. "Treat him well, old man, or my curse will follow you beyond the grave. May I die tonight if this is not so."

She turned and walked away across the polished floor, her layered skirts swirling. A servant opened the door for her. Inclining her head like a princess, she stepped outside.

With sudden horror, Nikki realized that his mother was serious—she truly did mean to leave him with the Gorgios. He raced after her, screaming, "Mama, Mama!"

Before he could reach her, the door swung shut in his face, trapping him in the sky-killing house. As he grabbed the knob, a footman caught him around the waist. Nikki kneed the man in the belly and clawed at the pale Gorgio face. The servant bellowed and another came to help.

Feet and fists flailing, Nikki yelled, "I am Rom! I won't stay in this ugly place!"

The earl frowned, revolted by the display of raw emotion. Such behavior must be beaten out of the brat, along with every other trace of his Gypsy blood. Kenrick had also been wild, spoiled by his doting mother. It was the news of Kenrick's death that had brought on the apoplexy that had turned the countess into the living corpse that she was now.

Harshly the earl ordered, "Take the boy to the nursery and clean him up. Burn those rags and find something more suitable."

It took two men to subdue the boy. He was still wailing for his mother as they carried his thrashing figure up the stairs.

His face a bitter mask, the earl looked again at the documents that proved that the dusky little heathen was the earl's only surviving descendant. Nicholas Kenrick Davies, according to the registration of his birth. It was impossible to doubt the bloodlines; if the boy weren't so dark, he might almost have been Kenrick at the same age.

But dear God, a Gypsy! A dark, foreign-looking, black-eyed Gypsy. Seven years old and as adept at lying and thievery as he was ignorant of civilized living. Nonetheless, that ragged, filthy creature was the heir to Aberdare.

Once the earl had prayed desperately for an heir, never dreaming that his prayers would be answered in such a way. Even if his invalid countess died and left him free to remarry, the sons of a second wife would be superceded by that Gypsy brat.

As he thought, his fingers clenched on the papers. Perhaps, if he was ever able to remarry and have more sons, something could be done. But meanwhile, he must make the best of the boy. Reverend Morgan, the Methodist preacher in the village, could teach Nicholas reading and manners and the other basics required before he could be sent to a proper school.

The earl turned on his heel and entered his study, slamming his door against the anguished cries of "Mama! Mama! Mama!" that echoed sorrowfully through the halls of Aberdare.

1

Wales, March 1814

THEY CALLED him the Demon Earl, or sometimes Old Nick. Hushed voices whispered that he had seduced his grandfather's young wife, broken his grandfather's heart, and driven his own bride to her grave.

They said he could do anything.

Only the last claim interested Clare Morgan as her gaze followed the man racing his stallion down the valley as if all the fires of hell pursued him. Nicholas Davies, the Gypsy Earl of Aberdare, had finally come home, after four long years. Perhaps he would stay, but it was equally possible that he would be gone again tomorrow. Clare must act quickly.

Yet she lingered a little longer, knowing that he would never see her in the cluster of trees from which she watched. He rode bareback, flaunting his wizardry with horses, dressed in black except for the scarlet scarf knotted around his throat. He was too far away for her to see his face. She wondered if he had changed, then decided that the real question was not if, but how much. Whatever the truth behind the violent events that had driven him away, it had to have been searing.

Would he remember her? Probably not. He'd only seen her a handful of times, and she had been a child then. Not only had he been Viscount Tregar, but he was four years older than she, and older children seldom paid much attention to younger ones.

The reverse was not true.

As she walked back to the village of Penreith, she reviewed her pleas and arguments. One way or another, she must persuade the Demon Earl to help. No one else could make a difference.

For a few brief minutes, while his stallion blazed across the estate like a mad wind, Nicholas was able to lose himself in the exhilaration of pure speed. But reality closed in again when the ride ended and he returned to the house.

In his years abroad he had often dreamed of Aberdare, torn between yearning and fear of what he would find there. The twenty-four hours since his return had proved that his fears had been justified. He'd been a fool to think that four years away could obliterate the past. Every room of the house, every acre of the valley, held memories. Some were happy ones, but they had been overlaid by more recent events, tainting what he had once loved. Perhaps, in the furious moments before he died, the old earl had laid a curse on the valley so that his despised grandson would never again know happiness here.

Nicholas walked to the window of his bedroom and stared out. The valley was as beautiful as ever—wild in the heights, lushly cultivated lower down. The delicate greens of spring were beginning to show. Soon there would be daffodils. As a boy, he had helped the gardeners plant drifts of bulbs under the trees, getting thoroughly muddy in the process. His grandfather had seen it as further proof of Nicholas's low breeding.

He raised his eyes to the ruined castle that brooded over the valley. For centuries those immensely thick walls had been both fortress and home to the Davies family. More peaceful times had led Nicholas's great-great-grandfather to build the mansion considered suitable for one of Britain's wealthiest families.

Among many other advantages, the house had plenty of bedrooms. Nicholas had been grateful for that the previous day. He never considered using the state apartment that had been his grandfather's. Entering his own rooms proved to be a gut-wrenching experience, for it was impossible to see his old bed without imagining Caroline in it, her lush body naked and her eager arms beckoning. He had retreated immediately to a guest room that was safely anonymous, like an expensive hotel.

Yet even there, he slept poorly, haunted by bad dreams and worse memories. By morning, he had reached the harsh conclusion that he must sever all ties with Aberdare. He would never find peace of mind here, any more than he had in four years of constant, restless travel.

Might it be possible to break the entail so that the estate could be sold? He must ask his lawyer. The thought of selling made him ache with emptiness. It would be like cutting off an arm—yet if a limb was festering, there was no other choice.

Still, selling would not be wholly without compensations. It pleased Nicholas to know that getting rid of the place would give his grandfather the ghostly equivalent of apoplexy, wherever the hypocritical old bastard was now.

Abruptly he spun on his heel, stalked out of his bedroom, and headed downstairs to the library. How to live the rest of his life was a topic too dismal to contemplate, but he could certainly do something about the next few hours. With a little effort and a lot of brandy, they could be eliminated entirely.

Clare had never been inside Aberdare before. It was as grand as she had expected, but gloomy, with most of the furniture still concealed under holland covers. Four years of emptiness had made the place forlorn as well. The butler, Williams, was equally gloomy. He hadn't wanted to take Clare to the earl without first announcing her, but he had grown up in the village, so she was able to persuade him. He escorted her down a long corridor, then opened the door to the library. "Miss Clare Morgan to see you, my lord. She said her business is urgent."

Taking a firm grip on her courage, Clare walked past Williams into the library, not wanting to give the earl time to refuse her. If she failed today, she wouldn't get another chance.

The earl stood by a window, staring out across the valley. His coat had been tossed over a chair, and his shirt-sleeved informality gave him a rakish air. Odd that he had been known as Old Nick; even now, he was scarcely thirty.

As the door closed behind Williams, the earl turned, his forbidding gaze going right to Clare. Though not unusually tall, he radiated power. She remembered that even at the age when most lads were gawky, he had moved with absolute physical mastery.

On the surface, he seemed much the same. If anything, he was even more handsome than he had been four years ago. She would not have thought that possible. But he had indeed changed; she saw it in his eyes. Once they had brimmed with teasing laughter that invited others to laugh with him. Now they were as impenetrable as polished Welsh flint. The duels and flagrant affairs and public scandals had left their mark.

As she hesitated, wondering if she should speak first, he asked, "Are you related to Reverend Thomas Morgan?"

"His daughter. I'm the schoolmistress in Penreith."

His bored gaze flicked over her. "That's right, sometimes he had a grubby brat in tow."

Stung, she retorted, "I wasn't half as grubby as you were."

"Probably not," he agreed, a faint smile in his eyes. "I was a disgrace. During lessons, your father often referred to you as a model of saintly decorum. I hated you sight unseen."

It shouldn't have hurt, but it did. Hoping that it would irritate him, Clare said sweetly, "And to me, he said that you were the cleverest boy he had ever taught, and that you had a good heart in spite of your wildness."

"Your father's judgment leaves much to be desired," the earl said, his momentary levity vanishing. "As the preacher's daughter, I assume you are seeking funds for some boring, worthy cause. Apply to my steward in the future rather than bothering me. Good day, Miss Morgan."

He was starting to turn away when she said quickly, "What I wish to discuss is not a matter for your steward."

His mobile lips twisted. "But you do want something, don't you? Everyone does."

He strolled to a decanter-covered cabinet and refilled a

glass that he had been carrying. "Whatever it is, you won't get it from me. Noblesse oblige was my grandfather's province. Kindly leave while the atmosphere is still civil."

She realized uneasily that he was well on his way to being drunk. Well, she had dealt with drunks before. "Lord Aberdare, people in Penreith are suffering, and you are the only man in a position to make a difference. It will cost you very little in time or money . . ."

"I don't care how little is involved," he said forcefully. "I don't want anything to do with the village, or the people who live in it! Is that clear? Now get the hell out."

Clare felt her stubbornness rising. "I am not asking for your help, my lord, I am demanding it," she snapped. "Shall I explain now, or should I wait until you're sober?"

He regarded her with amazement. "If anyone here is drunk, it would appear to be you. If you think your sex will protect you from physical force, you're wrong. Will you go quietly, or am I going to have to carry you out?" He moved toward her with purposeful strides, his white, open-throated shirt emphasizing the intimidating breadth of his shoulders.

Resisting the impulse to back away, Clare reached into the pocket of her cloak and pulled out the small book that was her only hope. Opening the volume to the handwritten inscription, she held it up for him to see. "Do you remember this?"

The message was a simple one. *Reverend Morgan—I hope that some day I will be able to repay all you have done for me. Affectionately, Nicholas Davies.*

The schoolboy scrawl stopped the earl as if he had been struck. His wintry gaze shifted from the book to Clare's face. "You play to win, don't you? However, you're holding the wrong hand. Any obligation I might feel would be toward your father. If he wants favors, he should ask for them in person."

"He can't," she said baldly. "He died two years ago."

After an awkward silence, the earl said, "I'm sorry, Miss Morgan. Your father was probably the only truly good man I've ever known."

"Your grandfather was also a good man. He did a

great deal for the people of Penreith. The poor fund, the chapel . . .''

Before Clare could list other examples of the late earl's charity, Nicholas interrupted her. "Spare me. I know that my grandfather dearly loved setting a moral example for the lower orders, but that holds no appeal for me.''

"At least he took his responsibilities seriously," she retorted. "You haven't done a thing for the estate or the village since you inherited.''

"A record I have every intention of maintaining." He finished his drink and set the glass down with a clink. "Neither your father's good example nor the old earl's moralizing succeeded in transforming me into a gentleman. I don't give a damn about anyone or anything, and I prefer it that way.''

She stared at him, shocked. "How can you say such a thing? No one is that callous.''

"Ah, Miss Morgan, your innocence is touching." He leaned against the edge of the table and folded his arms across his broad chest, looking as diabolical as his nickname. "You had better leave before I shatter any more of your illusions.''

"Don't you care that your neighbors are suffering?''

"In a word, no. The Bible says that the poor will always be with us, and if Jesus couldn't change that, I certainly can't." He gave her a mocking smile. "With the possible exception of your father, I've never met a man of conspicuous charity who didn't have base motives. Most who make a show of generosity do it because they crave the gratitude of their inferiors and the satisfactions of self-righteousness. At least I, in my honest selfishness, am not a hypocrite.''

"A hypocrite can do good even if his motives are unworthy, which makes him more valuable than someone with your brand of honesty," she said dryly. "But as you wish. Since you don't believe in charity, what do you care about? If money is what warms your heart, there is profit to be made in Penreith.''

He shook his head. "Sorry, I don't care much about money, either. I already have more than I could spend in ten lifetimes.''

"How nice for you," she muttered under her breath. She

wished that she could turn and walk out, but to do so would
be to admit defeat, and she had never been good at that.
Thinking that there had to be some way to reach him, she
asked, "What would it take to change your mind?"

"My help is not available for any price you would be
willing or able to pay."

"Try me."

Attention caught, he scanned her from head to foot with
insulting frankness. "Is that an offer?"

He had meant to shock her, and he had succeeded; she
turned a hot, humiliated red. But she did not avert her eyes.
"If I said yes, would that persuade you to help Penrieth?"

He regarded her with astonishment. "My God, you would
actually let me ruin you if that would advance your
schemes?"

"If I was sure it would work, yes," she said recklessly.
"My virtue and a few minutes of suffering would be a small
price to pay when set against starving families and the lives
that will be lost when the Penreith mine explodes."

A flicker of interest showed in his eyes, and for a moment
he seemed on the verge of asking her to elaborate. Then his
expression blanked again. "Though it's an interesting offer,
bedding a female who would carry on like Joan of Arc going
to the stake doesn't appeal to me."

She arched her brows. "I thought that rakes enjoyed seducing the innocent."

"Personally, I've always found innocence boring. Give
me a woman of experience any time."

Ignoring his comment, she said thoughtfully, "I can see
that a plain woman would not tempt you, but surely beauty
would overcome your boredom. There are several very
lovely girls in the village. Shall I see if one of them would
be willing to sacrifice her virtue in a good cause?"

In one swift movement, he stepped close and caught her
face between his hands. There was brandy on his breath and
his hands seemed unnaturally warm, almost scalding where
they touched. She flinched, then forced herself to stand utterly still as he scrutinized her face with eyes that seemed
capable of seeing the dark secrets of her soul. When she
was certain that she could bear his perusal no longer, he

said slowly, "You are nowhere near as plain as you pretend to be."

His hands dropped, leaving her shaken.

To her relief, he moved away and retrieved his glass, then poured more brandy. "Miss Morgan, I don't need money, I can find all of the women I want without your inept help, and I have no desire to destroy my hard-earned reputation by becoming associated with good works. Now will you leave peacefully, or must I use force?"

She was tempted to turn and flee. Instead she said doggedly, "You still haven't named a price for your aid. There must be something. Tell me, and perhaps I can meet it."

With a sigh, he dropped onto the sofa and studied her from a safe distance. Clare Morgan was small and rather slight of build, but she forcefully occupied the space where she stood. A formidable young woman. Her abilities had probably been honed while organizing her otherworldly father.

Though no one would call her a beauty, she was not unattractive in spite of her best efforts at severity. Her simple garments emphasized the neatness of her figure, and skinning her dark hair back had the paradoxical effect of making her intensely blue eyes seem enormous. Her fair skin had the alluring smoothness of sun-warmed silk; his fingers still tingled from feeling the pulse of blood in her temples.

No, not a beauty, but memorable, and not only for her stubbornness. Though she was a damned nuisance, he had to admire her courage in coming here. God knew what stories circulated about him in the valley, but the locals probably saw him as a major menace to body and soul. Yet here she was, with her passionate caring and her bold demands. However, her timing was dismal, for she was trying to involve him with a place and people that he had already decided he must forsake.

A pity he hadn't started on the brandy earlier. If he had, he might have been safely unconscious by the time his unwelcome visitor had arrived. Even if he forcibly ejected her, she would likely continue her campaign to enlist his aid, since she seemed convinced that he was Penrieth's only hope. He began speculating about what she wanted of him,

then stopped when he caught himself doing it. The last thing
he wanted was involvement. Far better to bend his brandy-
hazed brain to the question of how to convince her that her
mission was hopeless.

But what the devil could be done with a woman who was
willing to endure a fate worse than death in pursuit of her
goals? What could he ask that would be so shocking that
she would flatly refuse to consider doing it?

The answer came to him with the simplicity of perfection.
Like her father, she would be a Methodist, part of a close
community of sober, virtuous believers. Her status, her
whole identity, would depend on how her fellows saw her.

Triumphantly he settled back and prepared to rid himself
of Clare Morgan. "I've a price, but it's one you won't pay."

Warily she said, "What is it?"

"Don't worry—your grudgingly offered virtue is safe.
Taking it would be tedious for me, and you'd probably enjoy
becoming a martyr to my wicked lusts. What I want instead"—he paused for a deep swallow of brandy—"is your
reputation."

2

"**M**Y REPUTATION?" Clare said blankly. "What on earth do you mean by that?"

Looking vastly pleased with himself, the earl said, "If you will live with me for, say, three months, I will help your village to the best of my abilities."

She felt a clutch of fear. In spite of her bold words, she had never imagined that he might have a shred of interest in her. "In spite of the boredom you would have to endure," she said with defensive sarcasm, "you want me to become your mistress?"

"Not unless you do so willingly, which I don't expect to happen—you seem far too rigid to allow yourself to enjoy the sins of the flesh." His gaze moved over her again, this time with cool speculation. "Though if you changed your mind during the three months, I would be delighted to accommodate you. I've never had a virtuous Methodist schoolmistress. Would bedding one bring me closer to heaven?"

"You are outrageous!"

"Thank you. I try." He swallowed another mouthful of brandy. "To return to the subject at hand, though you would live here in a way that would make you appear to be my mistress, you would not actually have to lie with me."

"What would be the point of such a charade?" she asked, relieved but bewildered.

"I want to see how far you are willing to go to get what you want. If you accept my proposition, your precious village may benefit, but you'll never be able to lift your head there again, for your reputation will be destroyed. Would success be worth such a price? Would your neighbors for-

give your fall from grace even though they benefited by it?
An interesting question, but if I were you, I wouldn't trust
too much in their good will.''

Finally comprehending, she said tightly, ''This is only a
meaningless game to you, isn't it?''

''Games are never meaningless. Of course, they do require rules. What should the rules be here?'' His brows
drew together. ''Let's see . . . The basic terms would be my
help in return for your presence under my roof, and osten-
sibly in my bed. A successful seduction would be in the
nature of a side bet—a bonus that would be enjoyed by both
of us. In order to give me a sporting chance at seducing
you, I would be permitted to kiss you once a day, in a place
and time of my choosing. Any loveplay beyond that would
be by mutual consent.

''However, after that one kiss, you would have the right
to say no, and I could not touch you again until the next
day. After three months you would go home, while I would
continue my aid as long as it was needed.'' He frowned.
''Dangerous—if I let you draw me into your schemes, I
might not be free of the valley for the rest of my life. Still,
it's only fair that I risk something significant, since you will
lose so much if you accept my proposal.''

''The whole idea is absurd!''

He gave her a look of cherubic innocence. ''On the contrary, I think it would be quite amusing—I'm almost sorry
that you won't agree. But the price is too high, isn't it? Your
virginity could be sacrificed with no one the wiser, but reputation is a fragile, public commodity, easily lost, impossible to regain.'' He made a graceful, dismissive gesture
with his free hand. ''Now that I have established the limits
of your desire for martyrdom, I shall ask you once more to
leave. I assume you will not trouble me again.''

He had the wickedly self-satisfied expression of a Gypsy
horsetrader who had just sold a broken-winded beast for five
times its value. The sight caused Clare's temper to flare
violently out of control. He was so arrogant, so uncaring,
so utterly sure that he had bested her. . . .

Too furious to care about consequences, she snapped,

"Very well, my lord. I accept your proposal. My reputation in return for your help."

For a moment there was stunned silence. Then he sat bolt upright on the sofa. "You can't mean that! You would incur the scorn of your friends and neighbors, possibly be forced to leave Penreith, certainly lose your teaching position. Would it be worth sacrificing the life you've known for the fleeting pleasure of confounding me?"

"The reason I am agreeing to your proposal is to help my friends, though I won't deny that it pleases me to puncture your arrogance," she said coldly. "Moreover, I think you are wrong—a reputation that has been twenty-six years in the making may be less fragile than you think. I will tell my friends exactly what I am doing, and why, and hope that they will trust me to behave as I should. If my faith is misplaced and this game of yours costs me the life I have known . . ." She hesitated, then shrugged, her lips thin. "So be it."

Helplessly he said, "What would your father have said?"

The power had shifted to Clare, and it was a heady feeling. "What he always said. That it is a Christian's duty to serve others even if the personal cost is high, and that behavior is a matter between oneself and God."

"If you do this, you will regret it," he said with conviction.

"Perhaps, but if I don't, I will regret my cowardice more." Her eyes narrowed. "Is the great sportsman suddenly afraid to play a game he designed himself?"

Almost before she finished speaking, he was off the sofa and halfway across the room. He halted a yard away, his black eyes glittering. "Very well, Miss Morgan. Or no, I suppose I must call you Clare, since you are very nearly my mistress. You will get what you wanted. Take the rest of the day to settle your affairs in the village. I shall expect you here tomorrow morning." His gaze raked over her, this time critically. "Don't bother to bring much clothing. I'll be taking you to London, where you can be properly outfitted."

"London? Your obligations are here." Though it felt like

appalling impertinence, she forced herself to add, "Nicholas."

"Don't worry," he said shortly. "I shall fulfill my part of the bargain."

"But don't you want to know what needs to be done?"

"There will be time enough for that tomorrow." Relaxed again, he took a lazy step that brought them so close they were almost touching.

Clare's heart accelerated as she wondered if he intended to collect his first kiss. His overpowering nearness cut through the wrath that had sustained her so far. Uneasily she said, "I'll be off now. I've much to do."

"Not quite yet." He gave her a slow, dangerous smile. "We shall be seeing a great deal of each other over the next three months. Isn't it time to begin developing a closer acquaintance?"

He started to raise his hands, and she almost jumped out of her skin. Pausing, he said softly, "Perhaps your reputation is capable of surviving three months under my roof, but will you yourself be able to endure it?"

She licked suddenly dry lips, then colored when she saw him watching her slight, nervous movement. Trying to sound confident, she said, "I can endure whatever I must."

"I'm sure you can," he agreed. "My aim will be to teach you to enjoy it."

To her surprise, he didn't try to kiss her. Instead, he lifted his hands to her head and began drawing the pins from her hair. She became painfully aware of his intense, unnerving masculinity; of his deft fingers, and the triangle of tanned skin visible at the open throat of his shirt. Underlying the tang of brandy, he had a scent that made her think of piney forests and wild, fresh wind from the sea.

Pulse hammering, she held very still as the thick coils of her hair suddenly spilled free in an unruly torrent that fell past her waist. He lifted a handful of hair and let it drift through his fingers like thistledown. "It's never been cut?" When she shook her head, he murmured, "Lovely. Dark chocolate with a hint of red cinnamon. Is the rest of you like this, Clare—primly controlled, yet with hidden fire?"

Completely demoralized, she said hastily, "I'll see you tomorrow, my lord."

When she tried to twist away, he caught her wrist. Before she could panic, he lifted her hand and pressed the hair pins into her palm, then released her. "Until tomorrow."

Placing his hand in the small of her back, he guided her to the door. Before opening it, he looked down into her face, his mood shifting from teasing to complete seriousness. "If you decide not to go through with this, I won't think less of you."

Was he reading her mind, or did he merely understand human nature too well? Clare opened the door and bolted from the room. Fortunately, Williams was not around to see her disheveled hair and flaming cheeks. If he did, he would surely think . . .

Her breath caught. If she accepted the earl's challenge, she would be living here and Williams would see her every day. Would the butler's eyes be knowing or contemptuous? Would he believe her if she explained, or despise her as a liar and whore?

Feeling as if she were on the verge of shattering, she darted through an open door into a small, dusty drawing room. After closing the door, she sank onto a cloth-draped chair and covered her face with her hands. She scarcely knew Williams, yet she had been concerned about his opinion of her. It was a sharp, horrific demonstration of what she would experience if she persisted in this mad scheme. How much worse would it be when everyone in Penreith knew she was living with a notorious rake?

Realizing the sheer deviltry of Nicholas's game stirred her temper again. He had known exactly what he was asking; in fact, he was counting on her fear of public censure to discourage her.

The thought helped her regain her composure. As she straightened and began repinning her hair, she grimly recognized that anger and pride had goaded her to accept his absurd challenge. Not the most godly of emotions, but then, she was not the most godly of women, no matter how hard she tried.

When her appearance was restored, she slipped from the

drawing room and let herself out of the house, then made her way to the stables to collect her pony cart.

There was still time to change her mind. She wouldn't even have to face the earl in person to admit her cowardice. All she need do was stay away tomorrow, and no one, save herself and Nicholas, would ever know what had transpired.

But as she had said earlier, the real issue wasn't her and her pride, or even the earl and his stubborn selfishness. It was Penreith. That fact struck her forcibly as the road topped a small rise and the village came into view. She halted the cart and gazed down at the familiar slate roofs. It looked like a hundred other Welsh communities, with rows of stone cottages set into the lush greenness of the valley. Yet though there was nothing extraordinary about Penreith, it was her home, and she knew and loved every stone in it. The people were *her* people, among whom she had lived her whole life. If some of them were harder to love than others—well, she tried her best anyhow.

A square tower marked the Anglican church, while the more modest Methodist chapel was concealed among the cottages. She could barely see the mine, which was farther down the valley. The mine was by far the largest employer in the area. It was also the greatest threat to the community, a hazard as volatile as the explosives sometimes used for blasting.

The thought clarified her churning mind. She might have behaved badly today, succumbing to pride and anger, but the reasons for her mission were nonetheless valid. Fighting for the welfare of the village couldn't be wrong; the challenge would be for her to save her own soul from becoming a casualty of war.

The weekly class was the heart of Methodist fellowship, and Clare's group had its regular meeting that evening. That was convenient; she would be able to speak to her closest friends all at once. Still, as the group sang an opening hymn, her stomach twisted into a knot of anxiety.

The class leader, Owen Morris, led a prayer. Then it was time for members of the small group to share the spiritual joys or challenges they had experienced during the previous seven days. It had been a quiet week; all too soon, it was Clare's turn to speak. She rose to her feet and looked in turn at each of the five men and six women.

At their best, classes were a model of joyful Christian fellowship. When Clare's father had died, class members had supported her through the ordeal, as she had supported others in their troubles. The people gathered in this room were her spiritual family, the ones whose opinions she valued most.

Praying that her faith in them would not prove to be misplaced, she said, "Friends . . . brothers and sisters . . . I am about to embark on an enterprise that I hope may benefit all of Penreith. It is unorthodox—even scandalous—and many will condemn me. I pray that you will not."

Owen's wife Marged, who was Clare's closest friend, gave her an encouraging smile. "Tell us about it. I cannot believe that you would act in a way that would earn our censure."

"I hope you're right." Clare looked down at her tightly linked hands. Her father had been beloved of all of the Methodists in southern Wales, and the awe and affection he had inspired had spilled over onto her. Because of that, the other members of the local society gave her more credit than she deserved. Lifting her head again, she said, "The Earl of Aberdare has returned to his estate. I went today to ask him to use his influence to help the village."

Edith Wickes, who was never short of an opinion, looked horrified. "You spoke with that man! My dear, was that wise?"

"Probably not." Clare gave a terse description of the bargain she and Aberdare had struck. She did not mention how she felt, how the earl had behaved, or the fact that she must let him kiss her once a day. Nor could she bring herself to reveal the intemperance of her own reactions. Shorn of those details, the explanation didn't take long.

By the time she was done, her friends were staring at her with varying degrees of shock and concern. Edith spoke first. "You can't possibly go ahead with this!" she declared. "It's indecent. You'll be ruined."

"Perhaps." Clare lifted her hands in a gesture of supplication. "But you all know how matters are at the pit. If there is a chance that Lord Aberdare can change the situation, I have an obligation to try to secure his cooperation.''

"Not at the price of your reputation! A good name is a woman's greatest treasure.''

"Only in a worldly sense,'' Clare replied. "It is a prime tenet of our faith that each person must act according to his or her own conscience. We must not let ourselves be deterred by what the world might think.''

"Yes,'' Marged said dubiously, "but are you sure that you have a call to do this? You have prayed about it?''

Trying to sound confident, Clare said, "I am sure.''

Edith frowned. "What if Aberdare ruins your reputation and then doesn't do as he promised? You have naught but his word, and for all his title, the man is no more than a lying Gypsy.''

"To him the fate of the village is a game—but he is a man who takes games very seriously,'' Clare said. "I think, in his way, he is honorable.''

Edith snorted. "He's not to be trusted. As a boy, he was wild as a hawk, and we all know what happened four years ago.''

Jamie Harkin, who had been a soldier until he lost his leg, said in his slow, calm fashion, "We don't really know what happened then. Plenty of rumors, but no charges were ever placed against him. I remember Nicholas when he was a boy, and he was a decent lad.'' He shook his head. "Still, I don't like the idea of our Clare staying at the big house. We know her too well to think she'd stray, but others will talk and condemn. It could go hard with you, lass.''

Marged looked at her husband, who worked in the mine as a hewer. He was fortunate to have work, but she never forgot that it was hard and dangerous. "It would be wonderful if Clare could convince Lord Aberdare to improve conditions at the pit.''

"That it would,'' said Hugh Lloyd, a young man who also worked in the mine. "The owner and the manager don't give a damn . . .'' He colored. " 'Scuse me, sisters. What I meant is that they don't care what happens to us colliers. Cheaper to replace us than to install new equipment.''

"Too true,'' Owen said somberly. "In your heart, do you

truly believe this is right, Clare? You're brave to be willing to risk your good name, but no one would expect a woman to do something so offensive to natural modesty.''

Once more, Clare's gaze went around the room, touching each member in turn. Knowing herself inadequate, she had refused to become a class leader, and she would never have dreamed of preaching. But she was a teacher, and she knew how to command the attention of a roomful of people. ''In the days when members of our society were persecuted, my father risked his life to preach the Word. Twice he was almost killed by mobs, and he bore the scars of those assaults until the day he died. If he was willing to risk his life, how can I balk at risking something as trivial as worldly reputation?''

By their expressions, her friends were touched by her words, but still doubtful. Needing to feel that they supported her, she said persuasively, ''Lord Aberdare made no secret of the fact that his proposal was not a result of . . . of illicit lust, but simply a way to get rid of me. In effect, he made a wager about how I would react, and lost.'' She swallowed hard, then bent the truth until it was in danger of fracturing. ''My guess is that when he has me under his roof, he will decide to put me to work as a housekeeper, or perhaps a secretary.''

Relief showed on the concerned faces around her. A housekeeper—that was innocent enough. Only Edith muttered, ''Being a housekeeper won't save you if his lordship gets ideas. It's not for nothing they call him the Demon Earl.''

Suppressing a twinge of guilt over the fact that she had offered her friends a guess that might prove completely wrong, Clare said, ''Why should he have ideas about me? Surely he has his choice of immoral society women and'' —she searched for a term—''what do they call them—bits of muslin?''

''Clare!'' Edith exclaimed, scandalized.

Jamie Harkin chuckled. ''We all know such women exist. Some of them have even found the Lord and become good Methodists. Why be mealymouthed talking about 'em?''

Edith gave the old soldier a scowling glance. They had

clashed before; though the class members were bound by shared beliefs and mutual affection, they came from different ranks of society and didn't always agree about worldly matters. "What are you going to do about the school, Clare? You won't have time for teaching. Even if you did, most people in the village would be scandalized if you teach while staying at Aberdare under such irregular circumstances."

"I hope that Marged can take the regular classes." Clare looked at her friend. "Would you be willing to do that?"

Marged's eyes widened. "Do you think I could? Except for Sunday school, I've done no teaching, and I haven't anything like your learning."

"You can do it," Clare assured her. "The teaching itself is much like Sunday school—reading, writing, spelling, numbers, housekeeping skills. The main differences are that there is less study of scripture, and the older students are more advanced. Of course, during the time you are teaching, you would also draw the schoolmistress's salary."

As she had guessed, the prospect of wages tipped the balance, for Marged was ambitious for her three growing children. "Very well, Clare, I'll do my best."

"Wonderful! I've outlined the lessons and written notes on what different children are doing. If you come home with me after class, I'll give you everything you need." Then Clare turned to Edith. "Marged is going to be very busy for the next three months. It's a great imposition, but would you be able to take my Sunday school classes?"

The older woman looked first startled, then pleased. "Why, yes, my dear, if that would help you out."

Another member, Bill Jones, said, "Since I live just up the road, I'll keep an eye on your cottage."

His wife, Glenda, said robustly, "And anyone who speaks ill of you will get the rough edge of my tongue!"

Clare bit her lip, unexpectedly moved. "Thank you all so much. I am blessed in my friends."

Inwardly she vowed that she would never betray their trust.

* * *

"And here's the summary of what each student is study-ing," Clare gave Marged the last of the papers that she had written out after returning from Aberdare.

Marged scanned the sheets, asking an occasional ques-tion. When she was done, she said worriedly, "Three of them know almost as much as I do. After all, it hasn't been that long since I was a student in your adult class."

"The advanced pupils are the easiest of all. Not only do they largely teach themselves, but they help with the little ones. You'll manage very well," Clare assured her. "Re-member, if you have questions or problems, I'm only two miles away."

Marged's smile was a little tremulous. "As usual, you have everything wonderfully well-organized. I'm fright-ened, but—oh, Clare, it's so exciting that you believe I can do this! Five years ago, I couldn't even read. Who would have believed I'd ever be a teacher myself?"

"My biggest worry is that the school will turn out not to need me when I come back." Though Clare said the words lightly, she felt a pang at their truth. With experience, Marged would be a fine teacher, in some ways better than Clare. Though Marged was not as learned, she had more patience.

Business finished, Marged leaned back in her chair and sipped at the tea Clare had made. "What's he like?"

Caught unaware, Clare said, "Who?"

"Lord Tregar, or rather, Lord Aberdare as he is now." Marged slanted an impish glance at her. "Our Nicholas. It wasn't often that he was able to escape his keepers and come down to the village to play, but he's not a lad one would ever forget. You were younger, of course, so you wouldn't remember him as well. Mischievous and a little wild, but there was no harm in him, nor snobbery, either. He spoke Welsh as well as any of us. Not like the old earl."

"I didn't realize that he knew Welsh." Since the upper classes of Wales were usually very English in both language and customs, Clare was reluctantly forced to raise her opin-ion of Nicholas. "I spoke English when I visited him."

"I remember when he came down from Oxford with those three friends of his," Marged said dreamily. "Someone said that in London they were called the Fallen Angels. Nicholas, as dark and handsome as the devil. Lucien, blond and beautiful like Lucifer. Rafael, who's a duke now, and that Lord Michael, before he became the bane of Penreith. Maybe they were a little wild, but they were also the best-looking lads I've ever seen.'' She grinned. "Except for Owen, of course. A good thing he was courting me, or I might have been tempted to become a fallen woman.''

"Surely you exaggerate.''

"Only a little.'' Marged drained the last of her tea. "So now Nicholas is an earl, and home again after years of traveling in heathen places. Is he as handsome as he used to be?''

"Yes,'' Clare said repressively.

Marged waited hopefully for more details. When none were forthcoming, she said, "Were there any odd beasts running around the estate? They say that he sent some strange creatures back from his travels. It's been all I could do to keep the children from going up to investigate.''

"I didn't see anything more exotic than the peacocks, and they've always been there.'' Clare squared the stack of papers and handed them to her friend.

Taking the hint that it was time to go, Marged got to her feet. "You'll come to class meetings, won't you?''

"Of course.'' Clare hesitated. "At least, I will when I can. Lord Aberdare said something about taking me to London.''

Her friend's brows shot up. "Really? He wouldn't take a housekeeper there.''

"But he might if I were acting as his secretary,'' Clare said, uncomfortably aware that her answer was less than honest. "It remains to be seen what I'll be doing.''

Becoming serious, Marged said, "You be careful of Old Nick, Clare. He could be dangerous.''

"I doubt it. Lord Aberdare has too much arrogance to force a woman who isn't willing.''

"That's not what worries me,'' Marged said darkly. "The danger is that you'll be willing.'' On that ominous note, she left, to Clare's relief.

It didn't take long for Clare to pack the few possessions she would take to Aberdare, and there were no other chores to be done. Too restless to sleep, she drifted through the four rooms of the cottage, occasionally touching familiar objects. She had been born under this roof, had never lived anywhere else. The smallest chamber at Aberdare was grander, but she would miss her whitewashed walls and plain, sturdy furniture.

Lightly she skimmed her fingertips over the age-blackened lid of the carved oak chest. Clare thought it was a pity she would probably have no daughter to pass the chest to, for it had been handed down through the women of her family for generations. Inside the lid, "Angharad 1579" was chiseled. Sometimes Clare wondered about the life of that distant ancestress of hers. Probably Angharad had been the daughter and wife of smallholders who wrested a living from the land, but what had her husband been like? How many children had she borne? Had she been happy?

The overflowing bookcase at one end of the sitting room was the only note of luxury in the cottage. Thomas Morgan had been a son of the Welsh gentry who had been educated at Oxford and ordained as an Anglican vicar. After experiencing a profound spiritual conversion when hearing John Wesley preach, he had become a Methodist preacher himself. Though his rigidly traditional family had disowned him, he had never regretted his choice. Instead he had married the pious daughter of a smallholder and settled in Penreith, preaching and teaching the truth that had illuminated his own life.

Thomas had never lost his love of learning, and he had passed it on to his only daughter. Whenever he went on a preaching circuit, he had tried to find an inexpensive used book, and there had been many such circuits. Clare had read every volume in the cottage, many of them more than once.

Clare's mother had died twelve years earlier, quietly, the same way she had lived. Reverend Morgan had suggested that his fourteen-year-old daughter stay with other Methodist families when he went on a preaching circuit. Clare had flatly refused to leave the cottage, the only time she had ever defied her father. Eventually the reverend had acceded to her wishes, with the proviso that members of the society keep an eye on her when he was away.

Clare had started her first small, informal class when she was only sixteen, teaching adult women to read and write. Four years later, Emily, the young second Countess of Aberdare, had set up an endowment to establish a charity school. Dozens of villagers had worked together to fix up an abandoned tithe barn. Though teachers were usually male, Clare's experience had made her the logical choice for the new school, and she had taught there ever since. Over the years, half the people in Penreith had been her students at one time or another. The twenty pounds a year she earned would never make her rich, but it sufficed.

It had taken Nicholas Davies to pry Clare away from her home and her well-ordered life. As she looked into her small back garden, not yet planted for the year, she shivered, unable to suppress the feeling that she was seeing everything for the last time. Not literally, perhaps, but in her bones she was sure that one phase of her life was ending. Whatever happened at Aberdare would change her forever. Though she doubted that the changes would be for the better, she was committed to this course and would not turn back from it.

Finally, in a despairing quest for peace, she knelt and prayed, but there was no answer to her prayers. There never was.

Tomorrow, as always, she must face her fate alone.

3

NICHOLAS AWOKE with a pounding headache, which he richly deserved. He lay still, eyes unopened, and took stock of his situation. Apparently his valet, Barnes, had put him to bed in a nightshirt. Nicholas much preferred sleeping in his skin, but he supposed that he was in no position to complain.

He moved his head a fraction, then stopped, since it seemed in danger of falling off. He had been a damned fool and was paying the price for it. Unfortunately, he hadn't drunk enough brandy to obliterate his memory of what had happened the previous afternoon. As he thought of the pugnacious little wench who had stamped in and taken up his ridiculous challenge, he didn't know whether to laugh or cry. Knowing the consequences to his head, he did neither.

He had trouble believing some of the things he had said, but his memories were too clear to permit denial. Lucky that Clare Morgan hadn't come armed; she might have decided that it was her Methodist duty to rid the world of a parasitical nobleman. He almost smiled at the thought. He had rather enjoyed their encounter, though he devoutly hoped that after mature consideration she would decide to stay home and let their bargain lapse. A female like her could seriously unbalance a man.

The door swung open and soft footsteps approached. Probably Barnes, coming to see if he was awake. Preferring to be left alone, Nicholas kept his eyes shut and the footsteps retreated.

But not for long. Five seconds later, icy water sluiced

over Nicholas's head. "Bloody hell!" he roared, coming up swinging. He'd kill Barnes, he'd bloody kill him.

It wasn't his valet. Nicholas opened his bleary eyes to find Clare Morgan, who stood a safe distance away with an empty china pitcher in her hand.

At first he wondered if he was having an unusually vivid nightmare, but he could never have imagined the expression of sweet superciliousness on Clare's small face, nor the cold water that saturated his nightshirt. He snarled, "What the devil did you do that for?"

"Tomorrow morning has turned into tomorrow afternoon, and I've been waiting for three hours for you to wake up," she said calmly. "Long enough to have a cup of tea, organize my list of requests for Penreith, and make a brief survey of the house to see what needs to be done to open the place properly. Rather a lot, as I'm sure you've noticed. Or perhaps you didn't—men can be amazingly unobservant. From sheer boredom, I decided to wake you. It seemed like the sort of thing that a mistress might do, and I'm trying my best to fill the role you have assigned me."

She spoke with a hint of lilting Welsh accent and a rich, husky voice that made him think of aged whiskey. Coming from a prim spinster, the effect was startlingly erotic. Wanting to discomfit her, he said, "My mistresses always wake me up in more interesting ways. Care for me to explain how?"

"Not particularly." She took a towel from the washstand and handed it to him.

He roughly dried his hair and face, then blotted the worst of the water from his nightshirt. Feeling more human, he tossed the towel back to Clare.

"Do you get drunk often?" she inquired.

"Very seldom," Nicholas said dourly. "Obviously it was a mistake to do so this time. If I had been sober, I wouldn't have to endure you for the next three months."

With a look of demure malice, she said, "If you decide not to go through with this, I won't think less of you."

Nicholas blinked at hearing his own words thrown back at him. "You've a tongue like a wasp." He glowered at her until she began to look distinctly uneasy, then finished, "I like that in a woman."

To his delight, she blushed. Insults might not faze her, but compliments or shows of masculine interest did. Feeling cheered, he said, "Find my valet and send him in with hot shaving water. Then tell the kitchen to brew a very large pot of very hot coffee. I'll be down in half an hour." He threw the covers back and started to climb out of bed.

Averting her eyes, Clare said, "Very well, Nicholas," and beat a hasty retreat.

He chuckled as the door closed behind her. She really was a most intriguing female. If her natural forcefulness could be transmuted into passion, she would make a hell of a bedmate.

As he stepped onto the cold floor, he wondered if he would be successful at seducing her. Probably not; he suspected that her relentless virtue would outlast his patience.

But it would certainly be fun trying. Whistling softly, he stripped off his sodden nightshirt and considered when and where he should collect his first kiss.

When Lord Aberdare appeared downstairs in the breakfast parlor, exactly half an hour later, all traces of overindulgence had been removed. Except for his dark coloring and over-long hair, he looked every inch the fashionable London gentleman. Clare decided that she preferred it when he was informal; his present garb made her uncomfortably aware of the vast gap between their stations in life.

Then she remembered how he had looked in his nightshirt, with half his chest bare and wet fabric clinging to his muscular shoulders. That had been entirely too informal.

Wordlessly, she rose and poured him a cup of steaming coffee. Equally wordlessly, he gulped it down in three swallows, then held out his cup for more. The second cup vanished almost as quickly as the first. This time he refilled it himself, then took a chair opposite Clare. "You may begin your presentation about the ills of Penreith and the solutions you expect of me."

He was unnervingly businesslike. Glad that she was prepared, Clare said, "The problems are economic, with sev-

eral different causes. Things started getting difficult five
years ago, when your grandfather had Parliament enact a
private land enclosure act. With the upland commons fenced
off so Aberdare could run sheep, a number of cottagers were
driven into the village because they could no longer support
their families from the land. Jobs are few, and most of those
are at the coal pit. With so much cheap labor available, the
mine manager lowered wages. He also sees no reason to
buy better equipment, or to pay for even the most basic
safety precautions.''

Before she could elaborate, the earl held up a hand to
stop her. "How many men have died in the mine?''

"In the last four years, a total of sixteen men and four
boys have been killed in a variety of accidents.''

"That's unfortunate, but is it unreasonable? Mining has
always been hazardous. The colliers I've known take a certain pride in doing work that requires such strength and
courage.''

"Pride, yes,'' she agreed, "but they are not fools. The
hazards at the Penreith mine are far worse than they should
be—everyone who works there says it's a miracle that there
hasn't yet been a major disaster. Sooner or later, luck will
run out, and when it does dozens, possibly hundreds, of
people will die.'' Though she was trying to be coolly objective, her voice broke.

As she struggled to regain her composure, he said quietly, "I gather that you've lost friends in the mine?''

"Not just friends.'' She raised her head, her expression
rigid. "That's where my father died.''

Startled, Nicholas said, "What the devil was Reverend
Morgan doing in the pit?''

"What he always did—his work. There was a collapse.
Two men died outright and a third, a member of the Society,
was trapped by fallen rocks. The lower part of his body was
crushed, but he was still conscious. He asked for my father.
While other men tried to free the miner, my father held his
hand and prayed with him.'' After an unsteady breath, she
finished, "There was another rockfall. My father, the
trapped miner, and one of the rescue workers were killed.''

"One would expect no less from your father,'' Nicholas

said, his voice gentle. "Is it any comfort knowing that he died as he had lived—with compassion and courage?"

"Very little," she said bleakly.

After an awkward silence, he asked, "Why have you approached me? Though I own the land that the mine is on, it's leased to the mining company. The owner and manager are the ones in a position to make changes."

Clare's mouth tightened. "The manager, George Madoc, is impossible. Since he receives a percentage of the profits, he takes pleasure in pinching every penny he can, even at the cost of human lives."

"Is Lord Michael Kenyon still the owner? I would have thought he would be responsive to reasonable requests."

"Attempts have been made to communicate with him, but Lord Michael has not answered our letters and petitions. And no one has been able to talk to him in person, because he hasn't set foot in the valley in the last four years."

"Four years," Nicholas repeated, his expression enigmatic. "An interesting interval. But if Madoc and Lord Michael won't make changes, what do you think I can do?"

"Talk to Lord Michael," she said earnestly. "He is a friend of yours. If he can be persuaded to make improvements at the pit, perhaps nothing else will be required."

"Michael *was* a friend, but I haven't seen him in four years. More than that, actually. . . ." Nicholas's voice trailed off and he absently crumbled a piece of toast. "I have no idea where he is now, nor do I know if I would have any influence with him. He might be perfectly satisfied with matters as they stand."

"I've thought of that." Knowing that she was about to find out how far the earl would go to fulfill his part of the bargain, Clare rubbed damp palms along her gray skirt. "If the mine can't be changed, the solution is to create other kinds of employment. That is something you can do rather easily."

"I thought you would have a plan," he murmured. Slouching back in his chair, he folded his arms across his chest. "Proceed, Miss Morgan."

"To begin with, you are by far the largest landowner in the valley, yet you have done nothing to encourage more

scientific agriculture. Your tenants still use the same methods that were common in Tudor times. Improved breeding
and tillage would increase the wealth of the valley and create more jobs.'' She lifted a sheaf of papers and handed
them to Nicholas. ''I'm no expert, but I've studied reports
on scientific agriculture in England and noted techniques
that should be effective here.''

''There is something on which you are not an expert?''
After a brief glance at the papers, he set them on the table.
''Bringing local farming out of the Middle Ages should keep
me busy for the next decade or two, but in case I have some
spare time, do you have any other requests?''

Ignoring his sarcasm, she said, ''There is one major thing
you could do which would have effects almost immediately.''

''Oh? Carry on, Miss Morgan, I am panting to hear.''

''Perhaps you don't remember, but you own an old slate
quarry at the far end of the valley. Though it hasn't been
used in years, there's no reason why it couldn't be worked
again.'' She leaned forward, voice intense. ''Not only
would development be profitable for you, but it would provide jobs for those who are now out of work. The Penrhyn
quarries in Flintshire employ over five hundred men, and
the work is less dangerous than mining. In addition, Madoc would have to improve conditions at the pit or lose his
best workers.''

''I remember the quarry,'' Nicholas said thoughtfully. ''It
has probably roofed every building in the valley, but is there
enough slate there for worthwhile commercial development?''

''Indications are that the field is very large, and the quality has always been excellent.''

'' 'Indications,' '' he repeated. ''I suppose that means
you've been trespassing on my land while evaluating my
resources?''

She shifted uncomfortably. ''The quarry is near a public
right of way.''

''As long as you didn't frighten the sheep.'' His brows
drew together reflectively. ''The problem with slate is the
cost of getting the material to where it's needed. A tramway

would have to be built down to the river so the slate could go to the coast by barge.''

''What is a tramway?''

''It's a kind of road, made up of a pair of wooden or iron tracks. Horses pull wagons along the rails. They're expensive to build, which is probably why the coal pit doesn't have one, but they make it possible to move heavy materials much faster than using regular roads.'' He pondered again. ''At the coast, a new quay might have to be built as well.''

''But once the quay was built, you could ship the slate anywhere—across the channel to Bristol, north to Merseyside. You might also be able to recoup some of your costs by charging the coal pit for using the quay—their shipping facilities are inadequate. It could be very profitable for you, Lord Aberdare.''

''Stop using profit as bait,'' he said irritably. ''The topic doesn't much interest me.'' He drummed his fingers on the mahogany table. ''Do you have any idea how many thousands of pounds would be required to develop the quarry?''

''Not really,'' she admitted. ''I don't have a grasp of money on that scale. Is it more than you can afford?''

''I didn't say that.'' He got to his feet. ''Do you ride?''

She blinked in confusion at the change of topic. ''Some, but not lately—after my father died, I sold his horse. It was a placid old thing, so my riding experience is limited.''

''There should be something in the stables that will suit you. Meet me there in fifteen minutes in your riding habit. We're going to take a look at this quarry of yours.'' He turned on his heel and swept out of the room.

Clare was left feeling dazed, as if a thunderstorm had just rolled over her. But at least he was taking her ideas seriously.

However, he hadn't given her time to say that she didn't have a riding habit. With a faint smile, she rose and went up to the room that had been assigned to her. She would have to ride in the garments she had used in the past. Perhaps she would be able to shock the earl. She rather hoped so.

* * *

Clare entered the stables to find that Nicholas had arrived before her, and was in earnest conversation with the inhabitant of one of the large box stalls. The clicking heels of her old boots caused him to glance up at her.

He paused, arrested. "Are boy's breeches the Penreith version of a riding habit?"

"There are few women in the valley who ride, and even fewer who can afford to have an expensive gown with only one limited purpose," she said crisply. "I'm sorry if you disapprove, but this is what I've always worn on horseback, and it's all I have."

Nicholas gave her a lazy, dangerous smile. "I didn't say that I disapproved. Wear those breeches riding in London and you could start a new fashion. Either that or a riot."

Though Clare had never minded the sparseness of her wardrobe, she hadn't expected that his thorough examination of her buckskin-clad legs would make her feel so naked. Her face colored; with disgust, she realized that she had blushed more in the last day than the whole previous decade. Glancing toward the stall, she asked, "Is that the mount you chose for me?"

"Yes. Rhonda is a pure-bred Welsh pony." His long, graceful fingers stroked the dappled muzzle, causing the little mare to simper shamelessly. "Docile, well-mannered, and considerably more intelligent than the average horse. Too small for me, but she should do nicely for you."

As he opened the door of the stall and led Rhonda out, a groom emerged from the tack room carrying a sidesaddle. The earl said, "We won't be needing that. Get a regular saddle for Miss Morgan."

After giving her an interested glance, the groom obeyed the order and saddled the pony. Nicholas himself brought out the great black stallion he had been riding the day before, when Clare had first seen him. The horse danced out of his stall, high-spirited to a fault. As Clare stepped back nervously, Nicholas moved closer and breathed into the black nostrils.

The stallion quieted immediately. Seeing her surprise, Nicholas flashed a quick grin. "It's an old Gypsy trick to calm a horse. Useful when you're trying to steal one."

"No doubt you've had plenty of experience in that area," she said dryly.

As he saddled the stallion, he shook his head with regret. "I'm afraid not. One of the sad consequences of wealth is that there is no point in theft. The best meal I ever had was when I was a boy and shared a stolen hen and potatoes that were roasted over an open fire. Superb."

Knowing that she was being baited, Clare turned to Rhonda and checked the tightness of the saddle girth herself. Out of the corner of her eye, she saw the earl give a faint nod of approval at her thoroughness. He made a move in her direction, so she hastily mounted before he could help her.

Clare was nervous as they rode away from the stables, but the pony proved to be as well-behaved as promised. She relaxed and began to enjoy the ride, even though she knew that long-unused muscles would protest later.

Nicholas led the way to a trail that ran high up the edge of the valley. It was an unusually warm day for early spring, and the air was so clear that she could pick out individual trees on the far side of the valley.

It was several miles to the old quarry, and at first they rode in complete silence. Clare found that her gaze kept returning to Nicholas. He rode like a centaur, so at one with his horse that watching him was pure pleasure. Whenever she became aware of how great the pleasure was, she forced her attention back to her surroundings.

When the journey was half completed, the trail widened so that they could travel side by side. Nicholas said, "You ride better than I would have expected for someone who learned on that old slug of your father's. The beast had a mouth like granite."

She smiled. "If I seem competent, Rhonda must get the credit. It's pleasant to ride an animal that's so responsive and has such smooth gaits. Willow had his points, though. My father was an absent-minded horseman, and he never had to worry that Willow would bolt if neglected."

"Small chance of that. More likely Willow stopped and grazed whenever your father's mind wandered." Without a change in tone, he continued, "I'm curious about how bad my local reputation is. What do people in Penreith say about the melodramatic events of four years ago?''

Rhonda stopped and tossed her head unhappily as Clare's hands tightened on the reins. Forcing herself to relax, she said, ''It's believed that after years of trying to break your grandfather's heart, you finally succeeded by seducing his wife. When he found you in bed together, he suffered a fit of apoplexy that killed him. Your own wife, Lady Tregar, was horrorstruck when she discovered what had happened. Terrified that you would injure her, she fled Aberdare. The night was stormy and she died when her carriage went off the road and crashed into the river.''

When she fell silent, he said lightly, ''Is that all?''

''Isn't that enough?'' she said, her tone edged. ''Perhaps you'll be gratified to know that there was speculation that your grandfather really died of Gypsy poison, and that your wife's death may have been less accidental than it appeared. The fact that you left Aberdare that night and never came back was fuel for the fire. However, the magistrate's inquiry found no evidence of criminal conduct.''

Voice laced with irony, he said, ''Surely there are those who believe that Old Nick was capable of bribing a country magistrate to conceal the truth.''

''It was suggested, but the magistrate was much respected. Also, Lady Tregar's coachman swore that it was a genuine accident that resulted from her insisting that he go faster, against his better judgment.''

''Did the coachman ever mention where Caroline was going in such a tearing hurry? I've sometimes wondered.''

Clare thought a moment, then shook her head. ''Not that I know of. Does it matter?''

He shrugged. ''Probably not. I was merely curious. As you know, I left in a hurry, without learning all the details. Still . . . does the coachman live in the valley?''

''No. When you left, most of the servants were dismissed and had to go elsewhere.'' She was unable to resist adding, ''At least thirty people lost their jobs when the house was closed. Did you ever think of that when you went storming out?''

After a long silence, he said, ''To be honest, no.''

As she studied his profile, she saw a tightness that belied his casual manner. She had wanted to prick his conscience, yet now that she had, she found herself needing to ease his expression. "You had supporters as well as detractors. My father never believed that you could have behaved so badly."

Like her father, Clare had not wanted to believe the worst. She hoped that Nicholas would take this opportunity to deny the charges, offer some plausible explanation for what seemed like vicious immorality. Instead, he only said dryly, "Your father was a saint. I, however, am a sinner."

"You take great pride in that, don't you?" she said, disappointment sharpening her voice.

"Of course." His expressive brows arched. "One must have pride in something."

"Why not pride in your integrity, or your charity, or your learning?" she asked with exasperation. "The virtues of adults instead of the vices of small boys."

For a moment he looked startled and off-balance. Then he recaptured his insouciance. "At Aberdare, my grandfather laid claim to all the virtues. Vice was the only thing left to me."

Clare scowled at him. "The old earl has been dead for four years, and you're a grown man. Find a better excuse, or learn better behavior."

His expression darkened. "You scold more like a wife than a mistress."

Realizing that she had said too much, she said, "More like a schoolmistress than either."

"I'm sure that all your lessons will be sober, high minded, and worthy," he said thoughtfully. "But what lessons are you going to learn from me?"

Though Clare remained silent, she knew the answer to his question: any lessons she learned from Nicholas would be dangerous ones.

4

I T HAD BEEN years since Nicholas had visited the old
quarry, and then he had accepted it casually, without
deeper thought. This time, however, he studied the rocky
outcroppings more carefully. As he swung from his horse,
he said, "This whole area appears to be slate with a thin
covering of soil."

"A friend who knows about slate says it would take decades to quarry it all." Clare stopped her pony and prepared to dismount, then froze when Nicholas came to help
her.

He looked into her alarmed face and smiled reassuringly.
In her well-worn boy's clothing, she looked younger and
much less severe—an appealing urchin rather than a schoolmistress. "You must work on becoming more relaxed
around me instead of reacting like a hen that has been cornered by a fox." He helped her from the pony, then retained
her hand in his. "A mistress is supposed to enjoy her lover's
touch."

Her fingers fluttered anxiously for an instant, then stilled
as she accepted that he was not ready to release her. "I am
not a real mistress."

"You don't have to share my bed, but I intend to treat
you like a mistress in other ways. Which means that you'll
find the next three months much more pleasant if you let
yourself relax and enjoy it." Gently he caressed her slim
fingers with his thumb. "I like touching—female flesh is
delightfully different from that of males. Your hand, for example. Small-boned, rather delicate, yet it's not the soft,
helpless hand of a lady who never does anything more vigorous than lift a fork. An enchantingly capable hand. If you

should choose to use it for making love, it would be wondrously skilled.''

Her eyes widened and her hand shivered within his. It was not a reaction of distaste. Clare hungered for physical warmth, though he doubted that she knew that herself. He must use that hunger, slowly coax it into a craving so intense that she could no longer deny it. But he must go slowly, because she was going to fight him every inch of the way.

Again he wondered which would prove stronger: her virtue or his powers of persuasion. The uncertainty of the outcome made him feel more anticipation than he had known in years.

He released Clare and tethered both mounts, then put a casual hand on the small of her back and escorted her across the grass to the nearest outcropping of slate. Through the layers of coat and shirt, he felt her tense, then relax and accept the familiarity. As he savored her supple movements, he gave an inward smile. Intimacy was a web spun of many strands, and each small submission on her part was a point won for him.

When they reached the rocky projection, he moved away from Clare and examined the irregular layers of dark, light-absorbing stone. ''I never realized that slate breaks in such flat planes.''

''It doesn't always—this is a particularly high-quality vein. But even the beds that have the most clay mixed in will make good roofing slates.''

An idea occurred to him. ''Stand back.'' He lifted a sizable rock, then smashed it onto the outcropping with all his strength. There was an ear-piercing crack of sound and a spray of stone chips. A large slab of the outcropping sheered away, leaving several square feet of absolutely level surface.

He skimmed his palm across the slate. ''This might make a good surface for a billiard table.''

Her brows drew together. ''Why would you want to put slate on a billiard table?''

''Wood often warps, especially in damp areas like Wales,'' he explained. ''Fit together several slabs of this slate, cover it with green baize, and one might have a superior table.''

"That's a frivolous use of good slate."

"Here's a lesson for you, Clare. Frivolity is usually far more profitable than necessity." He dusted his hands and turned away. "I'll have the estate carpenter use some of this to resurface the table at Aberdare. If it works, we might have a profitable new market for the best of the slate." He draped a casual arm over her shoulders. "Show me the rest of the site."

They spent the next hour scrambling over the hillside, studying the extent and quality of the exposed slate, and laughing at the antics of the lambs that skipped around their grazing mothers. Nicholas found that it was as amusing to work with Clare as it was to skirmish with her, for her quick mind and direct manner made her unlike any woman he'd ever known. As a bonus, she looked enticing in her severe boots and breeches.

They ended by the lowest visible outcropping. Nicholas studied the slope, then pointed out a ridge that curled down to the southwest. "This looks like the best spot for the tramway. It isn't far to the river, and it's all Aberdare land."

"How soon would it be possible to start working the quarry?"

He considered. "Probably by midsummer. The tramway might not be completed, but finished slates can be held here until it is. Before work can begin, I'll have to go to London to arrange financing. We'll also have to visit a large slate quarry to study the techniques, and perhaps hire an experienced manager. Then there's the matter of the new quay on the coast. A site must be found, an engineer hired." He gazed absently at the valley, thinking of all the details that he would have to take care of; money was no substitute for personal attention.

"You're smiling," she said softly. "As if you're looking forward to the challenge."

"My feelings are mixed. I'd been thinking of selling Aberdare, but everything you've asked me to do will bind me more closely to the place, at least for the next year or two."

"Sell Aberdare!" she exclaimed, as shocked as if he

wanted to ship the whole estate—bag, baggage, and sheep—to China. "But you're Welsh—this has been the Davies home for centuries!"

"I'm no Welshman," he retorted. "I'm half Gypsy, and even though my grandfather liked to proclaim himself a descendant of Welsh kings, the truth is that generations of marrying English heiresses had made the Davies blood more English than Welsh. Aberdare represents only a small part of my fortune, and I would like nothing better than to turn my back on the place forever."

Observing her appalled expression, he said, "The idea shocks you more than anything else I've done, doesn't it?"

Rallying, she said, "Surely you can't sell even if you want to. Isn't the estate entailed so that you are only a life tenant, holding the property in trust for your own heir?"

He shook his head. "An entail has to be recreated in every generation. Ordinarily the resettlement is done on the heir's twenty-first birthday, or his marriage. However, my grandfather's own sons died before inheriting, and since the old boy never wholly accepted me as his heir, he kept putting off the resettlement. Since he died suddenly, it was still undone when I inherited. I think I can break the entail if I try."

"But you *were* his heir, and would have been even if his second wife had given him another son," she said, bewildered. "What did he hope to achieve by not accepting that?"

"He was praying for a miracle," Nicholas said dryly. "Very pious, my grandfather. He was sure that God would provide something better than an heir who was tainted by Gypsy blood."

Seeing through his mocking tone, Clare regarded him with too-perceptive eyes. "Is that why you hated him?"

Wondering why he had said more to a near stranger than he had ever revealed to his closest friends, he said, "That's no business of yours, my dear." He took her arm and headed up the hill to their mounts. "Has anyone ever pointed out that you're too clever by half?"

"It's been mentioned. Why do you think I'm a spinster?" She swung into her saddle, then looked down at him gravely. "Your grandfather had a reputation as a good Christian and

a conscientious lord. I'm beginning to think that the truth
must have been less flattering."

"Clever, clever Clare." He mounted his own horse and
turned it back the way they had come. "Why do you care
about such ancient history?"

"Isn't a mistress supposed to care about her lover?" she
asked softly.

Their glances met, and Nicholas felt something shift deep
inside him, creating a moment of strange vulnerability. This
woman could hurt him badly if he wasn't careful. Retreating
again to mockery, he said, "A mistress should care a little,
but not too much. Money and passion are the foundation of
this sort of relationship."

Refusing to be put off, she said, "Since I don't want
either of those things, where does that leave me?"

"As the patron saint of a slate quarry," he said promptly.
"Perhaps I'll call it the Great Clare." When she made a
face, he continued, "Speaking of your projects, I want to
visit the coal pit. Can you arrange that through your
friends?"

"I'm sure the manager, George Madoc, would be happy
to receive a visit from the greatest landowner in the area."

He made an impatient gesture. "It's not Madoc I want to
see, or at least, not yet. I'd rather go into the mine with a
knowledgable guide so I can see for myself the problems
that you mentioned."

Once again Clare felt that she was caught up in a tempest.
She had not expected Nicholas to move so quickly, or be so
determined to live up to his part of the bargain. "The leader
of my class-meeting is a hewer in the pit. I'm sure he'd be
willing to take you down and explain the hazards."

"Will doing so put his job at risk?"

"Perhaps," she admitted. "But if he should be discharged, you could hire him for the quarry. He's an out-
standing worker."

"Very well. Arrange it for as soon as possible, preferably
at a time when Madoc isn't about. No reason to borrow
trouble."

They both fell silent. It was near noon, and unseasonably
warm. Since Nicholas was bareheaded, Clare decided that

she too could take off her hat. After a long, cold winter, the sun's rays on her face felt wonderful.

Nicholas dismounted to open a gate that led into a pasture full of black Welsh cattle. Knowing that he would simply jump the fence if he were alone, Clare appreciated the courtesy.

As he closed the gate behind her, he remarked, "You're right that the local agricultural practices need attention. Driving the best cattle off to London every year has caused the quality of stock to deteriorate badly throughout Wales. While we're in London, I'll see about buying a couple of high quality bulls for breeding stock. Besides using them to improve the Aberdare herd, I'll make them available to the local smallholders."

Nicholas's deviltry must be contagious, for Clare found herself saying, "I suppose that providing a local stud service is the first thing a rake would think of."

Instead of being insulted, he gave a shout of laughter. "If you aren't careful, I might start to think that you have a sense of humor. A wicked one."

Rhonda slowed, and Clare realized that she was pulling at the reins again. Merciful heaven, but Nicholas could be charming. Seeking a safer subject, she said, "Is it true that you brought some unusual animals back from your travels?"

He grinned. "A few. Come along and I'll show you."

He swung his horse to the right and led her toward a higher, rockier section of the estate. They passed through another gate, this one in a high wall that looked newly built.

After closing the gate, Nicholas tethered his horse at the edge of a grove of sycamores, then went to assist Clare from her mount. "We'll go the rest of the way on foot."

Once again putting a light hand on her lower back, he guided her into the woods. Uneasily she recognized how pleasant it was to feel that she was being guarded and protected. That she was not alone . . .

Even though she jumped in surprise, it was a relief when the silence was shattered by a raucous, braying sound. The initial bellow triggered a chorus of similar cries. A little disappointed, she said, "It sounds like a herd of donkeys."

He smiled. "Wait."

They emerged from the woods by a small lake set in a rocky cup of ground. Clare stopped and blinked, not believing what her eyes were reporting. "What on earth?"

Waddling along the shore of the lake were a dozen or so of the strangest creatures she had ever seen. Perhaps two feet high, the black and white beasts walked upright like men, but seemed to have no feet at all. Their waddling gait was so irresistibly comic that she began to laugh.

Braying like a donkey, one creature got into a squabble with one of its fellows. After a brief tussle, the second ran squawking to the lake, then dived in headfirst and vanished.

"Clare, meet the penguins. Penguins, this is Clare." Nicholas took her hand and helped her through the rocks onto the pebbled beach. Though several penguins retreated into the high grass, the rest didn't seem to mind the intrusion. A few stood as still as statues with their black beaks held arrogantly high. Others scurried about as if the humans weren't there, tugging tufts of grass and stacking pebbles.

One ambled over and pecked hopefully at Clare's boot. Disappointed, it fixed her first with one beady eye, then tilted its head so it could see her with the other. She began laughing again. "I've read about penguins, but I had no idea they were so delightful! My children would love to see them. Could I bring my school here?"

When the earl quirked a brow, she remembered that the school was no longer hers, at least not for the next three months. But he said, "I don't see why not, as long as your students don't upset them."

Clare bent and touched the sleek head of the penguin that was still investigating her. The black feathers were short, stiff, and bristly. "I thought penguins only lived in very cold lands. Might Britain be too warm for them?"

"These are black-footed penguins from islands near the Cape of Good Hope, where the climate is more like Wales." He tossed a pebble. A penguin investigated, then collected it for its nest. "They seem to be thriving, though it was difficult getting them here. I had to fill a ship's hold with ice packed in straw and keep them there for the hottest weeks of the trip."

"They're amazingly clumsy."

"Only on land. They do their flying in the water, where they are as sleek and graceful as fish. Watch those two as they go into the lake."

Clare followed the direction of his gesture and saw how the bodies that were chunky and awkward on land became miraculously swift and sleek under the water. The penguins disappeared from view for long periods of time, then would rocket above the surface so swiftly that she could hardly see them before they vanished again. "I could watch for hours. I see why you went to the effort to bring them back."

He regarded the penguins pensively. "For a time I considered creating a menagerie made up exclusively of black and white animals."

"Was that because you always wear black and white yourself and wanted a place where you would fit right in?"

He grinned. "No, it was because I like zebras almost as much as penguins. Zebras are African creatures that look like black and white striped ponies. They race across the grasslands only a few inches apart, like a cavalry charge, or the trained horses at Astley's Circus."

Intrigued, Clare tried to imagine such a sight. "They sound interesting. Why did you change your mind?"

"Zebras are at home in the blazing African sun and the endless plains. I was afraid that in damp, rainy Wales, they'd fall into a decline and die on me. The peacocks complain about the weather constantly, but since I'm not the one who brought them here from India, I refuse to feel guilty."

"Everyone complains about the Welsh weather. It is the greatest single source of Welsh identity."

He chuckled. "True. Yet I missed the weather when I was away. It's always changing, which is more interesting than week after week of boring sunshine."

Three more penguins hurled themselves into the water. Nicholas said, "It's best to observe them below the surface. It's like watching an underwater ballet. They play together like otters." An expression of unholy mischief crossed his face. "Let's watch them. It's a warm day—perfect for a swim." He moved a dozen steps away from the pebble beach and stripped off his coat and waistcoat, then began to untie his cravat.

Penguins forgotten, Clare's jaw dropped. "You can't just take off your clothing and jump in the lake."

"Of course I can." He dropped his cravat on his other garments. "If you were a proper mistress, you would, too. Though in that case we might not get as far as the water."

"You aren't serious," she said nervously.

"Ah, Clare, how little you know me." He sat on a rock and tugged off his boots, then stood and unbuttoned the throat of his shirt. "I hope the penguins don't decide to use my clothing for nest-building—my valet would be furious."

As he pulled the shirt over his head, exposing a large swath of smooth, dark skin, she stammered, "S-stop. This isn't decent."

"Why? Penguins, zebras, peacocks, and all the rest of the earth's creatures go about in the skin God gave them. It's downright unnatural for humans to always cover themselves. In warmer parts of the world, they don't." Laughing, he tossed his shirt onto the growing mound of clothing.

His chest and shoulders were as beautifully muscled as a Greek statue, but warm with life, more inviting than marble could ever be. Clare was paralyzed, unable to look away from the ebony hair that dusted his chest, then arrowed down his hard midriff in a dark line that disappeared behind the edge of his pantaloons.

"Sure you won't want to join me? The water will be cold, but the sun is warm and a penguin ballet is a rare sight." He began unbuttoning his pantaloons.

Clare bolted. Without looking back, she gasped, "I'll wait with the horses."

His laughter followed her into the woods.

Clare ran until she could no longer see the lake, then stopped and clung to a tree, her heart pounding. As she struggled to regain her breath, she made an appalling discovery.

She had wanted, rather desperately, to stay and see his naked body.

Bark chipped away as her nails bit into the tree trunk. How could she want something so immoral? How could twenty-six years of irreproachable behavior be forgotten so quickly?

Her feverish mind sought for a calm, rational excuse for

going back to watch him swim. Perhaps . . . perhaps observing Nicholas now would diminish his air of masculine mystery, so that if he behaved so outrageously again she would be able to take it more in stride?

Even as she formulated the thought, she knew it was a lie. The simple truth was that her willpower was not strong enough to prevent her from returning. Face tight with self-reproach, she turned and quietly retraced her steps through the grove. When she reached the edge of the woods, she concealed herself behind a shrub, knowing that if Nicholas saw her, she would die of shame.

His back to Clare, he was walking into the water, his skin glowing golden in the sunlight. She stared, fascinated, at the strong arc of his spine and the taut muscles of his buttocks and thighs as they flexed with every step. He was gloriously pagan, as much in harmony with nature as the wind and the trees.

She caught her breath, heart aching with the knowledge that she could never be Eve to his Adam.

When the water was thigh-high, a penguin whizzed by him. Instantly he dived forward and vanished, staying under so long that Clare began to feel concerned. Then he surfaced halfway across the lake, laughing and surrounded by penguins, his black hair slicked over his head and neck.

How many other women had seen him like this and yearned over his beautiful, masculine body?

How many women had he casually seduced and forgotten?

The thought instantly sobered her. Nicholas was a rake and a philistine who made no attempt to deny that he had done despicable things. Clare's presence in his life was accidental and temporary; instead of mooning over him like a lovestruck milkmaid, she must concentrate on surviving the next three months with her dignity and reputation intact.

And yet the sight of him stirred emotions that she had not known she was capable of feeling.

Blindly she slipped into the woods and made her way back to the horses. Feeling shaky and horribly alone, she put her arms around Rhonda's neck and hid her face against the warm skin.

With a sick feeling in her stomach, she recognized that she was vulnerable to Nicholas's lethal charm. When she had accepted his challenge, she had believed herself too strong, too moral, to succumb to the weaknesses of the flesh. Yet a few hours in his company made her suspect that his wiles might be more potent than her principles.

If Clare was the woman people thought she was, she would have the strength to resist, but she wasn't.

She was a fraud.

All her life, she had worked hard to convince those around her that she was truly spiritual. She had been the model of a devout Methodist, helping those in need, offering comfort to those who were afflicted. And her charade had been successful, for it had never occurred to anyone to doubt the faith of Thomas Morgan's daughter.

Yet in her heart, she carried the shameful knowledge that she was an imposter. Never had she experienced the passionate inner knowledge of God that was the heart and soul of her religion. Not once had she known the ecstasy of divine grace, though she had seen it in those around her.

That failure had been her dark secret, never revealed to anyone. Not to her father, who assumed that her spirit was as true as his own; not to Owen Morris, who as her class leader was also her spiritual director.

It wasn't that she lacked faith. She truly believed that the world was shaped by divine purpose; that it was better to behave with kindness than cruelty; that service was life's highest purpose. Most of all, she believed—she needed to believe—that deeds were more important than words. When the time came for her to be judged, perhaps her works would outweigh her spiritual failings.

She pressed her fist to her mouth to suppress a despairing sob. It was horribly unfair—she was not an innocent pagan who could respond to Nicholas without guilt. Yet neither was her faith powerful enough to give her the strength to withstand him serenely.

But of one thing she was sure; the next three months were going to teach her about hell.

5

ONE OF THE penguins had absconded with Nicholas's cravat, but the rest of his clothing had been left alone. After roughly toweling himself off with his waistcoat, he dressed, then made his way back to the horses, whistling softly. Clare was sitting cross-legged beneath a tree, her expression remote. To his regret, there was no sign of the charming bashfulness she had exhibited when he had started to undress.

Offering her a helping hand, he said, "You should have joined me. The penguins were in fine form."

Ignoring his hand, she got to her feet unassisted. "I'm sure that I would have been so dazzled by you that I wouldn't have noticed them," she said witheringly.

"Ah, I am beginning to make an impression on you," he said with delight.

"I would never deny that."

Clouds had covered the sun and chilled the air, and the ride back was a quiet one. After stabling the horses, Nicholas escorted Clare into the house. He was pleased to see that she now accepted his casual touch as normal.

His good mood evaporated as soon as he stepped into his grandfather's house. As he ushered her into the main drawing room, he asked, "What do you think of this place, Clare?"

"It's very grand," she said after a slight pause.

He studied the room with distaste. "But do you like it?"

She frowned. "That's not a fair question. I'm a simple woman, with cottager tastes. I know how to appreciate an oaken chair, or a whitewashed wall, or a well-made quilt, but I know nothing of fine furniture, or art, or aristocratic style.''

"That doesn't mean your opinion is valueless. Does this house please your senses?''

"To be honest, I find it oppressive.'' Her gaze traveled around the room. "There's too much clutter. Every inch of space seems to be filled with patterns, or fabric, or bits of china whose value could feed a poor family for a year. No doubt everything is in the best of taste''—she ran a finger across the top of a picture frame, then frowned at the dust—"though the housekeeping could be improved. But I prefer my cottage.''

"Too much clutter,'' he repeated. "My sentiments exactly. Gypsies don't like being indoors at the best of times, and this house has always made me feel suffocated.''

"Do you think of yourself as a Gypsy?''

He shrugged. "When it suits me.'' He lifted a porcelain figurine that depicted a lion devouring an undutiful child. Not surprisingly, his grandfather had been fond of it. Nicholas had always wanted to smash it to pieces.

Well, why not? With one swift movement, he hurled the figure into the fireplace. It shattered with a satisfying crash.

Pleased, Nicholas turned to Clare, who was watching him warily. "I give you permission to change whatever you want,'' he said. "Pack away the clutter, hire more maids. Clean, paint, paper—whatever you think best. Since it's your fault that I'm going to spend more time in this mausoleum than I had planned, you can jolly well make it livable. Buy what you think necessary and have the bills sent to me. Not only will that pump money into the local economy, but you'll gratify Williams no end. He finds his post here rather boring, I think. I'll instruct him to follow your orders as he would mine.''

"Is it part of a mistress's job to redecorate her lover's house?'' she asked with dismay.

"Most mistresses would swoon with delight at the opportunity,'' he assured her. "Would you like to visit the attics? There are masses of furniture up there. You might find things that are more to your taste.''

Looking a little dazed, she said, "Later, perhaps. Before I make any changes, I will have to observe and think."

"Wise woman." He glanced at the ormolu clock on the mantel. "I must meet my steward now, so I'll leave you to your own devices for the rest of the afternoon. We dine at six. If you wish to bathe first, ring from your room. The staff should be able to manage hot water. Until dinner?"

He withdrew, already feeling less oppressed by the house. Three months of Clare's sturdy good sense should improve Aberdare immeasurably. Perhaps, in time, it might no longer feel so much like his grandfather's house.

Clare spent the next hour examining the public rooms. The basic layout and proportions were appealing, but the furnishings seemed to have been chosen more for grandeur than comfort, and there was too much of everything.

When she finished her survey, she went to her bedchamber, which was as large as the whole ground floor of her cottage. It was also cluttered, but the blue draperies and bed hangings were pretty. If she removed all the unnecessary furniture and the two dismal paintings of dead animals, it would be quite pleasant.

Feeling drained, she self-indulgently flopped across the bed, then folded her hands behind her head and thought about what had happened since she had arrived at Aberdare. It seemed as if days rather than hours had passed.

She was still incredulous that the earl had casually handed the reins of his household to her, with blanket permission to spend what she wished. But now that she had recovered from her surprise, she relished the prospect of improving this gaudy, dusty, neglected mansion. For the rest of the afternoon, she thought, made lists, and jotted down question to herself.

She was drawn from her plans when the clock struck five. Time to prepare for her first dinner with Nicholas.

Work had steadied her, and she no longer felt as emotionally fragile as she had by the lake. Nonetheless, being in such a grand house was unnerving. Even ringing for a bath made her uncomfortable, since the Morgans had never had any servants.

Trepidation vanished when the little maid who responded to the bell turned out to be a former student. Dilys was a sweet-natured girl who had always adored her teacher, and she accepted Miss Morgan's presence as if it were perfectly natural for a schoolmistress to be the guest of an earl.

For her part, Clare found that asking Dilys for a bath was no harder than asking a student to recite the times tables. However, she was unable to stop herself from helping when Dilys staggered into the room with two heavy coppers of steaming water. If she were a real lady, Clare supposed that she would have stood by and let the girl struggle.

The enormous hip bath was delightful; Clare had never had the luxury of so much hot water. She soaked for so long that she had to fix her hair and dress in a rush.

Only one of her gowns was suitable for evening wear, and it was old and had never been stylish. However, the rich blue fabric matched her eyes, and the neckline revealed several inches of smooth skin around her throat.

She glanced down at herself and tried to envision what she would look like in a fashionably low-cut gown. Regretfully she realized that even if she owned such a garment—and had the courage to wear it—the result would be unremarkable.

After brushing her hair and pinning it into a shining coil at her nape, she examined herself critically in the mirror. The moist heat of the bath had caused her dark hair to wave softly around her face, lessening her usual severity. Fortunately her complexion was good and she had naturally rosy Welsh coloring.

Her reflection showed that she appeared exactly as she was: a modest woman of modest means. For the sake of her pride, she looked as good as she was capable of looking, yet she was too ordinary to drive the Earl of Aberdare to uncontrollable lust. Thank heaven for that. It was bad enough that he viewed seducing her as a game; if his heart and loins were really in the pursuit, she might not be able to withstand him.

Wiping palms that were suddenly damp, she went downstairs to dinner. The day would soon be over, and she couldn't help wondering when the earl would collect his kiss. Even more important, how would she react when he did?

Nicholas was already in the family drawing room, pouring a drink from a decanter. Dressed in beautifully tailored black coat and pantaloons, he looked ready to dine with the Prince Regent. She paused in the doorway, momentarily struck by the sheer ridiculousness of the situation. What on earth was she, plain Clare Morgan, doing at Aberdare?

Hearing her steps, he looked up and halted in mid-gesture, his expression arrested. "You look lovely tonight, Clare."

There was such warmth in his voice that she shivered. Not only was he rich and handsome, but he had the ability to make a female feel beautiful and cherished. Perhaps that was an essential talent for a rake, for a woman would give a great deal to keep that expression in a man's eyes.

"Thank you," she said, trying to sound as if compliments were common in her life. "Would it be improper for me to observe that you are a sight to break any impressionable girl's heart?"

He looked hopeful. "Are you impressionable?"

"Not in the least." She tried to sound stern, but couldn't help smiling.

"A pity." He reached for a different decanter. "Would you care for a glass of sherry?"

She actually considered accepting for a moment, but shook her head. "No, thank you."

"That's right—Methodists avoid anything that might be considered strong drink." He set the decanter down and thought. "You drink ale, don't you?"

"Of course—everyone does."

He lifted a bottle. "Then try some of this German wine. It's milder than most ales." When she still hesitated, he said, "I swear this won't make you so drunk that you'll dance on the table." He gave an elaborate sigh of regret. "Unfortunately."

She chuckled. "Very well, I'll have some. But you needn't fear for your table—I don't dance, either."

"Good God, I'd forgotten that." He opened the bottle and poured her a glass of wine. "What do Methodists do to amuse themselves?"

"Pray and sing," she said promptly.

"I shall have to broaden your repertoire." He handed her one of the glasses. "Shall we drink to a mutually satisfactory conclusion to our association?"

"Very well." She lifted her glass. "Three months from now, may the mine be safer and the village of Penreith healthier, wealthier, and happier. In addition, I hope that you will have seen the spiritual light and become a sober and godly man, and that I will be home again, reputation and career intact."

He clinked the rim of his glass against hers, his black eyes gleaming. "My definition of 'mutually satisfactory' differs in several details."

"Which are?"

He grinned. "I'd better not say. You'd empty the rest of your wine over my head."

With mild wonder, Clare realized that she was bantering with a man. And not only was she carrying on a teasing conversation with suggestive undertones—she was enjoying it.

Her sense of being sophisticated and in control vanished when she made the mistake of glancing into Nicholas's face. He was studying her with a mesmerizing intensity that was as palpable as a touch. As she looked into his dark eyes, she felt trapped, unable to look away. Her blood swirled with unaccustomed heat, rushing to each spot touched by his slowly moving gaze. First her lips tingled, then her throat pulsed, almost as if he were caressing them with his fingertips.

When his gaze drifted to her breasts, her nipples tightened with yearning sensitivity. Merciful heaven, if he could affect her like this when he was a yard away, what would happen when he finally touched her?

Before she could become completely unnerved, she was saved by the soft gong of a dinner bell. Nicholas turned his head, freeing her from the spell of his gaze. "Shall we see what the cook is capable of? I haven't had a real meal since returning to Aberdare, so I have no idea how skillful he is. In fact, I don't know if the cook is a him or a her."

"I talked to Williams earlier, and he said that one of the

two maids, Gladys, has been pressed into service as temporary cook,'' Clare said, hoping that she sounded composed. ''You don't need a mock mistress—you need a
housekeeper to order your household.''

''Can't you be both?''

Once again he put his hand in the small of her back,
gently possessive. She flinched, for her gown and shift were
thinner than the garments she had worn earlier, and the effect was almost as intimate as if he had put his palm on her
bare flesh.

He noticed, of course. ''And here I thought that you were
becoming more at ease with me,'' he said softly. ''You
needn't be fearful, Clare.''

She scowled up at him. ''If I had any sense at all, I'd be
terrified. You're twice my size and probably four times my
strength, and I'm entirely at your mercy. The fact that I am
voluntarily under your roof means that you could do anything short of murder and most people would say that it was
only what I deserved for my shameless conduct.''

His face darkened. ''Let me repeat: I have no interest in
unwilling women. In spite of my worldly rank and greater
physical strength, you hold the ultimate power between us,
for you have the right to say no. For example . . .'' He
raised his hand and brushed her cheek with the back of his
knuckles.

The slow movement burned across her skin, seductive
and alarming. Clare felt suddenly vulnerable, as if his touch
was stripping away her common sense and exposing unad-
mitted longings.

He murmured, ''Shall I continue?''

With all her heart, she wanted to say yes. Instead she
snapped, ''No!''

His hand fell instantly. ''See how easy it is to stop me.''

He thought that she had done that easily? Apparently he
wasn't all-knowing. Nerves in shreds, she said, ''Why don't
you take your kiss for the day and get it over with? I'll enjoy
dinner more if I don't feel like a mouse being stalked by a
cat.''

He smiled lazily. ''My turn to say no. Anticipation is part
of the pleasure of lovemaking. Since I can only be sure of

one kiss, I wish to delay it as long as possible." He guided
her into the dining room. "So fear not—I promise not to
leap across the table before you've fortified yourself with
food."

He must know that her real fear was not that he wouldn't
stop, but that she would be incapable of saying no. The
thought strengthened her resolve. Yes, he was powerful and
infinitely more experienced than she, but that didn't mean
that she had to lose their contest. It was up to her to be
stronger.

That goal in mind, she encouraged him to talk about his
travels rather than more personal subjects. To her surprise,
he had traveled extensively on the Continent. After he mentioned a visit to Paris, she asked, "How did you manage to
see so much of Europe when Napoleon has closed the Continent to Britons?"

"By traveling with my disreputable kinfolk. Even Napoleon's armies can't stop Gypsies from going where they will.
When I joined a kumpania, I became just another Romany
horse trader. No one ever guessed that I was British." Giving up on his over-salted leek soup, he poured wine for each
of them.

She pushed away her own soup bowl with relief; it was
amazingly bad. "If you'd any taste for spying, traveling as
a Gypsy would have been a perfect disguise."

Nicholas broke out coughing. When she looked at him in
surprise, he managed to say, "Swallowed the wrong way."

Clare cocked her head to one side. "Was that coincidence, or a guilty reaction because you actually were involved in intelligence gathering?"

"You are definitely too clever for comfort." He sipped
his wine, expression thoughtful. "I suppose there's no harm
in telling you that an old friend of mine is active in intelligence work, and I sometimes passed on information that I
thought might interest him. Occasionally I acted as a courier
as well, if it fit into my own plans. I was never a serious
spy, though. That would have been too much like work."

She was intrigued by his reluctance to admit that he had
served his country. Perhaps he wasn't quite the wastrel he

pretended; then again, perhaps he had simply enjoyed the adventure of spying.

Williams and Dilys entered the room together. The girl, with nervous glances at the earl, cleared away the dishes from the first course. Williams placed a platter of scorched-looking lamb in front of his master, then served half a dozen other dishes. After dismissing the butler, Nicholas carved the lamb. "If the soup is any indicator, Gladys is out of her depth in the kitchen. This joint doesn't look too promising, either."

When Clare tasted the leathery meat, she had to agree. Nicholas winced when he tried his. "Something *must* be done about the food."

Seeing his speculative glance, Clare laid down her fork and gave him a warning scowl. "Yes, I'm a good cook, but I will not have time to work in the kitchen. And don't try to convince me that a mistress also has to cook for her lover."

"I wasn't thinking of wasting your valuable time in the kitchen." He smiled mischievously. "But a mistress can do interesting things with food. Shall I describe them?"

"No!"

"Another time, perhaps." He prodded a boiled potato with his fork. It promptly disintegrated into a shapeless white mass. "Do you know of a decent cook who is looking for a situation?"

"Not in the valley. You might be able to find someone in Swansea, but you'd probably be better off sending to London. There must be agencies that specialize in finding French chefs for aristocratic houses."

"French chefs are usually temperamental, and most would go mad with boredom in Wales. Aren't there any good Welsh country cooks around?"

Clare's brows drew together. "Surely that kind of food must seem very plain to a gentleman."

"I like country cooking as long as it's done well." After careful scrutiny, he pushed a sinister-looking lump to the side of his plate. "Even the penguins would sneer at this fish. Are you sure you don't know a competent person who could start soon—preferably tomorrow?"

His aristocratic impatience made her smile. "There's a woman in Penreith who worked at Aberdare as a kitchen maid before her marriage. She's not a formally trained cook, but whenever I've eaten at her house, the food has been wonderful. And she could use the work—her husband died in the pit last year."

Nicholas spooned a mysterious substance onto his plate. It was brown and it oozed. "What's this? No, don't tell me, I'd rather not know. If you can coax the widow up here tomorrow, I'll be eternally grateful."

"I'll see what I can do." Clare wrinkled her nose at the cold, gray, mushy Brussels sprouts. "I have a stake in the results myself."

After several more minutes of unenthusiastic chewing, Nicholas said, "Now that you've had time to reflect, have you devised a redecoration strategy?"

"Surveying the ground floor confirmed my original impression: cleaning and simplification will work wonders." Clare tried the apple tart, which proved to be flavorless but edible. "I won't do anything too radical—when you remarry, I'm sure your wife will have plans of her own."

Nicholas set his wine glass on the table with a force that threatened to shatter it. "You needn't concern yourself about that. I will never remarry."

There was a black edge to his voice that Clare had not heard before, and his face was dark as a thundercloud. He looked like a man who had loved his wife, and who mourned her deeply.

The late Caroline, Viscountess Tregar, had been the daughter of an earl, and she had brought a title and a fortune to her marriage. During her months at Aberdare she had seldom come into the village, but once Clare had seen her riding. Nicholas's wife had been tall and graceful and gloriously blond, so lovely that to see her was to stop and stare. It was not surprising to learn that her loss still hurt Nicholas. And his grief must be compounded by guilt over his own role in his wife's untimely death.

Again Clare wondered what had really happened on the fateful night when the old earl and Lady Tregar had died. It was hard to believe that Nicholas had been so crazed by lust that he had bedded his grandfather's wife in defiance of all decency. The second countess, Emily, was only a few years older than her step grandson, but though she had been attractive, no one would have looked at her twice if Caroline was in the room.

Unless . . . unless Nicholas had hated his grandfather so much that he had wanted to hurt the old man in the cruelest way imaginable.

The thought that Nicholas might have seduced the countess for such an ugly reason turned Clare's stomach. A series of dreadful pictures flashed through her mind: Nicholas and his grandfather's wife caught in flagrante delicto; the old earl collapsing with a fatal heart seizure; Caroline drawn by the commotion, then rushing hysterically from the scene, only to die as she fled from the monster she had married.

If that was what had happened, Nicholas was morally responsible for the deaths of his wife and grandfather, even if he hadn't killed them with his own hands. Yet Clare could not bring herself to believe that he had behaved so despicably. Though he might be wild, she had seen no wickedness in him.

But, she realized grimly, it was possible to believe that he had acted from impulse rather than calculated viciousness. If he had unintentionally precipitated the disaster, he would have ample cause to feel guilty.

Sickened, she pushed her plate away.

Unaware of her lurid thoughts, Nicholas said, "I agree. This is not a meal to linger over."

For a moment Clare felt disoriented; it was impossible to reconcile her nightmare imaginings with the charming, playful man who sat opposite her. She saw quite clearly that if she was to endure three months of his company, she must put speculations about his past out of her mind. Otherwise she would go mad. Already Nicholas was frowning at her, wondering what was wrong. With effort, she managed to say calmly, "Do I withdraw and leave you to your port now?"

His expression eased. "I'll skip the port. I find you much more interesting—just as a mistress should be."

"I don't feel very interesting at the moment." She got to

her feet. "May I go to my room now, or is it part of my bargain to keep you company all evening?"

He stood also. "I don't think it would be fair to force you to endure me all the time—but I would like it if you stayed willingly. It's still early."

There was a faintly wistful note in his voice. Perhaps he was lonely. She shouldn't be surprised, since he had no friends or family at Aberdare, but it had not occurred to her that he might suffer from common sorrows like loneliness.

Empathy proved stronger than her need for solitude. "How do fashionable people amuse themselves in the evening?" Seeing a familiar glint come into his eyes, she said hastily, "No, I won't do what you're thinking."

He chuckled. "Not only clever, but you can read my mind. Since you're rejecting my first choice, let's play billiards."

"Don't you know any respectable activities?" she said doubtfully. "Reading in the library would be a nice quiet way to spend the evening."

"Another time. Don't worry—there's nothing inherently immoral about billiards. The only reason decent folk condemn the game is because of the risk of falling into bad company." His mouth quirked up. "Since you're stuck with me already, I don't see how playing billiards can make your situation any worse."

She found herself chuckling as he lifted a branch of candles and led her from the room. Wryly she realized that the real danger was not bad company, but laughter. It would be hard to give that up when the time came to leave Aberdare.

6

THE BILLIARDS room was at the far end of the house. While Clare lighted the candles in the chandelier that hung from the middle of the ceiling, Nicholas built a coal fire to take the chill off the damp spring night. Then he removed the fitted velvet cover that protected the table. Dust flew in all directions and Clare sneezed.

"Sorry." He folded the cover and dropped it in a corner. "Another failure of housekeeping."

"I'm beginning to think my role as housekeeper won't leave time for me to be a mistress."

"I can live with dust," he said swiftly.

Clare gave the involuntary, hastily suppressed smile that fascinated Nicholas. Coaxing that smile was like trying to lure a shy foal to his hand; patience was the key.

He took a set of ivory balls from the equipment cabinet and laid them on the baize-covered table. "Do you want to use a mace or a cue stick?"

"What's the difference?"

He handed her the mace, which was a pole with a broad, flat head. "This is the old-fashioned way of playing billiards. The ball is pushed, rather like in shuffleboard, if you've ever played that. A player using a mace doesn't have to bend over." He set the mace against the cue ball and demonstrated, sending the object ball into a corner pocket.

"And the cue?"

He took off his coat so he could move freely, then bent over, lined up a shot, and stroked. The cue ball knocked a red ball into a pocket, then caromed off a second ball, which also dropped into a pocket. "The cue allows more flexibility and control. But I imagine you'll prefer the mace—it's more moral."

Clare's dark brows arched. "How can one piece of wood be more moral than another?"

"The mace saves a lady from bending over and exposing her ankles to whatever depraved males are present," he explained.

Her full lips quivered, and she pressed them together.

Amused, he said, "Why don't you go ahead and let yourself smile? It must be a tremendous strain trying to keep a straight face around me."

His sober, pious schoolmistress giggled. He wouldn't have believed it if he hadn't heard with his own ears.

"You're right," she agreed ruefully. "You haven't a serious bone in your body, and it's very hard to maintain my dignity. But I shall persevere." She lifted the mace in one hand and the cue in the other. "It won't matter which of these I use, because I suspect I've fallen into the clutches of a billiard sharp."

He rolled a red ball across the green baize toward a pocket. Halfway across the table, it hit a bump and skipped to the right. "This table is so warped that skill won't count for much. I'm looking forward to seeing how the slate surface will work."

"What are the rules?"

"There are a number of different games, and players can make up others at their pleasure. We'll start with something simple." He gestured toward the table. "I've put out six red balls, six blue, and one white cue ball. The cue ball is used to knock the others into pockets but mustn't go in itself. Each of us will take a color. If you choose red, you will get a point for each one you pot, and lose a point if you accidentally knock in a blue. The person shooting continues until missing a shot."

Clare set down the mace and walked to the other side of the table, then bent over and tried a stroke with the cue stick. The hard wooden tip hit the polished ivory cue ball off-center, and the ball rolled weakly to one side. She frowned. "This is harder than it looks."

"Everything is harder than it looks. That's the first law

of life." He came around the table to her side. "Let me demonstrate. I promise I won't look at your ankles."

The smile tugged at her lips again. "Liar."

"Suspicious wench." He lifted his cue stick and went through the shooting procedure step by step. "Put most of your weight on the right foot and bend from the hips. The fingers of your left hand support the stick. Sight along the cue and try to hit the ball dead center." He demonstrated again.

When Clare bent over to try, he leaned back against the table, folded his arms across his chest, and blatantly studied her ankles. She ostentatiously ignored him.

The ankles were well worth watching, as was the rest of her. Clare didn't have the kind of spectacular figure that attracted male attention from across a crowded room, and her clothing was designed to disguise rather than enhance. Yet her figure was trim, and when she relaxed, she had a natural grace that drew the eye. He looked forward to seeing what she would look like in more flattering garments. Even more, he would like to see her in no garments at all.

After Clare had learned the basics, they began a game. Nicholas gave himself a handicap: his shots wouldn't count unless his ball caromed off two cushions before going into a pocket. The combination of that restriction and the unevenness of the playing surface kept them from being hopelessly mismatched.

To his amusement, his sober schoolmistress played like an enthusiastic child, scowling when she miscued, glowing with satisfaction when she potted a ball. He wondered how often she allowed herself to do something strictly for pleasure. Very seldom, he suspected; she had probably spent all her time on hard work and good deeds since she was an infant.

But she was clearly enjoying herself now. She had potted two reds in a row and was now stretched over the table as she carefully lined up a third. Several strands of hair had come loose and they curled enticingly around her face. Her position also emphasized the delightful curve of her derriere. He was strongly tempted to stroke it.

With regret, he suppressed the impulse so that the harmonious atmosphere wouldn't be wrecked. When her bristles weren't up, Clare was excellent company—intelligent and dryly witty, with an understanding of human nature that made up for her lack of worldly experience.

She took her shot, but didn't hit the cue ball squarely. It squirted to one side. "Drat! Another bad stroke."

He grinned. While billiards might not be inherently immoral, there was no denying that talking about balls, shafts, strokes, and pockets was pleasantly suggestive for those of lewd mind, like himself. Fortunately Clare, in her innocence, did not recognize the latent ribaldry of their conversation. "Strong language, Clarissima," he said with mock disapproval. "Perhaps exposure to billiards really does weaken the moral fiber."

She put her hand over her mouth to conceal her smile. "I suspect that the fault is the bad company, not the game."

Nicholas gave her an appreciative glance, then leaned over the table and lined up his next shot. He moved with lazy grace, his white shirt emphasizing the width of his shoulders and the narrowness of his waist. Bad company indeed; dark and diabolically handsome, he was every romantic girl's dream, and every protective father's nightmare. She forced her gaze away from her companion to the table.

During the course of the evening he had learned how to avoid the worst of the table's bumps. Even with the complication of having to bounce the object ball off the cushions, he managed to pot his last four balls to end the current game.

"It's fortunate that we're not playing for any stakes," she observed. "You would have beggared me by now."

Generous in victory, he said, "For a beginner, you're doing very well, Clare. You've narrowed the gap with every game. With practice, you could turn into a billiards sharp yourself."

She was absurdly pleased, even though it was a disgraceful kind of compliment. "Shall we play another game?"

The mantel clock began striking the hour. Glancing over to it, she said with surprise, "Eleven o'clock already." The day was almost over, and the moment of truth was at hand. Clare's relaxed mood evaporated instantly.

In the vain hope that he might not remember that he was entitled to a kiss, she said, "Time to retire. I've a great deal to do tomorrow—go into Penreith and find a cook, arrange for you to visit the pit, make sure that my friend Marged is managing all right with the school. All kinds of things."

She set her cue stick on the rack and turned toward the door. Before she could take a step, Nicholas's cue shot straight out, the hard tip banging into the wall beside her and barring her exit. He drawled, "Aren't you forgetting something?"

She flinched. "I haven't forgotten. I was hoping you had."

He was watching her with the expression of a charming predator. "Not when I've been waiting for my kiss all day."

He lowered the cue and stepped forward. When he raised his arm she skittered back, then felt like a fool when she saw that he was only returning his stick to the rack.

When he had done so, he turned a thoughtful gaze on her. "Is being kissed by me such a terrible prospect? I've never had any complaints in the past. Quite the contrary."

Her back was to the wall and she couldn't retreat any farther. "Just go ahead and do it," she said tightly.

Sudden insight lit his eyes. He put his hand under her chin and raised it so that she was looking directly at him. "Clare, have you never been kissed with . . . with amorous intent?"

Unable to deny the humiliating fact, she said flatly, "No man has ever wanted to."

In this, as in billiards, he was generous, not ridiculing her inexperience or her fear. "I guarantee that there are men who have dreamed of kissing you, but you intimidated them so much that none dared try." He began stroking her lips with his thumb. "Relax, Clarissima. My aim is to persuade, not terrorize."

His rhythmic movements were profoundly sensual, and the effect was even more unsettling than when he had released her hair the day before. Her lips softened and parted slightly, and instinctively she touched her tongue to his thumb. She tasted salt and maleness, then flushed in embarrassment when she recognized the forwardness of her behavior.

Ignoring her subtle withdrawal, he said, "If this is a first kiss, I'll start simply. After all, we have three months ahead of us." He placed his hands on her shoulders and bent his head.

Her face tightened as she steeled herself for his onslaught. But instead of kissing her mouth, he pressed his lips to the tender skin at the base of her throat.

Clare gasped as her pulse beat against the seductive pressure of his mouth. She had thought herself prepared, but she found that she had no defenses against this unexpected caress. Heat and a hint of moisture; melting sensations that flowed downward, weakening her and throbbing in secret, shameful places.

"Your skin is lovely," he murmured as his lips traced the sensitive junction between throat and shoulder. "Celtic silk, smooth and alluring."

She felt that she should be doing something, but had no idea what. Hesitantly she laid her hands on his waist, feeling taut muscles beneath the luxurious cambric of his shirt.

He exhaled warm, teasing breath into her ear, then lightly nipped the lobe, his teeth an erotic contrast to the gentleness of his lips. Her fingers moved restlessly over his ribs.

When he began kneading her shoulders and upper arms, her eyes closed and she drifted, flotsam in a sensuous sea, both of her hands working against him like a kitten nursing. Locks of loosened hair fell over her shoulders, brushing across her sensitized flesh with feather lightness. She felt as if she were made of wax that could be molded into any form she desired.

She felt a faint tugging behind her neck, then his hand slid lower, his open palm warming the area between her shoulder blades. With icewater shock, she realized that he had unfastened the button that secured the top of her gown. As he started to finger the next button, she spun away from him. "Isn't there a time limit to kissing?" she asked with a brittle sham of composure. "Surely this one must be over."

He made no attempt to prevent her from escaping. Per-

haps his breath had quickened, but he seemed otherwise
unaffected by the embrace. ''A kiss has no set length,'' he
replied mildly. ''It's finished when one of the participants
decides that it is.''

''Very well. Today's kiss is over.'' She reached back and
refastened the button with unsteady hands.

''Was the experience as bad as expected, Clarissima? You
didn't seem to dislike it.''

She would rather not have answered, but honesty compelled her to say, ''I . . . did not dislike it.''

''Are you still afraid of me?''

He touched her fallen hair with a butterfly's delicacy. She
might not have noticed that touch, except that she noticed
everything he did. She closed her eyes for a moment, then
opened them and met his gaze steadily. ''Aristophanes said
that boys throw stones at frogs in jest, but the frogs, they
die in earnest. You're going to break my life into splinters,
then move on without a second thought. Yes, my lord, you
terrify me.''

He became very still. ''Only things that are rigid can
break. Perhaps your life needs to be splintered.''

''That sounds very profound.'' Her mouth twisted. ''Your
life was shattered four years ago. Are you better or happier
for it?''

His expression hardened. ''It is definitely time to retire.
I'm going into Swansea tomorrow, so I'll see you at dinner.'' He lifted the dusty velvet cover and tossed it over the
table.

Clare took a small branch of candles from the top of the
equipment cabinet and left the room at a pace that was almost a run. She didn't stop until she reached her bedchamber. There she locked the door, set down the candlestick
and sank into an upholstered chair, her hands pressed to her
temples.

One day, and one kiss, had passed. How on earth would
she survive another ninety?

Not only had she enjoyed the embrace of a man who was
not her husband and whose intentions were strictly dishonorable, but she could not prevent herself from yearning for
the next day's embrace. For the sake of her soul, she should

leave Aberdare immediately. The village could take care of itself. No one had asked her to sacrifice herself for Penreith; it had been strictly her own idea of duty.

The thought of leaving cooled her overheated thoughts. The earl was willing to do things that would benefit hundreds of people, and it would be madness to forfeit that because of a spinsterish attack of nerves. She was overreacting to what had been a startling new experience; tomorrow she would be less susceptible to his wiles.

After changing into her flannel nightgown and braiding her hair into a long plait, she climbed into the enormous bed and ordered herself to fall asleep. She would need all of her strength to hold her own against the Demon Earl.

Nicholas stood in front of the fireplace and gazed idly at the dying coals. The house felt less dismal with her in residence, but she was having an unsettling effect on him. Perhaps that was because he was unused to innocence. Clare's blend of inexperience and cool-eyed practicality was oddly endearing. And for a moment, before her common sense took over, she had yielded to his touch, as pliant as sunwarmed willow.

He wanted to be the one to teach her that desire was not a sin. And he wanted, dammit, to do it tonight.

Cursing the bargain that prevented him from making further attempts to seduce her until the next day, he restlessly drummed his fingers on the marble mantel. Memories of Clare's wide eyes and silken skin were going to make it difficult to get to sleep.

Suddenly he put back his head and laughed. He might be frustrated, but he also felt more alive than he had in a long time. And the credit must go to his Methodist minx.

Quietly Clare opened the door of the school and stepped into the back of the plain, whitewashed room. Most of the students were working individually while Marged conducted a low-voiced lesson in arithmetic with the youngest children.

Heads turned at Clare's entrance, followed by whispers and giggles. Marged also glanced up. With a smile, she yielded gracefully to the inevitable. "Time for lunch. Say hello to Miss Morgan, and then it's outside with you all."

Released, the children foamed around Clare like the sea, as if she had been gone for months rather than a day and a half. After accepting their greetings and making appropriate comments ("So you've learned subtraction, Ianto. Wonderful!"), she went forward and gave Marged a hug. "How are you managing?"

Laughing, her friend perched on the edge of the battered desk. "Yesterday I didn't think I'd survive. If you had been here, I would have begged on bended knee for you to take the school back. But today is going more smoothly. In another fortnight, I think I'll have the knack of it." She fingered a lock of fair hair as she sought for words. "It's hard work, but so satisfying when I explain something and a child's face lights up with understanding. I can't begin to describe the feeling." She gave a little laugh. "Of course, you know what that's like."

With a small pang, Clare realized that though she believed passionately in education, it had been years since she had felt such pleasure in the actual act of teaching. Too often she was inwardly bored by the drills, the constant repetition. Perhaps that was why she enjoyed the challenge of dealing with Nicholas; it was a pleasure matching wits with a crafty, unpredictable adult whose intelligence was the equal of hers.

Feeling vaguely guilty about her thoughts, she said, "Lord Aberdare wants to go into the mine to see what conditions are like there, and he'd rather not do it under George Madoc's guidance. Would Owen be willing to take him through?"

Marged bit her lip. "If Madoc finds out, he might make trouble for Owen."

"I know that's a danger," Clare admitted, "but if the worst happened and he was discharged, I'm sure his lordship will find other work for him. Don't tell anyone but Owen yet, but Aberdare says he's willing to reopen and expand the slate quarry."

"So you've been successful! Clare, that's marvelous."

"It's a bit early to count our chickens, but so far, so

good. He's also willing to speak with Lord Michael Kenyon about the mine, but I think he wants to see the problems for himself rather than take the word of a mere female.''

"It will be good if he does go into the pit—no one can really understand who hasn't been there." Marged thought a moment. "Madoc always goes home for a two-hour meal in the middle of the day, so tomorrow should be as good a day as any to take his lordship into the pit. I'll check with Owen when he comes home tonight. If there's a problem, I'll send a message to Aberdare, but if you don't hear to the contrary, bring him over a bit after noon." That settled, she turned her bright-eyed gaze on Clare. "How are you getting along with the Demon Earl?"

"Well enough." Clare lifted a dull quill and penknife from the desk and automatically started to sharpen the pen. "He was not at all pleased that I decided to take him up on his challenge, but he has accepted my presence with good grace.''

"What kind of work will you be doing there?"

The penknife jerked and almost sliced into Clare's forefinger. "It looks like I'll be a glorified housekeeper. He's given me license to hire staff and clean and rearrange the place to make it more livable.''

"What does Rhys Williams think of all this?"

"I talked with him this morning before coming to Penreith, and he's delighted. It's been hard trying to care for that huge house with only two maids." She made another cut on the quill, trying for a better point. "I spent the morning in the village hiring people to work temporarily, with the possibility of permanent positions if the earl decides to keep the house open.''

"I'm sure you had no trouble finding willing workers."

Clare nodded. "Not only did every single person accept, but they all went up to Aberdare as soon as we finished talking. Rhys Williams must have at least a dozen people scrubbing and dusting, and Mrs. Howell is busy in the kitchen. The house may need redecorating, but at least it will be clean soon.''

"Has Lord Aberdare done anything to live up to his rakish reputation?''

The knife split the quill in half. "I'm sorry—I've ruined your pen." Clare set the penknife carefully back on the desk. "To me, he seems more lonely than rakish. Perhaps he still mourns his wife. He seems to like having me as a companion—someone to tease."

"That sounds more interesting than housekeeping."

"Oh, I almost forgot. I met the famous 'strange animals,' and they're penguins—the most fascinating creatures. Lord Aberdare said the children could come and see them."

"Splendid! Perhaps in a few weeks, when the weather is better, we can have a school picnic. We shouldn't have any trouble borrowing a couple of wagons."

From there, they drifted into talk of the school. After Clare had answered Marged's questions, she took her leave and drove back to Aberdare.

Stepping into the front hall was like entering a whirlwind. The hall and the adjacent drawing room were full of hard-working people, and since they were all Welsh, they were singing in harmony and with as much skill as enthusiasm. The music lent a festive air to the activity, and gave Clare a brief vision of what an ungloomy Aberdare might be like.

As she looked around her, bemused, Rhys Williams turned away from polishing the brass light fixtures and greeted her. She had never seen his long face so animated. "The house is coming alive," he said proudly. "I decided to take your advice and concentrate our efforts on the hall and the drawing room, since that will make the most impact on the earl."

"It's having an impact on me." Clare shook her head in awe when she stepped into the drawing room. "It's amazing how much it helped to remove the ugliest furniture and ornaments." So much had been taken away that there were now gaps that needed filling. "His lordship said there are furnishings stored in the attic. Is anything suitable for the drawing room?"

"There are some fine pieces there. I'll take you up now." The butler hung his polishing rag over a doorknob, took Clare's bonnet and shawl away, then led her upstairs. "During these last years, when the house was so dreadfully dull, I would sometimes think what I would do with the place if

it were mine. The prospects and proportions of the rooms
are lovely, and with a little effort Aberdare could be magnificent. But I could do nothing without his lordship's orders."

They stopped to light lamps, then started up the last narrow
flight to the attics. Clare said, "Since the earl has given permission to make changes, tell me your ideas. Perhaps we can
put them into effect."

Williams led her through a forest of shadowy shapes into
a smaller attic. "I would return these pieces to the drawing
room, where they used to be. The furniture is old, from the
middle of the last century, but beautifully made, and there's
a natural elegance in the designs." He pulled a dustcover
from a small sofa. "Exiled by the whims of fashion. Lady
Tregar was the one who installed the crocodile-legged so-
fas." He gave a faint sniff. "Clear proof that good breeding
and good taste don't necessarily go together."

Clare smiled. She had the best of both worlds; not only
was Williams willing to accept her orders, but he still treated
her with the frankness of a fellow Penreithian. Knowing she
shouldn't gossip, but unable to resist the opportunity to learn
more, she said, "What was Lady Tregar like?"

The butler's expression became impassive. "I really can't
say, Miss Morgan. I was the underbutler then and very seldom saw her ladyship. She was very beautiful, of course."
After a pause, he said, "Would you like to see her portrait?"

"Why, yes. I didn't know there was one."

"The old earl had it commissioned at the time of his
grandson's marriage." Williams led Clare from the main
attic into a smaller one. A large wooden rack divided into
slots ran the length of one wall, with fabric-draped rectan-
gles occupying most of the spaces. "I had the carpenter
build this so the paintings could be stored safely."

He pulled one out and removed the sheet that covered it,
then raised his lantern to light the portrait. It was a superb
rendition of a young woman in the costume of a Greek
nymph. She stood in a flower-strewn meadow with the wind
blowing her golden hair and molding the white draperies to
her lush figure.

Clare studied the flawless face, the cool green eyes and the faint smile that hinted at hidden mysteries. This was the woman who had married Nicholas and shared his bed, and now haunted his nights with grief and guilt. ''I saw Lady Tregar once in the distance, but she is even lovelier than I realized.''

''I have never seen her equal,'' Williams said simply.

''Why is the portrait here rather than downstairs?''

''I believe that the dowager countess sent the painting up here just before she closed the house and moved to London.''

That would have been Emily Davies, the old earl's second wife. Had she loved her husband's unruly grandson and been jealous of Nicholas's exquisite wife? That would account for banishing the portrait to this hidden corner.

Clare's expression hardened. This house had known too many dark emotions; perhaps it was time to expose some of them to the light of day. ''This portrait would look good over one of the drawing room fireplaces. Have it taken downstairs.''

Williams started to protest, but changed his mind. ''Very well, Miss Morgan.'' After a moment's thought, he suggested, ''Do you want to put this one over the other fireplace? It used to hang in the drawing room. The dowager countess had it stored at the same time as the portrait of Lady Tregar.''

He drew out another picture and uncovered a full-length likeness of the old earl. Though the white hair showed that it had been painted toward the end of his life, his posture had lost none of its vigor and his face was as arrogant as ever. An impressive man, but Clare knew that Nicholas wouldn't want to look at him every day. ''Leave this one up here. I'll see if there's something suitable among the other paintings.''

She found two charming landscapes that deserved to be hung downstairs. The last picture was another portrait, and this time the face looking out from the canvas belonged to Nicholas himself. He was posed holding the reins of a horse and with hounds lying at his feet. Clare caught her breath, unable to resist the carefree charm of that handsome, laughing youth. This was the Nicholas who had fascinated her when she was a child.

Then she frowned, perplexed. The clothing was wrong, too old-fashioned, and the coloring wasn't dark enough. "Could this be his lordship's father?"

Williams squatted and peered at the small plaque set in the frame. " 'The Honorable Kenrick Davies.' " The butler straightened. "He left home before I started here. The one time I looked at this painting, I assumed it was of Master Nicholas."

"Hang it over the fireplace that is nearer the hall, and put Lady Tregar over the other one." Clare dusted her hands against her skirt. "With luck, we might have the drawing room completed by the time Lord Aberdare returns from Swansea."

And when he came back, she wanted to be there to see his reaction to the portrait of his long-dead wife.

7

L ATE AFTERNOON sun was slanting in the windows as they finished rearranging the drawing room. Clare thanked everyone who had taken part, then dismissed them for the day.

Before going upstairs to bathe, she made a last survey of the drawing room. A critic might point out that the walls needed repainting and the upholstery fabrics were past their prime, but the overall effect was very attractive. Hoping Nicholas would be pleased, she stepped into the hall and inhaled happily. The new cook, Mrs. Howell, had been busy all day, and tantalizing scents of roasting meat and baking bread drifted through the house.

To her dismay, the earl chose that moment to walk in the door, hatless, wind-tousled, and coiled whip in hand. "Hello, Clare," he said with a smile. "Did you have a productive day?"

Crossly she wondered why mud spattered on his boots and driving coat made him seem dashing, while smudges on her dress made her dowdy. Life was not fair. Wishing that he had been delayed another half hour, she replied, "Very. And you?"

"I located the engineer who built most of the tramways in Merthyr Tydfil, and I found a good site for the coastal quay. I'll tell you more over dinner." He sniffed. "Something smells delicious. You were successful at luring a cook up here?"

"Yes, and that's not the only success." She beckoned him into the drawing room, trying not to look as nervous as she felt.

He stepped inside, then halted and gave a soft whistle of

amazement. "Good Lord, the place is so bright and appealing that it's hard to believe this is Aberdare. How did
you accomplish so much in such a short time?"

"I can't take the credit. The ideas came from Williams,
and the hard work from the servants I engaged this morning." Wanting reassurance, she went on, "You approve of
the results?"

"Very much." Nicholas gave her a devastating smile,
then began to investigate his surroundings. Touching a blos-
som in a vase full of spicy-scented carnations, he said,
"Where did you find flowers this early in the spring?"

"Believe it or not, they're from the Aberdare greenhouse.
For the last four years, the gardener has continued to raise
flowers and vegetables because no one told him to stop."

The earl looked startled. "Old Iolo, with the peg leg?"
When Clare nodded, he said, "It's sobering to think how
much power I had over Aberdare when I wasn't even thinking about the place. Iolo, Williams, the rest of the skeleton
staff of servants who have performed their jobs through the
years—I don't deserve that kind of loyalty."

"No, you don't," Clare agreed with a hint of tartness.
"If it's any comfort, the loyalty was more to their wages
than to you personally. Though I believe that Iolo has been
selling the unused flowers and produce at the Penreith market, so he hasn't done badly out of your absence."

"Still . . ." Nicholas's voice drifted off as he looked up
and saw the portrait of Kenrick Davies. After a long silence,
he said quietly, "My father?"

"So the plaque says. The painting was in the attic. You've
never seen it before?"

"Never. My grandfather probably had it moved upstairs
when he disinherited my father." He studied the picture
intently. "I see why my parentage was never disputed."

"Do you remember your father at all?"

"A little. He laughed a great deal. I suspect that living
as a Gypsy was a game to him. He enjoyed the life, but if
he hadn't died of a fever, I think that eventually he would
have returned to the Gorgio world."

He turned and began strolling down the room. "I like the

way you arranged the furniture in conversational groupings. It gives the room a greater sense of intimacy.''

Clare was pleased; that had been one of her own ideas. She drifted along the wall, watching his expression and reactions to learn what he liked best and least. He evaluated the changes tactilely, lightly skimming his palm over the shining surface of a satinwood table, prodding the deep cushions of a chair with his coiled whip, using the toe of his boot to test the depth of a magnificent Persian carpet that had been rolled in the attic.

Glancing over at Clare, he opened his mouth to speak, then froze. *"Where the bloody hell did that come from?"*

His explosive rage was so unexpected that Clare was momentarily paralyzed. Then she remembered that she was standing below the portrait of Lady Tregar. She swallowed, then said, "From the attic."

Nicholas raised his driving whip and lashed out at her with a furious snap of his wrist. Clare gasped and instinctively threw up her arm to protect her face.

There was a faint whistling sound, followed by a vicious crack. Clare felt nothing, and for a confused moment she wondered if she had been hit and numbed by the impact.

Only when Nicholas drew the whip back and struck again did she realize that she had not been the target. The thong slashed savagely across the painted face of his dead wife.

He snarled, "Get rid of it. *Now!*"

He spun around and stalked from the room, slamming the door with a force that rattled the glass chimneys of the lamps.

Stunned, Clare sank into a chair. She had expected that he would react to the portrait with surprise, perhaps grief, and she had mentally prepared a little speech about coming to terms with his loss and getting on with his life. But his fury left her previous assumptions in tatters. It was possible that his fury was a result of a husband's grief and guilt—but the expression on his face had been far more akin to hate than love.

Hands shaking, she rang for Williams. He appeared promptly, expression wary. "His lordship didn't like the redecoration?"

"He loved the way the drawing room looks. It was the portrait that he hated." She indicated the painting. "It needs to be removed. Immediately."

The butler's eyes widened when he saw that the portrait had a neat X slashed across Lady Tregar's beautiful face. His gaze slanted over to Clare, but he asked no questions. "I'll take it down right now. Do you want the space left blank?"

Clare made an effort to think clearly. "Hang that painting of the old castle against a sunset. It's about the same size."

Then she went upstairs and ordered a bath. This time Dilys had help in bringing up the hot water, and both girls were talking cheerfully. The house was coming alive.

The steaming water eased her anxiety as well as her sore muscles. She decided to proceed with the evening as if the flare-up hadn't happened. That meant dressing and making herself available as a dinner companion—always assuming that Nicholas was talking to her after what had happened.

After drying herself, she dressed her hair more severely than the night before. She had to wear the same blue gown, since she owned nothing else that was suitable. Braced for trouble, she went down to dinner.

The morning room was empty when she reached it, but Nicholas appeared as the clock began striking six. He was dressed as impeccably as the night before. "Shall we go into dinner directly? I'm anxious to test the cook's skill."

She felt cowardly gratitude that he seemed willing to pretend that the scene in the drawing room hadn't taken place. But when she took his arm, she became aware of the tenseness of the muscles beneath his elegant black sleeve. His anger had not abated, but at least it wasn't directed at her.

He began to relax as dinner was served by Williams and one of the newly hired footmen. After the food had been placed on the table and the two servants were about to withdraw, Nicholas said, "Williams, I understand that you contributed substantially to the improvements in the drawing room. Well done."

The butler blushed pink with pleasure and shot a grateful glance at Clare. "Thank you, my lord. It was my pleasure."

Clare had to admire Nicholas, who had obviously learned that a few appreciative words were an effective way of earning loyalty. From what she had heard, it was a lesson that the old earl had never mastered.

As Nicholas carved the joint, he remarked, "Roast lamb again, but this time cooked as it should be. A suet crust with mountain ash berry jelly on the side, I believe?"

"Exactly. One of Mrs. Howell's specialties."

The roast potatoes were crisp and hot, the asparagus tender, and the sauteed trout known as *gwyniad* flaked delicately away from the bone. It was the best meal Clare had had in months. If Nicholas had sneered at the simplicity of the food, she would have been tempted to pour the leeks in cheese sauce over his head, but he ate with obvious enjoyment.

After having second helpings of everything, he pushed his plate away with a happy sigh. "Double Mrs. Howell's salary."

Clare almost dropped her fork. "But you don't know how much she's earning."

"Whatever it is, she's worth more."

"As you wish, my lord." She smiled. "Yesterday's unsuccessful cook, Gladys, is now the head housemaid. She's excellent at cleaning."

He chuckled and poured himself more wine, then began describing what he had accomplished in Swansea. When he was finished, Clare outlined the arrangements she had made in the household, and told him of the mine visit that was scheduled for the next day. It was a curiously domestic conversation.

The servants silently cleared away the dishes and brought hot coffee while Clare and Nicholas discussed what needed to be done next. She was surprised when the clock struck ten. Feeling suddenly tired, she got to her feet. "It's been a busy day. I'm going to bed now."

He said softly, "Come here."

Her fatigue instantly vanished in a surge of wary anticipation; given what had happened that afternoon, she had half expected him to forgo his kiss.

He pushed his chair away from the table but remained

seated. When she was close enough, he caught her hand and pulled her toward him until she was standing by his chair. With his face a few inches below hers, she saw how ridiculously long his eyelashes were. He really was too handsome to be believable.

Still holding her hand, he said lazily, "Where shall I kiss you tonight?"

The fact that her leg was pressed against his hard thigh undermined her judgment. Trying for her best schoolmistress voice, she said, "I assume the question is rhetorical because you've already made up your mind."

He smiled. "Not yet."

His gaze went to her throat, where he had kissed her the night before, and she felt her pulse beat harder. When his gaze shifted to her mouth, she touched her tongue to her lower lip. Surely tonight he would kiss her on the mouth.

He surprised her again, this time by pressing his lips into her hand. At first he simply exhaled softly into the sensitive flesh, his breath a warm caress. Then his tongue began teasing the center of her palm. "A woman's body is a symphony," he murmured, "and every part of you is an instrument crying out to be played."

Her fingers curled involuntarily and brushed his cheek. Under the dark, smoothly shaven skin she felt the faint prickle of whiskers, a texture that was startlingly erotic in its maleness.

His firm lips moved higher and he drew her little finger into his mouth. Pressure, heat, and moisture, a dimly understood essence of desire. Her breath quickened and her body slackened. As if she were mesmerized, she drifted lower until she settled on his knee. Dimly she realized that her behavior was appalling, but she had no more volition than a leaf in the wind.

His mouth traced a path down to the pale fragile skin inside her wrist. Enchanted, she gave a breathy exhalation and relaxed against him. With her free hand, she stroked his hair. Ebony softness, thick, sensual, alive.

Once more she experienced the feeling of melting, and she wondered helplessly how he could reduce her to this state so quickly. She knew she should call a halt, but the yielding warmth flowing through her was so gently delicious that she couldn't bear to end it.

Until she realized that his other hand was on her thigh, and he was slowly stroking upward. For the space of a heartbeat, she considered letting him continue until he reached the throbbing between her thighs. He would ease it . . .

Then sanity returned. "Enough!" She scrambled off his lap, staggering in her haste to get away. She almost shrieked when he grabbed her wrist, until she recognized that he was merely keeping her from falling.

"Nowhere near enough, but tomorrow is another day." As he released her wrist, his breathing was also faster than normal. "Sleep well, Clarissima."

She stared at him with wide, stark eyes, like a deer cornered by a hunter. Then, as she had the night before, she picked up a candle and hastened from the room.

He lifted his napkin from the table and absently began folding it. She was unlike any other woman he'd ever known; certainly she was nothing like Caroline. . . .

He had forgotten about the portrait, or rather, had blocked its existence from memory. It was a damnably accurate likeness, and seeing it unexpectedly was almost as great a shock as it would have been to see Caroline herself. Foolish of him to think that he could forget her while he was living in this house.

Finding that he had twisted the linen napkin into a noose, he tossed it onto the table in disgust. Far better to think about Clare and her sweet femininity than about the past.

When they had begun their little game, he had been able to objectively consider the fact that he might fail to seduce her, but that was no longer an acceptable outcome. This was one game he was going to win. In the meantime, he would indulge in the one activity that had always provided solace. He got to his feet and headed for the most distant corner of the house.

When Clare reached the safety of her bedchamber, she threw open a casement window and inhaled a lungful of cool, moist air. Outside a gentle spring rain was falling, and the steadiness helped calm her nerves. Ruefully, she thought that no one in Penreith would recognize her as the cool, collected schoolmistress to whom they had entrusted their children.

She was beginning to think that Nicholas really was the devil; he certainly was a genius at offering temptation. The trouble was that she reacted to Nicholas with her senses. She must learn to use her mind, be rational instead of emotional. Then she would be able to resist him.

It sounded so easy when he wasn't around.

Leaving the window open, she changed into her nightgown and slid into the wide bed. It took time for her to relax, but eventually the restful beat of rain began to lull her to sleep.

As she drifted between waking and slumber, a whisper of music began weaving through the raindrops, like fragments of a dream. At first she simply enjoyed it.

Then realization of the improbability jarred her to wakefulness. How could there be music in the middle of the night in an almost empty house? And *such* music—a delicate tune as elusive as fairy song.

The hair at the nape of her neck began to prickle as she tried to remember if there had ever been talk of ghosts at Aberdare. Not that she believed in ghosts, of course.

She slipped out of bed, went to the open window, and listened hard. At first she heard nothing but rain and the distant bleat of a sheep. Then another haunting phrase brushed the edges of her hearing, a sound as profoundly Welsh as the stony hills that guarded the valley. And though she heard it through the night air, it seemed to originate in the house.

While many of the younger servants would be moving into the house the next day, tonight there were only six people sleeping at Aberdare. She wondered if Williams might be a musician who practiced in the middle of the night. But he had grown up in the village, and she had never heard that he was unusually musical.

With a sigh, she lit a candle and donned her shoes and her old wool robe. Curiosity about the music would keep her awake, so she might as well try to locate the source.

Candle in hand, she unlocked her door and stepped into the hall. The flame danced in the drafts, and the wavering shadows and drumming raindrops made her feel that she had wandered into a Gothic melodrama. She shivered and briefly considered waking Nicholas, but dismissed the idea. The Demon Earl naked in bed was far more dangerous than any ghost. Soft-footed, she set out through the darkened house.

Her quest led her to a room in the most distant corner of the ground floor. A faint light showed under the door, which she found reassuring; presumably ghosts didn't need lamps.

Cautiously she turned the knob. When the door was half open, she halted in astonishment. The inhabitant of the room was no phantom.

But a ghost would have surprised her less.

8

SINCE A COVERED pianoforte stood in the shadows, Clare assumed that she had found the music room, but it was Nicholas who drew her fascinated gaze. He sat on a chair by the flickering fire, his face dreamy and a small harp resting against his left shoulder. In contrast to the stillness of his expression, his fingers danced across the metal strings, calling forth a melody that rang like singing bells.

Though she would have recognized him anywhere, his expression made him seem like a stranger. He was no longer the flippant aristocrat or the menacing rake, but the embodiment of a legendary Celtic bard—a man with gifts and griefs beyond those of the common man.

The vulnerability in his face called to Clare, whispering that perhaps she and Nicholas were not so different after all. And such thoughts were dangerous.

He began singing in Welsh, his low voice filling the room with a baritone as sweet and rich as dusky honey.

Maytime, fairest season,
Sweet are the birds, green are the groves . . .

After two more lines, the music shifted from joyous spring to a minor key lament.

When cuckoos sing in the high tree tops,
Greater grows my grief.
Smoke stings, sorrow cannot be hidden,
For my kinsmen have passed away.

Softly he repeated the last line, all the world's anguish in his voice.

Though the tune was unfamiliar to her, Clare recognized

the words as a poem from the medieval *Black Book of Caer-marthen,* one of the most ancient Welsh texts. Tears stung her eyes, for the familiar words had never touched her so deeply.

When the last notes had faded away she sighed, mourning all that she had lost, and all that she would never have.

Hearing the sound, Nicholas's head whipped up, his fingers clashing the strings in a harsh chord as vulnerability instantly transformed into hostility. "You should be asleep, Clarissima."

"So should you." She stepped into the room and closed the door behind her. "Why do you call me that?"

His expression eased. "Clare means clear, bright, direct. Clarissima would be the superlative form in Italian. Most clear, most direct. It suits you."

She came forward and perched on the edge of a chair near him. "I didn't know you were so musically accomplished."

"It's not a widely known fact," he said dryly. "In ancient times, a Welsh gentleman had to be skilled in the harp to be considered worthy of his rank, but that has changed in these uncivilized days. Behold my secret vice."

"Music is not a vice—it's one of life's great joys," she said lightly. "If this is a sample of your wild and wicked ways, I have to wonder if you're the rakehell that the world thinks."

"My serious vices are public. Since playing a harp has distressingly angelic overtones, I conceal it so as not to ruin my reputation." He plucked a brief, bawdy refrain. "You and I both know the value of reputation."

"An amusing explanation, but pure rubbish." She regarded him thoughtfully. "Why did you look daggers when I found you?"

Perhaps it was the midnight intimacy that made him give her a real answer instead of more flippancy. "A gentleman appreciates music, as he does art and architecture, but he doesn't waste his time performing it. If, God forbid, a man of breeding insists on playing an instrument, he should choose something like the violin or pianoforte. A gentleman most emphatically does *not* waste his time on anything as plebian as a Welsh harp.'' He pinched a string and ran his fingertips down so that it wept like a heartbroken elf.

Clare shivered at the agonized sound that came from the instrument. ''I assume that you're quoting the old earl. But it's hard to believe that he could dislike your music. You play and sing superbly.''

Nicholas leaned back in the chair and crossed his legs at the ankle, the harp loosely clasped in his arms. ''Most of the Welsh common folk would rather sing than eat. Gypsies will dance until their feet bleed. My grandfather did not approve of such excesses. The fact that I wanted to play a harp was proof of my tainted, common blood.'' Idly he plucked a series of wistful notes. ''This was one reason I learned to speak Welsh. *Cymric* is an ancient, primitive tongue, a language for warriors and poets. I needed to speak it to do justice to the harp.''

''Where did you learn to play so well?''

''From a hill shepherd called Tam the Telyn.''

''Thomas the Harp,'' she said, translating to English. ''I once heard him play when I was a child. He was marvelous. It was said fancifully that he was the harper of Llewelyn the Great, come back to remind us of Wales' ancient glory.''

''Perhaps Tam really was one of the great bards returned—there was an uncanny quality to him. He made this harp with his own hands, in the medieval style.'' Nicholas stroked the carved forepillar. ''The soundbox is hollowed out of a single piece of willow, and like the ancient harps it's strung with wire rather than gut. Under his instruction I made one like it, but the tone wasn't quite as rich. Tam left me this when he died.''

''You're better than any harpist I've ever heard compete in an *eisteddfod*. You should enter one sometime.''

''Not bloody likely, Clare,'' he said, nostalgia vanishing. ''I play for myself alone.''

''Is that because you can't bear the thought that people would admire you? You seem much more comfortable with scorn.''

''Quite right,'' he said silkily. ''Everyone has to have an ambition, and mine is to be a soulless monster, an affront to all decent God-fearing people.''

She smiled. "I can't believe that anyone who makes music like you do is soulless. My father never would have thought so highly of someone who was truly wicked."

He strummed the harp again, calling forth a gentler air. "If not for your father, I would have run away from Aberdare. I'm not sure that he did me a favor in persuading me to stay, but I have to admire his skill at taming a wild child."

"How did he do that? My father talked very little about his work, since he considered that he was only God's instrument."

"Did you know that my mother sold me to my grandfather for a hundred guineas?" Before Clare could express her horror at his casual words, Nicholas struck the strings again. Deep, doom-laden notes shivered through the air. "When I came to Aberdare, I was seven and had never spent a night in a house. Like a trapped bird, I became crazed, fighting desperately to escape. They locked me in the nursery and barred the windows to prevent me from battering my way out. The old earl summoned your father, whose spiritual achievements he respected. Perhaps he thought Reverend Morgan could cast out my demons."

"My father was no exorcist."

"No. He simply came into the nursery with a basket of food and sat on the floor by the wall, so that his head was near the level of mine. Then he began to eat a mutton pie. I was wary, but he seemed harmless. Also, I was getting hungry because I hadn't eaten in several days—whenever a footman brought food, I'd thrown it at his head.

"But your father didn't try to force me to do anything, nor did he scold when I stole a mutton pie from the basket. After I'd wolfed it down, he offered me a drink of ale and a currant griddle cake. He also gave me a napkin, along with a gentle suggestion that my face and fingers would be improved by wiping.

"Then he began telling me stories. Joshua and the walls of Jericho. Daniel in the lion's den. Sampson and Delilah— I particularly liked the part where Sampson pulled the temple down, since I'd felt like that ever since I'd come to Aberdare." Nicholas rested his head against the back of the chair, firelight gilding the chiseled planes of his face. "Your father was the first person to treat me like a child rather than a wild animal to be subdued. I ended up curled under his arm, sobbing.''

Clare felt like crying herself as she imagined the desolate, forsaken boy. To be sold by his own mother! Swallowing the lump in her throat, she said, ''My father was the most compassionate man I've ever known.''

Nicholas nodded. ''The old earl had chosen well—I doubt that anyone but Reverend Morgan could have persuaded me to accept the situation. He told me that Aberdare was my home, and that if I cooperated with my grandfather, eventually I would have more freedom and wealth than any Gypsy had ever known. So I went downstairs to the old earl and proposed a bargain.''

He made a face. ''Obviously I have a propensity for strange bargains. I told my grandfather I would do my best to be the kind of heir he wanted—eleven months a year. In return, I must have one month to return to the Rom.

''Naturally the earl didn't like the idea, but Reverend Morgan persuaded him that this was the only way to get me to behave. So your father became my tutor. For the next two or three years, he came to Aberdare almost every day that he wasn't on a preaching circuit. Besides the usual academic subjects, he taught me how to act like a Gorgio. Eventually I was fit to be sent to a public school where I could be beaten into the semblance of a proper English gentleman.'' He gave her an ironic glance. ''Before I left, I gave him the inscribed book that you used to try to blackmail me.''

Refusing to feel guilty, she said, ''So you preserved your heritage by returning to your mother's people every year. That was a remarkably clear piece of thinking for a child.''

''Not clear enough.'' He plucked a mocking spray of notes. ''I thought that I could don the Gorgio life like a suit of clothes and be unchanged when I took it off. But it wasn't that simple—if one is always acting a role, eventually the pretense starts becoming real.''

''It must have been difficult straddling two different worlds,'' she said. ''Did you ever feel that you were neither fish nor fowl nor good red herring?''

He laughed without humor. ''That's a fair description.''

"The more I hear, the less surprising it is that you hated your grandfather."

Nicholas bowed his head and picked a series of single notes that ran up an octave and down again. "To say that I hated him is . . . too simple. He was my only kin, and I wanted to please him, at least some of the time. I learned manners and morals, Greek and history and agriculture, yet I could never satisfy him. Do you know what my unforgivable crime was?"

When Clare shook her head, he said, "Hold out your hand."

When she extended it, he held his hand next to hers. Beside her milky Celtic complexion, his was like rich coffee with cream. "The color of my skin—something I couldn't change even if I wanted to. If my coloring had been lighter, I think that eventually my grandfather would have been able to forget my heritage. Instead, every time he looked at me he saw a 'damned black Gypsy,' as he so charmingly put it." Nicholas flexed his long, supple fingers, studying them as if for the first time. Bitterness in his voice, he said, "Ridiculous, and certainly unchristian, to hate someone for the color of his skin, yet such trivial things can change the pattern of a life."

"You are perfect exactly as you are," Clare said intensely.

He looked startled. "I wasn't fishing for compliments."

"That wasn't a compliment—it was an objective aesthetic judgment," she said loftily. "A well-bred female would never compliment a man in such a vulgar fashion."

He smiled, his expression easing. "So I am now classified with Greek urns and Renaissance paintings."

"More interesting than either." She cocked her head to one side. "Was life easier when you traveled with the Gypsies?"

"In most ways. My mother was an orphan with no close family, so I would join whatever kumpania was closest to Aberdare. They would always take me in, like a stray puppy." He hesitated. "I enjoyed the visits, but as time passed, I started to see my kinfolk with different eyes. Though the Rom think themselves completely free, in fact they are trapped by their own customs. Illiteracy, the treatment of women, the pride in dishonesty, usually at the cost of those Gorgios who could least afford it, the cleanliness taboos—eventually I could no longer accept such things without question.''

"Yet you have provided a Gypsy campsite at Aberdare."

"Of course—they are my kin. Any of the Rom can stay as long as they wish. In return, I ask them not to pester the people in the valley."

"That must be why there hasn't been any trouble with Gypsies for years," Clare said, intrigued. "When I was little, I remember that my mother would bring me inside and bolt the door whenever they came to town. She said that Gypsies were thieves and heathens and that they stole children."

He chuckled. "The first two things may be true, but the Rom have no need to steal children—they have plenty of their own."

"I used to dream about being stolen by the Gypsies," she confessed. "I thought it would be nice to be wanted so much."

Unfortunately, Nicholas caught what she had revealed by her remark. "Did you feel unwanted, Clarissima? I sometimes wondered what it would be like to have Reverend Morgan for a father. A man of unshakeable virtue, compassionate, with time for everyone who needed him." He struck a soft, wistful chord. "Yet saints may not be the easiest people to live with."

She felt as if he had stabbed her. How dare this rake see what no one else ever had—what she scarcely admitted even to herself. Lips stiff, she said, "It's very late. Now that I know you're not a ghost, I need to get some sleep."

"How quickly you flee from a question," he murmured. "You're obviously one of those people who enjoys probing others, but doesn't want anyone to see inside her."

"There's nothing to probe." She stood. "I'm a simple woman and I've led an uncomplicated life."

He laughed. "You are many things, but simple isn't one of them. You simmer with intelligence and suppressed emotions." He strummed the harp in a deliberate tempo that made her think of a cat stalking a bird. "Do you need to feel wanted, Clarissima? I want you. You have the mysterious, subtle complexity of fine wine—a drink to be savored over and over again. Lovely ankles, too—I'm glad you decided to use the cue for playing billiards."

Not dignifying that remark with a reply, she tugged her shapeless robe around her and walked toward the door. He plunked at the harp strings with every step.

She moved faster, and so did the harp.

She stopped, and the notes did also.

She whirled around. "Don't mock me!"

He stilled the strings with one hand, then set the harp on the floor. "I'm not mocking—I'm inviting you to share in the banquet of life, which includes laughter." He rose to his feet, his face a collection of dramatic planes and shadows in the firelight. "It includes desire as well. Passion is the best way I know to forget life's sorrows."

She shivered. "I see why you're called the Demon Earl, for you talk the devil's theology."

"In the course of my education, quite a bit of religion was shoved down my throat. I don't recall hearing that pleasure is inherently wicked. Evil is hurting others, while passion is a source of mutual joy." He started to walk toward her. "It's past midnight—another day. Shall I collect my next kiss?"

"No!" She whirled and dashed out the door.

The last thing she heard was soft laughter. "You're right—it would be a pity to use it so early. Until later, Clarissima."

As she hastened through the hallways to the safety of her room, she thought a little wildly that whoever said it took a long spoon to sup with the devil was right, for Nicholas's thinking was beginning to make sense to her.

Not only was she halfway to perdition—she was beginning to look forward to it.

9

WHEN THEY came into sight of the mine, Nicholas reined in his horse and studied their destination. It was not a pleasant scene. The tallest structure was a chimney that poured dark smoke into the cloudy sky. Waste stone was heaped around the grimy buildings, and no trees grew for hundred of yards.

Clare said, "The main shaft is right in the middle of those buildings. It's used for ventilation, access, and lifting the coal out." She gestured toward the left. "You can't see it from here, but there is also a small older shaft, called the Bychan. These days it's used mostly for ventilation, and sometimes for access to the south end of the pit."

Though they were over a quarter of a mile away, the pounding of a steam engine was clearly audible. "Is that racket from the engine that pumps water from the pit?" Nicholas asked.

"Yes, it's an old Newcomen engine. The modern Watts engines are much more powerful."

He set his horse in motion and they rode down the hill. "Is the engine one of the problems?"

She nodded. "Not only is it too small for a mine this size, but it's almost a hundred years old and unreliable."

"Why hasn't it been replaced? When Michael Kenyon bought the mine, he planned to modernize the equipment so production could be increased."

"Lord Michael did make some improvements in the first few months, but he soon lost interest and left the running of the mine to George Madoc," she explained. "The mine has several old adits—underground tunnels that drain water from the lower levels—so Madoc decided that it would be a waste of money to buy a better pump. That's also his excuse for using an old-fashioned whim gin to raise and lower loads. A modern steam winding engine would be faster, more powerful, and much safer."

"Short-sighted thinking on Madoc's part. New equipment would be expensive, but would pay for itself fairly soon. I'm surprised that Michael didn't maintain control of the mine's daily operations—he always had a shrewd head for business."

Nicholas glanced at Clare. "As you know, the Davies family used to own the mine, but my grandfather considered it more bother than it was worth. Michael became interested in the mine when he visited me. He thought that with better management it could be very profitable, so he made an offer. My grandfather was delighted to be rid of the nuisance of running the mine as long as he retained ownership of the land."

"So that's why the mine changed ownership," she said dryly. "No one bothered to explain to the people who worked there. It was said that Lord Michael took a passing fancy to the valley, so he bought a house and a business on impulse."

"There's some truth to that—Michael *did* fall in love with this part of Wales the first time he visited Aberdare. As a younger son, he wasn't in line to inherit any land from his family, so he bought Bryn Manor at the same time he acquired the mine." A thought occurred to Nicholas. "Has he neglected the house as thoroughly as he has the mine?"

"As far as I know, Lord Michael hasn't set foot in the valley for years. At least another fifteen jobs were lost when Bryn Manor was closed." Clare accompanied her second sentence with a pointed glance.

Nicholas winced. "The gentry hasn't done very well by the valley, has it?"

"Things have been going wrong for years. Only desperation could have driven me to seek the aid of a reprobate like you."

Seeing the mischievous gleam in her eyes, he said promptly, "At least that is turning out well. Look at the splendid opportunity for Christian martyrdom that I'm giving you."

Their gazes met, and they both burst out laughing. Damn, but he liked this woman and her tart sense of humor. She was more than capable of holding her own against him.

They both sobered as they reached the grim buildings. He asked, "What's the ghastly racket coming from that big shed?"

"The coal is being screened and graded. Most of the above-ground employees work in there."

He brushed at the smudges appearing on his white cuff. "It also appears to be the source of the coal dust that covers everything in sight."

"Since you like wearing black, you shouldn't mind." She gestured toward a shed. "We can leave the horses here."

As they dismounted, a compact, muscular man came forward. Clare said, "Lord Aberdare, this is Owen Morris."

"Owen!" Nicholas held out his hand. Raising his voice to be heard over the noise of machinery and rattling coal, he said, "Clare didn't mention the name of my guide."

The miner smiled and shook hands. "I wasn't sure you would recognize me after all these years."

"How could I forget you? I showed other boys how to tickle trout, but you're the only one who ever developed a real knack for it. Is Marged well?"

"Aye. Even lovelier than when we married," Owen said fondly. "It's pleased she'll be that you remember her."

"She was well worth remembering. Of course, I scarcely dared say hello to her, for fear that you'd break my neck." As he spoke, Nicholas studied his old friend's face. Under the coal dust Owen had the usual miner's pallor, but he seemed healthy and happy. Even as a boy, he had had an enviable inner serenity.

Owen said, "You'd best change to pit dress. It would be a pity to ruin your fancy London clothes."

Nicholas obediently followed Owen into a shed and stripped off his outer clothing, then put on a shirt, loose jacket, and sturdy trousers similar to what Owen wore. Though the coarse flannel garments had been carefully washed, they were still impregnated with ancient grime. He grinned as he added a heavily padded felt hat to complete the outfit. His London tailor would have vapors at the sight of him.

"Knot these through a buttonhole," Owen ordered as he handed over two candles. "Do you have flint and steel?"

Nicholas did, but if he hadn't been reminded, he would have left them in his own coat. As he transferred the tinderbox to the pocket of his flannel jacket, he said, "Anything else?"

The miner scooped a handful of soft clay from a wooden box and used it to form a lump around the base of two candles. "Take one of these. When we have to crawl, you can use the clay to fix the candle to your hat."

They went outside and found Clare waiting, also dressed in pit costume. In the baggy garments, she looked like a young boy.

"You're coming with us?" Nicholas asked with surprise.

"It won't be my first trip down pit," she said coolly.

With a surge of irrational protectiveness, he wanted to forbid her to go, though he had the sense to hold his tongue. Not only had he no right to give Clare orders, but she had more experience with mines than he did. And, judging by her expression, she'd probably bite him if he tried to stop her. He smiled to himself. Not that he'd mind being bitten, but this wasn't the time or place.

They had to circle around the whim gin to reach the pit mouth. The gin was a huge spindle that resembled a water wheel lying on its side. Turned by a team of horses, it powered the squealing pulleys that hung over the main shaft.

As they approached, a heaping basket of coal reached the top of the shaft. Two laborers swung the load to one side and dumped the contents into a wagon. As the coal rumbled into the wagon, an older man came out of a hut. "This your visitor, Owen?"

"Aye. Lord Aberdare, this is Mr. Jenkins, the banksman. He's in charge of all that goes in or comes out of the pit."

Nicholas offered his hand. After a startled moment, the banksman took it, gave a hasty shake, then touched the brim of his hat. "An honor, my lord."

"On the contrary—visiting the pit is my privilege. I'll try to stay out of people's way." He surveyed the open shaft. "How do we get down?"

Mr. Jenkins braked one of the pulleys to a halt and gave a rusty chuckle. "Light your candle from the one in the hut, then grab hold of the rope, my lord."

Looking closer, Nicholas saw that the rope had a cluster of loops attached at varying levels. "Good God, that's how people come and go from the pit? I thought that metal cages were the usual method."

"In modern mines, they are," Clare answered.

But Penreith was primitive and unsafe, which was why Nicholas was here. He watched Owen light his candle, then step into a loop and sit down, one hand casually holding the rope. Acutely aware that he was leaning over a sheer drop of hundreds of feet, Nicholas did the same. He felt that he was being tested. Being a peer of the realm counted for nothing here if he didn't have the courage to do what every miner did daily.

Settling into the loop was nowhere as difficult as watching Clare do the same. As she stepped out over the abyss, Nicholas again had to clamp down on his protective instincts.

With a creak, the pulley began to turn and they dropped into the darkness, hanging from the rope like a cluster of onions. The candle flames swayed wildly as smoky air rushed past them. They revolved as they descended and Nicholas wondered if miners ever got dizzy and fell. Clare was perched slightly above him, so he kept his gaze on her slim back. If she had showed any signs of imbalance, he would have grabbed hold of her instantly. But she was as calm as if she were taking tea by her own hearth.

As the light at the top of the shaft diminished, he saw that a red dot below them was expanding. Earlier Clare had mentioned that a fire burned at the bottom of the shaft as part of the ventilation system. That explained the smoke and heat of the air rising around them; in effect, they were going down a chimney.

He glanced down again and saw that the fire had partially disappeared, obscured by a huge black object that was hurtling upward at lethal speed. Instinctively he tensed, though God only knew what he could do to prevent a collision.

With an explosive impact of air, the object whipped by them, missing Owen by inches. The miner didn't even blink. Nicholas expelled his breath with relief when he saw that it was only a basket of coal. Still, if the rope that held them had swayed more, one of them might have been struck. The mine definitely needed a steam winding engine and lift cages.

After about two minutes their descent slowed and they came to a halt several feet to one side of the roaring ventilation fire. As they unlooped themselves from the rope, Nicholas saw that they were in a large gallery. Several feet away, dust-blackened figures were loading another basket for lifting. He remarked, "This place bears a distinct similarity to the infernal regions your father used to describe with such relish."

Clare smiled a little. "I should think you'd feel at home here, Old Nick."

He smiled back, but one thing he did not feel was at home. The Romany half of him had always craved fresh air and open spaces, both of which were in short supply in a pit. He coughed and blinked his stinging eyes, remembering why curiosity had never led him to come down here when he was a boy.

"We'll go to the western coal face," Owen said. "It's not so busy at that end, so you'll be able to see more."

Half a dozen tunnels led from the main gallery. While crossing to the one that would take them to their destination, they dodged small wheeled wagons full of coal. "That's a corf," Owen explained as the first rolled by, pushed by two adolescent boys. "Holds five hundredweight of coal. The lads who push are called putters. Larger pits have rails for the corves—makes the work easier."

They entered a passage, Owen in the lead, followed by Clare, with Nicholas bringing up the rear. The roof was not quite high enough for Nicholas to stand erect. He became conscious of a damp, stony smell that was quite different from the earthy scent of a newly plowed field.

Over his shoulder, Owen said, "Gas is a great problem.

Chokedamp collects in the bottom of abandoned workings—
that will suffocate you. Firedamp is worse because it explodes. When it gets too thick, there's a fellow who crawls
in and sets fire to the gas, then lies down and lets the flames
run over him.''

"Jesus, that sounds suicidal!"

Owen glanced over his shoulder. "It is, but that doesn't
mean you should take the Lord's name in vain. Even if you
are a lord," he added with a faint twinkle.

"You know I've always been a profane sort, but I'll try
to watch my tongue," Nicholas promised. It occurred to
him that Clare must also find his language offensive. Perhaps he should start swearing in Romany. "Now that you
mention it, I've heard of burning gas off, but I thought the
practice had been abandoned because of the danger.''

"This is a very traditional mine, my lord," Owen said
dryly.

"If you're going to scold me for bad language, you'll
have to start calling me Nicholas again." He wiped his forehead with the flanneled back of a wrist. "Is it my imagination, or is it warmer here than on the surface?''

"It's not your imagination," Clare answered. "The
deeper the mine, the warmer the temperature." She glanced
over her shoulder. "Closer to the infernal regions, you
know.''

Nicholas's smile lasted until his foot came down on a soft
object that shrieked, then shot away with a scrabble of claws.
As he struggled to regain his balance, he bashed his head
into the ceiling and doubled over swearing. In Romany.

Clare turned back in concern. "Are you all right?''

He tested his head gingerly. "The padded hat seems to
have saved me from bashing my brains out. What did I step
on?''

She touched his forehead with a cool hand. "Probably a
rat. There's plenty of them down here.''

Owen, who had also stopped, added, "A bold lot, too.
Sometimes they snatch food right from the lads' hands.''

Moving forward again, Nicholas said, "Has anyone considered bringing down a cat?''

"There are several, and they lead fat, happy lives," Clare said. "But there are always more rats and mice."

A faint metallic rattle sounded ahead of them, and as they came around a bend Nicholas saw that a metal door ahead blocked the tunnel. Owen called, "Huw, open the door."

The door swung open with a creak and a small boy, perhaps six years old, stuck his head out. "Mr. Morris!" he said with pleasure. "It's been that long since I've seen you."

Owen stopped and ruffled the boy's hair. "I've been working the face on the east side. How's life as a trapper?"

Huw said wistfully, "It's easy, but it do grow lonesome sitting in the dark all day. And I do not like the rats, sir, not at all."

Owen took one of his spare candles and lit it, then handed it to the child. "Your da won't let you have a candle?"

Huw shook his head. "He says they're too dear for a child who only earns fourpence a day."

Nicholas frowned. The boy was working in this black hellhole for only four pennies a day? Appalling.

Owen dug a boiled sweet out of his pocket and gave it to Huw. "I'll see you when we return."

They moved through the door and continued down the passage. When they were out of earshot, Nicholas said, "What the hell is a child that young doing down here?"

"His father wants the money," Clare said in a hard voice. "Huw's mother is dead and his father, Nye Wilkins, is a drunken, greedy brute who brought the boy down pit when he was only five."

"Half the miners owe their allegiance to the chapel, the other half to the tavern," Owen added. "Five years ago, our Clare stood up in chapel and said that children belonged in school, not the pit. Quite a discussion there was, but before the day was done, every man in Zion chapel had promised not to put his children to work before the age of ten."

"It would take a brave man to face her down. I wish I'd been there," Nicholas commented. "Well done, Clare."

"I do what I can," she said bleakly, "but it's never enough. There are at least a dozen boys Huw's age in the pit. They act as trappers, sitting in the dark all day by those doors that control how air moves through the shafts.''

They passed a shaft that had a length of timber nailed across it. Nicholas asked, "Why is this tunnel blocked off?''

Owen paused. "At the end, the rock changes suddenly and the coal vein disappears.'' His brows drew together. "Odd that it's blocked—there are plenty of dead shafts.''

"Maybe the chokedamp is particularly bad in this tunnel,'' Clare suggested.

"Likely that's it,'' Owen said.

They continued on, flattening themselves against the craggy walls whenever a corf was pushed by. Eventually they reached the end of the shaft. In a narrow, irregularly shaped space, a dozen men were laboring with picks and shovels. After brief, incurious glances at the newcomers, they proceeded with their work.

"These are hewers,'' Owen said. "They're working longwall, which means that as coal is removed, the waste stone goes behind them and the props are moved forward to support the work space.''

They watched in silence. Soft clay was used to fix candles in various spots, leaving the hewers' hands free. Each had a corf sitting behind him to hold his coal, since a hewer was paid for the amount he cut. Nicholas was fascinated at the way the men contorted their bodies to get at the coal. Some knelt, one lay on his back, still another was doubled over so that he could undercut the bottom of the seam.

His gaze lingered on the hewer at the very end of the shaft. In an undertone, he said, "That fellow down there has no candle. How can he see to work?''

"He doesn't,'' Clare replied. "Blethyn is blind.''

"Are you serious?'' Nicholas said incredulously. "Surely a pit is too dangerous for a blind man. And how can he tell if he's cutting coal or waste?''

"By touch and the sound of the pick striking,'' Owen said. "Blethyn knows every twist and turn in the pit—once when flooding drowned our candles, he led six of us out to safety.''

One of the hewers said, "Time to set another charge.''

Another straightened and wiped sweat from his face. "Aye. Bodvill, it's your turn to set the gunpowder."

A broad, taciturn man set down his pick, lifted a large hand drill, and started to bore into the rock face. The other hewers put their tools into their corves and began rolling them back along the tunnel. As the observers stood aside, Owen explained, "When the hole is deep enough, it will be packed with black powder, then lit with a slow fuse."

"The explosion won't bring down the shaft?"

"Not if it's done right," Clare answered.

Hearing tension vibrate through her terse words, Nicholas gave Clare a puzzled look and saw that she also appeared on the verge of explosion. For an instant he wondered why. Then the obvious answer hit him and he felt like kicking himself.

He had half-forgotten that her father had died down here, but Clare obviously hadn't; her taut profile spoke vividly of what it was costing her to be in the mine. He wanted to put his arms around her and say something soothing, but he quelled the impulse. Judging by her expression, she did not want sympathy.

The last hewer to leave the area was a squat fellow with massive muscles and a pugnacious jaw. When he was even with the visitors, he stopped and squinted at Nicholas. "You're the Gypsy Earl, ain't you?"

"I've been called that."

The man spat at his feet. "Tell your bloody friend Lord Michael to keep an eye on Madoc. Old George lives better than any mine manager ought to." The hewer turned back to his corf and pushed it down the tunnel.

As the man disappeared, Nicholas asked, "Do you think Madoc might be skimming the mine's profits?"

"I really can't say," Owen said uncomfortably. "That's a harsh accusation to make."

"You're too fair," Clare said. "Put a greedy manager under a careless owner and embezzlement is guaranteed."

Nicholas said, "If that's true and Michael finds out, I wouldn't like to be in Madoc's shoes. Michael has always had a fierce temper."

Bodvill withdrew the drill and began packing black powder into the hole. "Time for us to go," Owen said. "There's something else I want to show you on the way back."

After retracing their steps for a short distance, they turned into a shaft that led to a vast gallery whose ceiling was supported by massive square pillars. Lifting his candle to illuminate the area, Owen said, "I wanted you to see pillar and stall mining. Larger veins are usually worked this way. It has advantages, but maybe half the coal is left in the pillars."

Intrigued, Nicholas studied one of the supports and found that the roughly cut surface had the dark shine of coal.

Suddenly Owen yelled, "Mind your head, boyo!" As he spoke, he grabbed Nicholas's arm and yanked him backward.

A chunk of rock crashed right where Nicholas had been standing, shattering into fragments when it hit the floor. Shaken, he looked up at the craggy roof. "Thanks, Owen. How did you see that in time?"

With a touch of humor, Owen said, "Caves are made by God and are very stable. Being made by man, mines are always falling to pieces. Working in one, you learn to keep one eye on what's above you. It takes wits and strength to be a collier."

"Better you than me," Nicholas said dryly. "A Rom would die if forced to work down here."

"Dying is easy—too easy in this particular mine." Owen gestured at the shadowy cavern. "Madoc wants to start robbing the pillars—taking more coal out of them. Says it's wasteful to leave them like this."

Nicholas frowned. "Won't that bring the roof down?"

"It could." Owen pointed at one of the wooden beams. "Enough props would make it possible, but Madoc doesn't like paying for any more timber than he has to."

Nicholas grimaced. "I'm beginning to thoroughly dislike Mr. Madoc, and I haven't even met him."

"Wait until you do meet him," Clare said acerbically. "Your dislike will turn to sheer loathing."

"That's an unchristian statement, Clare," Owen said with gentle reproach. "Come you, it's time we left."

As she followed him out of the gallery, Clare said repentantly, "You're right. I'm sorry."

Nicholas wasn't sorry to be heading back. As he fell in behind Clare, he kept one eye on the ceiling and the other on the graceful sway of her hips. It was time to start thinking about what he would do with today's kiss.

As they reached the main shaft and turned toward the pit head, Owen cocked his head. "The pump has failed again."

When Nicholas listened, he realized that the steady, distant thump of the engine had ended, leaving profound silence. "Does this happen often?"

"Once or twice a week. I hope the engineers can fix it quickly. With all the spring rain, there will be flooding if the pump is down for more than an hour or two." He began retracing their steps.

Nicholas started to follow, then paused at the sound of a hollow boom. It echoed eerily through the passages and galleries and sent vibration shivering through the rock under their feet.

Owen said over his shoulder, "Bodvill's charge."

Abruptly Clare whirled about to face the way they had come, her expression urgent. "Listen!"

Startled, Nicholas turned and looked in the same direction. Visibility was blocked by a bend about two hundred feet behind them, but the air was compressing strangely, and something was rushing toward them with a liquid sound he could not identify.

Before he could open his mouth to ask what was happening, a huge wave exploded around the bend, filling the entire shaft as it roared toward them with lethal speed.

10

A S SOON AS the wave appeared, Owen barked, "Climb the walls and hang on! I'll try to help Huw." His candle vanished as he raced away.

Clare grabbed Nicholas's arm and tugged him toward the nearest wooden prop. "Quickly! We need to get as close to the ceiling as possible."

Understanding, Nicholas dropped his candle, grabbed Clare around the waist, and lifted her as high as he could. She scrambled upward, finding footholds in the roughly cut rock, and Nicholas followed. The wildly swinging candle stuck on her hat brim showed a crook in the timber that left several inches of space between the prop and the rocky wall. He managed to hook one arm around the wood and the other around Clare.

Then the raging waters struck, drowning the candle and submerging them completely. The current battered furiously, and it took all of Nicholas's strength to maintain his hold on the timber. Something heavy hit them and whirled away, almost knocking Clare from his grasp.

As he strained to hold her against the force of the water, she wrapped herself fiercely around him. Once her grip was secure, he turned her against the current until her back was braced against the rocky wall and his body sheltered hers. Another object struck him, gouging his ribs and knocking out what little breath he had left, but this time Clare was spared.

The seconds ticked away and the flood did not diminish. As the burning in his lungs became unbearable, he began to wonder if it was their fate to drown here, far from the wind and the sky. He pressed his face against Clare's hair, feeling the silky tendrils swirl across his cheek. What a waste. What a bloody waste of two lives. He had thought he would have more time. . . .

His vision darkened and Clare's clasp was weakening when the current began to ease. Sensing that the water level might be dropping, he turned his face up and discovered that there was now a narrow band of air between the water and the ceiling.

Even as he sucked air into his desperate lungs, he slid his arm down Clare's back and under her hips, then lifted her so that she could breathe. Her head came above the surface and she broke into a spasm of coughs, her slim body shaking convulsively. In the dangerous darkness she seemed very fragile, and his arm tightened around her again.

For long minutes, they simply clung to each other and reveled in the luxury of breathing. The water slowly dropped until it was about a foot below the ceiling, then held steady. Nicholas asked, "Do you have any idea what the devil happened?"

Clare coughed again, then managed to say, "The gunpowder charge must have opened a hidden feeder spring. It happens sometimes, but the flooding isn't usually this bad."

"And the steam pump is broken down," he said grimly. "I hope it's repaired soon."

The cold current still tugged at them, and his hold on the timber was their only support. He explored with his left foot until he found a solid ledge, which reduced the strain on his arm. He wondered how long they would be trapped; eventually fatigue and cold would start to take their toll. "If the water starts rising again, we'll have to try to swim out, but in the darkness we would risk getting lost in a cross passage. For the time being, I think we're better off staying here and praying that the water goes down more."

With an attempt at lightness, Clare said, "You, praying? I must have water in my ears."

He chuckled. "My friend the notorious Michael was a soldier before he decided to become rich instead. He said once that there are no unbelievers on the battlefield."

He felt a small ripple of amusement from her, but it passed quickly. When she spoke, her voice was tight. "Do you think Owen and Huw were able to escape the flooding?''

''They should be safe,'' he said, hoping his optimism was not misplaced. ''Owen was some distance ahead of us, and I don't think it was much farther to the door the boy operates. They may be clinging to a prop, like we are, but with luck they made it through the door and closed it behind them. That would have slowed the water and given them time to reach a higher level.''

''Dear God, I hope so,'' she whispered. ''But there may have been other miners caught by the flooding. Bodvill probably didn't withdraw this far when he set the charge off.''

She was shaking violently. Guessing why, he asked, ''Was your father killed in this area?''

''No. That happened at the other end of the mine.'' After a long silence, she burst out, ''I hate this place! Dear God, how I hate it. If I could close the pit tomorrow, I would. So many have died here. So many . . .'' Her voice faded away and she hid her face against his shoulder.

''Did you lose someone else special?'' he said quietly.

At first there was silence, except for the ripple of moving water. Then she said haltingly, ''Once . . . once I had a sweetheart. We were both very young—I was fifteen, Ivor a year older. But I admired him, and he admired me. We watched each other. Sometimes after chapel we talked, trying to say what we felt, using words anyone could overhear.'' She shuddered, then finished in bleak words more vivid than melodrama. ''Before matters could go very far, there was a gas explosion. He was burned alive.''

Growing up in the valley, Nicholas had seen the innocent passion of the young villagers as they found their life's partners. Though a cynic would say that such affairs were rooted in mere animal lust, Nicholas had known better; he had only to think of Owen's courtship of Marged. From the beginning, the two had been bound by such sweet, awkward radiance that it had hurt to see them together. Nicholas had been bleakly envious; he had never been that innocent.

At fifteen, Clare would have been much like Marged— pure of spirit and loyal of heart. Would young Ivor have been worthy of her gift of first love? Clare would never know, just as she would never have to risk betrayal, for her sweetheart had died when their budding love had still had infinite possibilities.

Ever since they had reached the pit, Nicholas had been forcing himself to suppress his protective instincts for Clare. Now he abandoned the struggle and offered what solace he could. He whispered, "Such courage you have to venture into the depths." Inclining his head, he touched his lips to her wet face, tracing a path across the curve of her cheek.

She gave a soft, wondering sigh when their lips met, her head falling back against his shoulder. Her mouth was warm, a tantalizing contrast to her cool cheek. The water supported her weight, and it was easy to mold her yielding body against his. Their saturated clothing compressed and warmed where they touched, creating a feeling of nakedness. She didn't seem to mind that his thigh was between hers, or that her breasts were flattened against his chest.

At first he kept the kiss simple, almost chaste. But there was nothing chaste about the desire she aroused in him. Experimentally, he parted his lips a little. Her mouth opened under his and there was a delicate exchange of breath.

Emboldened, he touched her lips with his tongue. She made a small, surprised movement, and for a painful moment he thought that she would decide that she had had her kiss for the day. But instead, her tongue shyly touched his, and her hands made light brushing motions down his back.

She tasted sweet as summer wine. He knew that it was insane to feel such desire when their lives were in peril, yet for a mad moment he forgot the water, the blackness, the menace of their circumstances. Only Clare was real. He raised his knee so that she settled more firmly over his thigh, her legs lying along his. She responded with her whole body, as fluid as the water that surrounded them. There was something utterly erotic about her tentative explorations, a hint of innocent wantonness.

Clare had expected to be sensually assaulted when Nicholas finally gave her a traditional, mouth-to-mouth kiss. What she had not expected was such ravishing tenderness. Instinctively she knew that this embrace was different from the previous two, when he had been coolly testing her response and befuddling her expectations. This kiss was sharing, for danger had made them comrades instead of antagonists.

And the danger was not yet over. Reluctantly she turned her face away. "I . . . I think it's time to stop."

"Think? You're not sure?"

Before she could answer, his mouth found hers again, weaving an enchantment that dissolved her fragile common sense. She pressed closer to him, then shivered when his hand drifted upward and brushed the side of her breast. His light touch stirred a shocking amount of excitement.

With it came guilt, and acute embarrassment when she realized that her loins rubbed against his in a most disgraceful fashion. She broke away again, saying firmly, "I'm sure."

He caught his breath, then slowly released it in a sigh of soft regret. "What a pity." The arm that held her close began to loosen, a fraction of an inch at a time.

She wriggled back along his thigh so they weren't quite so intimate. But it was hard to be dignified when they were twined around each other and to let go would be to risk drowning.

The thought rekindled the terror she had felt when the flood had almost dragged her under. Nicholas had been the only safety in a world gone mad. If he had not been so strong, so tenacious, she would have become one more of the mine's victims. "You saved my life, my lord. Thank you."

"Pure selfishness on my part. Without you, my household would instantly fall apart."

His teasing restored her sense of humor. "But without me to complicate your life," she pointed out, "you would have been free to leave Aberdare."

"Whoever said that life should be simple?" He nuzzled his face into the angle between her throat and shoulder.

She caught her breath. Their original agreement had covered kisses; in her naivete, she had not known how many seductive ways there were for a man to touch a woman. Trying to distract herself from awareness of their physical closeness, she said, "The water has dropped another foot or so."

"So it has. Shall we find out if it's low enough for me to stand without drowning?" He took her hand and laid it on the prop, then disengaged himself and moved away.

Her fingers skidded off the wet wood, leaving her unsupported in the water. She gave a choked cry and grabbed for the timber, but she had drifted and could find only slippery stone that gave her no purchase.

Instantly he caught her and drew her back to safety. "I should have asked if you know how to swim."

She shook her head. Recalling that he couldn't see her, she said, "I'm afraid not."

"Very well, we'll try again more carefully."

This time Nicholas placed both her hands around the prop and made sure that her grip was secure before he moved away. "The water comes about to my chin," he said, "and the current isn't too bad. I think it's time to leave. You, Miss Morgan, will have to ride on my back. I don't want to lose you in the dark."

"I couldn't agree more," she said. "Speaking of the dark, do you have flint and steel? Perhaps we can light a candle."

"You still have yours? I lost my candles when the flood hit. Should have tied them tighter. Let me check my tinderbox." More splashing as he located the box and raised it above the surface. After a moment he said regretfully, "Sorry, the tinder is soaked. A pity I'm not really Old Nick—if I was, I could light a candle by snapping my fingers."

The water moved against her as he approached. "I'm backing up to you," he explained. "Climb aboard."

She wrapped her arms around his neck and her legs around his waist, finding his muscular frame much more secure than the timber. He locked his left arm around her left leg, then started wading through the water, right arm held in front of him so he wouldn't walk into a wall.

Clare said, "If I put my arm to the side, I can keep track of the side wall."

"Good idea—that should keep us on course."

He moved with slow grace through the water, his hip muscles flexing voluptuously against her inner thighs. Abruptly she recalled a fragment of conversation she had overheard from two older women. One was a widow who had said bawdily that she was longing to feel a good man between her legs again. Clare had turned away from the vulgar comment, but now she better understood it. Though this was not what the widow had in mind, Nicholas's movements were causing a thick, tense pleasure to form deep inside her. She wanted to roll her hips against him to soothe the ache at the juncture of her thighs.

Instead she buried her heated face against the back of his neck. After this indecent intimacy, how could they return to a safe relationship? But of course she hadn't been safe since she had gone to Aberdare to win his cooperation.

As her thoughts churned, her fingers skimmed the right wall, feeling the roughness of worked stone punctuated by an occasional prop. Twice they passed open shafts.

Then she touched something different. Cool and slick but yielding, with stubby bristles. Her hand trailed along and touched fabric. She gave a small shriek and jerked away.

"What's wrong?" Nicholas said sharply.

Voice shaking, she said, "Th . . . there's a drowned man here."

He stopped walking. "Is there a chance he's still alive?"

Remembering the flaccid feel of the skin, she shuddered and shook her head. "I don't think so."

"Probably the luckless Bodvill—something heavy struck me during the first burst of flooding, and it could have been a body. If he's beyond help, we'll have to leave him, Clare."

His matter-of-fact tone helped her compose herself. Her worst fear had been that the body was Owen's, but her friend was clean-shaven and this poor man wasn't.

Nicholas began moving forward again. When a safe distance had been covered, she wiped her hand on her thigh—a meaningless gesture when she was almost completely submerged—and started skimming the wall again.

The shaft seemed endless, far longer than when they had had light. She was beginning to wonder if they had somehow turned off the main tunnel when Nicholas stopped again. "Hang on. We've hit a dead end." After a moment, he said, "No, the tunnel continues, but the ceiling drops below the waterline."

Clare frowned, tried to remember. "We came through a section with a low roof. I don't think it was very long. Do you remember? You would have had to duck your head."

"To be honest, I wasn't paying that much attention. All I remember is that sometimes I could walk upright and sometimes I couldn't." There was a frown in his voice. "I don't want to take you under water without knowing how long this section is. Can you hold onto a timber while I reconnoiter?"

The last thing Clare wanted was to be alone in a flooded shaft with a floating corpse, but she said calmly, "There's a prop about ten feet behind us. I'll be fine there."

He backed up until she was next to the prop. "Can you get a firm grip?"

"This timber is well-designed for holding," she assured him.

He dropped a quick kiss on the forehead, then said with mild chagrin, "Sorry, I forgot. Have I used up tomorrow's kiss?"

"I think that under the circumstances, I won't charge it to your account," she said gravely.

"In that case . . ." His arms went around her and he kissed her again, on the mouth and at much greater length.

The embrace sent welcome warmth right down to her chilled toes. She tried to sound stern when he finally stepped away. "You are impertinent, Lord Aberdare."

He chuckled. "Of course." Then, no longer encumbered by a passenger, he swam to where the ceiling lowered.

Clare listened intently, following his actions by sound. He paused to draw a series of deep breaths, filling his lungs as much as possible. Then, with the quiet ripple of an otter sliding into a stream, he was gone.

The water around her immediately seemed ten degrees colder. Clare shivered as dreadful possibilities occurred to her. If they had strayed from the main shaft, Nicholas could be heading into unsuspected dangers. Firmly she told herself to stop worrying; the Demon Earl had already proved that he could take care of himself, and her as well.

Nonetheless, it seemed like forever before he returned, gasping for breath when he broke the surface. When he could speak again, he swam toward Clare. "The tunnel slants up a bit, so the water is shallower on the other side. I think we can make it, but it will be uncomfortable—you'll be pushed to the limit of your lung capacity. Will you trust me to get you through?"

"Of course—you need me to keep your household organized." It was easy to joke when he was with her again.

He laughed and drew her through the water until they were at the end of the high-ceilinged section. "Breathe deeply several times and take hold of my left hand with both of yours. When you're ready, squeeze twice."

She followed his orders, locking her hands around his. When she signaled her readiness, he dived under the surface, towing her behind. He swam on his side, his legs making powerful scissor-like strokes below Clare. It was an effortless way to travel, but he had been right about the discomfort. Though she did trust him, as she ran out of air she could feel panic rising. She wanted to flail wildly to the surface. Instead, as her heart pounded like a drum, she exhaled slowly.

When she couldn't have lasted a second longer without gulping water into her burning lungs, he kicked upward and they broke into air. Again she clung to Nicholas while she struggled for breath. "Brave girl," he murmured, stroking her back.

"Not brave," she gasped. "And not a girl. What I am is a very cross spinster schoolmistress."

He laughed and kissed her again. She had the right to stop him—he was already well over his limit—but she didn't. His kisses gave her courage, and she needed all she could find. She would worry about her morals when they were safe above ground.

Desire throbbed through her, revitalizing her fatigued body. It took time to realize that the pulsing rhythm was not only inside her, but all around them, shivering through the stone and water. Lifting her head, she said with relief,

"The pump is working again." Cautiously she felt for the floor and found that she could stand and keep her face above water, though only just.

"Hallelujah. This calls for a celebratory kiss." Again he drew her into his arms and sought her mouth with his.

Laughing, she pushed away from him. "Don't you think of anything but kissing?"

"Occasionally," he admitted, "but not by choice." He caught her into his arms and lifted her so that their mouths were level.

Each time it was easier for her to melt into his kiss. Once again, she found herself floating in a heady mixture of water and desire. Paradise in a coal pit. . . .

Struggling for sense, she leaned back and said, "If we don't stop this, the water will start boiling."

"Clarissima!" he said with pleasure. "That's the nicest thing you've ever said to me."

Fortunately he didn't try to kiss her again, since her will-power was at a very low ebb. After setting her down, he put an arm around her shoulders and they went on.

They soon reached a wall, which gave a metallic rattle when Nicholas investigated with his free hand. "I think we've reached the door where Huw was trapper."

The area seemed mercifully free of small drowned bodies. Nicholas ducked down and went through the submerged door, then called for Clare to follow.

When she came up on the other side, blinking, she was overjoyed to see approaching candles. Half a dozen men were splashing toward them through waist deep water, Owen in the lead. He called, "Clare, Nicholas, is that you?"

"We're both here and fine," Nicholas answered as he helped Clare to her feet. "Did you get Huw out safely?"

"Aye, though it was a near thing. After swimming to a higher level, I had to take him up to grass. The poor mite was terrified of staying in the pit."

"There's a drowned man back in the shaft," Clare said soberly. "Have there been any other casualties?"

"That would be Bodvill, rest his soul," Owen said. "But no one else was killed or hurt badly. We are lucky."

One of the other miners said, "We'll go after Bodvill now."

"He's not far beyond the section where the ceiling is lower," Nicholas said.

The miner nodded, then led three of the other men toward the metal door. The water had been falling steadily, and it was now possible to take lighted candles through.

As Clare and the others began splashing toward the main gallery, Owen said, "Sorry it took so long to reach you. There's a section ahead that was impassable until the pump was repaired."

"No harm done, though I've spent more enjoyable afternoons," Nicholas said dryly. "Is every day like this, or was the excitement arranged for my special benefit?"

Owen sighed. "I only wish that today was unusual."

The accident would have one good outcome, Clare thought as she slogged wearily through the water. Now that Nicholas's attention had been engaged, she was willing to wager that soon there would be changes at the mine.

11

KNOWING HOW exhausted Clare was, Nicholas wrapped a firm arm around her as the creaking rope lifted them to the surface. After carrying her through the flooded mine, he certainly didn't want to lose her on the last leg of the trip. She leaned against him wearily, apparently glad for his support.

At the top, he swung over to solid ground, then helped Clare dismount. The wind was freezing through their soaked clothing.

Huw waited anxiously at the top. His expression lightened when he saw Owen, who had come up at the same time as Nicholas and Clare. "It's glad I am that you're safe, Mr. Morris. This is a wicked place."

Owen patted the boy on the shoulder. "Mining is not so bad, Huw, though it's not to every man's taste."

"I swear to Lord Jesus that I won't go down there again," the boy said in a solemn voice that was vow, not blasphemy.

As he spoke, the whim gin brought several more men to the surface. One of them, a tall, lanky fellow with a red face, bellowed, "I heard that, Huw-boy, and I don't want to hear it again. To stop your whimpering, I'm going to take you down pit again right now."

The child's small face went dead white. Quavering but determined, he said, "N . . . no, Da, I won't go."

"I'm your father, and you'll do what I tell you," the man growled. Stepping forward, he reached for Huw's wrist.

The boy shrieked and scuttled behind Owen. "Please, Mr. Morris, don't let him take me."

Owen said mildly, "The lad almost drowned, Wilkins.

He needs warm food and his bed, not another trip down pit.''

"This is none of your affair, Morris." Wilkins made another lunge for his son, almost falling over in the process.

Owen's face hardened. "You're drunk. Leave the boy alone until you're sober."

The miner exploded like gunpowder, waving a bony fist and snarling, "Don't tell me what to do with my son, you canting Methodist bastard."

Owen sidestepped neatly. Then, with visible satisfaction, he downed his assailant with a well-placed blow to the jaw. As Wilkins lay stunned on the ground, Owen knelt by the child. "You had best come to my house for tea, Huw," he said gently. "Your da is in a temper today."

Nicholas winced at the distress in the boy's face, for it reminded him of his own childhood. And the way Owen talked to Huw made Nicholas think of Reverend Morgan.

Not liking the memories stirred, he turned away in time to see Wilkins stagger to his feet, his short-handled miner's pick in his hand. Face ugly with rage, he raised the pick and started to swing at the back of Owen's head.

As shouts of warning rose, Nicholas stepped forward and wrenched the pick from the other man's hands, twisting it with such force that Wilkins fell to the ground again. Roaring, the miner started to scramble to his feet.

Nicholas kicked the other man in the belly, sending him sprawling on his back. Then he lowered the pick and rested the center of the heavy metal head on Wilkins' throat. The miner smelled of cheap whiskey. He wasn't fit to keep a dog, much less a child. "I have an offer for you," Nicholas said coolly. "The boy is willful and has no taste for the pit, so he's obviously no use to you. May I take him off your hands for, say, twenty guineas? That's as much as he'll earn in years as a trapper, and you won't have the cost of food or clothing."

Blinking confusedly, Wilkins said, "Who the devil are you?"

"I'm Aberdare."

Wilkins' face twisted. Heedless of his precarious position, he sneered, "So the Gypsy has a taste for little boys. Is that why your lady wife couldn't stand the sight of you?"

Nicholas clenched the handle of the pick convulsively, fighting the urge to ram the tool through the man's throat. "You haven't said whether you'll part with your son," he said when he had regained his control. "Twenty guineas, Wilkins. Think how much whiskey that will buy."

Mention of money gave the miner pause. After laborious thought, he said, "If you want the brat, you can have him for twenty-five guineas. God knows he's worthless. Does nothing but whine and wail and ask for more food."

Nicholas glanced at the gathered miners who had silently watched the scene. "You'll all bear witness to the fact that Mr. Wilkins is voluntarily relinquishing all rights to his son Huw for the sum of twenty-five guineas?"

Most of the onlookers nodded, their expressions showing their disgust for a man who would sell his own son.

Nicholas removed the pick so Wilkins could climb heavily to his feet. "Give me your direction. The money will be delivered this evening. My steward will need a receipt for the boy."

After Wilkins nodded, Nicholas tossed the pick aside and said silkily, "Now that you are standing, would you care to make any more slanders about my personal life? I'm not armed—we can discuss your statements strictly man to man."

Though the miner outweighed Nicholas by at least two stone, his gaze slid away. Under his breath, so only Nicholas could hear, he muttered, "Bugger who you want, you Gypsy bastard."

Weary of Mr. Wilkins, Nicholas turned away and said to Owen, "If I pay Huw's expenses, will you foster him with your own children? Or if that's not possible, do you know another suitable family?"

"Marged and I will take him." Owen lifted the boy in his arms. "Would you like to come with me for always, Huw? Mind, you'll have to go to school."

Tears filled the child's eyes. He nodded, then buried his face against Owen's neck.

As Owen patted Huw's back, Nicholas reflected cynically

on the power of money. For a mere twenty-five guineas, a child could have a new life. Of course, noble blood was more expensive; Nicholas had cost the old earl four times as much. No doubt the price would have been higher if he hadn't had the Gypsy taint.

Face set, he turned away. What mattered was that Huw was going to people who would treat him with kindness.

Throughout the scene, Clare had been watching in silence, her blue eyes penetrating. When Nicholas glanced at her, she said, "There may be hope for you yet, my lord."

"Don't get any wrongheaded ideas about my philanthropy," he snapped. "I acted from sheer perversity."

She smiled. "Heaven forbid that you should be associated with a good deed. Why, you could be drummed out of the Society of Rakes and Rogues for that."

"They can't expel me, I'm a founding member," he retorted. "Go change into your dry clothes before you freeze to death. And you're going to need a bath—you're wearing so much coal dust that you look like a chimney sweep."

"So do you, my lord." Still smiling, she went into the smaller shed where she had left her garments.

Nicholas, Owen, and Huw went into the other shed. Though Owen usually worked until later, the flood had thrown normal operations into chaos, so he had decided to take Huw home early.

As he changed into his own clothes, Nicholas said quietly, "You're sure Marged won't object to your bringing home a child?"

"She won't mind," Owen assured him. "Huw's a bright, good-natured lad, and more than once Marged has said she wished he was ours. Since Wilkins wouldn't let the boy go to Sunday school, she has been teaching him his alphabet and numbers when she has the chance. Feeding him, too. Poor lad is always hungry."

As they talked, Huw tugged off his wet, ragged shirt, revealing a bony back striped with ugly welts. Nicholas frowned when he saw the marks. "I'm tempted to go outside and tear Wilkins' head off. Or would you rather do the honors?"

"Don't tempt me," Owen said ruefully. "It's better to

let it alone now that Wilkins has agreed to give up the boy. He spent years in the army, and he loves any excuse to fight. No point in making him more of an enemy than he is already. Besides," he continued piously, "our Lord was against violence."

Nicholas grinned and pulled on his coat. "This from a man who laid Wilkins out as neatly as any professional boxer?"

"Sometimes one must be firm with the ungodly," Owen said with a twinkle in his eyes. "Even Jesus lost his temper and drove the moneychangers from the temple."

Huw came over and took Owen's hand trustingly. Again Nicholas thought of Reverend Morgan. Buying the boy from his brutish father had been one of Nicholas's better impulses.

As the three of them left the shed, Nicholas saw that Bodvill's body had been brought up the shaft and was being laid beside the banksman's hut. Supervising was a massive man with miner's muscles, expensive clothing, and an undeniable air of authority. Owen muttered, "That's Madoc."

Nicholas had guessed as much. Though he wanted to meet the manager, he would prefer to do it under other circumstances. He looked around for Clare and saw that she was emerging from the other shed, dressed in her boy's riding clothes. Given the number of people milling around, it would be easy to collect her and the horses and leave unobtrusively.

Luck wasn't with them. As Madoc turned away from the drowning victim, his gaze fell on Clare. "What are you doing here, you little troublemaker?" he barked. "I told you to keep your pious arse away from the pit."

Here was another head that should be torn off, but Nicholas had come to the pit to investigate, not start a war. Before Clare could answer, he stepped forward and said peacably, "If you're angry, blame me. I asked Miss Morgan to bring me here."

Madoc swung around. "Who the hell are you?"

"The Earl of Aberdare."

The manager looked momentarily disconcerted. Then his

bluster returned. "You're trespassing, Lord Aberdare. Get off the property, and stay off."

"The mining company leases this land from the Davies estate," Nicholas said with deceptive calm. "Remember, I still own it. Better manners might be in order."

With visible effort, Madoc curbed his anger. "I apologize for my abruptness, but there's been a fatal accident and it's a bad time for visitors." His eyes suddenly narrowed as a thought struck him. "Have you already been down pit?"

"Yes. A memorable experience," Nicholas said with massive understatement.

Madoc swung around, glaring at all the assembled workers. "Who's responsible for taking Aberdare down?"

Guessing that anyone admitting to the deed would be discharged on the spot, Nicholas gave Owen a warning glance, then said, "Again, the fault is mine. I may have given the impression that I had your permission. Your employees were most helpful."

The manager appeared to be on the point of apoplexy. "I don't care if you are an earl and the owner of this land," he growled. "You've no right to sneak around behind my back and lie to my laborers. I've half a mind to call the law on you."

"Go right ahead," Nicholas said pleasantly. "I haven't seen the inside of a jail lately, and I'm due. But my old friend Lord Michael Kenyon still owns the mine, doesn't he? I've been meaning to call on him now that I've returned. He might not approve of such discourtesy on his premises."

Madoc's uneasiness showed in the sharpness of his reply. "Go right ahead. His lordship gave me full authority over the mine, and never once has he disapproved of my actions."

"I'm sure he finds it a great comfort to have a manager who is so conscientious," Nicholas said with irony. He glanced at Clare, who had quietly brought out the horses. "Shall we leave, Miss Morgan? I've seen everything I wish to see."

She inclined her head and they both mounted. Nicholas could feel Madoc's gaze boring into his back as they rode from the premises. If looks could kill, he would be a dead man.

When they were well away from the mine, he said, "I've made two enemies and it isn't even teatime. Not a bad day's work."

"It's not a joke," Clare said sharply. "Nye Wilkins is the sort who might get drunk one night and decide to set fire to your stables as a way of getting even for humiliating him."

"And Madoc is worse. I see why asking him to make improvements has been a waste of time. A very dangerous man."

She looked at him in surprise. "I've always felt that, but I thought my judgment was colored by my dislike of the mine."

"Madoc is a bully and petty tyrant who will fight to the death to maintain his power. If threatened, he would be as vicious as a weasel," Nicholas said thoughtfully. "I've seen his sort before. It amazes me that Michael hired such a man, much less that he's satisfied with Madoc's performance. I'm beginning to wonder what the devil Michael has been doing for the last few years. He can't be dead or I would have heard, but he has become amazingly neglectful of things that are important to him."

"Perhaps they no longer seem as important," she suggested. "People can change in four years."

"True. Yet it surprises me that Michael would change in the direction of indifference. He always cared a great deal about things. Often he cared too much." Idly Nicholas stroked his horse's neck, his mind on the past. "When I get to London, I'll ask our mutual friend Lucien where Michael is, and what he's been doing. Lucien knows everything about everyone."

Remembering that Marged had mentioned the name, Clare said, "Is Lucien another of your Fallen Angel friends?"

Nicholas looked at her in astonishment. "Good Lord, has that old nickname made it all the way to Wales?"

"I'm afraid so. Where did the name come from?"

"The four of us—Lucien, Rafael, Michael, and me—became

friends at Eton," he explained. "In London, we often
went about together. The fashionable world loves nick-
names, and some hostess dubbed us the Fallen Angels because we were young, a little wild in the way young men
often are, and two of the group had the names of archangels.
It meant nothing."

"The story I heard was that you were all as handsome as
angels, and as wicked as devils," she said demurely.

He grinned. "Gossip is a wonderful thing—much more
interesting than the truth. We weren't saints, but neither did
we break any major laws, bankrupt our families, or ruin any
young ladies' lives." He considered. "At least, none of us
had at the time we acquired the nickname. I can't vouch for
what anyone has done in the last four years."

Hearing the regret in his voice, she said, "You must be
looking forward to seeing your friends again."

"I am. Michael may have fallen off the face of the earth,
but Lucien has a post at Whitehall and Rafe is active in the
House of Lords, so they are almost certainly in London
now." He glanced at her. "We'll leave day after tomorrow."

Clare's jaw dropped. "You're really taking me to London?"

"Of course. I said so the day you came to Aberdare with
blackmail on your mind."

"But . . . but you had been drinking. I thought you'd
forget, or think better of it."

"What could be better than getting you a suitable wardrobe? Although the way that old shirt clings is quite fetching. Are you wearing anything underneath it?"

Her hands tightened on the reins, slowing her pony. Since
she seemed fated to be constantly embarrassed by Nicholas,
she must learn not to let her emotions affect her riding, she
thought with disgust. "I couldn't bring myself to put dry
clothing over wet undergarments."

"A good decision for both practical and aesthetic reasons, except that you appear to be on the verge of freezing."
He peeled off his coat and tossed it to her. "Though it's
against my principles to encourage females to wear more
clothing, you'd better put this on."

She tried to give the coat back. "Then you'll freeze."

"I've spent too many nights sleeping under the stars to be bothered by the cold."

Surrendering to the inevitable, she wrapped the coat around her. The folds were warm with Nicholas's body heat and held a faint, masculine scent that she could have identified anywhere. Wearing the coat was like having his arms around her, only safer.

It would be interesting to see London, but the visit would surely end the odd closeness that was growing between them. In the metropolis he would have his friends, and probably his old mistresses, to fill his time. He would scarcely remember Clare's existence. Her life would be much easier.

She really should be more grateful for the prospect.

The rest of that day fell into what was becoming a pattern. Clare took a long bath and washed the smell and filth of the pit from her body and hair. Then, even though she was still shaky from her brush with drowning, she conferred with Williams about the house redecoration. Today the servants had concentrated on cleaning and reorganizing the dining room, with splendid results. She and Williams planned what rooms would be worked on in her absence. Then they made lists of wallpapers and fabrics for her to buy in London.

After another of Mrs. Howell's excellent dinners, Clare and Nicholas retired to the library. There he busied himself with correspondence and calculations, working with a degree of concentration that belied his wastrel reputation.

Clare welcomed the opportunity to browse through the library, which contained riches beyond her wildest dreams. If she and Nicholas were on friendly terms when the three months were up, perhaps he would let her borrow books occasionally.

She glanced up and studied his profile as he frowned over a document. As always, he amazed her: stunningly handsome, both aristocrat and Gypsy, as unpredictable as he was intelligent. He and she were as different as chalk and cheese, and it was impossible to imagine a future when they could be friends. More likely, the three months of this ridiculous challenge would end in disaster, and it wouldn't be the Demon Earl who would suffer.

Telling herself sharply that no one had forced her to come to Aberdare, she returned to her survey of the bookshelves. The collection was well-organized, with sections of literature in half a dozen languages. A few were even in Welsh.

Other sections were devoted to subjects such as history, geography, and natural philosophy. Clare's father had sometimes borrowed theological texts; though the old earl had considered it his duty to stay within the Church of England, he had had Dissenter tendencies. Probably that was why he had chosen a Methodist preacher to educate his grandson.

Set in the middle of the section was a large Bible richly bound in tooled leather and gilt. Guessing that it was the Davies family Bible, Clare pulled the volume from the shelf and laid it on a table. Absently she paged through, reading some of her favorite verses.

There was a family tree in the front, and she found it moving to see the different hands and inks that had carefully recorded births, deaths, and marriages. Faint smudges that might have been tears blurred one death date. A faded, century-old entry recorded the birth of one Gwilym Llewellyn Davies, the exuberantly added "At last, a son!" at the side. The infant had grown up to become Nicholas's great-grandfather.

But as she examined the chart, she understood why the old earl had been so concerned about an heir. The family had not been prolific and Nicholas had no near relations, at least not in the male line. If he held to his determination not to remarry, the earldom of Aberdare would probably die with him.

She turned the page to look at the most recent records. The old earl's two marriages and three sons were written in his own forceful hand. Though all three of the sons had married, there were no entries for children under the names of the two oldest.

Her mouth tightened when she looked at the notation by Kenrick's name. In contrast to the ink used everywhere else, Kenrick's marriage to "Marta, surname unknown," and the birth of "Nicholas Kenrick Davies" were recorded in pencil. It was more proof of how reluctantly the old earl had accepted his heir. If only he had shown Nicholas one-tenth the warmth that Owen had extended to Huw, who was not even of his own blood!

Thinking sadly of the waste, she turned to the next page. Several folded papers slipped out. She glanced at them, then looked more closely and murmured, "How odd."

She had not meant to disturb Nicholas, but he leaned back in his chair and stretched lazily. "What's odd, Clarissima?"

"Nothing very important." She went to his desk and laid the documents down under the light of the oil lamp. "Those two papers are notarized copies of the parish registers that recorded your parents' marriage and your birth. Both are worn and stained, as if they were carried too long in a pocket."

She pointed at the other two. "These documents are also duplicates, though they were copied rather badly. The oddity is that they have no legal value because they haven't been attested by a notary, yet they're folded and stained very much like the originals. I suppose your grandfather had the copies made, but I can't see what use they would be, or how they became so worn."

Nicholas lifted one of the unnotarized copies. Abruptly the tendons sprang taut on the back of his hand, and the air seemed to crackle, electric and feverish, as if lightning had struck.

Clare glanced up and saw that he was staring at the document with the same annihilating rage that he had shown when he had slashed the portrait of his wife. She caught her breath, wondering what could have triggered such fury.

He picked up the other copy and crumpled the two papers viciously in his hand. Then he rose from his chair, stalked across the room, and hurled the documents into the fire. Flames blazed up, then slowly faded back to the dull red of coals.

Shaken, Clare asked, "What's wrong, Nicholas?"

He stared into the fire, where the papers were slowly crumbling to ash. "Nothing that need concern you."

''The reason for your anger may not be my concern, but the anger itself is,'' she said quietly. ''Shouldn't a good mistress encourage you to speak of whatever is troubling you?''

''Perhaps a mistress should ask, but that doesn't mean I have to answer,'' he snapped. Perhaps regretting his curtness, he added more moderately, ''Your good intentions are duly noted.''

She decided that she preferred Nicholas's maddening whimsy to his imitation of a brick wall. Suppressing a sigh, she replaced the other papers and reshelved the Bible. He ignored her, his face like granite as he prodded the fire with a poker.

''Tomorrow is Sunday and I'm going to chapel, so I'll retire now. Good night.'' She said the words for politeness's sake, not expecting acknowledgment, but Nicholas glanced up.

''A pity that the kissing is over for the day,'' he said with brittle humor. ''Shortsighted of me to use my allotment when we were in the mine.''

His fury had passed, leaving an expression perilously close to desolation. God only knew why the papers had affected him so, but Clare couldn't bear seeing such grief in his face. With a boldness that would have been unthinkable four days before, she crossed the room and placed her hands on his shoulders, saying shyly, ''Your kiss is over, but I can kiss you, can't I?''

His gaze locked with hers, his black eyes haunted. ''You can kiss me whenever you want, Clarissima,'' he said huskily.

She felt his muscles tense, but he held still, waiting for her to take the initiative. Raising herself on tiptoe, she touched her lips to his.

His arms came around her with unmistakable hunger. ''Ah, God, you feel so right.''

Their mouths mated, deep and ardent. The initiative passed from her to him, and what she had intended as a quiet good-night embrace became far more.

When they had kissed in the mine it had been dark, sparing her the shocking intimacy of looking into his eyes. Embarrassed by his penetrating gaze, she let her lids drift shut, only to find that without the distraction of sight her other senses intensified. A spatter of rain against the window, the wet velvet roughness of his tongue against hers. A tangy scent that was smoke and piney soap and Nicholas; his breath, rough and wanting, or perhaps it was her breath, too. The crunch of coals collapsing into the grate; the soft rub of palms against fabric as he stroked her back.

The sound of an opening door.

Shocked back to awareness, she ended the kiss and looked past his shoulder. Standing in the doorway was one of the new maids, Tegwen Elias, a young chapel member with high moral standards and an unbridled tongue.

The two women stared mutely at each other, Tegwen's face showing horrified disbelief.

The sight jarred Clare into a sickening awareness of her own sinful behavior. What she was doing was wrong, and nothing could mitigate that stark fact.

The maid's momentary paralysis ended and she whirled away, closing the door behind her.

All his attention on Clare, Nicholas was unaware of the byplay. "If you've caught your breath," he said, running a seductive hand over her hip, "can I persuade you to another kiss?"

She stared up at him, torn by the bitter contrast between what she experienced in his arms, and what she had seen in Tegwen's eyes. Unevenly she said, "No. No, I must go."

He lifted a hand, as if to stop her, but she brushed by and left from the room, scarcely seeing her surroundings.

If only she had left ten minutes sooner.

The room felt very empty without Clare in it. Nicholas stared into the fire, wondering what it would take to stop her mind from warring with her body. It was the same each time they came together. First, she was shy and a little doubtful. Then, she would begin to respond, opening like a flower at dawn. Finally, with shattering abruptness, she would remember that she was not supposed to enjoy what was so utterly natural.

He ground his fist into the mantelpiece with frustration.

Once she overcame her religious priggishness, she would make a superlative mistress: sensual, intelligent, understanding. Her passion for good works might occasionally be tiresome, but that would be a small price to pay for having her in his bed.

He didn't doubt that once she became his mistress, she would be content to stay with him when the three months were up. Not only would she want to, but it would be effectively impossible for her to return to her life in Penreith. The trick was to get her into his bed in the first place.

He was getting damned tired of her vanishing like a rabbit down a burrow every time her conscience caught up with her.

12

CLARE SLEPT badly that night. It had been easy to gloss over the gravity of her behavior when she was under Nicholas's spell. A kiss was only a kiss, more naughty than sinful. But seeing herself through Tegwen's eyes had forced her to confront her own behavior. No longer could she deny her weakness, her lustful craving.

As she lay sleepless, she heard the beckoning sound of Nicholas's harp. More than anything on earth she wanted to follow that siren song, to forget her pain in the warmth of his embrace. But that would be like a moth trying to cure its attraction to the candle by diving into the flame.

She rose in the morning with heavy eyes and a heavier heart. The thought of going to chapel made her hands shake, but she could not stay away. She had never missed a Sunday service in her life, and doing so today would be an admission of guilt.

As she donned her sober gray Sunday dress, she wondered if Tegwen would be at the service, and if the girl would tell others what she had seen. Bleakly she realized that the question was not if but when; Tegwen would hardly be able to wait until she could share the scandalous news. The girl loved being the center of attention, and the story of the schoolmistress kissing the Demon Earl would be irresistible. If the news wasn't out yet, it would be very soon.

While driving to Penreith, Clare overtook the new cook, Mrs. Howell, who was on her way to the chapel. Mrs. Howell accepted a ride cheerfully and spent the rest of the journey thanking Clare for finding her the situation at Aberdare. Apparently she had not yet heard anything that impugned Clare's morals.

They arrived just as people were taking their seats. Ordinarily Clare would have found comfort in the familiar benches and whitewashed walls, the wooden floor that gleamed with lovingly applied wax. Today, however, she found herself watching to see if any of the other worshippers were regarding her oddly.

A quick scan of the congregation showed that Tegwen was not present. As Clare slipped into her usual place by Marged, her friend smiled and nodded toward Huw, who sat between Owen and Trevor, the oldest Morris son. Huw's narrow face glowed with happiness and his small body was clad in warm, sturdy garments that had been outgrown by one of his new foster brothers. For the first time in his short life Huw had a real home. When Clare thought of what the boy had endured in the pit and at the hands of his brutal father, her own problems seemed less important.

The deacon in the pulpit named a hymn and the singing began. Music was an integral part of Methodist worship, and it brought Clare closer to God than prayer ever had. As she raised her voice her tension began to dissolve.

Her peace lasted only until a late arrival entered and took a seat in the back. Amid the soft rustle of whispers, Clare heard her own name. Feeling ill, she closed her eyes and steeled herself for what was to come.

Zion Chapel had no permanent preacher, so worship was conducted by members of the congregation and visiting ministers. Today's sermon was being given by a preacher named Marcross from the next valley, but he broke off as the whispers increased in intensity. Voice thunderous, he said, "And what, pray tell, is more important than the word of God?"

More muttering and a creak of wood as someone stood. Then a harsh female voice rang through the chapel. "There is wickedness among us today. The woman to whom we have entrusted our children is a sinner and a hypocrite. Yet she dares sit with us in the house of the Lord!"

Clare's mouth tightened as she recognized the speaker as Tegwen's mother. Gwenda Elias had strong opinions about a woman's place, and had never approved of Clare's teaching or of Clare herself. And now Mrs. Elias had a weapon to punish Clare for every disagreement the two women had ever had.

Marcross frowned. "Those are grave charges, sister. Do you have proof? If not, be silent. The house of God is no place for idle gossip."

Every head in the congregation turned to Mrs. Elias. She was a tall, heavyset woman, her face carved by lines of righteousness. Raising one hand, she pointed at Clare and boomed, "Clare Morgan, daughter of our beloved former preacher and teacher of our children, has succumbed to wicked lust. Not four days ago, she moved into the house of Lord Aberdare, the one they call the Demon Earl. She claimed she would be his housekeeper. Yet last night, my daughter Tegwen, who works at Aberdare, found this shameless slut in the earl's embrace, half-naked and behaving with utter indecency. It was only God's grace that my innocent child did not catch her in the act of fornication." Her voice trembled theatrically. "Thank heaven your dear father is not alive to see you now!"

The eyes of the congregation turned to Clare. Her friends, her neighbors, her former students, regarded her with shock and horror. Though many faces showed disbelief, others— too many—showed that she had already been condemned.

Looking uncomfortable at being caught in a local dispute, Marcross said, "What have you to say for yourself, Miss Morgan? Fornication is always a sin, but it would be particularly despicable in someone like you, who holds a position of trust in the community. A murmur of agreement rose.

The blood drained from Clare's face, leaving her faint. She had known this would be difficult, but the reality was more painful than she had dreamed possible. Then Marged took her hand and squeezed it. Glancing up, Clare saw concern in her friend's face, but also faith and love.

Her support gave Clare the strength to rise to her feet. Gripping the back of the pew in front of her, she said with as much composure as she could muster, "Tegwen was one of my students, and she has always had a rich imagination. I cannot deny that she saw a kiss last night. I was feeling . . . grateful to Lord Aberdare, both because he saved my life yesterday, and because of actions of his that will benefit the village.''

Briefly she closed her eyes, searching for words that would be honest, yet not incriminate her too badly. "I won't pretend that what I did was either wise or right, but a kiss is hardly fornication, and I swear that I was as decently clothed then as I am this moment.''

A child piped up, ''What's fo'ncation?''

Almost as one, women with young children and unmarried daughters rose and hustled their offspring outside. More than one woman cast a longing glance over her shoulder as she left, but there was no question of letting children be exposed to such a subject. As Marged collected her brood, she gave Clare a sympathetic smile. Then she, too, withdrew.

When the room had been cleared of innocents, Mrs. Elias resumed the attack. "You can't deny that you are living with the earl, nor that you have behaved indecently.''

''Your own daughter is living under Lord Aberdare's roof,'' Clare pointed out. ''Aren't you concerned for her virtue?''

''My Tegwen lives with the other servants and scarcely sees the earl, but *you* are with him constantly. Don't try to deny it! Even if you are telling the truth and you are not yet his mistress,'' the sneer in Mrs. Elias's voice underlined her disbelief, ''it will only be a matter of time until you surrender your virtue. We all know about the Demon Earl, how he seduced his grandfather's wife and caused the deaths of the old earl and his own wife.''

Her voice choked with genuine emotion. ''I was chambermaid to Lady Tregar, and she herself told me of her husband's infidelities, great tears in her beautiful eyes. He broke her heart with his adultery. Then, when his wickedness was discovered, he frightened her so badly that she ran away to her death.'' Her tone turned venomous. ''You are so smug, so sure of your virtue, that you think you can consort with Satan and not be corrupted. For shame, Clare Morgan, for shame! As Thomas Morgan's daughter, you've always thought yourself better than others. Yet I tell you now that if you stay in the devil's house, you will soon be carrying his brat!''

Anger stirred in Clare, giving her strength. ''Who are you more interested in condemning—me or Lord Aberdare?'' she said sharply. ''I know that you loved your mistress, and that you still grieve for her. Yet no one but the earl himself knows what was between him and his wife, and it is wrong for us to sit in judgment. Yes, his lordship has a black reputation, but from what I have seen of him, he is less wicked than he is painted. Does anyone here have personal knowledge of vicious behavior on the part of the earl? If so, I have never heard of it. Has he ever seduced one of the village girls? No one in Penreith has ever named him father of her child.'' She paused, her gaze running over the congregation. ''I swear before God that I will not be the first.''

The silence was broken when Gwenda Elias snapped, ''So now you are defending him! To me, that's clear proof that you are succumbing to his lures. Very well, go to that devil, but don't take any of our children with you, and don't ask our forgiveness when you have ruined yourself!''

A man muttered, ''She has admitted to indecent behavior. Can't help but wonder what she isn't admitting.''

Clare's fingers whitened as her fingers tightened on the pew back. Perhaps submissiveness and confession would be more Christian, but part of her nature that she had never recognized demanded that she fight back. Looking at the man who spoke, she said, ''Mr. Clun, I sat with your mother every night for a week when she was dying. Did you think I was a liar then?''

She found another accusing face. ''Mrs. Beynon, when I helped you clean your cottage after it flooded and sewed new curtains for your windows, did you think I was immoral?'' Her icy glance moved on. ''Mr. Lewis, when your wife was ill and you were out of work, I collected clothing and food for you and your children. Did you think me corrupt then?''

All three of the people she singled out looked away, unable to meet her glance.

In the silence, Owen Morris rose to his feet. As a deacon and class leader, he was one of the most respected men in the society. "Justice belongs to the Lord, Mrs. Elias. It is not for us to forgive or condemn." His grave gaze went to Clare. "There is not another member of our chapel who has served others more than Clare Morgan. When the earl demanded that she work for him in return for his assistance to the village, she voluntarily took leave from the school so that no hint of scandal would touch the children. Her reputation has always been above reproach. If she swears her innocence, should we not believe her?"

A murmur of agreement spread through the room, but it was far from unanimous. Mrs. Elias snapped, "Say what you will, I refuse to worship under the same roof as a female who consorts with Lord Aberdare." She turned and marched toward the door. After a moment, others, both male and female, got to their feet and started to follow.

For a moment Clare froze, horrified at the knowledge that the congregation was on the verge of shattering, and she was the cause. If something wasn't done immediately, the chapel members would divide into pro-Clare and anti-Clare factions. The result would be hatred, not the love that was the purpose of their fellowship. She cried, "Wait!"

The exodus paused as people turned to her. Voice shaking, she continued, "I admit that my actions are not above reproach. Rather than split the congregation of Zion Chapel, which my father loved so much, it is better if I alone withdraw." She took a deep, shuddering breath. "I promise that I will not return until I am no longer under a shadow."

Owen started to protest, then quieted when she shook her head. Struggling to keep her chin high, she walked toward the door. One unidentified voice said admiringly, "As fine an example of Christian generosity as I could ever hope to see."

Someone else hissed, "She's wise to leave before she's thrown out. For all her education and superior ways, she's no better than she should be."

Clare had to pass two members of her class meeting. Edith Wickes scowled, not quite condemning but certainly disapproving. Jamie Harkin, the former soldier, reached out to touch her hand and give an encouraging smile. His sympathy almost triggered the tears that threatened to spill out.

She nodded to him, then opened the door and walked into the cool spring morning.

The children were playing games while most of the mothers hovered near the windows, listening to what was happening inside while keeping the curious unmarried girls at a safe distance. Marged came over and gave Clare a hug. "Oh, Clare, love," she whispered, "you do be careful. I've teased you about the earl, but this is not a laughing matter."

"It certainly isn't," Clare agreed. She tried to smile. "Don't worry, Marged. I promised I won't let him ruin me."

Unable to face anyone else, she collected her pony cart and drove away. It was horrible knowing that, within a day, everyone in Penreith would be talking about her, and that many of her fellows would not give her the benefit of the doubt.

Far worse was knowing that the doubters were right; she *had* behaved wantonly, she *was* susceptible to Nicholas's diabolical temptations. And in spite of her brave vow that she would preserve her virtue, she knew, with bleak certainty, that if she didn't leave Aberdare soon, there was a dreadful likelihood she would cooperate in her own ruination.

Knowing that Clare had gone to chapel, Nicholas had ridden out early to visit the shepherd who grazed flocks in the highest hills of Aberdare, the pastures that Tam the Telyn had once used.

He was riding back when he saw movement on the track that led to the ruins of the medieval castle that was the original Aberdare. Shading his eyes, he squinted across the valley. To his surprise, he saw that Clare's pony cart was moving slowly up the steep hill.

He watched until the cart reached the point where the track became too steep for the cart. Clare climbed out and tethered the pony, then continued the climb by foot.

The sun had come out, so she was probably going to the castle to enjoy the view, which was the best in the valley. Deciding to join her, he cantered across the valley and up the track. Unlike her pony, his stallion was capable of climbing all the way to the castle. Leaving his mount in a corner where it would be sheltered from the wind, he went in search of Clare.

He found her on the highest parapet, the wind whipping her gown and shawl and adding vivid color to her cheeks. Apparently unaware of his approach, she was gazing down at the valley. From this high vantage point, Penreith was a collection of toy-sized buildings and the mine only a wisp of smoke. In sheltered dells that faced south, daffodils were opening their golden heads.

Speaking quietly so not to startle her, he said, "A splendid prospect, isn't it? This was my favorite place when I was a child. The height and stone walls give the illusion of safety."

"But safety *is* only an illusion." She turned to face him, her face stark. "Let me go, Nicholas. You've had your amusement. Now I want to go home."

Sudden fear stabbed through him. "You're asking to be released from our bargain?"

"Now that you're going to London, you don't need my company." Wearily she brushed at tendrils of hair that had escaped her bonnet. "You've seen for yourself what needs to be done to help the village, so you don't need me for that, either."

"No!" he said explosively. "I will do nothing for Penreith unless you fulfill your part of the bargain."

"Why not?" she said, bewildered. "You care about people—it's obvious from the way you behaved at the mine, by what you did for Huw. Surely by this time you must want to help the villagers for their own sakes, not because of our foolish wager."

"You overestimate my altruism," he snapped. "The day you move back to Penreith, I will leave Aberdare. The pit and the village can go to hell for all I care."

Her eyes widened with shock. "How can you be so selfish when you can help so easily?"

"It is my nature, my little innocent," he said sarcastically. "I was taught well and truly by my nearest and dearest. Selfishness has served me far better than trust or generosity ever did, and I will not abandon it now. If you want me to play savior, you will damned well have to pay the price.''

''And the price is my life!'' she cried, tears shimmering in her eyes. ''This morning I was publically condemned in the chapel by people whose respect I thought I had earned. Even the most loyal of my friends are worried about what I am doing. It has taken only four days to undermine twenty-six years of virtuous living. Because of your whim, I am losing my friends, my work, everything that has given meaning to my life.''

It hurt to the heart to see her anguish, but to yield would be to lose her. ''You knew the price would be high at the beginning,'' he said coldly, ''and you said then 'so be it.' It's easy to be brave when nothing is asked of you, but now that you have run into the first difficulty, you are showing what you are made of. And you're a coward, Clare Morgan.''

She stiffened, the tears drying in her eyes. ''You dare speak of cowardice, a man who responded to crisis by running away from home for four years?''

''The issue is not my failings but yours,'' he retorted. ''If you want to leave, go. Preserve your precious virtue if that is what is most important to you. But I'm not fool enough to put my time and money into your projects for no more return than a superior smile. If you leave before the three months are up, the slate quarry will stay closed, I will make no attempt to improve conditions at the mine, and Aberdare will sit empty, without servants, until I can find a way to sell it.''

Her eyes narrowed with fury. ''Do you think that holding me prisoner will make me more willing to share your bed?''

Anger had driven her to accept his challenge in the first place, and if he was not careful, anger would drive her away. Softening his voice, he said, ''I am not your jailer, Clare. The decision is yours alone. I know that it must hurt terribly to be condemned by your fellows. Yet from what I know of Methodist beliefs, what truly matters is your conscience before God. Can you truly say that you are ashamed of what has passed between us?''

She gave a brittle laugh. "So must the serpent have spoken to Eve."

"Very likely," he agreed, "for the knowledge that the serpent offered was carnal. Adam and Eve ate the apple, became aware of their nakedness—their sexuality—and were expelled from Eden. Personally, I've always thought that Eden must have been a boring place—perfection always is. With no capacity to do evil, there is also no chance to do good. The world we live in is a harder place than Eden, but far more interesting, and passion is one of the great compensations."

"Obviously as a boy you learned enough religion to know how to subvert it," she said sharply, "but you missed the lesson on mercy. The world must be full of beautiful, experienced women who would welcome your attentions. Why do you insist on keeping me with you against my will?"

"Because, though there are women more beautiful, it is you that I want." He stepped closer and put his hands on her upper arms. "Can you honestly say that you dislike my attentions?"

She stiffened. "Whether I like them is not the point."

"Isn't it?" When he kissed her, her chilled lips swiftly warmed under his. He murmured, "Is this against your will?"

She made a raw, ardent sound deep in her throat. "No, damn you, it isn't! That's why I fear you."

There was desperation in her response, and he sensed that she found his embrace as much consolation as menace. If he could bind her to him now, she would be his forever.

Without breaking the embrace, he drew her a few steps along the parapet into the shelter of a wall. As the wind swirled her skirts around his ankles, he untied her appalling bonnet. A small tug and it dropped away, freeing the rich darkness of her coiled hair. He slipped his hand under her shawl and cupped her breast, kneading the gentle swell as his thumb teased her nipple to hardness. She gasped, then arched against him.

Her slightest response inflamed him easily, so easily. His hips moved against hers, trapping her between himself and the rough stone wall. She shifted restively, not trying to escape, more as if she instinctively sought how best to fit against him.

As he delved the liquid depths of her mouth, he slid his hand around her back and located the hooks that secured the top of her high-necked gown. The first unfastened easily, and the second. He paused to stroke her satiny skin, then eased her gown and shift down to expose the pale expanse of her shoulders.

Her scent was lavender and thyme, as modest as Clare herself but with a sweet, wild tang. He began to lay butterfly kisses down the arc of her throat and along the angle of her collarbone. Feverishly she rolled her pelvis against him.

He responded with a groan, his whole body becoming rigid. Through the layers of cloth that separated them, she felt a tremor in the hard ridge that pressed against her belly.

"Ah, Clare, you bewitch me," he said hoarsely.

She wanted witchery so that she need not think of the devastating choice she must make. Yet by staying in his arms, perhaps she had already chosen.

Lost in swirling sensation, she was slow to understand that the bitingly cold air on her left leg was caused by his inching her skirt and petticoat above her knee. His warm hand glided over her garter and he began caressing her inner thigh, tracing sensual patterns on the bare skin. Her breathing fractured and a dangerous craving radiated through her.

What saved her was not shame for her wickedness, but realization that secret parts of her body were becoming hotly moist. Not understanding why but obscurely embarrassed, she summoned all her strength and gasped, "No more."

Voice rough with urgency, he said, "If you want an end to doubting, let me continue. I swear you will not regret it."

"You can't guarantee that. It's far more likely that I would never forgive myself." Tears stung her eyes again as she caught his upper arms, holding him away from her. "Why are you so determined to ruin me?"

He expelled his breath with ragged slowness. "Don't cry, Clare. Please don't cry." He loosened his clasp, then turned and slid down to sit against the wall. Catching her hand, he tugged her down onto his lap, enfolding her so that her head was against his shoulder. While she struggled with her emotions, he stroked her tenderly, as if she were a frightened child.

As the fever that had invaded her body began to ebb, she forced herself to face her dilemma. There was still time to leave Nicholas and return to her normal life in the village. There would be some scandal, but it would fade soon. Leaving was the simple, safe, moral solution.

Yet if she chose it, for the rest of her life she would have to bear the guilt of her cowardice. Nicholas had the power to change hundreds of lives for the better, and for her to withdraw would be not only cowardly but selfish.

Sacrificing her reputation and her way of life to help the village was far more painful than she had expected. Yet she could have borne it easily if she disliked what he was compelling her to do; as a suffering martyr, her conscience would have been clear. The bitter irony that caused this maelstrom of guilt and doubt was the fact that Nicholas was giving her the greatest happiness of her life.

He was a rake and an adulterer, a man of avowed selfishness who had no desire to use his wealth and power for anything but gratifying his own desires. Yet he moved her deeply in ways she had never known. And strangely, even though their values were wholly antagonistic, he understood her as no one else ever had.

The gusty spring wind ruffled her skirts and teased at her hair. It was bitingly cold in this shaded corner of the parapets, but Nicholas was an island of warmth and comfort. She sighed, her hand tightening on his solid upper arm. Against all morals and sense, she felt safe with him.

He said softly, "Roses in the cheeks—a cliché used by every lovestruck swain who ever wrote bad poetry to his sweetheart. Yet nothing better describes the lovely color in your face. Welsh roses blooming on flawless Celtic skin." He brushed her cheek with the back of his hand. "Don't leave, Clare."

Even if she had made up her mind to return to Penreith, her resolve would have crumbled under the tenderness in his voice. Amazingly, it seemed that Nicholas truly wanted her with him; she was something more than an idle whim.

Though she had been too disabled by passion to appreciate that fact when they were locked in each other's arms, now she recalled his hunger, the way he had trembled at her response.

Yet the fact that she could affect him didn't guarantee her safety; it was more likely that they would simply go up in flames together. Thinking out loud, she said sadly, "If I leave now, I should be able to mend my tattered reputation. To stay is to forfeit the only life I have known. To be ruined."

"I cannot agree that passion always brings ruin. If physical intimacy creates joy and no one is hurt, how can it be wrong?"

"I suspect that men have been saying that to innocent maidens ever since the Fall," she said dryly. "And women who are fool enough to believe it are left to bear their babes in a lane and raise them in the workhouse. Who says that no one is hurt?"

"Making babies casually is wrong, a crime against the child as well as the mother," he agreed. "But pregnancy is not an inevitable result of passion. There are reasonably effective methods of prevention."

"Interesting if true," she said, "but even where there is no risk of pregnancy, casual coupling would be wrong."

He shook his head. "I think that if methods of preventing babies were widely known, ideas of right and wrong would change. Our current sexual morality exists to protect women, children, and society from the dangerous consequences of careless passion. If there were no consequences—if men and women could freely decide whether or not to share their bodies based on desire, not morality—our world would be very different."

"But would it be a better place? Perhaps for men, who could satisfy their lusts, then leave with a light heart and a clear conscience. I don't know if women can be so heedless."

"Some can, Clare," he said, an edge to his voice. "Believe me, there are women as reckless and heartless as any man."

"I'm sure that you've known any number of females of

that sort.'' She sighed ruefully. ''What a pagan you are,
Nicholas. An amoral, silver-tongued devil who can make
sin look sweet. You think that if I am forced to be in your
company, eventually I will succumb to your heathen
charms.''

He kissed her forehead lightly. ''It's my fondest hope.''

Her laughter was tinged with exasperation, and a little
anger. He was making this very difficult for her.

It was time to determine her course. She toyed with one
of his buttons as she gathered her thoughts.

First, she had to stay for the sake of the people who would
benefit from the earl's aid; her sense of duty would allow
nothing else. That being the case, she must strive to get
through the next three months with as little damage as possible. Grimly she accepted the knowledge that staying meant
she would be guilty of numerous minor offenses against morality. She would have to pray that refraining from worse
sins would count for something.

A sudden, tantalizing thought struck her. Nicholas was a
man of the world, used to gratifying his desires. Surely he
would soon weary of mere kisses. If he became frustrated
enough with her refusal to allow the ultimate intimacy, he
might ask her to leave, yet feel honorbound to fulfill his end
of the bargain.

Intrigued, she played with the idea, turning it around in
her mind. To have any chance of success, she would have
to learn to inflame his desire, while herself maintaining
enough willpower to keep saying no. Sensuality was a dangerous game and he was far more skilled in it than she. But
perhaps that advantage would be countered by the fact that
men's passions were greater than women's. Her mind made
up, she said slowly, ''My conscience will not allow me to
leave when staying will do so much good. But I warn you—
your goal is seduction, and mine is to make you decide that
I'm not worth the trouble.''

He exhaled with relief, then smiled at her with breathtaking sweetness. ''I'm very glad you're staying. It will be
interesting to see what you do to vex me, but I don't think
you'll succeed.''

''We'll see about that, my lord.'' As she looked into his

dark eyes, she felt a wicked stir of anticipation. She was no longer a helpless victim of his superior experience and strength. Her power over him was limited, but by God, she would wield it to the best of her ability.

13

CLARE PEERED out the window of the traveling coach, wide-eyed at the sight of London in the dusk. "I never imagined that there were so many people in the world," she breathed.

Nicholas chuckled. He was seated beside her, lounging casually against the upholstery with his arms folded across his chest. "Country mouse comes to city."

She scowled with mock irritation. "The first time you came to London, I'm sure you were utterly nonchalant."

"Not in the least," he said cheerfully. "I was seventeen and so enthralled that I nearly fell out the carriage window. One may love London or hate it, but one is never indifferent. I intend to see that you experience some of the city's variety while you're here."

The carriage swerved and the driver of a passing cart hurled a stream of filthy abuse at their own coachman. Clare listened, her brow furrowed. "Is that carter speaking a foreign language? I can't understand what he's saying."

"He's speaking a particularly dreadful form of cockney, the East London dialect, as well as using words that a well-bred young lady should not recognize," Nicholas said repressively.

She gave him a mischievous glance. "Can you explain his remarks to me?"

His brows arched. "Though I have every desire to corrupt you, foul language is not the way in which I wish to do it."

She smiled and looked out the window again. The long journey from Wales to London had been fast-paced and tiring, but she had enjoyed it. Since the painful scene at the castle had forced her to come to terms with her situation, she had become more relaxed with Nicholas, and their relationship was now marked by considerable teasing.

Better yet, she had learned that it was possible to enjoy his caresses without being overwhelmed. The single daily kiss had developed into a delightful session that lasted until Nicholas's hands started wandering dangerously. When that happened, Clare would call a halt. He always obeyed promptly. She sensed that, like her, he was holding back a little, enjoying the kisses without allowing himself to be swept away by desire.

The situation couldn't last; sooner or later Nicholas would unleash the full power of his sensuality in a really determined effort to seduce her. When that day came, she thought she would have the strength to resist, for every day she felt stronger, more his equal, at least within the narrow confines of their odd relationship. Meanwhile, she would enjoy London.

The streets gradually became cleaner and quieter, and eventually the carriage lurched to a halt. The coachman opened the door and lowered the steps and Nicholas helped Clare down. It was almost dark, and all she could see of Aberdare House was the broad classical facade. "Is this place also in dire need of a housekeeper?" she asked.

"Several days ago I informed my London agent that I would be coming, so the house should be clean and have a temporary staff." He offered his arm. "Of course, as mistress of the household, you may make changes as you see fit."

Wryly she realized that this was another, subtler, form of seduction. It was intoxicating to be treated like a lady, to have her opinions respected. Knowing that the situation was temporary helped her keep it in perspective.

As they climbed the marble steps, her sense of well-being began to erode. Until now, it had amused Nicholas to have Clare for a companion. But London would hold many other, more exciting amusements. In fact, he might become bored with her and send her home before the week was out.

Then she would have won, wouldn't she?

The grand rooms and lavish furnishings of Aberdare House proved to be in good condition, though years of emptiness had given it the impersonal air of a hotel. Nicholas blandly introduced Clare to the small staff as his cousin, as he had when booking separate rooms at inns on the trip to London.

At first, the servants didn't know quite what to make of Clare. She guessed that she seemed too dowdy to be an aristocratic relation, but she was an even more unlikely candidate to be a mistress. However, the servants were Londoners and hard to shock, so they shrugged their collective shoulders and obeyed her orders in return for their generous pay. She found that she was indifferent to their private opinions of her; there was much to be said for living among strangers rather than with people whom she had known her whole life.

Clare awoke to her first day in the city bubbling with excitement. When she came downstairs, Nicholas was already in the breakfast parlor, drinking coffee and reading the *Morning Post*. He rose politely when she came in. "Good morning, my dear. Did you sleep well?"

"Not really—Mayfair is almost as noisy as the Penreith mine. But I expect I'll get used to it." Clare glanced at the *Morning Post*. "Imagine, being able to read a newspaper the very day it's published rather than weeks later! Such luxury."

Smiling, he poured her a steaming cup of tea. "London is the center of the world, Clare. Much of the news is made here."

After she had selected a breakfast from the heated dishes on the sideboards, they both took seats. Nicholas said, "I've been looking at the society notes. No mention of Lord Michael Kenyon or the Earl of Strathmore, but the Duke of Candover is in town."

Clare felt a touch of alarm. "A duke?"

Accurately interpreting her expression, he said, "That's Rafe. Don't worry, he may be a duke and richer than Croesus, but he never allows it to make him insufferable. He's a great believer in restrained gentlemanly behavior."

"I've always been curious about what makes a man a gentleman, apart from money and the right ancestors."

He grinned and folded the newspaper. "According to Rafe, an English gentleman is never rude except on purpose."

"I don't find that a comforting definition," she said with a smile. "I suppose the Earl of Strathmore is your friend Lucien."

"Precisely. Don't worry, exalted though they might be, my friends are a tolerant lot—they have to be, to put up with me." He smiled remiscently. "I met Lucien at Eton when four boys decided that anyone as dark and foreign-looking as I should be beaten. Lucien thought the odds were unsporting, so he came into the fray on my side. It cost us both black eyes, but we managed to drive the others off and have been friends ever since."

"I think I approve of the Earl of Strathmore." Clare finished her eggs and sausage. Not as good as Mrs. Howell's, but quite acceptable. "Are any of the Fallen Angels married, or is that against the Code of the Rakes?"

"As far as I know they're all single, though I've been away so long that anything could have happened." He dug into his pocket and pulled out several banknotes, then handed them to Clare. "Take this. London is an expensive place, and you'll need some pin money."

Clare gave him a bemused smile and fingered the notes. "Twenty pounds. The same as my salary for a year's teaching."

"If you're implying that the world is an unfair place, I won't argue the point. Perhaps the Penreith school endowment should raise your salary."

"Twenty pounds is generous—there are schoolmasters in Wales who earn as little as five pounds a year, though usually they have other jobs as well. I also receive gifts of food and services from many students and their families. I don't know if I belong in a world where twenty pounds is pin money." She started to slide the notes back across the table.

"You can belong in any world that you choose," he said sharply. "If twenty pounds seems extravagant, keep it for running away money. You'll need it to return to Penreith if I become unbearable, a possibility that can't be ruled out.''

As usual, his nonsense distracted her. "Very well, though it seems strange to take money from you."

His eyes twinkled. "If I were paying you for immoral purposes, I wouldn't be getting my money's worth. However, the twenty pounds is to defray the costs of my bringing you to London against your will."

She surrendered and pocketed the notes. "You're very hard to win an argument with."

"Never argue with a Gypsy, Clare—we're not constrained by either logic or dignity." He got to his feet and stretched luxuriously. "When you finish your breakfast, it will be time to do something about your wardrobe."

She looked quickly down at her teacup. There was something downright indecent about the way he stretched; his catlike sensuality was enough to distract the soberest lady.

Once she had thought herself sober, but that was getting harder to remember all the time.

The elegant dressmaker's shop had the name "Denise" discreetly painted on the small sign that hung above the door. There was nothing discreet about Denise herself, though; as soon as they entered the salon, a buxom blond squealed and boldly hurled herself into Nicholas's arms.

"Where have you been, you Gypsy rogue?" she exclaimed. "I've been breaking me heart for you, I have."

He lifted her into the air and kissed her soundly, then patted her generous backside when he set her back on her feet. "I'm sure you say that to all the lads, Denise."

"Yes," she admitted candidly, "but in your case I mean it." Dimples emerged. "At least, I mean it as much as I ever do.''

Clare watched in silence, feeling invisible and slightly homicidal. While she had known that Nicholas was free with his kisses, she didn't enjoy seeing the proof, especially not with a blowsy wench like this one.

Before her temperature could rise to dangerous levels, Nicholas said, "Denise, this is my friend Miss Morgan. She needs a complete wardrobe from the shift out."

The dressmaker nodded and slowly began to circle around her new customer. When she had completed her survey, she announced, "Rich colors, simple lines, provocative without being vulgar."

"My thoughts exactly," Nicholas said. "Shall we begin?"

Denise ushered them into a lushly carpeted fitting room, where they were joined by a seamstress and a very young apprentice. Clare was ordered to stand on a platform in the middle of the room. Thereafter she was treated as an inanimate dummy while Nicholas and Denise draped her in fabrics and discussed styles, colors, and materials.

Denise's cheerful manner encompassed Clare as well as Nicholas, and soon Clare's initial irritation faded. It tickled her sense of humor to have the full attention of two people who cared more about her clothing than Clare herself did, particularly since the garments under discussion were so different from what was considered appropriate in Wales. If she had had to select a wardrobe on her own, she would have given up from sheer confusion at the number of choices.

To occupy her mind, she thought about what she would like to see and do during her visit to London. Only once did fashion break into her preoccupation, when Denise draped a length of blue silk around her shoulders and said, "Perfect color, isn't it?"

"Your eye is unerring," Nicholas agreed. "That will make a splendid evening gown."

As they began to discuss possible designs, the apprentice came forward to rewind the silk on the bolt. But as the material rippled around her throat, Clare involuntarily caught a handful, unwilling to let it go. It was the loveliest fabric she'd ever seen, shimmering with every shade of blue imaginable and with an exquisite, cloudlike texture. She pressed her cheek into the silk and rubbed against it like a cat until she saw that Nicholas was watching her. She dropped the fabric in embarrassment.

"There's nothing wrong with enjoying something that is beautiful," he said with gentle amusement.

"That silk is vain and extravagant," she said sternly,

though her skin still sang where the fabric had caressed it. "There are better ways for you to spend your money."

"Perhaps," he agreed, his amusement increasing, "but a gown made from that will do wonderful things for your blue eyes. And you'll feel wonderful when you wear it." ·

She wanted to deny that she would derive any special pleasure from having such a beautiful, useless garment, but she couldn't; her treacherous heart yearned for the blue silk. She had known that accepting Nicholas's challenge would test her virtue, but it was depressing to see how susceptible she was to greed, vanity, and worldliness. Mentally she recited every scriptural passage she could remember that warned of the folly of vanity.

It didn't make her stop wanting the blue silk.

After styles and fabrics had been chosen, Nicholas asked if there were any finished garments available that would fit Clare. Denise produced three gowns with the tart comment that since the lady who had ordered them hadn't paid for the last lot, she could jolly well wait for these.

To try on the first dress, Clare withdrew behind a screen. Assisted by the seamstress, Marie, she donned a shift of muslin so fine it was almost translucent. Then the seamstress laced her into a short, lightweight corset. Clare expected the worst, for she almost never wore stays, but the garment proved less uncomfortable than she had expected.

Marie murmured, "Mam'zelle has such a small waist that this is scarcely necessary, but it will improve the line of the gown." The seamstress took her measurements to use in making the other dresses. Then she dropped a gown of rose-colored challis over Clare's head. The back fastenings were complicated; Clare was beginning to see why fashionable ladies needed maids.

Before allowing Clare to look at herself in the wall mirror, Marie produced a sprig of creamy silk roses and tucked them into Clare's dark hair. "*Tres bien.* Accessories and a different hairstyle are needed, but this will please *Monsieur le compte.*"

When Clare was finally permitted to see herself, she blinked in surprise at her image. The rose challis made her skin glow and her eyes look enormous. She looked like a lady—an *attractive* lady. Even, heaven help her, rather dashing. She studied the neckline of the gown uneasily. Not only was it cut alarmingly low, but the stays pushed her up in front. Though Clare knew herself to be modestly endowed, in this fashionable gown she looked quite . . . bountiful.

Suppressing the desire to cover her bare chest with her hands, she shyly emerged from behind the screen. Nicholas and Denise broke off their discussion to stare. While the dressmaker nodded with satisfaction, Nicholas circled around Clare, his eyes glowing with approval. "I knew this gown would become you, but even so, I'm impressed. Only one alteration is needed."

He used the edge of his hand to draw a line across the front of her bodice. "Cut the decolletage to here."

She gasped, as much because he was touching her breasts—in public!—as because of the shockingly low neckline he wanted. "I refuse to wear anything indecent!"

"What I'm suggesting is rather moderate." He drew another line across her breasts, this one barely clearing her nipples. "*This* would be indecent."

Appalled, Clare glanced at Denise. "Surely he's jesting?"

"Not at all," the dressmaker said briskly. "I have customers who won't buy a gown unless they're in danger of popping out. Keeps the gentlemen interested, they say."

"I should certainly think it would," Clare muttered, unmollified. "But it's not for me."

"You smolder better than any woman I ever met." Nicholas gave her his devil's smile. "The decolletage I am suggesting is more daring than you want, and more conservative than I would like. Isn't that fair enough?"

She had to laugh. Reminding herself that she would never wear these garments in front of anyone she knew, she said, "Very well. But if I catch lung fever, on your head be it."

"I'll keep you warm," he said, the gleam in his eye definitely dangerous.

Hastily Clare retreated behind the screen, telling herself that it didn't matter that these strangers assumed she was his mistress. The next garment was a day dress and the

neckline was somewhat more respectable, though still low
enough to raise every eyebrow in Penreith.

During a moment when there was no one near enough to
hear, Clare quietly asked Nicholas, "What sort of clients
does Denise have? I don't have the feeling that this is an
establishment for the extremely respectable."

"Perceptive of you," he replied. "The females who come
here are those who want to look as alluring as possible.
Though some are society women, many are actresses and
courtesans." He cocked his head to one side. "Does that
offend you?"

"I suppose it should," she admitted, "but I would be out
of place in a society salon. Besides, I rather like Denise."

Their conversation ended when the young apprentice
brought in a tray of tea and cakes to sustain them. Nicholas
and Denise began an energetic discussion of the stockings,
shoes, gloves, cloaks, and unmentionable undergarments
that would be required. Merely listening to them made Clare
tired.

Nicholas, however, was thriving. When they left the shop
after three hours, he said exuberantly, "Now, my dear, I
am going to introduce you to the most sensual experience
of your life."

"Oh, no," she said with dismay. "I'm trying to be a
good mistress, but I don't think it's fair for you to humiliate
me."

"Did I say anything about humiliation?" He helped her
up into the curricle, then took the reins from his groom,
who climbed onto the back of the vehicle.

As they plunged into the London traffic, she said warily,
"Are you taking me to some kind of . . . of orgy?"

"Why, Clare!" he said, glancing at her askance. "You
shock me. What do you know about orgies?"

"Not much, though I understand that they are vile and
lascivious and involve numerous people behaving like barn-
yard animals," she said scathingly.

He laughed. "Not a bad definition. Orgies come in all
sorts, of course, but I suppose that there must be at least
three parties present to qualify. They don't all have to be
human, of course."

As Clare choked with embarrassment, a dray shot from a side street, almost colliding with them. Nicholas deftly managed to stop the curricle and avoid an accident, but the filthy cockney drayman wasn't satisfied. A long-dead cigar dangling from his mouth, he began shouting curses about bloody flash coves who thought they owned the roads.

"What a disagreeable fellow," Nicholas remarked. "He needs to be taught manners."

With a powerful snap of his wrist, he cracked his whip and the cigar vanished from the drayman's mouth. The cockney was left with a ragged stub clenched between his teeth and an astonished expression.

Impressed but appalled, Clare gasped, "Good heavens, if you had misjudged, you might have taken that man's eye out."

"I do not misjudge," Nicholas said calmly. He snapped the whip again, and the drayman's cap came sailing through the air to land on Clare's lap. She felt a faint hiss of air, but the thong of the whip moved so swiftly that she couldn't see it.

As she gazed at the crumpled cap in mute fascination, Nicholas told her, "Though it is said that a man who is a good whip can take a fly off the ear of one of his lead horses, there are few who actually can do it." The whip cracked once more, and the hat went whirling back through the air to land on the head of the befuddled drayman. "I, however, am one of the ones who can."

Performance over, Nicholas resumed threading through traffic. "To return to the fascinating topic of orgies, it is a common male fantasy to bed two women at once. In fact, bed is the wrong term—so much space is required that one is likely to end up on the floor. Having an inquisitive mind, I once decided to indulge in this particular fantasy. I suppose that the result could be termed an orgy." He turned the curricle into a broader street. "Do you know what my most vivid memory of this orgy is?"

Face flaming, Clare clapped her hands over her ears. "I don't want to hear any more!"

Ignoring her protest, Nicholas said with relish, "Carpet burns on the knees, that's what I remember. In order to keep either of the ladies from getting bored, it was necessary to crawl back and forth constantly. An exhausting experience, and I limped for a week.'' He paused pensively. ''It taught me that some fantasies are better off remaining in the mind.''

Clare went off into helpless laughter. ''You're deplorable,'' she gasped, thinking that only Nicholas could turn a hopelessly bawdy story into something hilarious. Perhaps, after all, his ''most sensual experience'' would not turn out to be so dreadful.

Yet she was not prepared when he pulled the curricle up in front of an enormous Gothic church. Recognizing the building from a print she had seen, Clare said incredulously, ''Surely this is Westminster Abbey.''

Nicholas tossed his reins to the groom, then assisted Clare from the curricle. ''Right you are.''

For a time, they stood in silence while her eager gaze scrutinized the facade. No print could do justice to the size, or the power, of the structure. Every line of the abbey and its twin towers soared toward the heavens, a wordless tribute to the faith of those who had built it.

Nicholas took her elbow and they moved toward the entrance. If he had not been guiding her, she would have fallen over her own feet, for she could not take her eyes off the building.

The interior was even more glorious than the exterior. Though other visitors and worshippers were scattered about, the enormously high roof made the people seem insignificant and gave a paradoxical sense of privacy. Dark shadows, glowing jewel-toned windows, pointed arches, a forest of enormous columns; Clare was so dazed by the visual richness that she had trouble grasping the abbey as a whole.

She held Nicholas's arm as they wandered up a side aisle. ''This is a building designed to impress humans with the power and majesty of God,'' she murmured, not wanting to raise her voice.

''All of the great places of worship do that,'' he replied quietly. ''I've been in churches, mosques, synagogues, and Indian temples, and all of them were capable of making a man think that there is something to this religion business.

But I've also been in shrines smaller than Zion Chapel in Penreith, and some of those seemed the holiest of all.''

She nodded absently, too overwhelmed to keep up a rational discussion of religious architecture. The walls were lined with monuments to famous Britons. Incredible to think that she was walking over the bones of so many great men and women: Edward I, called Longshanks, and Henry VIII. Elizabeth the Virgin Queen and her cousin and enemy, Mary Queen of Scots. Geoffrey Chaucer, Isaac Newton, and the William Pitts, both Elder and Younger. When they reached the chapel of Edward the Confessor, who had been both king and saint, she said in a hushed voice, ''Is every important figure in English history buried here?''

He gave a low laugh. ''No, though it can seem that way. The combination of spectacular architecture and history is rather overwhelming.'' He pulled out his pocketwatch and checked the time, then turned and started back along the south aisle.

They had gone only a short distance when the silence was shattered by a torrent of music. Clare caught her breath and a shiver fizzed up her spine. It was an organ; no other instrument would have had the power and majesty to fill such a huge church.

The organ was joined by a choir of angels. No, not angels, though the voices were truly angelic. Hidden somewhere in the complex spaces of the abbey, scores of male voices lifted in triumphant song. The music resonated from the stone walls, echoing and concentrating with a stunning power that paradise itself would be hard-pressed to match.

Nicholas gave a soft, enraptured exhalation. ''They're practicing Easter music.'' He took Clare's hand and stepped back into the shelter of a niche that was partially obscured by a flamboyant memorial sculpture.

Relaxing back against the stone wall, he closed his eyes and gave himself over to listening, absorbing the throbbing measures as a flower absorbs sun. She had known that he loved music from his own harp playing, but his face now made her realize that ''love'' was not a strong enough word. He had the expression of a devastated angel seeing the possibility of redemption.

Slowly, insensibly, she drifted closer to him until her back brushed his white linen shirt. One of his arms went around her waist, folding her against him. There was nothing carnal about the embrace; rather it was a way of sharing an experience too profound for words. Closing her own eyes, she allowed herself to revel in the moment. The transcendent power of the music. The strength and warmth of Nicholas. Joy.

The third piece was Handel's "Hallelujah Chorus," a piece of music as electrifying as it was unmistakable. *For the Lord God omnipotent reigneth* . . . She shivered under the impact of emotions that resonated from the depths of her soul.

King of kings and Lord of lords . . . Spiritual faith and passion, beauty and love, sensuality and tenderness, sacred and profane—all were jumbled together in an inseparable mass that brought wistful tears to her eyes. *Forever and ever and ever* . . .

Perhaps the juxtaposition of such disparate emotions was blasphemous, but she was unable to separate them, any more than she could have said where she ended and Nicholas began. She simply existed, wanting nothing more of life.

When the choir finished, the organ went into a thunderous solo that threatened to loosen the ancient stones of the abbey. Slowly Clare came out of her trance. She opened her eyes to a scowl from two passing ladies. Reminded that Nicholas's arm was still around her waist, reluctantly she pulled away from him.

She turned and looked up at him, and couldn't look away. Softly he said, "I've always thought that hell must be the absence of music."

A sense of closeness, of connection, pulsed between them. And there was something different about him. It took a moment for her to realize that, for the first time, his expression was utterly open. Usually his quick tongue and eloquent face disguised the fact that he held himself back, but now the barriers were down. What she saw in his eyes was vulnerability, and she wondered how long it had been since he had let anyone see that deeply into him. Or if he ever had.

Then she began to wonder what he might be seeing in her

eyes. Uneasily she looked away, breaking the connection between them. She had to clear her throat before she could speak. "That was wonderful. And you were right—it was the most sensual experience of my life."

"And utterly respectable." He offered his arm to her.

Clare could still feel the phantom warmth of that arm around her waist. She slipped her hand into the crook of his elbow and they walked wordlessly from the abbey. After the choir, anything else would be anticlimactic.

Outside a brisk wind was chasing fragments of cloud across the sky in ever-changing patterns. Nicholas hailed the curricle, and soon they were threading their way through the Westminster traffic. The quiet streets of fashionable Mayfair were a relief, and Clare was looking forward to reaching Aberdare House. In fact, after the stimulation of the dressmaker and the abbey, she might commit the self-indulgence of a nap.

Nicholas, however, had not yet run out of surprises. As they passed down a peaceful residential street, he suddenly reined in his horses. "The knocker is up, so the family must be in residence."

Handing the reins to the groom again, he jumped lightly to the pavement and reached up to help Clare.

"Who's in residence?" she asked as she alighted beside him.

Eyes gleaming, he guided her up the steps and rapped on the door with the lion-head knocker. "Why, my dear old granny."

Granny. Grandmother? But his father's mother had died years before, and if his mother's Gypsy mother was alive, she wouldn't be living in a house in Mayfair.

Understanding hit her as the door began to swing open. Clare realized with horror that he must be talking about his grandfather's young widow: Emily, the dowager Countess of Aberdare—the woman who was widely believed to have been Nicholas's mistress, and who had been at the center of the scandal that had cost two lives.

14

A S CLARE entered the house with Nicholas, she felt a distinctly unchristian desire to wring his neck. It was common knowledge in Penreith that on the night when the old earl and Caroline had died, servants had found Nicholas in the countess's bedroom. In spite of that strong circumstantial evidence, Clare had been reluctant to draw the obvious conclusion. Though at the time she thought she was being nonjudgmental, in retrospect she supposed that she simply hadn't wanted to believe Nicholas could be so base. Now, however, she was likely to learn the truth by seeing the two of them together, and she found that she didn't want to know what had actually happened.

As the dignified butler admitted the visitors and asked their names, a naked toddler ran shrieking through the front hall. It quite ruined the formal effect. A panting nursemaid came racing through in hot pursuit of the child, followed a few seconds later by a laughing lady in her mid-thirties.

Her gaze went to the visitors, and her expression changed. "Nicholas!" she exclaimed, holding her hands out to him. "Why didn't you tell me you'd returned to England?"

He caught her hands, then kissed her on both cheeks. "I only arrived in London yesterday, Emily."

Clare watched in stiff-faced silence, thinking that she had seen Nicholas kiss entirely too many women today. The dowager countess was glowing with health and happiness and looked a decade younger than when she had lived in Aberdare. And judging by the obvious affection between the two, it was easy to believe that they had been lovers.

Nicholas turned and drew Clare forward. "Perhaps you remember my companion."

After a moment of perplexity, the countess said, "You're Miss Morgan, the Penreith schoolmistress, aren't you? We met when Nicholas was setting up the endowment for the school."

It was Clare's turn to look perplexed. "Nicholas set up the endowment? I thought the school was your project."

"Since my husband tended to disapprove of Nicholas's progressive ideas, it was better for me to do the public part," the countess explained. "I hope the school is doing well. Are you still the schoolmistress?"

"Most of the time," Nicholas interjected. "She's taken a three-month leave of absence in an attempt to educate me."

The countess's curious gaze went from him to Clare and back again, but before she could comment, the young nursemaid returned, her bare-bottomed charge gurgling in her arms. "I'm sorry, ma'am," she said apologetically. "I don't know how Master William managed to sneak off like that."

The countess leaned forward and kissed her son's cheek. "Amazingly inventive, isn't he?" she said proudly.

" 'Ventive, 'ventive, 'ventive!" the child echoed.

"So this is my godson." Laughing, Nicholas took William away from the nursemaid. "Considering how much he hates wearing clothing, he's going to be inexpensive to dress in years to come. Maybe he has some of the Gypsy love of freedom."

Clare couldn't stop herself from looking for a resemblance between Nicholas and William. If there was one, she didn't see it; the child was blond and blue eyed, a proper English baby. He was also too young to be the product of a four-year-old liaison.

The countess's light voice interrupted her thoughts. "Forgive my rudeness, Miss Morgan. As you can see, everything is at sixes and sevens, but would you care to join me for tea? Nicholas and I have a great deal to talk about."

Nicholas chuckled and handed William back to his nurse. "It's clear what you've been doing for the last several years."

The countess blushed like a schoolgirl as she ushered her guests into the drawing room and rang for refreshments.

Clare sipped tea and nibbled cakes while the other two exchanged news. Was this why she was in London—to watch
Nicholas charm other women? The thought made her feel
distinctly hostile.

After half an hour, Nicholas drew a round, brightly
painted wooden object from his pocket. "I brought a small
present for William. It's from the East Indies, where it's
called a yo-yo." He looped the silk string around his finger
and made the toy run up and down the string, accompanied
by a soft singing sound.

The countess said, "My brother had a similar toy when
we were children, but his was called a bandalore. Let's see
if I remember how to make it work." Her attempts were
unsuccessful. The third time the yo-yo ended up hanging
limply from the string, she returned it to Nicholas. "I'm
afraid I'm out of practice."

"If you don't object, I'll take it up to the nursery and
demonstrate it for William."

"He'll be enchanted." The countess rang for the butler
and ordered him to take Nicholas to the nursery.

Clare felt uneasy about being left alone with the countess,
but that faded when the other woman turned candid hazel
eyes toward her. "Please forgive Nicholas and me for our
rudeness—four years is a long time, and the scapegrace
hardly ever wrote."

"I'm sure you're glad that he's home again, Lady Aberdare," Clare said in a neutral tone.

"Yes, even though it reminds me of that dreadful time."
The countess picked up one of the butter cakes. "Inciden-
tally, I don't use the title anymore, Miss Morgan. Now I'm
plain Mrs. Robert Holcroft. Or Emily to a friend of Nicholas's."

"You've abandoned the title? That's almost unheard of. I
thought women in your position usually keep their former
rank if they remarry commoners."

Emily's face hardened. "I never wanted to be a countess.
Robert—my husband—and I grew up together, and always
knew that we wanted to marry. But he was the younger son
of a squire with few prospects, while I was the daughter of
a viscount. When Lord Aberdare made his extremely flat-

tering offer, my parents insisted that I accept it even though he was forty years older than I.''

''I'm sorry,'' Clare said awkwardly. ''I had no idea. You looked so serene that no one in Penreith guessed that the marriage was not to your taste.''

''Lord Aberdare wanted a young brood mare to give him more children.'' She began crumbling the butter cake between her fingers. ''He was quite . . . conscientious about exercising his conjugal rights, but I proved to be a disappointment to him. It was a difficult time. Nicholas was a . . . great comfort to me.'' The butter cake had been reduced to a mound of golden crumbs.

To Clare, it sounded like an oblique confession that Emily and Nicholas had been lovers, but that the affair had not been casual, lustful seduction. At least, not on Emily's part. Though Clare could not condone adultery, she understood how an unhappy woman could slip into an affair with a handsome, charming step-grandson who was close to her own age. Not knowing what else to say, she remarked, ''William is proof that it wasn't your fault that there were no children borne of your first marriage.''

''Don't think I haven't found satisfaction in that knowledge,'' Emily said dryly. ''Wherever the fourth Earl of Aberdare is now—and I suspect that it's a very hot place—I hope he knows that I am not barren.'' She touched her abdomen. ''And in the autumn, William will have a brother or sister.''

''How lovely. Congratulations.'' No longer able to contain her bemusement, Clare continued, ''But why are you telling all this to a stranger?''

Emily shrugged. ''Because you're easy to talk to. Because Nicholas brought you here. Because you're from Penreith. I suppose the last reason is the most important. If you live in the valley, you must know the scandal surrounding the death of my husband and Nicholas's wife. Heaven only knows what stories went around, though the rumors could hardly be worse than the truth. I left Wales as soon as I had buried my husband. At the time I was too numb to care what anyone thought, but this seems like a chance to set the record straight.''

Clare wondered how Nicholas had felt about the affair. Had he loved Emily? Did he still? But of course she couldn't ask. Instead, she said, "There was a great deal of wild speculation about what had happened, but the scandal is half forgotten by now. With you and Nicholas gone from the valley and no one else knowing the facts, the gossips had precious little to work with."

"Good." Emily's brows drew together. "Robert helped me put that dreadful time behind me. Nicholas, I think, has been less fortunate. Perhaps you can help him, as Robert helped me."

A little helplessly, Clare said, "This is a very strange conversation."

"I suppose it is." Emily smiled. "I don't know exactly what is between you and Nicholas, but he wouldn't have brought you here if he didn't care about you. He needs someone to care about him. Someone he can trust."

Before Clare could explain that the situation was not what Emily thought, Nicholas himself returned from the nursery. As conversation became general again, Clare decided it was just as well that she had been unable to respond, because she didn't know what to think, or what to say. She had been raised in a world of blacks and whites, where right was right and wrong was wrong. Unfortunately, the area around Nicholas was all shades of gray.

A few minutes later, as Clare and Nicholas were taking their leave, Emily's husband returned home. Robert Holcroft was a stocky blond man with a contagious smile. When introduced to Nicholas, he shook hands eagerly, saying how much he had looked forward to this meeting. If he knew that Emily and Nicholas had been lovers, it didn't show in his manner.

As they drove away in the curricle, Clare said, "I'm glad to know that Lady Aberdare is happy now. When she left the valley after burying her husband four years ago, it was as if she had dropped off the face of the earth. No one in Penreith had any idea what happened to her."

"She wanted to forget her years in Wales, and one can hardly blame her," Nicholas said dryly. "She married Holcroft one year to the day after my grandfather's death. He's a barrister by training, but now he's a rising star in Parliament. Someday he'll be a cabinet minister.''

"What district does he represent?"

"Leicestershire." Nicholas slowed the curricle, then turned left into a quieter street. "I control the seat, and when Emily wrote that Holcroft wanted to go into politics, I gave it to him. From what I hear, he's working out well— seems to be both cleverer and more principled than the fellow who preceded him."

Startled, she said, "You control a district in Leicestershire?"

"Among others. Our corrupt political system gives me effective control of seats in three different counties. Though the Aberdare title is rooted in Wales, these days the majority of the family fortune is generated elsewhere."

Clare was struck by how little she knew about Nicholas, or about the wealth and power a man in his position wielded. "No wonder Mr. Holcroft was so happy to meet you, since you're his political patron. Is that also why you're William's godfather?"

Nicholas smiled. "I'd like to think that friendship enters into it. Emily was an island of warmth and sanity at Aberdare."

He didn't sound like a man suffering from a broken heart. Obviously he was very fond of Emily, but Clare took irrational satisfaction in the knowledge that she had not been the great love of his life. "If you were able to put Holcroft into Parliament, you must have kept fairly close track of your affairs while you were out of the country."

"Every six months or so, a box of legal papers would catch up with me, and I would send instructions back to my man of business." He gave her an ironic glance. "I'm not quite as irresponsible as my reputation implies."

"No one could be," she said tartly.

Nicholas laughed. "You're a perfect Welsh rose: delicate, sweet-scented, and well-equipped with thorns." He reached out and brushed her chin with his gloved knuckles. "And it's the thorns that make you interesting."

As compliments went it wasn't much, but Clare cherished

it anyhow. She was much better at thorniness than she was at conventional charm.

Clare carefully lined up the cue ball, then stroked. The cue stick skidded against the ivory ball and veered off, missing the object ball. "Drat! I misstroked again." She raised the cue and scowled at the tip. "The problem is that the wood is so smooth and hard. Would it be illegal to put a different material on the end—something that would not skid as much as bare wood?"

"I think it would be legal, but no true billiard lover would approve. The challenge is to play well in spite of the equipment, not because of it." Nicholas leaned over, his muscles flexing under his white lawn shirt, and neatly potted a ball. "At least this table is flat compared to the one at Aberdare, which resembled a plowed field in midwinter."

"By the time we go home, that table should have its new slate top. It will be interesting to see how it works."

Since her first day in London had been full of drama, it was pleasant to spend the evening quietly with Nicholas. And there were advantages to her being a novice billiard player, because she spent most of her time watching him shoot. Moving around the billiard table with easy, pantherlike grace, he was a sight to please any female. With a small tingle of pleasure, she wondered when he would collect today's kiss. If he didn't do it soon, she might kiss him herself. He seemed to like it when she did that.

Nicholas stroked again. After the cue ball bounced showily off three cushions, it knocked the object ball into a pocket.

Before Clare could compliment him, a lazy voice drawled from the doorway, "A certain skill at billiards is the mark of a gentleman, but to play *too* well is the sign of a misspent youth."

"Lucien!" Nicholas dropped his cue on the table and went to give the newcomer an exuberant hug. "I see you got my note. I'm glad you could come by tonight."

Lucien murmured, "Still as unrestrained as ever, I see," but Clare noticed that he returned the embrace with obvious affection.

While the men exchanged greetings, she studied the newcomer, who was dressed with an elegance just short of dandyism. He was almost as handsome as Nicholas, but in a blond, utterly English way. Among the Fallen Angels, he had obviously been Lucifer, the morning star who had been the brightest and most beautiful before he had rebelled against heaven. He also moved as quietly as a cat, for neither Clare nor Nicholas had heard him approach.

After disentangling himself from his friend, Nicholas performed the introductions. "Clare, you'll have gathered that this is Lord Strathmore. Lucien, my friend Miss Morgan."

Were she and Nicholas friends? As a description, it left much unsaid. Smiling, she said, "It's a pleasure to meet you, my lord. Nicholas has often spoken of you."

"Lies, all lies," he said promptly. "They were never able to prove anything."

As Clare laughed, he bowed elegantly over her hand. When he straightened, she saw that his eyes were an unusual green-gold that made her think of cats again. He studied her curiously, as if trying to deduce her position in the household. No proper spinster would be spending an evening alone at a man's house. On the other hand, even her new gowns couldn't make Clare look like the sort of female with whom Nicholas would misbehave.

Lord Strathmore said, "You're Welsh, Miss Morgan?"

"And here I thought my English was flawless."

"A touch of Welsh accent adds music to a voice." His smile proved he rivaled Nicholas in charm as well as looks.

Nicholas said, "Clare, do you mind if we finish the game later?"

She smiled. "I'll concede—I've no chance of winning."

"In that case . . ." Nicholas handed the cue to his friend. "Think you can pot the last two balls?"

Lucien bent over the table and stroked. The cue ball whizzed about the table, knocking first one, then the other, of the object balls into pockets. "I, too, had a misspent youth."

After the laughter died down, Clare said, "I'll retire for the night. I'm sure you two have much to talk about."

Nicholas draped an arm around her shoulders. "Don't go

yet. I want to ask Lucien about Michael Kenyon, and the answer to that concerns you as much as me.''

Lord Strathmore frowned, but said nothing until the three of them were settled in the library, the two men drinking brandy while Clare sipped on a very small sherry. She and Nicholas sat in adjacent wing chairs while Strathmore lounged on a sofa opposite. The room was lit mostly by the coal fire, which created a warm, peaceful glow.

After briefly describing the situation at the Penreith mine, Nicholas said, ''Michael seems to have completely abandoned the business, which doesn't seem like him. Do you know where he is now? I've had no contact with him since I left England, but I'd like to see him soon if possible.''

Lucien raised his brows. ''You didn't know that he went back into the army?''

''Good God, I had no idea. When he sold out, he swore that he'd had enough of soldiering to last him the rest of his life.''

''No doubt he meant it at the time, but he bought another commission not long after you left the country.''

Nicholas frowned, and Clare saw concern in his eyes. ''You're not going to tell me that the silly beggar has gone and gotten himself killed, are you?''

''Don't worry, Michael is indestructible. He spent most of the last four years fighting the French on the Peninsula. He's a major now, and something of a hero.''

Nicholas smiled. ''That sounds like him. Better to unleash that ferocious temper on the enemy rather than on his friends.''

Lucien looked down into his glass and swirled the brandy around. ''Speaking of his temper, did you and Michael lose touch because you'd had some kind of quarrel?''

''No. Actually, I hardly saw him for some months before I left the country, even though he was in Penreith for much of that time. He was very involved with plans and improvements for the mine, which is why it's so surprising that he has neglected it since.'' Absently Nicholas reached over and covered Clare's hand. ''Where is he now—with the army in France?''

''No, you're in luck. He came down with fever in winter

camp and was shipped home at Wellington's personal order. He's in London now, pretty well recovered from his illness, though he's still on sick leave.'' Lucien fell silent and regarded his brandy glass broodingly.

"You've seen him then, and you're concerned about him,'' Nicholas guessed. "What's wrong?''

"Too much war, I imagine,'' Lucien said slowly. "I met him in the park riding one morning. He's lean as a wolf, and I felt wildness just under the surface. Or perhaps it's desperation. The country may have benefited by his army service, but I don't think he has.''

"Is he staying at Ashburton House? I want to call on him.''

"No, he's taken rooms, but I don't know where.'' Lucien smiled wryly. "Though he seemed pleased to see me, he wasn't volunteering any information. Reminded me of a fox that's gone to earth. Though he's been in London for several months, he hasn't made much attempt to see his old friends.''

"You can find where he's staying—you always know everything about everyone.''

"But I very seldom tell all I know.'' Lucien glanced up, his eyes glowing golden in the firelight. "It might be better if you don't try to see him. When Michael and I were talking, your name came up and—well, I won't say that he literally bared his teeth like a wolf, but that's the impression I got.''

Nicholas's fingers tightened on Clare's. "It's a nuisance if he's having a tantrum, but I need to talk to him about the Penreith mine. If he doesn't want to run it properly, he can sell the lease back to me, but that is my land and those are my people, and I will not permit the present situation to continue.''

Clare glanced at him, surprised at his intensity. It sounded very much as if Nicholas had made her cause his own, in spite of his threat to walk away if she left him.

"You're as stubborn as Michael is,'' Lucien said with a trace of exasperation. "If there are going to be fireworks, meeting in a public place is probably a good idea. Rafe is having a ball next week, and Michael said he'd be attending.

Of course you'll be invited as soon as Rafe knows you've returned."

"Perfect." Nicholas relaxed and smiled at Clare. "Rafe's balls are famous. You'll find it interesting."

Lucien frowned. "I'm not sure that it is the sort of event you should take Miss Morgan to."

"No?" Nicholas's glance was challenging. "The highest sticklers might not approve of Rafe's entertainments, but he would never permit real vulgarity. I think she'll enjoy it."

"It's still no place for a respectable unmarried female."

"But I am not respectable," Clare said smoothly as she got to her feet. "Nicholas can tell you about it if you're curious. I'm very glad to have met you, Lord Strathmore. Nicholas, I'll see you tomorrow."

He also rose. "I'll be back in a moment, Luce."

He escorted her into the hall and closed the door to the library behind him. "Did you think you'd be able to escape without surrendering your kiss for the day?"

She chuckled. "I was hoping you wouldn't forget." She stepped into his arms and turned her face up.

As always, his kiss was intoxicating, stirring pulses throughout her body. One of his hands wandered down to cup her buttock, pressing her tightly against him. She almost broke away. Then a mischievous demon pointed out that Nicholas would have to return to his friend soon, so it was safe to tease him in a way that she wouldn't dare otherwise.

Delicately she nipped his lower lip with her teeth. He gasped and his hands began working convulsively, kneading her body as if he was trying to absorb her into himself. Amazed at her own boldness, she slid her hand down between them until it came to rest on that fascinating, alarming ridge of male flesh. He hardened instantly, his whole body going taut. "Luce can go home while we continue this upstairs," he gasped.

A little flustered by the intensity of his reaction, she broke away from his embrace. "Mustn't be rude to a friend you haven't seen in years," she said breathlessly.

As she started up the stairs, he caught her hand and turned her toward him. In a soft, mesmerizing voice, he asked,

"Shall I join you later tonight and show you what comes next?"

She felt a shiver that was part fear, part excitement. She was teasing a tiger, and if she wasn't careful, the tiger would make a meal of her. Disengaging her hand, she said lightly, "After such a tiring day, I need a full night's sleep."

"Soon you'll say yes." His black eyes bored into hers, demanding and promising. "I swear it."

"Don't count on that, Nicholas. Remember, your object is to seduce me, and mine is to drive you to distraction."

He gave a crack of laughter. "You're a minx, Clare. But this is one contest I aim to win."

She gave him her sweetest smile. "Prepare yourself for failure, my lord." Then she whisked upstairs, exhilaration sizzling in her veins.

Her animation lasted until she entered her room. After locking the door, she leaned against it as her gaze traveled over the sumptuous bedchamber. Gilded cherubs cavorted on the ceiling, gold velvet hangings swathed the magnificently carved bed, and her feet rested on a Chinese carpet that probably cost more money than she would earn in her entire life. She felt a wave of disorientation. Merciful heaven, what was plain, sensible Clare Morgan of Penreith doing in such a place?

Good intentions had led her to Nicholas in the first place, but it was unholy anger that had made her agree to his devil's bargain. Ever since then, the two of them had been circling each other in an elaborate dance, advancing and separating while drawing ever closer. At the center of the circle lay ruin, both spiritual and social. Yet still she danced, for she had never felt so alive in her life. If all sin was so sweet, so exciting, no wonder mankind was a race of sinners.

For an instant, she imagined her father standing before her, regarding her with a grave disappointment that hurt more than anger would have. She knew she wasn't living up to his standards. She had never been able to, and since meeting Nicholas she had been awash in pride, anger, and lust.

Desolation engulfed her, and a great and terrible despair.

For the first time since leaving Penreith, she knelt and attempted to pray. *Our Father, who art in heaven . . .*

An ethereal father in heaven was no help, not when set against the warm, solid reality of Nicholas. He wanted her. Though his desire might be fleeting, as much the urge to win a game as to indulge his lust, it was real and powerfully compelling. No one had ever wanted her so intensely.

It meant so much to be wanted.

It would be easier to resist Nicholas if he were evil, but he was no more a devil than he was a saint. She suspected that he was best described by the words pagan and amoral. But he was kind to her, and sometimes she sensed in him a loneliness as great as her own. She was learning that loneliness was even more compelling than desire. . . .

She tried to force her mind back to the prayer, but she broke again at *Lead us not into temptation . . .*

It was too late, for temptation surrounded her. She suspected that the major reason she hadn't succumbed to it was because of her competitive desire to beat Nicholas at his own game. If she were being honest, she would have to admit that virtue had very little to do with her resistance.

If she managed to preserve her virginity, she would be able to go back to Penreith and face down the gossip, for her conscience would be clear. But what would become of her if she surrendered? She could not imagine returning to her old life if she was a ruined woman. Yet there could be no future for her with Nicholas, who wanted to bed her mostly to prove that he could. Marriage was out of the question, and she could never live as his mistress even if he continued to want her.

Abandoning the Lord's Prayer, she sent up a silent cry from the heart. *Dear God, help me find the strength to break away from this dangerous dance before I destroy myself.*

She repeated the words again and again in the most desperate prayer of her life. But though she held herself silent and listened, there was no sign that anyone had heard. She felt no presence, no inner certainty of what path she should follow. She was alone, without guidance. The only reality was the seductive dance, which spiraled down into darkness, danger, and desire.

As she wept into her hands, she felt more alone than ever before in her life.

As Nicholas reentered the library, Lucien was adding brandy to both their glasses. "Miss Morgan says that she is not respectable, and that you could tell me about it if I am curious." He took a small sip of spirits. "Which I am, very."

In a few succinct sentences, Nicholas outlined the bargain he and Clare had made: her presence in return for his influence in improving the lot of the residents of Penreith.

Though he deliberately gave no details, when he finished Lucien muttered an oath under his breath. "Bloody hell, Nicholas, what devil has gotten into you? You've had your share of wild escapades, but I've never known you to ruin an innocent."

"Clare is no innocent," Nicholas retorted. "She is twenty-six years old, well-educated enough to qualify as a bluestocking, and admirably tough-minded. She is with me by her own choice."

"Is she?" Lucien's eyes took on the green glitter that meant he was not about to let the discussion lapse. "If you feel a desire to strike a blow against womankind, find a bitch who deserves it. Don't ruin a decent woman by using her conscience and her caring heart as weapons against her."

Nicholas banged his brandy glass down on the side table. "Damnation, Luce, I've never given you the right to censure me. That's why I always acted as an amateur rather than becoming an official member of your furtive little organization."

Lucien raised one hand. "Pax, Nicholas. I don't particularly enjoy meddling, but I'm concerned by the situation, and it looks like no one else will speak for Miss Morgan."

"I've no intention of hurting her."

"But you already have. You must have some idea what the gossip is like in a village. It will be very hard for her to return to her old life."

Nicholas stood and paced restlessly across the library. "Good. She can stay with me."

"As a permanent mistress?" Lucien's voice was startled.

"Why not? I could do worse, and often have."

"If you feel that way about the girl, then marry her."

"Never," Nicholas said flatly. "I married once, and that was once too often."

After a long silence, Lucien said softly, "I've often wondered what happened between you and the beauteous Caroline."

Nicholas spun on his heel and glared at his friend, his expression taut to the point of shattering. "Luce, the only way a friendship can endure is by having limits that can't be crossed. If you value our friendship, you'll mind your own business."

"Obviously it was even worse than I suspected. I'm sorry, Nicholas."

"Don't be. At least she had the consideration to die." Nicholas retrieved his glass, then raised it in a mocking salute. "To Caroline, who taught me so many useful lessons about life and love." He drank the rest of the brandy in one long swallow.

Lucien watched in silence. He had assumed that four years would have been long enough for Nicholas to recover from the disaster that had sent him flying from England, but that didn't seem to be the case. Lucien was beginning to feel as concerned about Nicholas as he was about Michael.

But he had learned lessons himself in the last difficult years. One of them was that there wasn't much a man could do for a friend . . . except to be a friend.

15

CLARE SLEPT very little, but in the dark reaches of the night she found a bleak kind of balance. A good Methodist should be guided by inner knowing, and the only inner knowledge she had was that she wanted to be with Nicholas for as long as possible. Not as his lover; she doubted that she would ever be able to forgive herself for such a devastating moral lapse.

But as she looked back at the time she had spent with him, the scenes were etched in her mind in vivid color. Next to that, the rest of her life appeared in shades of faded gray. This was the high noon of her life, and she sensed that when the three months were over, nothing and no one would ever move her as deeply as Nicholas. That being the case, since she was undoubtedly going to hell anyhow, she might as well enjoy the time with him rather than berate herself for her wickedness. She would have the rest of her life for repentance.

Though she dressed with care, she assumed that Nicholas would sleep late, since he had probably stayed up until the wee hours with Lord Strathmore. She was surprised when he emerged from the breakfast parlor as she came down the stairs.

He met her when she reached the bottom step and blocked her path. Without saying a word, he drew her into his arms and kissed her. Since she was standing on a step, they were almost the same height, which proved wonderfully convenient. His embrace held tenderness and a surprising element of yearning. As she wrapped her arms around his neck, she wondered if he too had experienced loneliness in the night.

When the kiss ended, they stayed in each other's arms. A

little shyly, Clare said, "You've claimed your kiss very early."

"I like to surprise you. If you want another today, you'll have to initiate it yourself. I'll cooperate if I'm in the mood." Though his words were light, his eyes searched hers intently. "I'm going to be tied up with business for most of the day, but I'll be back by late afternoon. Is there anything you would particularly like to do this evening?"

"I've always had a secret yen to visit Astley's Amphitheatre," she confessed. "Would that be possible?"

His eyes began to sparkle. "You've a taste for clowns and equestrians? Easily done—there should be a show tonight. Think about what else you'd like to see in London. There should be guidebooks in the library." He put an arm around her waist and they went companionably in to breakfast.

The day set the pattern for the week to come. Nicholas spent part of his time on business and the rest with Clare. He seemed to enjoy seeing the sights of London as much as she did.

In the mornings they rode together in the park, and in the afternoons they visited everything from the crown jewels in the Tower to the Egyptian Hall to Week's Mechanical Museum, which featured an appalling clockwork tarantula. She refused to go to Madame Tussaud's Waxworks, knowing that lifelike figures of victims of the French Revolution would give her nightmares. Nicholas even took her to cabinetmakers and fabric shops so that she could select the new furnishings needed for Aberdare.

Several times Lucien joined them for dinner, his cool amusement a contrast to Nicholas's vivid enthusiasm. Lucien's attitude toward Clare was courtly and a little protective, as if he were her older brother. Though she found his reserve a bit intimidating, she liked him a great deal.

For safety's sake, she tried to keep the kissing sessions light and playful. Nicholas didn't force the issue, though his drifting hands covered more and more territory, and she found herself disinclined to make him behave.

Altogether it was an idyllic week, though she suspected that it was the calm before an approaching storm. What form the storm would take she couldn't guess, so she refused to worry about it. Time was trickling away, and the best she could do was wring every drop of enjoyment from the hours spent with Nicholas.

Clare bent over the billiard table, lined up her shot and stroked. As soon as the cue struck the ball she knew that she had hit slightly off center, but this time the cue stick didn't skid away. Instead, the ball rolled forward and knocked the object ball into the pocket. "Hallelujah!" she said gleefully.

The London household needed little supervision. Since Clare had no talent for idleness, she divided her free time between the library and the billiards room, with the goal of becoming skilled enough to defeat Nicholas. Her progress had been slow until she had a cobbler in the next street cut a round leather button and glue it to the tip of the cue. Today she was using the modified cue for the first time, with remarkable results.

She tried another shot, then a third, and successfully potted a ball each time. Lifting the cue, she regarded the tip with satisfaction. The leather softened the impact of the stroke, reducing the number of miscues and giving her much better accuracy. Smiling, she applied herself to practice. Nicholas would definitely have a surprise the next time they played.

"Just a moment longer, miss." The maid, Polly, slipped in one last hairpin. "There. Perfect."

Clare studied her reflection, impressed. The maid had managed to style her long hair into soft coils that were elegant without being fussy. "You've done a wonderful job. I was afraid you would do something horribly complicated that would make me feel as if I were wearing birds' nests on my head."

"It isn't that many years since women *did* wear birds' nests in their hair, not to mention model ships and vases of fresh flowers," Polly said. "My granny was a lady's maid, and she used to tell me stories about those old wigs." She edged a wave into the perfect position. "But you've wonderful hair, so thick and shiny. A simple style shows it off best.''

"Now for the gown.'' Clare stood and raised her arms while Polly dropped the blue silk dress over her head. It had been delivered that afternoon, just in time for the Duke of Candover's ball, and this would be the first time Clare put it on.

While Polly hooked hooks and tied tapes behind her, Clare stroked the skirt, loving the fluid, luxuriant texture of the fabric. Tonight would probably be the only time she would ever wear it, since she doubted that the future would hold many balls.

When Polly finished, Clare turned to look at herself. This was her first formal evening gown, and she was stunned by the image in the full-length mirror. Clare looked like a complete stranger—a provocative, sophisticated stranger.

Seeing her expression, Polly said encouragingly, "You look splendid, miss.''

"I don't even recognize myself.'' The shimmering, iridescent hues of the silk made her complexion glow with delicate color and her eyes shine like enormous sapphires. She turned a little, watching the way the silk clung to an impossibly small waist, then flared over her hips. As she regarded the expanse of bare flesh exposed by her decolletage, her brows drew together in perplexity. "How can a gown and stays change a perfectly ordinary figure into one that's practically voluptuous?''

"You have the best kind of figure, miss. Some would call it average, but you're round enough to look lush in the right dress, and small enough to look slim the rest of the time. You can appear almost any way you want to.''

Clare shook her head doubtfully. "I'm not sure I'll have the courage to wear this in public.''

"There will be lots of ladies with lower necklines.''

"But will they be ladies?'' Clare said gloomily.

"This will help. His lordship sent it.'' Polly lifted a velvet-covered box and opened it.

Clare's eyes widened when she saw the triple rope of pearls. Nicholas was certainly treating her like a mistress, even though he wasn't getting his money's worth.

Polly lifted the necklace and fastened it around Clare's neck. The cool pearls caressed her skin, the soft white echoing the silk flowers woven into her hair. They also made her feel a bit less bare. "Thank you for your efforts, Polly. You've managed to turn a sow's ear into a silk purse."

The maid sniffed. "All I did was make the best of what you already had. I know ladies who would kill to have a complexion like yours, and without a trace of powder or rouge."

Gesturing at her image, Clare said, "But I'm a stranger to myself. I don't know who that woman is."

"That's you, miss, though maybe not a you that you're well acquainted with." Polly frowned. "There must be a better way to say that, but I don't know what it is."

The clock struck nine. Time to go down to Nicholas. Clare draped a luxuriant kashmir shawl around her shoulders, then went into the hall and down the stairs.

He waited in the hall below, looking even more diabolically handsome than usual. As always he wore black, which was set off by his white shirt and an embroidered white on white waistcoat. Hearing her footsteps, he glanced up with a smile. "Hasn't anyone explained that fashionable ladies are never punctual, Clare?"

"I am neither fashionable nor a lady."

He started to return an answer, but when she came into the circle of lamplight, he caught his breath. "No one seeing you now would believe that."

The frank desire in his eyes embarrassed her. It also made her feel deeply, powerfully feminine, yet she could not stop herself from saying, "You're not going to perjure yourself by saying I'm beautiful, are you?"

As she descended the last few steps, he replied, "Perhaps not beautiful."

Her heart twitched; apparently she had wanted him to perjure himself.

"Bewitching is a better word." He took the end of her shawl so that it unwound when he circled around her. "Irresistible." The shawl slithered to the floor and pooled around Clare's slippers. He leaned forward and touched warm, firm lips to the sensitive juncture of throat and jaw. "A potent mixture of innocence and sensuality."

A strange, intoxicating feeling shivered through Clare, as much a product of his admiration as his kiss. All of a sudden she felt that she *was* that woman in the mirror—alluring, intensely female, as capable of playing the games of love as Nicholas. It was like being possessed by the spirit of another woman—one who was not at all respectable.

"I'm glad you approve." She raised her hand and traced the planes of his face with her fingertips, taking care not to disturb the crisp folds of his cravat. He had just shaved and his jaw was very smooth. "Have I mentioned lately that you are undoubtedly the handsomest man in Great Britain, if not the whole of Europe?"

He chuckled and reached for her. "Shall we continue this exchange of compliments upstairs?"

Gracefully she eluded his grasp, knowing that her movement would release the scent of her perfume, a haunting wild rose fragrance that Polly had suggested. "It's time we were going. We mustn't miss the chance to find Lord Michael."

"You're learning to be dangerous, Clarissima," he murmured, desire and amusement warring in his face.

"I'm studying with the best."

He laughed, then retrieved the shawl and draped it around her shoulders. The light brush of his hands sent fire racing through her veins. She took his arm and they went out to the waiting carriage.

As they settled inside, Clare asked, "Why did Lord Strathmore say this wasn't a suitable place to take me? Does the duke throw orgies?" She let her hand rest on his and stroked his palm with her thumb.

"Nothing like that, though it's true that few families would let their unmarried daughters attend. Rafe's entertainments are considered fast—the sort of occasion where a man might take his mistress, and perhaps meet his wife who is attending with her lover." Nicholas twined his fingers with Clare's and rested their hands on his knee. "Most of the women will be from fashionable society, but some will be high-grade courtesans."

"How can I tell the difference?"

"The most flamboyant will be society women," he explained. "The courtesans will be a bit more discreet."

She smiled. In the intimate darkness of the carriage, it was easy to flirt. Polly had been right: the provocative woman in the mirror had been real—a dangerous part of herself that Clare had never acknowledged. Yet as she let her knee brush his as if by accident, she did not regret what she was becoming. She would do that later.

In the darkness Nicholas's mouth found hers for a long, leisurely kiss that intensified when he slid his hand under the shawl and caressed the back of her bare shoulders. Thirty seconds more, and she would melt at his feet and let him do whatever he willed.

Remembering that offense was the best form of defense, she put her hand on his knee and squeezed. A tremor went through him. "Definitely dangerous," he said in a voice that wasn't quite level. His hand moved to her breast. "Do you want to learn how far it is possible to go in a carriage?"

She gave a gurgle of laughter. "You said that the duke's house is quite near yours."

"That isn't what I meant and you know it, minx."

Her nipple hardened as his thumb teased it through the silk. Much more of this and they would be testing the limits of the coach in earnest. She drew a deep breath, then said, "Time to stop, I think."

His hand moved from her breast to the safer territory of her waist. "For the rest of the night?"

She thought. "Enough for now. It's too early to give up touching for the rest of the night."

"I quite agree." He settled back against the velvet-covered seat, but kept her hand in his.

As Clare steadied her breathing, she realized that trust was what made this mad game possible. Whenever she said to stop, Nicholas stopped, and his self-control gave her the freedom to play the role of siren. She smiled into the darkness and wondered what the next phase of the game would be.

16

AS THEY waited in a short receiving line at Candover House, Clare said, "Have you seen the duke since returning to London?"

"I paid a call, but he wasn't in, so I left a card." Nicholas smiled. "Rafe sent back a note inviting me to the ball, with a threat to drag me here by the scruff of the neck if I didn't come voluntarily."

"You'll probably be unable to do much except say hello to each other," she remarked. "I've always heard that a London ball has to be a great crush to be considered fashionable."

"Rafe doesn't follow fashion, he sets it. Since he doesn't enjoy unruly crowds, his gatherings are a more comfortable size. Makes them more exclusive, as well."

She gave him a teasing glance. "Does he not bother to invite unmarried girls since they aren't allowed to come?"

"Rafe has no interest in well-bred virgins," Nicholas said dryly. Gesturing to the woman standing by the host, he added, "That's Lady Welcott, his current mistress, according to Lucien."

"A married woman?"

Nicholas nodded. "The only kind of female Rafe has any interest in. They know the rules and don't cause trouble by falling in love with him."

Sounding very much like a preacher's daughter, Clare said, "Is adultery a way of life in fashionable society?"

He shrugged. "Since many aristocratic marriages are made for reasons of family and property, it's hardly surprising when people look elsewhere for pleasure."

Was that why Nicholas had been unfaithful to his wife?

Even Clare's glorious gown didn't give her the courage to ask that question. Instead, she said, "Surely the duke is in a position to marry a woman of his choice rather than for dynastic reasons."

"He came close once—fell head over heels for a girl when he was just down from Oxford. I never met her, since I was still at university, but he wrote me some incoherent drivel to the effect that she was a goddess come to earth and they would become officially betrothed when the Season was over. It was the only time I've ever known Rafe to sound unbalanced."

"Did the girl die and he's never met another woman who was her equal?" Clare asked sympathetically.

A hard glitter in his eyes, Nicholas replied, "No, she betrayed him. Isn't that what love means?"

Clare felt as if all the air had been knocked out of her lungs. Then she sputtered, "That is, without a doubt, the most cynical remark I have ever heard in my life."

"Is it? My experience says otherwise. Everyone who has ever claimed to love me—" His voice cut off abruptly.

Realizing that he had accidentally exposed one of the painful truths that made him what he was, she took his unresponsive hand in hers. "I suppose that some people claim to love when the real motive is neediness, or a desire for control, or something equally selfish," she said thoughtfully. "Yet there are also people like Owen and Marged Morris, and Emily and Robert Holcroft. Do you think their love involves betrayal?"

His hand slowly tightened on hers. "No, I suppose not. Perhaps honest love is a talent, or simply luck, that some people have and others don't."

"I've sometimes thought that myself," Clare said wistfully. "If you don't believe in love, what do you believe in?"

After another pause, he said, "Friendship, I suppose."

"One can do worse than believing in friendship," she said, "but deep friendship is also a kind of love."

"I suppose so." He gave a self-mocking smile. "But since the stakes are much lower, betrayal is less likely, which makes friendship much safer."

They reached the head of the receiving line, and Clare
got her first clear look at the Duke of Candover as he talked
to the couple ahead of them. The duke was tall, handsome,
and almost as dark as Nicholas, with an aristocratic air that
she guessed was as natural to him as breathing. Polite,
pleasant, controlled—the very picture of a proper English
gentleman.

The previous guests moved on and the duke turned to
them. His face immediately lit up. "Nicholas! I'm glad you
were able to come." He shook hands with real enthusiasm.
"We probably won't have much time to talk tonight, so I
hope you'll join me for luncheon at White's tomorrow."

Just as Clare had approved of Lucien for fighting beside
an outnumbered schoolboy, she now liked the duke for his
obvious pleasure in the reunion. Though Nicholas had a low
opinion of love, he obviously had the gift of making friends.

Drawing Clare forward, he said, "Rafe, this is my friend
Miss Morgan."

Their talk had given her a new appreciation of what it
meant that he introduced her as a friend. Smiling, she said,
"It's a great pleasure, Your Grace."

He bowed elegantly. "The pleasure is mine, Miss Morgan." Unlike Nicholas, his eyes were a very English gray,
and she saw both curiosity and masculine approval in the
cool depths. Completing the introductions, he said, "Lady
Welcott, the Earl of Aberdare and Miss Morgan."

The duke's mistress was several years older than he, perhaps forty. She was a handsome, fair-haired woman with a
worldly air; not the sort to fall hysterically in love with a
man who had no taste for untidy emotions. Clare thought
of the "goddess come to earth" who had brought Rafe to
this, and repressed a sigh. Poor duke. So many people
wanted love, yet there never seemed to be enough to go
around.

Lady Welcott gave Clare a perfunctory nod, but her eyes
brightened when she turned to Nicholas. "Lord Aberdare,"
she said warmly, extending a hand. "You may not remember, but we met when you were Viscount Tregar. At Blenheim, I believe."

He bowed over her hand. "Of course I remember. I never forget an attractive woman."

Lady Welcott was too sophisticated to simper, though in Clare's jaundiced opinion it was a near thing. Fluttering her fan gracefully, her ladyship said, "Now that you've returned to Britain, I hope we'll be seeing more of you in London."

"Very likely you will." His smile was charming; his smiles always were.

Though the duke seemed mildly amused by the interaction, Clare had to repress a desire to kick either Nicholas or her ladyship in the ankle. Nicholas slanted an amused glance at her, and Clare was sure he could read her thoughts. Smoothly he said, "We're holding up the line. If we don't have a chance to talk tonight, Rafe, I'll see you at White's tomorrow."

He took Clare's arm and led her into the enormous entry hall, then turned left toward the ballroom. "To succeed in society, Clare, you must learn to control your expression. I was afraid you were going to bite Lady Welcott."

"I've no desire for social success," she said acidly. "And surely it was rude of her aging ladyship to drool over you in front of me."

He grinned. "Do I detect a hint of jealousy? I thought it was one of the seven deadly sins."

"Jealousy isn't, but envy is, along with covetousness, lust, anger, gluttony, pride, and sloth," she retorted.

"I know the list well." His eyes were dancing. "Everyone needs ideals to aspire to."

She had to laugh. "You're disgraceful."

"I try," he said modestly.

They stepped through an arch of scarlet flowers into a large ballroom, where beautifully dressed men and women drifted about between dances. Yet even though it was Clare's first grand society event, what drew her astonished attention was not the people but the decor.

The walls and high ceiling had been painted black, which absorbed much of the light from the chandeliers and gave the room a mysterious, shadowy atmosphere. The blackness also made a spectacular backdrop for the well-lit marble statues that stood on pedestals around the edges of the room.

All of the sculptures were of life-sized females clad in wispy classical draperies that bared large parts of their bodies. Clare remarked, "The Greeks and Romans were a fast lot, weren't they?"

Nicholas grinned. "Watch the statues for a while."

She did as he suggested, then gasped when one of the figures changed position. "Merciful heavens, they're alive!"

"Rafe likes his balls to be memorable." Nicholas indicated another "sculpture," where a soulful man was leaning against the pedestal and talking to the handsome female figure above him. "They are probably ladies of the evening who are being paid handsomely to cover themselves with white lead and powder, then stand still for the evening. I imagine that fellow is trying to make a private arrangement with his favorite nymph."

"The duke won't mind?"

"Well, he wouldn't like it if his statue went off into an alcove with the fellow, but I imagine that they can do as they please when the ball is over."

Clare watched the false sculpture close a whitened eyelid in a slow wink for the gentleman who was stroking her feet. Her clothing was so minimal that it was clear that her remarkable figure owed nothing to artifice. "I'm beginning to understand why people wouldn't bring their innocent daughters here," she said rather faintly.

Musicians in the gallery struck up a tune and dance sets started forming, with men and women lining up opposite each other. Clare found her foot tapping to the music.

"Would you like to dance?" Nicholas asked.

"I don't know how," she said, not quite able to keep regret out of her voice.

"Mmm, I'd forgotten that dancing is un-Methodist." He glanced down at her tapping foot. As she tucked her slipper under her hem, he said, "This is a rather simple country dance. If you watch once, you should be able to participate when another is played, if your conscience permits."

After consideration, she said, "My conscience has been numb with shock for weeks. Dancing can hardly make it worse."

The first country dance was followed by a similar one,

and Clare and Nicholas joined in. It was delightful, and she only tripped over her feet once, luckily when he was close enough to catch her. Guilt firmly suppressed, she enjoyed herself greatly.

The next dance was a waltz, so they withdrew to the side of the ballroom. Nicholas said, "Does the wicked waltz look like it will bring about the fall of western civilization?"

"Probably not." She studied the gliding couples. "It seems as if it would be very nice with a partner one liked a great deal, and rather nasty with a partner one didn't like."

"If you're interested, I can get a dancing master to teach you. It's a bit complicated to try without instruction."

A tempting offer, but her conscience proved to have a little life left in it. "Thank you, but I can't imagine that I will have any opportunity to waltz in the future."

"We'll see," he said cryptically.

A voluptuous redhead suddenly swept up to Nicholas. Completely ignoring Clare, she hugged Nicholas and squealed, "Darling Old Nick, you've come home. You must call on me. Number 12 Hill Street. My current protector won't mind."

He calmly peeled her off his chest. "That's what you said last time, Ileana, and I ended up fighting a duel at Chalk Farms. Fortunately your man of the moment was a damned bad shot, since I could hardly deny the justice of his complaint."

"Henry wasn't good at much of anything—that's why I invited you over that time." Unrepentant, she rapped his wrist with a folded ivory fan. "When can you come?"

"Sorry, I'm otherwise occupied." His gaze went to Clare's rigid face. "Besides, I never make the same mistake twice."

The redhead's coquettishness turned to a pout. "I was only being polite for old times' sake, you know." She opened her fan and wielded rapidly. "It's not as if I need you. My current protector is six foot four, with *everything* in proportion."

Instead of being insulted, Nicholas gave a shout of laughter. "Quite right, Ileana, you shouldn't waste your time on a paltry fellow like me."

The redhead's rouged lips tugged into a reluctant smile, and for the first time she looked at Clare. "Enjoy yourself while it lasts, duckie. There's no one like Nicholas, in or out of bed."

As Ileana undulated away, Clare said waspishly, "Are the females here divided between those you've bedded in the past, and those who hope to bed you in the future?"

His mouth quirked up. "It's probably a waste of breath for me to tell you not to be upset, but notice that I didn't take her up on her offer. Though I'm guilty of attempted seduction, the destruction of your reputation, and numerous lesser charges, one thing I will not do is humiliate you in front of other people."

He put his hand on the nape of her neck and slowly massaged. Her tension began to ease. Ruefully she realized how well he understood her. Though she was innocent of most of the deadly sins, she was certainly guilty of pride, and it would have been unbearable if Nicholas had publically favored that coarse tart over herself. "I thought you said the courtesans would be more discreet than the ladies."

"Every rule has exceptions."

A familiar voice broke in. "Good evening, Nicholas, Miss Morgan." Lord Strathmore ambled up to them. "I think I saw Michael heading for the card room, though I wasn't close enough to be sure it was him."

"Perhaps I can run him to earth," Nicholas replied. "Will you stay with Clare until I return?"

"Of course."

As Nicholas cut through the crowd, Strathmore said reflectively, "There goes living proof of the value of crossbreeding."

Startled, Clare said, "What do you mean?"

Strathmore nodded toward Nicholas's retreating back. "Compare him to the rest of these overbred aristocrats."

She laughed, understanding immediately; there wasn't a man in the ballroom who had Nicholas's magnetic vitality. "I see what you mean. Next to him, everyone else seems half-alive." She glanced mischievously at her companion. "Are you overbred?"

"Of course. The founder of the noble house of Strathmore was a lusty robber baron, but the blood has thinned over the centuries. Marrying a Gypsy or two might improve the stock." He gave her an angelic smile. "Since I have never been known to let my passions run away with me, Nicholas knew it would be safe to leave you in my care."

"I should think that lack of passion would be a failing in a rake."

"I'm not a rake, except by association." He smiled. "But I am widely assumed to have dark, mysterious secrets."

Lightly she said, "So you're a spymaster, not a rake?"

Strathmore's frivolous manner dropped away and he said sharply, "Did Nicholas tell you about . . . ?" He halted, then made a face. "I think I just said too much."

Though Clare's comment had been mostly banter, Strathmore's reaction led her to a quick deduction. "Nicholas mentioned once that his travels on the Continent included a bit of information gathering and courier work for an old friend. Since you work in Whitehall, it's not a bad guess that he meant you."

"You have the mind of an intelligence officer yourself." Lucien's smile made him look younger and much less world-weary. "While I admit that I'm not quite as useless as I pretend, I'd appreciate it if you kept your deductions to yourself."

"This conversation has been so oblique that I can't imagine mentioning it to anyone, Lord Strathmore."

"A brain *and* discretion." He gave an elaborate sigh. "Why don't I ever meet females like you? I'll have to settle for asking you to call me Lucien, as my friends do. Then I can call you Clare, if you don't object."

"I'd like that, Lucien."

He offered his arm. "Now that we're officially friends, shall we find a glass of punch? It's rather warm in here."

With a smile, she tucked her hand in his elbow and they made their way across the ballroom to an alcove where wine punch cascaded into a crystal pool from a jar held by a naked mermaid. This time it was a real statue, though if live mermaids were available, Clare was sure that the duke would have hired one.

Strathmore held a glass under the stream of punch for Clare, then filled one for himself. "Are you enjoying your first ball?"

"Yes, but I hope it's not obvious that I don't belong."

"You look composed and very much at home," he assured her. "No one would guess that you are a schoolmistress from Wales who is being dragged willy-nilly into an alien world."

He escorted Clare back to the ballroom so they could watch the dancers. "Nicholas deserves a good beating for what he's doing to you, yet I can understand his impulse."

"I'll hope that's a compliment."

"It is." His levity dropped away. "You don't need me to tell you that Nicholas is far more complicated than he pretends. He always was, and after that disastrous business four years ago, God only knows what's going on below the surface of his whimsical Gypsy mind. He needs something or someone, and you're the best hope in sight. Though you have every reason to resent what he's doing to your life, I hope you will be patient with him."

"In fairness, I have to say that the situation is as much of my making as his. I didn't have to ask for his help in the first place, nor did I have to take him up on his ridiculous challenge." Clare thought about the rest of what Lucien had said. "But I'm of no real importance in his life, except to the extent that I've involved him in Penreith." She grinned. "I've sometimes thought that Nicholas doesn't know whether to treat me as a mistress or a pet."

Lucien smiled appreciatively, but shook his head. "You are more than either of those things to him, though I doubt that he himself really understands what."

Lucien's comments were interesting, but Clare didn't believe them. As she sipped her punch, she decided that the very cool, allegedly over-bred Lord Strathmore was secretly a romantic.

It was easier to believe that than to believe she was important to Nicholas.

17

HALF THE guests at the ball wanted to stop Nicholas to welcome him home. Besides friendly greetings, he also received three blatant propositions and five broad hints; a good thing he had left Clare with Lucien. Not that he minded her jealousy; he found it rather endearing. Every day Clare was becoming more and more a woman, and less and less the virtuous schoolmistress.

By the time Nicholas reached the card room, Michael Kenyon was long gone, if indeed he had ever been there. Nicholas asked several men if they'd seen Lord Michael, but no one seemed sure. Finally, in frustration, he went back to find Clare and Lucien.

As he passed through the entry hall, he saw a man covered with travel dust admitted and hasten over to the Duke of Candover, who was still receiving latecomers. On hearing the message, Rafe gave a whoop, then turned and raced up the stairs two at a time. Nicholas tried to guess what could have aroused such a reaction in a man whose legendary calm rivaled Lucien's, but imagination failed him. With a shrug, he went into the ballroom, where a quadrille was in progress.

It took several minutes to locate Clare, but Lucien's height and bright hair made a good beacon. As Nicholas approached them, the music abruptly stopped in the middle of a measure. In the sudden silence, Rafe's voice boomed out over the ballroom. "My friends, I have wonderful news."

Nicholas looked up and saw that the duke was standing in the gallery with the small orchestra. In a voice pulsing with excitement, Rafe announced, "I've just received word that Napoleon has abdicated. The war is officially over."

At first there was a stunned silence. Then a single voice raised a wild cheer. More and more people joined in to produce a roar that rattled the rafters of Candover House.

Adding his own exhilarated shout to the din, Nicholas pushed his way toward Clare; kissing her was a perfect way to celebrate. To his intense disgust, Lucien, who was closer, beat him to it with a jubilant embrace that swept Clare from her feet.

After Lucien returned her to the floor, Nicholas gathered her into his own arms, saying to his friend, "I suppose it would be churlish to cut out your liver, but next time find a girl of your own."

Unintimidated, Lucien grinned and pounded him on the back. "The war that has been going on since we were in short coats is over! By all things great and wonderful, we've done it!"

Giddier than he'd ever seen her, Clare wrapped her arms around Nicholas and kissed him exuberantly. When she came up for air, she said with awe, "Even though Napoleon's forces have been on the defensive for the last year, it's hard to believe that the end has arrived. Finally, finally, we'll have peace."

Nicholas thought of the war-ravaged areas of Europe he'd seen, and his arms tightened around Clare. "Thank God the fighting never reached British soil. Our losses were light compared to what most of the nations of Europe have suffered."

Still beaming, Lucien said, "With luck, I'll never have to do a blessed useful thing in my life."

Nicholas laughed. "After all you've done for your country the last few years, you're entitled to spend the rest of your life lying around like a turnip."

Similar scenes of exultation surrounded them. Nearby stood an older man in a Guard's uniform with an empty sleeve. His remaining arm circled his wife while both of them wept unashamedly. Even the "statues" abandoned their roles and jumped to the floor to join in the celebration. A cheer went up for Wellington, then for his troops.

Nicholas glanced up at the musicians' gallery again, then stiffened. "Isn't that Michael up there talking to Rafe?"

Lucien peered upward. "So it is. Probably wanted to learn if Rafe has any details. God knows that from the look of him, Michael has paid a higher price for victory than most."

"With luck, the announcement has put him in a good mood."

Taking Clare's hand, Nicholas threaded his way through the rapturous crowd, Lucien right behind them. Clare almost had to run to keep up. They climbed the entry hall staircase, then turned left into a long, dimly lit corridor that must parallel the upper wall of the two-story ballroom.

At the far end of the corridor, the duke and a tall, rangy man emerged from a door that led to the musicians' gallery. Behind them the orchestra struck up a triumphal march that was muted when the duke closed the door.

As the duke and his companion came down the corridor, talking earnestly, Clare studied Major Lord Michael Kenyon. Lucien had described him as lean and wolflike, and it was true that his recent illness had left him thin almost to gauntness. Yet the strong bones of his face were still ruggedly handsome, and he moved with an athlete's sureness. He seemed like a worthy addition to the Fallen Angels. Especially, she thought with amusement, since his glossy chestnut hair fitted nicely between the black or blond extremes of the other members.

With his quarry in sight, Nicholas slowed his pace. "Congratulations, Michael. As one of the men who fought for this victory, you have more reason to celebrate than most."

Lord Michael froze, the animation in his face dying as he swung about. His eyes were a dark, haunted green. "Trust you to ruin a happy moment, Aberdare," he said harshly. "Under the circumstances, I'll forgo what I swore I'd do if I ever saw you again, but get the hell out of my sight before I change my mind."

Nicholas still held Clare's hand, and she felt his fingers chill. She realized, with painful empathy, that in spite of Lucien's warning, Nicholas had not truly believed that his old friend had become an enemy.

Even now he must not believe it, for he said mildly,

"That's an odd greeting after years of separation. Shall we try again?" He stepped forward and offered his hand. "It's been too long, Michael. I'm glad to see that you've survived the Peninsula."

The other man jerked back as if he was faced by a viper. "Do you think I'm joking? You should know better."

The duke said sharply, "If there are matters to be discussed, my study is a better place than this hall."

By sheer force of will, he shepherded everyone into a room just down the corridor. As he lit several lamps, Rafe said, "Tonight is a time for beating swords into plowshares. If something has been festering over the years, Michael, now is a good time to settle it."

As crosscurrents of emotion surged through the room, Clare realized that she had become almost invisible. These men had met in the harsh conditions of a public school and had grown up together. Like all groups of friends, they would be connected by a web of shared experiences that had developed over many years—memories of joy and sorrow, of conflict and support. Now one of them was threatening to tear the fabric asunder.

The major had withdrawn behind the duke's desk, and his raging gaze made Clare think of a predator at bay. "This is not your affair, Rafe. Nor yours, Lucien." To Nicholas, he said with what sounded like genuine sorrow, "When I heard that you'd left the country, I thought you'd have the decency to stay away."

Voice tight as a drum, Nicholas replied, "Would you mind telling me what you think I've done?"

"Don't play the innocent, Aberdare. The others may believe you, but I don't."

Rafe started to speak, but Nicholas held up his hand to stop him. "Forget my alleged wrongdoing for a moment, Michael. I need to talk to you about a matter that is strictly business. Your mine in Penreith is being run in a highly dangerous manner. Not only is your manager endangering the workers, but there have been suggestions that he's skimming the profits as well. If you haven't the time or inclination to deal with it yourself, sell the company back to me so I can do what is needed."

After an incredulous moment, the major gave a laugh that sent chills down Clare's spine. "If Madoc is irritating you, I should raise his salary."

Clare knew that her own anger was mirrored by Nicholas, but he kept his voice admirably even. "Don't turn the mine into a bone between us, Michael. The men whose lives are at risk are innocent of whatever you're holding against me."

"You've turned into an old woman, Aberdare," the major said coldly. "Mining has always been dangerous, and it always will be. Miners know and accept that."

"There is a difference between courage and foolhardiness," Nicholas retorted. "In the last couple of weeks, I've inquired about accidents and deaths at similar mines. The Penreith pit is four or five times more dangerous than the others, and there's a potential for major catastrophe. I've seen it with my own eyes."

"You've been in my mine?" The green eyes narrowed. "Keep the hell out in the future. If I hear that you've trespassed, I'll have Madoc set the law on you."

"I'm beginning to understand why you left him in charge—you talk exactly like him," Nicholas said dryly. "If you don't believe what I say, investigate yourself. I guarantee that unless you're the sort of officer who enjoyed seeing his men slaughtered, you'll admit that the mine is in dire need of improvement. You're the only one in a position to make changes quickly, so damn it, live up to your responsibilities."

Michael's face twisted. "There is no way in hell I will do anything to oblige you."

"Remember that I own that land—if you refuse to improve conditions, I'll find a way to break the lease. I'd rather not take it to the law, because lives might be lost while the courts decide, but if I have to, I will." Nicholas's voice hardened. "And by God, if men die needlessly while you're sulking, I'll hold you personally responsible."

"Why waste time waiting for a crisis?" Michael pulled crumpled gloves from his pocket and stepped around the desk. Before anyone realized what he had in mind, he slapped the gloves viciously across Nicholas's face. "Is that clear enough? Name your seconds, Aberdare."

In the shocked hush that followed, the distant sounds of revelry were clearly audible. Clare felt the numbness of nightmare. This couldn't be happening—Lord Michael couldn't want a fight to the death with a man he hadn't seen in years; a man who had been a close friend.

Nicholas's cheek reddened from the force of the blow, but he did not strike back. Instead he scrutinized his old friend as if seeing him for the first time. "War can drive men mad, and that's obviously what has happened to you." He turned to Clare, and she saw anguish in his eyes. "I won't fight a lunatic. Come, Clare. It's time to go."

He took her arm and led her to the door. As he raised his hand to the knob, Lord Michael's bitter voice snarled, "Coward!"

A hissing sound cut the silence, ending in a hard *thunk!* as the tip of a wicked-looking knife buried itself in the door between Clare and Nicholas. She stared at the quivering haft, horrified at how close that lethal blade had come.

Quietly Nicholas said, "Don't worry, Clare. If he had wanted to hit me, he would have." He took hold of the knife and wrenched it from the wood, then turned to face the other man. "I won't fight you, Michael," he said again. "If you want to kill me, you'll have to make it cold-blooded murder, and I can't believe you've changed that much."

Eyes burning, the major said, "Your faith is misguided, Aberdare, but I'd rather kill you fairly. Fight, goddamnit!"

Nicholas shook his head. "No. If you want to think me a coward, go ahead. I am supremely indifferent to your delusions." He took Clare's arm again.

Michael began drumming the fingers of his left hand on the mahogany desk. "Does your little whore know that you killed your grandfather and your wife?"

In a blur of movement so swift that Clare couldn't follow it, Nicholas raised his arm and hurled the knife back across the room. It sliced into the desk a quarter inch away from Michael's fingers. "Clare is a lady, something you are obviously incapable of recognizing," he said in a voice that was no longer even. "Very well—if you want to fight, so be it. But since you're the challenger, the choice of weapons is mine."

Lucien started to speak, but Michael cut him off. Voice gloating, he said, "Any time, any place, any weapon."

"The time—now," Nicholas said flatly. "The place—here. And the weapons—horsewhips."

The major's face turned a dull red. "Horsewhips? Don't mock me, Aberdare. The choice is between pistols and swords. Even hand-to-hand fighting with knives if you want, but not with something as trivial as a whip."

"Those are my terms. Take it or leave it." Nicholas gave an ice-edged smile. "Think how satisfying it will be to horsewhip me—*if* you're good enough, which I don't think you are."

"I'm good enough to flay your hide off as you deserve," Michael growled. "Very well, let us begin."

Rafe exploded, "This has gone far enough! You've both lost your minds. I won't allow this on my property."

Lucien said quietly, "If Michael is determined on violence, I'd rather it took place here with both of us present."

Lucien and Rafe exchanged a long look. With deep reluctance, the duke said, "Perhaps you're right."

Nicholas said, "Will you act for me, Luce?"

"Of course."

The major turned his ire on Lord Strathmore. "The Arabs have a saying: the friend of my enemy is my enemy. Let him find someone else."

Face set, Lucien said, "I count you both my friends, and the most important duty of a second is to try to resolve the dispute without bloodshed. You can start by telling me what your complaint is so that Nicholas has a chance to answer it."

Michael shook his head. "I will not speak of what happened. Nicholas knows, whether he admits it or not. If you insist on acting for him, we are no longer friends."

"If so, it is by your wish, not mine," Lucien said gravely.

Michael looked at the duke. "Will you act for me, or are you also going to side with that lying Gypsy?"

Rafe glowered at him. "Damned irregular to have an affair of honor where a man doesn't know why he has been challenged."

The major repeated, "Will you act for me?"

Rafe sighed. "Very well. As your second, I will ask if there is anything Nicholas can do—an apology, some other way of addressing your grievance—that will resolve the dispute."

Michael's lips stretched in a humorless smile. "No. What he did can never be rectified."

Rafe and Lucien exchanged another glance. Then the duke said, "Very well. The garden behind the folly should be suitable, and it's cool enough that there shouldn't be any guests in the shrubbery. I'll get two matched whips from the stable tackroom and meet you there."

They filed out of the study and followed Rafe down the hall toward the back of the house. When Clare came with them, Lucien frowned. "You shouldn't come. A duel is no place for a woman."

She scowled back. "Every aspect of this ridiculous duel is abnormal, so I doubt that my presence can make anything worse."

As Strathmore hesitated, Nicholas said, "Save your breath, Luce. Clare can keep a score of small children in order, so she can certainly outface any of us."

Clare thought he looked less perturbed than any of them. Having seen his skill with a whip, she knew that he could more than hold his own, but Lord Michael's attitude chilled her. He was a man possessed, and if he couldn't kill Nicholas in a duel, heaven only knew what he would do instead.

They went down a narrow back staircase, then outside. Clare shivered as she stepped into the cold April night. Nicholas took off his coat and dropped it around her shoulders. "Here. I won't be wearing this."

She nodded and pulled the warm wool folds around her. It was hard to remember that half an hour ago she had been having a wonderful, thoroughly frivolous time.

The garden was enormous for a London house, and at the far end the ball was almost inaudible. Behind the folly was a small courtyard intended for summer dancing. Torch holders stood around the area, and Rafe and Lucien proceeded to light and set an armful of torches brought from the stables. The wind whipped the flames, causing shadows to flare wildly across the garden.

The major seemed calmer now that action was imminent. Like Nicholas, he stripped off his coat and cravat. Nicholas went one further by taking off his waistcoat, shoes, and stockings so that he was barefoot.

With the field prepared, Rafe and Lucien solemnly examined the two carriage whips and agreed that they were substantially similar. When the whips were offered to the combatants, Nicholas took the one that was closest, gave it an experimental crack, then nodded acceptance. Michael did the same, his eyes blazing with anticipation.

The duke said, "There are no codified rules for a whip duel, so we'll set them now. Stand back to back, walk eight paces each when I tell you to start, then turn. I'll drop my handkerchief. After it reaches the ground, strike at will." He turned a hard stare at both men, his gaze lingering on the major. "The duel is over when Lord Strathmore and I agree that it is. If either of you fails to stop when I call time, then by God, we'll stop you. Is that understood?"

"Crystal clear," Nicholas said. His opponent didn't bother to reply.

Lucien walked away from the other men and drew Clare back to the edge of the courtyard. "Stay back here," he said in a low voice. "A carriage whip has quite a range."

She nodded silently, and tried not to think of what might happen. Though a whip might not be lethal, it could destroy an eye in an instant. She doubted that Nicholas would deliberately maim his opponent, but Michael might think that blinding his enemy would be a suitable vengeance for whatever grieved him.

In eerie tableau, the duelists went through the required ritual, standing back to back, then pacing out the steps after the duke called "Now!"

When the two men had turned to confront each other, Rafe raised his handkerchief, then threw it down. Clare stared at the light muslin square, mesmerized, as it floated earthward. Just before the handkerchief reached the ground, a puff of breeze caught the fabric and it skimmed sideways above the flagstones.

Not noticing that the handkerchief hadn't yet touched, or perhaps unable to wait a moment longer, Lord Michael

struck out. Caught off guard, Nicholas threw up his left arm
to protect his face. The whip curled around his forearm with
an ugly snapping sound, ripping through his shirt and scor-
ing the flesh below.

As crimson stained Nicholas's sleeve, the major's gloating
voice announced, "First blood, Aberdare."

"Next time I do this, I'll remember to start early, too."
As he spoke, Nicholas slashed back. There was a faint,
menacing whistle, then a thin red line blazed across his
opponent's cheek and jaw. Michael couldn't suppress a gasp
of pain, but it didn't stop him from striking again. This time
he cut at the other man's feet. Nicholas leaped into the air
like a dancer and the vicious leather thong passed below
him. Even before he had landed, his whip snapped back. A
ragged slit appeared across Michael's chest, and again blood
flowed.

Undeterred, the major struck again. As Nicholas twisted
away, taking the lash on his shoulder, Clare pressed a fist
to her mouth to stop herself from crying out. She had seen
fights between schoolboys and once between drunken miners, but what she saw now had the primal savagery of war.

With a snarl, Michael bounded forward so he could strike
at closer range. "I've waited years for this, you bastard."

Amazingly, Nicholas flicked his wrist and his thong intercepted the other man's. As the leather strips twisted
around each other, he said, "Then you can wait a little
longer."

He jerked on his whip in an attempt to disarm Michael.
The other man was dragged to his knees but managed to
hang onto the handle of his weapon. For almost a minute,
the men strained against each other, muscles knotted. Then
the thongs abruptly separated, causing both men to lurch
backward.

Rather than strike back immediately, Nicholas crouched
like a wrestler and moved sideways, his whip raised and
ready. Michael fell into the same stance and they began
circling each other, their smooth, gliding movements belied
by the fierce concentration on their faces.

Even in the uncertain light there was no confusing the
two men. Nicholas the Gypsy was light-footed and swift,

one step ahead of his opponent's probing lash, while Michael the warrior was aggressive and grimly determined to destroy his enemy. There was no sound except the faint scrape of the major's boots against the flagstone.

When Nicholas successfully evaded another slash, Michael panted, "You're good at running, you filthy Gypsy."

"I'm not ashamed of what I am, Michael." With a powerful snap of his wrist, Nicholas slashed another hole in the other man's shirt. "Can you say the same?"

His taunt ignited an explosion of rage. The major launched a wild assault, flailing his whip back and forth to produce a continuous torrent of lashes. As the ugly sounds of leather striking flesh echoed across the courtyard, an agonized gasp escaped Clare. Why didn't Nicholas slide away again instead of enduring so much punishment with no more than a raised arm to protect his head?

She learned why when Michael stepped forward into a lunge that put most of his weight on one foot. It was the moment Nicholas had been waiting for. He struck out with lethal precision, and his hissing thong curled round and round Michael's booted ankle.

Though the lash itself did little damage, when Nicholas yanked his whip with both hands the other man fell hard, too off-balance to catch himself. His momentum sent him rolling across the ground and his head cracked audibly against the flagstones.

Suddenly it was over, leaving Michael lying still as death in a frozen silence broken only by Nicholas's harsh breathing. Clare spent an instant giving thanks that Nicholas had won. Then she darted across the courtyard and knelt by the fallen man. She had tended her share of schoolyard injuries, which stood her in good stead as she gently examined his bleeding head.

Nicholas dropped down beside her. His shirt was in ribbons and blood oozed from at least a dozen slashes, but a quick glance assured Clare that his injuries were superficial. He himself paid no attention to them, for all his attention was on the unconscious man. Voice shaking, he asked, "Is he hurt badly?"

Clare didn't answer until she had checked Michael's pulse

and breathing as well as the head wound. "I don't think so. Concussion certainly, but I don't think his skull is fractured. Head wounds always bleed freely, so they look worse than they are. Does anyone have a handkerchief?"

One with an elegantly embroidered C was thrust into her hand. Firmly she pressed the folded cloth to the wound.

Nicholas murmured, "Thank God it isn't worse. I wanted to slow him down, not kill him."

"Don't blame yourself," Lucien said soberly. "He forced this quarrel on you. If you'd chosen pistols or swords, one of you would be dead now."

"It was stupid of me to let myself be drawn into any kind of fight," Nicholas said, his anger at himself obvious. "You saw how Michael behaved earlier. Do you think he'll accept this as a final resolution of his grievance?"

The silence that followed was answer enough.

When the first handkerchief was saturated, Clare used another, this time with a Strathmore S on it. Fortunately the bleeding had almost stopped. Nicholas retrieved his cravat and she used it to tie a crude bandage that held the second handkerchief in place. Glancing up, she said, "He should be moved as little as possible. Can he stay here, Your Grace?"

"Of course." Wry admiration in his eyes, the duke added, "Since you seem to fit into this gang of ruffians so well, you had better call me Rafe."

Clare sat back on her heels. "I don't know if I'm capable of calling a duke by his first name."

"Don't think of me as a duke. Think of me as someone who failed miserably at Nicholas's fish-tickling lessons."

She smiled, realizing that his humor was a sign of relief that nothing worse had happened. "Very well, Rafe."

The duke continued, "Luce, do you think the two of us can get him indoors? I'd rather not involve any of the servants."

"We can manage," was the terse reply. "He weighs at least two stone less than he ought."

As the two men gently raised Michael from the flagstones, his ripped shirt fell away, exposing an appalling mosaic of scars that ran from his left shoulder to his waist.

They all stared, shaken, and Nicholas swore under his breath.

"He was wounded by shrapnel at Salamanca," Rafe said grimly. "Obviously it was worse than he said at the time."

As Michael was lifted to his feet, he seemed to regain a little consciousness, enough so that he wasn't quite a dead weight as his friends slung his arms over their shoulders.

Nicholas donned his stockings and shoes, then collected the whips. As he and Clare followed the others into the house, she gave thanks that the duel hadn't ended in disaster. But she had little sense of relief, for she feared that Nicholas was right; tonight's duel would not satisfy Lord Michael's fury.

18

FACE FINE-DRAWN by tension, Nicholas refused treatment for his injuries. He did accept a loose cloak from Rafe, since putting on his own closely cut coat was out of the question. Within a few minutes, he and Clare were heading home in his coach. The ball guests were still so busy celebrating that no one gave them a second glance when they left the house.

There was no talk as they rumbled through the streets of Mayfair. Nicholas sat on the opposite side of the carriage, balanced on the front edge of the seat rather than leaning on his abused back. He also moved stiffly when he helped her from the carriage at Aberdare House.

Once they were inside, she said, "Before you go to bed, I want to clean and treat those lacerations." She gave him her no-nonsense schoolmistress look. "I know that you delight in being stoic, but there are limits."

He gave her a self-mocking smile. "Agreed, and I've reached them. Where do you want to hold your surgery?"

"Your room, I suppose. I'll change out of this gown and be along after Polly finds me some medical supplies." She went to her own room, where Polly was napping. She woke quickly and helped Clare undress, then went for bandages and medications.

Perhaps as punishment for her worldliness, Clare's blue silk gown had been ruined by Lord Michael's blood and her contact with the ground. She donned her practical white flannel nightgown and covered it with a handsome red velvet robe that was part of her London wardrobe. After brushing out her hair and braiding it into a loose plait, she sat down to wait for Polly's return.

The nervous energy that had carried her through the duel and ride home disappeared, leaving her suddenly exhausted. She leaned back in the wing chair, pressed her hands to her temples, and began to shake as the stresses of the night caught up to her. Every blow struck in that ghastly duel was permanently engraved in her memory. If Lord Michael had gotten his wish and they had fought with pistols or swords . . . She shuddered and tried to change the direction of her thoughts.

Though she had felt murderous when she saw Lord Michael attacking Nicholas, now that the duel was over her heart ached for the major. Though his wild accusations against Nicholas were the product of a disturbed mind, he obviously believed them, for his torment had been genuine. She sighed. He was not the first soldier to be destroyed by war, and sadly, he wouldn't be the last. Perhaps in time his mind would heal; she hoped so.

But in the meantime, he was a very real danger. Though Nicholas didn't think his old friend capable of cold-blooded murder, Clare was not so sure. Perhaps it was time to return to Wales. Michael had implied that he would not have gone in search of Nicholas; with luck, out of sight would prove out of mind.

When Polly returned with a tray containing bandages, medications, and a basin of warm water, Clare forced her weary body from the chair. After taking the tray, she sent the maid to bed and went down the hall to Nicholas's bedchamber. The door was slightly ajar, so she pushed it open and went in.

Nicholas knelt on the hearth, adding coals to the fire. Clare almost dropped the tray when she saw him, for her first impression was that he was naked. A second glance showed that he had a towel wrapped around his loins. It was the absolute minimum necessary to make him decent, and rather less than what she required for peace of mind.

It was unnerving to see at close hand the beautiful, muscular body that she had shamefacedly admired when he swam with the penguins. Still more unnerving was the sight of his injuries. Belatedly she realized that he had stripped off most of his clothing so she could treat his wounds. The thought steadied her; she was here as a nurse, not a mistress.

He finished fixing the fire and set the screen into place, then stood and lifted a goblet from the table. "Care for some brandy? Tonight might be a good time to temporarily suspend your objections to strong drink."

After a brief mental debate, she said, "The Methodist rule is to make decisions according to what is in one's heart, and my heart says that something calming would be welcome."

He poured a small amount of brandy and handed the glass to her. "Drink carefully. It's much fiercer than sherry."

"Shouldn't you be encouraging me to drink more? I've heard that getting a female tipsy is a standard seduction technique."

"I've considered doing that, but it wouldn't be sporting," he said with dry humor. "I'll seduce you fair and square."

"No, you won't, fairly, squarely, or otherwise," she retorted. Though the first taste of brandy made her choke, she appreciated the soothing afterglow.

As she sipped, her gaze followed him as he prowled around the room, glass in hand. In his near-naked state, he was a most distracting sight. Trying to be objective, she noted that his arms and the upper part of his chest and back had sustained all of the damage. His beautiful muscular legs were unmarked. . . .

Clinical, Clare, remember to be clinical. Setting down her glass, she said briskly, "Time to get to work. Sit on that stool, please."

Silently he obeyed. She began by gently washing the lacerations with warm water to remove grit and fragments of cloth that had been driven in by the lash. He stared across the room, occasionally sipping at his brandy. She tried not to be distracted by the ripple of taut muscles when he shifted position. All carnal thoughts vanished whenever the pain passed the limits of stoicism and he involuntarily winced.

As she sprinkled basilicum powder on the open wounds, she said, "The lacerations are messy and must feel beastly, but they're fairly shallow, and none are still bleeding. I expected the damage to be worse.''

"Whips are more destructive when the victim can't avoid the lash, as when a soldier is tied to a post and flogged,'' he said absently. "A moving target doesn't incur as much damage.''

She transferred her attention to his left forearm, which was cut and bruised in several places. His fingers tightened around his glass as she cleaned dried blood from a gash on his wrist. "Odd that all of the damage is to your upper body. Lord Michael has no imagination—he kept striking at the same area.''

Nicholas reached for the decanter and poured himself more brandy. "He was trying to break my neck. If he'd been able to wind the thong around my throat and jerk it, as I did with his ankle, he'd have had a good chance of success.''

She stopped, appalled. "You mean he was deliberately trying to do the one thing that might kill you?''

Nicholas raised his brows. "Of course. Michael said that he wanted me dead, and he's always been a man of his word.''

Clare's hands began shaking. After a quick look at her face, Nicholas stood and guided her into a nearby wing chair. She buried her face in her hands, unable to escape a horrific vision of what would have happened if the major had managed to wrap his whip around Nicholas's neck.

"Sorry—I shouldn't have told you,'' Nicholas said as he returned to his stool. "There was no chance he would succeed. Once or twice I've seen similar brawls among the Gypsies, so I'm familiar with the basic motion of whip fighting.''

After a brief, intense battle with incipient hysterics, she looked up. "He really is mad, as you said. Do you have any idea why he fixed his madness on you rather than someone else?''

"Wouldn't it make more sense to ask if Michael was correct when he accused me of killing my wife and my grandfather?''

She made an impatient movement with her hand. "I think he was only trying to shock, and their sudden deaths made convenient ammunition. Besides, I doubt that he cared about my reaction. He was more interested in antagonizing you, and in trying to drive a wedge between you and your other friends.''

Nicholas rose and began pacing again. ''So coolheaded. But surely the thought has crossed your mind that I might be a murderer.''

''Naturally I considered the possibility four years ago, when the deaths occurred.'' She linked her fingers together in her lap, determined to be as cool as he thought she was. ''However, though you have flashes of temper, I simply don't think you have that kind of violence in you.''

He toyed with the bellpull, twining it around the post of the bed. ''Are there different kinds of violence?''

''Of course,'' she replied. ''It's easy to believe that Lord Michael is capable of murder. I think Lucien would be also, under extreme circumstances—certainly he can be as ruthless as necessary. But though you can be dangerous, as you proved tonight, you would rather laugh or walk away from a difficult situation. I can't imagine you killing except in self-defense, and even then only if you couldn't avoid it.''

His mouth twisted. ''I damn near killed Michael tonight.''

''That was an accident,'' she said sharply. ''Did you think I wouldn't notice how you held back? He's skilled with a whip, but you're better. You could have sliced him to pieces if you chose. Instead, you allowed yourself to be hurt much worse than necessary while you waited for a chance to disable him.''

''You notice a great deal.'' He drifted to the walnut dresser and began stacking coins by size. ''Too much, perhaps.''

I notice everything about you, Nicholas. Her fingers locked more tightly. ''My father's work brought many kinds of people to our home. I couldn't help but learn something of human nature.''

''You've deftly analyzed Michael, Lucien, and me in terms of our capacity for violence,'' he remarked, all his attention on the coins. ''What about Rafe?''

She pondered. ''I scarcely know him. My guess is that

he is like you—the kind of man who won't look for a fight, but who will acquit himself well when trouble can't be avoided.''

"You're even more dangerous than I thought," he said with a hint of amusement. "You're quite right about me walking away—I think it's bred into all Gypsies. We've always been persecuted—to survive as a race, we had to learn to fold our tents and steal away rather than wait to be slaughtered.''

"He who fights, then runs away, will live to run another day," she misquoted.

"Exactly." Losing interest in the coins, he began fiddling with his silver card case. "You asked why Michael chose me as his target. My best guess is that his anger is because of the old earl. Though he was estranged from his own father, the Duke of Ashburton, for some reason Michael and my grandfather got on well. The old earl said in as many words that he wished Michael was his heir instead of me.''

Nicholas took the engraved cards from the case and spread them into a fan between his thumb and forefinger. "My grandfather was a healthy, vigorous man right up until the night he died. Perhaps Michael really does believe I killed the old boy with some subtle Gypsy poison or black magic spell.''

Thinking that he was unnaturally dispassionate about what must have been deeply hurtful, she asked, "Did you envy Michael for the way he got on with your grandfather?''

He snapped the cards together and returned them to the case. "I might have minded when I was younger, but by the time Michael moved to Penreith, I no longer cared. If it made the two of them happy for Michael to play surrogate grandson, they were welcome to it. I spent most of my time elsewhere.''

Clare wondered if the old earl had deliberately set the two young men against each other as a way of hurting his grandson. Could the earl have been that devious, and that cruel? If so, he had much to answer for. And, like Emily, Clare hoped he was answering for it in a very hot location.

Deciding she should finish her work so she could go to her room and collapse, she took a pot of herb salve, cornered Nicholas by the dresser, and began spreading the salve on minor wounds, where the skin was raw but not bleeding.

He sucked his breath in when she touched a tender spot on his back, but didn't move. "What about your capacity for violence, Clare? You'll never convince me that you're a milk-and-water miss who would never say boo to a penguin."

"I believe that peace is better than war, and that turning cheeks is better than breaking heads." She spread salve on a scrape that ran from his collarbone to his ribs. "But though I'm not particularly proud to admit it, I suspect I could be violent on behalf of those I care about. If some villain came to the school and threatened my children, for example." Or if someone threatened Nicholas.

She went back to the tray for a bandage. "I'm going to cover the worst of the lacerations with this." She wrapped his wrist, then began winding the muslin strip around his chest.

Casually he asked, "How does Lucien kiss?"

"What?" She was so startled she almost dropped the bandage. "Oh, that's right, he kissed me when Napoleon's abdication was announced. It was quite a nice kiss, I suppose—I didn't really notice." She looped the end of the bandage under his arm and tied a neat knot on top of his shoulder. The muslin looked very white against his dark skin. "He wasn't you."

"Next time Lucien needs to be taken down a peg or two, I'll tell him how unimpressed you were with his skill."

"Surely you wouldn't . . ." She looked at him uncertainly. "Oh, you're joking."

"Of course—whimsy is my strong suit." Nicholas stepped away and rolled his shoulders, testing to see how much they hurt. "Why did you say that Lucien has a ruthless streak? You're right, but it's surprising that you deduced that after meeting him only a handful of times, and when he was on his best behavior."

She began stacking her medical supplies on the tray. "It's just something I feel about him. Though he plays the dilettante very well, there is something inside him that makes me think of polished steel." She smiled a little. "I startled him by guessing that his Whitehall post involves gathering intelligence, and that you worked for him."

"Good Lord, you figured that out? You should be in intelligence work yourself." Nicholas finished the last of his brandy, then looked consideringly at the decanter.

"Take some laudanum," she suggested. "The effects will be milder than trying to numb the pain with brandy."

"I don't need either." His mouth tightened and he set his empty glass by the decanter. "Thank you for patching me up. I'm sorry that your first ball ended like this."

"Well, it was certainly an unforgettable experience." She lifted the tray and walked toward the door.

"Clare. Don't go yet," Nicholas said, a strained note in his voice.

She turned back to the room. "Yes?"

He was staring out the window into the quiet street, his breathing too quick and his right hand clenching and unclenching on the edge of the drapery. When he didn't reply, she said, "Was there something else?"

Speaking as if each word was being wrenched out of him with hot irons, he said, "Clare, will you . . . stay with me for the rest of the night?"

"You want me to sleep with you?" she said stupidly, more surprised than when he had asked her about Lucien's kiss.

He turned from the window, and the sound of his harsh breathing filled the room. She realized that it was the first time he had looked directly at her since they met Lord Michael, and she was shocked by the stark anguish in his eyes.

It was suddenly, blindingly obvious that his detachment had been a charade. She felt like kicking herself. Though she was supposed to be perceptive, she had utterly failed to understand his uncharacteristic restlessness and refusal to meet her eyes.

Now his carefully constructed facade had shattered, revealing what lay beneath. Her heart ached for him; though she had guessed that it must be bitterly painful for a man who believed in friendship to be repudiated by a close friend, the reality was far worse than she had imagined.

Misinterpreting her expression, he said haltingly, "Not as a mistress, but . . . as a friend." His hand clenched again and the tendons stood out like iron cords. "Please."

She wanted to weep for his vulnerability. Instead she set down the tray and said quietly, "Of course, if you wish it."

He crossed the room and enfolded her in a fierce embrace. She protested, "I don't want to hurt you."

"You won't," he said tightly.

She didn't believe him, but it was clear that his need for closeness far outweighed the physical pain. His yearning was almost palpable—for warmth, for friendship, for anything that could ease the betrayal he had suffered tonight.

Carefully to avoid his injuries, she linked her arms around his waist and rested her head against his cheek. They stood that way for a long time. When his breathing had returned to a more normal rate, he released her and said, "You're shivering. Climb into bed where it's warm and I'll join you in a minute." He went into his dressing room while she dowsed the lamps, took off her robe, and laid it over a chair. Illuminated only by the glowing coals in the fireplace, she slipped into his bed. Though she felt shy, she did not for a moment doubt that she was doing the right thing, for compassion mattered more than propriety.

A minute later he returned wearing a nightshirt. She smiled a little, guessing that the garment was in deference to her maidenly sensibilities, since it looked as if it had never been worn. With the bandages covered he looked normal, except for the desolation on his face.

He slipped into bed on her left so that she was on his less-injured side. After kissing her lightly on the lips, he drew her head onto his shoulder and laced his fingers into her hair. "I didn't want to be alone," he whispered.

"I'm also glad not to be alone tonight," she said honestly as she fitted herself against his side. Though she was aware of his pain, both physical and emotional, she also knew that her presence eased him as nothing else could have.

The reverse was also true.

He spoke only once more, saying bleakly, "He always called me Nicholas."

And now Michael used only the impersonal "Aberdare." She made a silent vow: no matter what the future held, she would not become one of the people who had betrayed Nicholas's friendship.

19

THOUGH NICHOLAS hadn't expected to sleep, Clare's soft warmth overcame his grief and pain. He awoke with the dawn and lay very still, not wanting to disturb the woman slumbering in his arms. The worst was over; he had survived other betrayals, and he would survive this time. But it would have been much harder without Clare beside him.

The night before, he had thought he was dissembling rather well, right up until the moment when she started to leave. Then a crippling wave of despair had engulfed him. In that moment he would have gone down on his knees and begged if that would have persuaded her to stay.

It would have been better if he had managed to restrain himself until she was safely gone, for it was always a mistake to reveal weakness. But he had never made a practice of regretting what couldn't be changed, and he didn't now.

Certainly he didn't regret having Clare in his bed. A trace of exotic perfume still lingered, triggering a vivid memory of how dazzling she had looked. This morning, in her relentlessly plain nightgown and with her hair escaping her braid, she was adorable, more enticing than the most expensive courtesan.

He indulged himself in the fantasy that they were already lovers, and that soon he would wake her with a kiss that would be the first step toward fulfillment. His gaze went to her mouth. Even when she pursed her lips into her best schoolmistress glare, she could not suppress the natural fullness. In the muted morning light, her lips were so luscious he could barely restrain himself from sampling them.

Mentally he reviewed the most memorable kisses they

had shared. The list was lengthy, for Clare had proved to be an apt pupil in the arts of sensuality. The fact did not surprise him; he had learned early that intelligent women made the best bedmates. When they became lovers, she would be without peer.

But since that hadn't happened yet, he must control his desire. He didn't think that restraint would be a problem— until he realized that he was already stroking her slim body.

When he ordered himself to stop, his hand drifted to a halt on her breast, but refused to be lifted away. Through the no-nonsense flannel, he felt her heart beating against his palm.

It was time to remove his hand. He told himself that, forcefully, and managed to raise his hand a couple of inches—far enough for his fingertips to begin teasing her nipple to tantalizing hardness.

He didn't know whether to laugh or swear. His body's refusal to obey would be amusing, if it wasn't so dangerous.

She gave a sigh of contentment and snuggled closer, her hand sliding lower on his torso. For an instant desire gained the upper hand, and he leaned forward. He would give her a deep kiss so that she would be aroused by the time she was fully awake. He looked forward to removing the flannel nightgown and uncovering her silken skin. When he kissed her breasts she would make that delicious choked sound deep in her throat. Then her eyes would drift shut as her yearning body conquered her overactive mind. The fantasy was so vivid that it almost overwhelmed him.

But of course he couldn't do any of that. For a moment he felt paralyzed, caught between lust and conscience. To break the deadlock, he thought back to the worst moment of his life, an event so stomach turning that it dampened his desire. Not entirely, but enough so that he could move.

After gently working his right arm out from under her head, he slid from the bed, wincing as all his dormant cuts and bruises flared to painful life. But in spite of his care, Clare awoke.

Her long dark lashes swept up and she regarded him gravely. In her deep blue eyes he saw shyness, but no regret. "Were you able to sleep?"

"Better than I expected."

She sat up cross-legged, blankets tangled around her, and regarded him with drowsy curiosity. "You keep saying that you're going to seduce me, yet you're passing up a perfect opportunity. Mind you, I appreciate your restraint, but it does seem odd."

He smiled wryly. "I asked you to stay as a friend, the kind of request you would find very hard to refuse. To take advantage of that would be dishonorable."

She gave a soft, throaty chuckle. "Male codes of honor are very strange and inconsistent."

"Undoubtedly true." His gaze went to the throat of her nightgown, where a small triangle of bare skin showed. Since it was the only visible part of her, it became amazingly erotic. Lucky he was wearing the voluminous nightshirt, which concealed his simmering state of arousal. Trying to move his mind to higher things, he explained, "Honor, like Methodist faith, is a highly individual commodity. I have no qualms about seducing you and ruining your reputation, but I can't do it by deception."

"What kind of Gypsy are you?" she said teasingly. "I thought guile was a way of life among your mother's people."

He smiled. "It is, but I've been corrupted by conventional British morality."

She nibbled at her lower lip, which made him want to do the same. The idea was so appealing that he almost missed her remark when she said, "Will we be going home soon? London has been delightful, but there is much to be done in Penreith."

"Trying to get me out of the line of fire?"

"Yes," she admitted. "I can't imagine that Lord Michael will be pleased by the outcome of last night's encounter."

"No, but he's not going to shoot me in the back," Nicholas said reassuringly. "Nor will I allow myself to be goaded into another fight of any kind."

Clare looked unconvinced. "I hope you're right, but I'd still like to return to Wales soon. I've seen about as much of London as I can absorb."

"Most of my business should be settled within the next few days," he said. "Then we can go."

"Good." Looking happier, she scooted off the bed. "Time I was getting back to my own room. It's early enough that none of the servants need know where I spent the night."

"Does it matter what they think?"

She smiled ruefully as she donned her velvet robe. "Perhaps not, but since I wasn't raised as an aristocrat, I haven't your sublime indifference to other people's opinions."

As she put one hand on the doorknob, he felt the same tearing sensation that he had experienced the night before when she had started to leave. It was much milder this morning, but quite unmistakable. Knowing that he was being a damned fool, he said, "I think I'll collect my kiss for the day."

She turned back to the room, looking a little wary. "Shouldn't it be saved for later?"

"You can always have more if you wish." He closed the distance between them in two strides and drew her into his arms. Though she caught her breath when she felt his erection through their nightclothes, she didn't pull away.

With luxurious slowness he nibbled the lower lip that had attracted him earlier. Her mouth opened and her rough exhalation caressed his cheek. When their lips melded and his tongue slid into heated, welcoming depths, her tongue greeted his, touching delicately, then darting away in a brazen invitation for pursuit.

The kiss went on and on, breathtaking and pulse-pounding. Dimly he realized that he had pinned her against the door and that their pelvises were rubbing together in a profoundly erotic simulation of intercourse. Her robe and gown lifted easily and he cupped her bare buttock in one hand, pressing her more tightly to his groin. "Ah, Clare," he said hoarsely. "You are so lovely. So desirable."

He shouldn't have spoken, for his words caused her to open her dazed eyes and whisper, "It's time . . . to end this kiss."

He was so far gone that he almost didn't remember their bargain. When he did, he groaned aloud. "Yesterday there

was no official kiss. Can I collect it now?'' Without waiting
for an answer, he pressed his lips to her throat.

She gasped, but managed to say, ''No! Yesterday is over,
and you can't collect kisses retroactively. Besides, there
were plenty of unofficial ones.''

The primitive male part of his brain was not yet ready to
give up. He kneaded her buttock, molding the smooth, firm
curve. ''Then can I take tomorrow's?''

She gave a half-hysterical giggle. ''If we were counting
future kisses, your account would be somewhere around
1830. Enough, Nicholas.''

Enough. His breath rattled out of him. *Remove your hand,
even though it abhors the emptiness. Let her robe drop over
her shapely bare legs. Set your palms on the door and push
away from it, and her. Look somewhere else, not at her ripe
lips and passion-drugged eyes.*

Honor. Remember honor.

*Now open the door so she can get the hell out before it's
too late.*

One thing more needed to be said. ''Clare.'' He swallowed hard and moved a safe distance away. ''Thank you
for staying.''

She gave him a smile of great sweetness. ''That's what
friends are for.'' Then she slipped out.

He gazed at the closed door for a long time, body and
mind both throbbing with needs, some simple, some not.

Who would have thought that the prim schoolmistress
could be so sensual?

And who could have predicted that the irritating female
who had come to Aberdare to bully him would become his
friend?

The dignified doorman at White's greeted Nicholas as if
his last visit had been the day before. The exclusive club
looked exactly the same as it had four years before; only
change would have been surprising.

Since Rafe hadn't arrived yet, Nicholas wandered into the
reading room and picked up a copy of *The Times*. As expected, Napoleon's abdication dominated the news, along

with speculations about the future and self-congratulatory articles about the triumph of British courage and wisdom.

Hearing a familiar voice, he glanced up and saw Rafe heading toward him. Halfway across the room, the duke was intercepted by an ebullient young man who burbled, "Have you heard the news, Your Grace? They say that Napoleon's dynasty will be set aside and the Bourbons be restored to the French throne."

Impaling the young man with a glance, Rafe said in freezing accents, "Indeed?"

The young man flushed, then backed away, mumbling apologies.

Nicholas watched sardonically. When Rafe reached him, he said, "You're even better at terrorizing the impertinent than you were four years ago."

"I should hope so," Rafe replied with a lazy smile. "I've been practicing."

Nicholas had to laugh. "How many people in the world are allowed to see you as you really are?"

"The arrogant side of me is quite genuine. Since you lack arrogance yourself, you have trouble recognizing it in others," Rafe observed. "But if you want to know how many people I actually relax with, the number is about six."

In a rare show of affection, he put a friendly hand on Nicholas's shoulder. Caught unprepared, Nicholas flinched.

"Damnation." Rafe hastily dropped his hand. "Sorry—you seem so normal that I forgot that your back must look like a chessboard. How bad is it?"

Nicholas shrugged even though it hurt. "Nothing to signify."

Rafe didn't appear convinced, but he let the subject drop. "Do you mind if we go directly to the coffee room? I was so busy being a host last night that I didn't eat much, and I seem to have missed breakfast as well."

"Fine." As they headed toward the coffee room, Nicholas added, "After last night, I wasn't sure you would want to keep our engagement. Michael will look on this meeting as consorting with the enemy."

"Don't be ridiculous—I'm not going to drop one friend

because another is temporarily addled.'' Rafe smiled a little. ''Besides, he won't know about it.''

In the coffee room, cold meats and other dishes were set on a sideboard. Few tables were occupied this early, so after selecting food they found a quiet corner where they could talk privately. Seeing the duke, a waiter brought a bottle of hock without being asked, then withdrew. When they were alone, Nicholas asked, ''How is Michael this morning?''

Rafe sliced a pickled onion in half and ate it with a piece of beef. ''Physically he's all right, apart from a devil of a headache. Clare's diagnosis was confirmed by the doctor who examined him.'' He gave Nicholas a speculative glance. ''I liked her very much. She has a cool head on her shoulders.'' After a moment's thought, he added, ''Very nice shoulders, too.''

''Yes to both observations,'' Nicholas agreed, not in the mood to discuss his eccentric relationship with Clare. ''I'm glad that he wasn't seriously injured, but what about his mental state?''

''When I visited him this morning, he was civil but very withdrawn, almost as if we were strangers. He didn't refer to the duel at all.'' Rafe hesitated, as if considering whether to say more. ''When I mentioned your name, the shutters went up. Not a hint as to why he exploded last night, or if he intends to seek you out again.''

''If he does, I won't let him goad me into another fight,'' Nicholas said once more.

''Not even if he insults Miss Morgan?''

Nicholas's mouth tightened, but he said, ''Not even then. My patience can outlast his insults. Nor do I care if he threatens to tell the world I'm a coward—I don't have that kind of pride.''

''You might not fight, but that doesn't mean he won't.''

Nicholas looked at the duke sharply. ''No matter how angry he is, Michael is not going to try to kill me out of hand.''

Rafe looked troubled. ''I wish I were sure of that.''

Nicholas snorted. ''You know Michael—he can be a stiff-necked idiot, but he would never behave dishonorably.''

"Four years of war can change anyone. He said as much himself."

Because it was Rafe talking, Nicholas gave serious thought to the possibility. He had known Michael Kenyon for more than twenty years, through good times and some bad. Michael had always had a fierce temper—and an equally fierce sense of honor. Dangerous, yes. Treacherous, never. Nicholas shook his head. "He can't have changed that much—not Michael."

"No doubt you're right and I'm worrying too much." Rafe topped up their glasses with hock. "Actually, he'll be too busy to pursue a vendetta. He said this morning that since the war is over, he'll sell his commission rather than return to the army."

"Good. Without battle to feed his madness, in time he should become himself again."

"I certainly hope so." With determined cheerfulness, Rafe continued, "Did you really remember meeting Jane Welcott at Blenheim, or were you only being polite?"

"I remembered, though the circumstances were not ones that a gentleman could disclose." Nicholas grinned. "Even I won't."

"No need—I can imagine." Rafe sampled the jugged hare. "I think the lady and I are about to reach a parting of the ways. She has become rather tedious lately."

Since it wasn't the sort of statement a wise man commented on, Nicholas addressed himself to his pork pie. Rafe's light, civilized liaisons seldom lasted more than six months, and Lady Welcott wasn't the woman to change that.

He thought of Clare, with her stubbornness, exasperating morality—and her honesty and warmth. Though his little Welsh rose had her full share of thorns, he would rather spend a week with her than a year with any of Rafe's polished, worldly ladies.

He took another bite of pork pie. The weeks were slipping by, and it was time he made Clare his mistress. He must use the next few days well, since he guessed that she would yield more easily in anonymous London than in the valley, where reminders of her old life were everywhere.

He finished his glass of hock. She must be well and truly

his before the three months were up. No other outcome was acceptable, for he would not let her go.

Pushing away his empty plate, he asked, "What have you been doing while I was out of the country? Do you still race that marvelous red roan?"

"No, but he sired an equally marvelous colt," Rafe replied. The conversation moved easily from horses to politics and beyond. Nicholas enjoyed himself thoroughly; Rafe, like Lucien, was someone with whom he could pick up immediately, no matter how long it had been since the last meeting.

Once Michael had been like that.

Angrily pushing aside the thought, Nicholas got to his feet. "I've a meeting with my solicitor, so I must be on my way. I'll be returning to Wales in a few days, but I expect I'll be back in London before too long."

"Good. Think about coming down to Castle Bourne for a few weeks this summer."

"If my affairs in Penreith are in order, I'd be delighted. If I can't get away, you're always welcome at Aberdare."

As the two men shook hands, Rafe said gravely, "I know you're not concerned about what Michael might do, but . . . do me a favor, please. Be careful."

It was a sobering note on which to part.

Clare was intensely glad that Nicholas spent the day away from Aberdare House; she needed time to recover from the dizzying effects of their morning embrace. Spending the night with him had made her very susceptible, and she had come within a hair's breadth of surrender. It amazed her that she had been able to call a halt when she had been a whimpering imbecile.

Thank heaven he'd used his kiss for the day, for she still felt vulnerable and over-sensitive. Perhaps she should count the kiss on the throat that he'd taken while trying to wheedle one other. If she charged it to his account, she would be protected from his potent persuasions for another day.

By the time Nicholas returned for dinner, she had managed to calm her carnal instincts. As long as she didn't spend another night with him, her virtue would be in no danger.

When they finished, he said, "Will you join me in the library? I'd like you to look at the Penreith mining lease. Maybe you'll see something that the solicitor and I have missed."

"You're looking for a way to break the lease so you can take over the mine?"

"Exactly." He made a face. "My solicitor assures me that anything can be brought to court, but this particular lease is so simple that it's hard to find a weak point. A long, complicated document would be easier to challenge."

Though they often discussed business, it was the first time he had asked for Clare's help on such a matter, and she felt flattered. In fact, she realized as they walked to the library, his whole manner was different this evening. A wonderful idea struck her: now that they were acknowledged friends, perhaps he would abandon his campaign of seduction.

Their relationship had been a strange mix of challenge and companionship, but she felt that it had changed the night before: what was between them now was deeper and warmer than simple lust. Nicholas knew how her life would be damaged if he seduced her, and surely he wouldn't want to ruin the life of a friend.

The more she thought about it, the surer she became that she no longer had to fear his advances. Supporting her theory was the fact that he hadn't once touched her since returning home, which was unusual in a man who loved to touch.

Though she would miss his kisses—dreadfully!—she wouldn't miss the dangerous game they had been playing. For weeks she had been balancing on the edge of a cliff, one step away from falling into the abyss. It would be safer, and far more comfortable, to spend the rest of the three months like brother and sister. And at the end, she could return to Penreith with her life intact.

She wasn't fool enough to think that Nicholas would embrace celibacy. Once he gave up hope of bedding her, he would soon find a more accommodating female. The thought did not enthrall her; in fact, it turned her stomach. But as long as she didn't know the details, she could bear it. Better to be his friend than one in an endless procession of quickly forgotten bedmates.

In the library, he handed her a copy of the lease and she sat down to study it. While she read, he picked up his harp and began playing softly.

After going over the document three times, Clare laid it back on the desk. "I see what you mean about simplicity. All this says is that Lord Michael Kenyon or his assignees have the right to remove coal from the designated tract for twenty-one years. If the leasing fee was based on the amount of profit, you might have had a case if Madoc is embezzling, but since the fee is a fixed sum, that won't work."

"And unfortunately, the five hundred pounds rent is paid promptly every Lady Day," Nicholas said. "I checked in the hopes that the company had ever been late paying, but no such luck."

"Is there a chance that the mine shafts have extended beyond the limits of the leased land?"

His brows went up. "That's a good thought. The area leased is quite large and probably the mine has stayed within the boundaries, but I'll have it looked into. Any other ideas?"

"Sorry, that's the best I can do."

He smiled. "Your idea is better than my solicitor's. He suggested filing a suit on the grounds that Michael used undue influence to persuade my grandfather to lease him the mineral rights, thereby depriving me of part of my lawful inheritance. It's a feeble argument—not only is five hundred pounds a fair price, but my grandfather was mentally competent when he signed the lease. Still, if we keep thinking about it, perhaps we can come up with a legal challenge that will work."

He began to play the harp again, and this time he sang along in Welsh. Clare kicked off her slippers and settled into the sofa with her feet tucked under her. On the second song he persuaded her to join in. Though her voice was unremarkable, a lifetime of hymn singing had made it strong and flexible, and like all her countrymen she loved music.

They drifted from song to song, sometimes in English,

other times in Welsh. Clare sang when she knew the words, and listened in contentment when she didn't. It was the kind of evening friends enjoyed together, and she enjoyed every minute and every note. Admittedly, Nicholas looked impossibly romantic as he bent over the harp, his whole body engaged in the act of making music, but he couldn't help that. What mattered was that they could enjoy each other's company without strain.

At least, that's what she thought until he began singing love songs. Every one of his glances was a caress, every heart-tugging phrase was aimed at her, and she was halfway to ruination before she recognized the danger. Without a single touch, he was melting her resistance and preparing her for his bed.

Her dreamy contentment vanished. As she sat up on the sofa, she said accusingly, "You're trying to seduce me again."

He finished the song he was playing, then gave her a smile of lazy innocence. "I haven't touched you since this morning."

She frowned. "But the songs you're singing are designed to turn any female's head."

His smile widened. "I certainly hope so."

Her earlier hopes crashed as she realized that nothing had changed. "I had hoped that you had decided to stop trying to seduce me," she said bitterly. "If we are friends, how can you want to wreck my life?"

"The trouble is, I genuinely do not see passion as destructive." His fingers danced across the strings. "I see it as—liberation. Fulfillment. As I said when we first agreed on this bargain, if I win, we both win."

"And if I win, you lose," she said tartly. "An idea that I prefer." She rose to her feet, slipped on her shoes, and headed for the door. It was irrational to feel betrayed—the belief that Nicholas had ended their struggle had been entirely in her own head—but nonetheless she felt deeply hurt. When he had needed her the night before, she had instantly set aside her compunctions to help him, but he was not responding in kind.

She was almost to the door when he began singing again.

She recognized the tune, which was by a twelfth-century poet-prince called Hywel ap Owain Gwynedd. But never had it sounded as magical as when Nicholas sang:

My choice is a maid, wondrous slender and fair,
Beautiful and tall in her purple-hued cloak.

Compelled by the music, she halted, then slowly turned back to him. As the dark fire in his eyes dissolved her anger and resistance, his velvet voice spun a tale of yearning, of a man longing for a woman.

My choice art thou—how reckest thou me?
Why wilt thou not tell, who in silence art sweet?

Step by reluctant step, she crossed the room to him. His eyes blazed and his voice soared to the song's conclusion.

I have chosen a maid, and no regret have I,
It is proper to choose a lady sweet and fair.

As the last notes died away, he raised a beckoning hand and said softly, "This kiss must come from you."

So potent was his spell that she raised her hand to take his. Gypsy magic. Musical magic.

Old Nick, with all his demonic power.

With self-disgust, she saw how close she was to yielding. Her hand dropped. "You're like a spider, spinning a web of sound to trap a foolish fly. But it won't work this time."

His smile was a little wistful. "To become part of another being is the ultimate union. It is what humans strive for when they mate, but even at best, they achieve it only briefly." Deep, melancholic chords flowed from the harp and twined around his words. "Who is to say that the fly doesn't enjoy that ultimate union which is the end of aloneness?"

Exasperated by his ability to make anything sound romantic, she snapped, "That's a lovely metaphor, but the reality is that the fly becomes the spider's *dinner*. The fly dies while the spider goes on to devour other fools." She spun on her heel and marched toward the door. "Find yourself another victim."

She heard the hum of strings as he set the harp on the floor and followed her across the room. "Clare."

Reluctantly she turned to him. "You have no right to stop me—you've used your kiss for today, and tomorrow as well."

"Don't think I don't know that," he said ruefully.

He loomed over her, so close that the warmth of his body caressed her. But not touching. "I can't kiss you, but you can kiss me." He gave her an entrancing Gypsy smile. "I'll resist if you'd like that."

Her anger overflowed. "This isn't a joke, damn you!"

"Why are you so distressed?" he asked quietly.

She blinked back the tears that threatened. "You claim to believe in friendship, but it's strictly on your terms. You're stone selfish, Nicholas, like every man I ever met."

He rocked back, and she saw with satisfaction that her words had hurt him. After a pause, he said, "Perhaps friendship between men and women is rare because the sexes view it differently. Obviously you think our friendship should be platonic, while I think that friendship enhances passion." His fingertips skimmed her hair, as light as gossamer. "Yes, I want to make love to you, and there is some selfishness in that. But if I simply wanted to satisfy lust, it could be more easily done elsewhere. With you, passion would mean far more."

The tenderness in his voice almost undid her, but if she softened, she was lost. Anger was safer. "Your beguiling Gypsy tongue could sell coals in Newcastle, but it's not going to work this time. No matter how you dress it up, the fact is your desires come first, and what I want is a distant second."

She knew she was being irrational and would not have been surprised if he lost his temper, but his answer was mild. "You were the one who said that you care more about the people of Penreith and the miners than about your own welfare," he pointed out. "I'm doing my best to see that they get the prosperity and safety you wanted. Passion is my end of the bargain, and I'm merely trying to make you want that, too. And I've succeeded, haven't I? That's why you're so upset."

Honesty compelled her to admit, "You're right, but that doesn't make me any less angry. Good night, Nicholas."

She swept out the door and slammed it behind her. He was trying to make her forget her own best interests, but by God, she was going to turn the tables. He wanted her, and she was going to use that fact to make him feel as harrowed as she did.

Yet he had the last word, for as she lay in her bed, she heard him play the lilting melody of "The Raggle Taggle Gypsies, O!" The words of the old ballad danced through her mind, telling the tale of the high-born lady who gave up her silk and gold and her new-wedded lord, and ran away with the raggle taggle gypsies.

The lady of the ballad was an immoral wench, and needed her head examined if she preferred a cold open field to a goose feather bed. Yet if the Gypsy who lured her away resembled Nicholas, Clare couldn't blame the lady one bit.

20

CLARE AWOKE the next morning less angry, but no less determined to teach Nicholas a lesson. But what was a suitable revenge?

The ceiling of her bedchamber was painted with a rustic scene of satyrs chasing giggling nymphs, and the answer came to her as she gazed at their amorous antics. Pursuit and retreat was a pattern that played itself out between male and female over and over again—the wary female fleeing, wanting to save herself for the best possible mate; the male giving chase, wanting to conquer another female. It had been the pattern of Clare's relationship with Nicholas.

Since that pattern lay at the heart of her predicament, her vengeance should be in kind—it was time to play the nymph to his satyr. She would act like a proper trollop until he was half mad with desire. Then she would walk away, leaving him to suffer the worst torments of frustration.

Of course her desire for revenge was distinctly unchristian. However, after a month with Nicholas, her soul was so tarnished that another moral lapse couldn't make it much worse.

She was more concerned by the knowledge that she would be acting with an immaturity that ill became a grown woman. She had never behaved in such a petty fashion in her life. Regretfully she realized that it was a sign of her moral deterioration that she looked forward to it.

More seriously, there was a risk that she would be carried away by passion and give Nicholas exactly what he wanted. If that happened, she would deserve it, but she believed that she would be able to resist him. After all, she had managed to say no after spending a languorous night in Nicholas's arms, an act of willpower that still amazed her.

The greatest danger was that if Nicholas became too aroused, he would not be able to stop when she told him to. Again, if that happened she could hardly blame him for the results. But she had faith in his self-control, having seen it demonstrated again and again. He was not a lust-crazed boy of twenty, nor was she Helen of Troy, whose face had launched ten thousand ships.

She smiled with anticipation and tucked her hands behind her head. Now that she had decided on her strategy, it remained only to choose when and where she would put it into effect.

Nicholas was relieved to see that Clare's anger had passed by the next day. Though she was quiet, she didn't sulk. On his part, he meticulously avoided claiming another kiss to compensate for the extra two he had taken the morning before.

But he really must find the right way to seduce the stubborn wench. The trouble was that Clare was unlike any female he'd ever known. Most women melted if given rich clothing and jewels; Clare consented to wear them mostly to uphold her part of their bargain. Most women became soft and dewy-eyed when men courted them with poetry or love songs; though Clare was not unaffected, it wasn't enough to make her forget her tiresome morality.

If she had been genuinely devout, he could have better understood her resistance, but he was convinced that her piety was skin-deep. Underneath, she had a streak of purely pagan sensuality; he had seen occasional flashes of it. He suspected that what really kept her virtuous was sheer stubbornness. She had sworn he would not seduce her, and she would uphold that vow if it killed both of them. Pig-headed wench.

But great though her obstinacy was, it couldn't match his.

The day after the kissless day, Clare appeared for dinner looking particularly fetching. Nicholas watched admiringly as she crossed the drawing room toward him. She wore a rose-colored gown that managed the neat trick of being both demure and provocative. Her hair was also styled a new way, and he yearned to run his fingers through the soft confection of waves and ringlets. She didn't look like a rustic schoolmistress; she looked like a sophisticated lady with a bit of the devil in her.

"You look especially lovely tonight." He offered her his arm. "Is your maid willing to return to Wales with us?"

"Polly is excellent, but I don't need a maid," Clare said with mild surprise. "I've done without one all my life."

"Most of your fashionable new clothing requires assistance for dressing. Also, she is very good at styling hair."

"Very well," Clare said agreeably. "I'll ask Polly if she is willing to spend two months in Wales, until I go home."

He hated it when she talked about leaving him, but he didn't comment; hearing his long-term plans for her would merely aggravate her stubbornness. As he pulled out her dinner chair, he said, "I've taken care of my most pressing business, so we can return to Aberdare day after tomorrow."

Her face lit up. "I'll be ready."

"Before I start work on the slate quarry, I'd like to visit Penrhyn to see how a large-scale quarry is run." He took his own seat. "If we rode up through central Wales, it would take two or three days each way. Do you think you could ride that far?"

"As long as the pace isn't too fast," she said. "I would enjoy a spring ride through the uplands."

"Good. Plan on going a week or so after we return to Aberdare."

The meal was a lengthy one, for conversation flowed freely. It was so late when they finally finished their coffee that Nicholas wouldn't have been surprised if Clare had excused herself to go to bed. Instead, she looked at him with such innocence that he was immediately suspicious.

"Are you in the mood for billiards?" she asked. "I've been practicing, and I'd like to play against an opponent."

He was agreeable, so they adjourned to the billiard room. Clare lifted her cue stick and slid it idly through her fingers. "Shall we play for some kind of stakes?"

"You must have been practicing in earnest," he said, amused. As he lowered the chandelier that hung over the table, he asked, "What did you have in mind?"

A gleam came into her eyes. "If I win, you aren't allowed to kiss me anymore."

"Not acceptable," he said promptly, "unless the opposing stake is that tonight you aren't allowed to say no if I win."

"*Not* acceptable," she replied. "Any other suggestions?"

While he lit the wax candles, he considered alternatives. "We can play strip billiards, with the loser of each game having to remove an item of clothing."

"Surely that isn't a standard game!"

"No, but I've played cards based on the same principle, and there's no reason why we can't do it with billiards. The loser is whoever is stripped down to the skin first." He grinned as he raised the chandelier and secured the rope. "Are you game?"

She thought about it. "All right, though if I get down to my shift, I'll forfeit rather than take it off."

"Fair enough. We should start with the same number of garments." He mentally counted. "If I take off my coat, I'll be wearing ten items, which should match what you have, unless you're wearing extra petticoats under that charming gown."

Blushing a little, she did her own mental inventory, then nodded. "Ten it is. Shall we begin?"

"Ladies first."

After he set up the balls, Clare bent over for her first stroke. Her levity dropped away and she lined up the shot with flinty concentration.

A female playing billiards offered a myriad of delights: trim ankles, an irresistibly rounded derriere, an enticing amount of decolletage. And while Nicholas was admiring the view, the little hussy proceeded to pot all six of her blue balls one after another, winning the game before he had a chance to shoot.

Laughing, he said, "You *have* been practicing." He pulled off a polished Hessian boot and set it by the wall, then started another game. After potting four of his reds, he missed the fifth when the ball hit a soft spot in a cushion and caromed badly

It was Clare's turn again, and once again she sank all six of her balls. After Nicholas pulled off his other boot and set it by the first, he said, "Let me see your cue stick."

She handed it over and he inspected the tip. "This button is made of leather?" When she nodded, he asked, "May I try a couple of shots with it?"

After she granted permission, he experimented with the cue, with startling results. When he returned the stick, he said, "Clarissima, you may have just revolutionized the ancient art of billiards. I've never seen a cue that allowed such control."

"I've been amazed at the results myself." She bit her lip. "Since I have a superior cue, it isn't fair for you to have the handicap of having to make difficult carom shots when I don't. We should be playing equally." She smiled roguishly. "I don't want to take advantage of you."

"You can take advantage of me anytime you want," he said with a cheerful leer.

He expected a withering glance in answer to his suggestive remark, but instead she said, "Later, perhaps." Her remark was accompanied by a sweep of long dark lashes. "But for the moment, let's play billiards. I'll do carom shots, too."

"That should make us roughly equal." While she started another game, he lounged against the table and tried to define what made her seem different tonight.

Much as he would like to believe that she had decided to stop resisting and enjoy the inevitable, he couldn't. The little witch probably wanted to put him in his place by crushing him at billiards. And with her improved cue and undeniable skill, she would have succeeded if her innate fairness hadn't made her choose to equalize the odds by matching his handicap.

He found it hard to take his eyes off her, for a subtle eroticism marked all her movements. As she potted her second ball, he realized that Clare had the air of a successful courtesan—the kind of woman who was absolutely sure of

her femaleness, and of her power over men. Though he
didn't believe that she had been practicing a courtesan's arts
along with her billiard game, she was certainly revealing
her innate sensuality as never before.

He was so absorbed in his thoughts she had to raise her
voice and repeat, "Nicholas, it's your turn," before he
heard.

He bent over the table and lined up his shot. Because he
played billiards very well and lacked a killer competitive
instinct, he had become casual over the years, but Clare's
new skill put him on his mettle. He efficiently cleared the
table of his balls, and it was her turn to take something off.

Obligingly she kicked off one of her kidskin slippers, revealing a flash of ankles. As she put her stockinged foot
down, she said, "Mmm, this carpet feels wonderful." Her
toes curled sensuously into the lush pile.

Nicholas was tempted to lie down so she could walk on
him and do the same. Instead he set up the balls again with
a mental vow to play his best so he could see more of her.

Conversation dwindled and tension rose as they applied
themselves like a pair of hardened billiard sharps. Since
their abilities were well matched, irregular patches on the
surface and bad ricochets off the cushions decided most
games.

Nicholas's cravat came off and joined his boots, then Clare
gave up her other slipper. When she lost the next game as
well, she sat down and lifted her skirt to her knee.

He watched, mesmerized, as she extended a shapely leg
in the air and removed her left stocking. She rolled the pale
silk over her calf and ankle with the demure explanation,
"A garter will stay up without a stocking but not the reverse, so I thought the stocking should come off first."

"Very logical," he agreed, his mouth dry. Though she
primly covered her ankles again, he missed his next shot.
Smiling mischievously, Clare potted her balls with six
strokes.

After taking off his gray velvet waistcoat, he knelt and
built up the fire, since it was a cool night and they were
both losing clothing at a rapid rate. He smiled to himself as

he added more coal; the one advantage he had left was that being naked would bother him a lot less than it would Clare.

Her next stocking came off with just as much ceremony as the first. He watched appreciatively, but managed to keep his head and shoot well. Unfortunately the cushions didn't cooperate on his fourth stroke. Clare took over and won the game.

He removed his first stocking, and a few minutes later lost the second as well. The carpet *did* feel good under bare feet.

Anticipation about what Clare would do next sharpened his focus and he won the next game. Up came her skirt again, this time far enough to reveal the ribbon garter tied above her knee. To his delight, it was decorated with a dainty pink satin rose. She took her time untying the ribbon. After putting her foot down, she regarded the garter thoughtfully. Then she glanced up with a wicked smile and tossed it to him.

He caught the garter with one hand and discovered that the satin still retained the warmth of her body, as well as a faint trace of the fragrance she was wearing. As she started the next game, he twined the ribbon around his fingers until it cooled to room temperature and he could no longer detect her scent.

He tied the garter around his wrist, then bent over the table and neatly potted four balls. The fifth caromed wildly and it was Clare's turn again. She came and took her stance next to him, so close that her skirts fluttered around his bare foot when she leaned over. He could have moved, of course, but he didn't.

As she lined up her shot, he admired her trim backside But when his hand began reaching out to pat, he hastily moved away before he could commit a disastrous faux pas; a gentleman *never* interfered with an opponent's stroke.

She potted the ball, then shifted to a new position. Though all her attention seemed to be on the table, her bare toes brushed his as she moved. His gaze became riveted on her feet. The left one lifted in the air, leaving her balanced on the right when she shot. He'd never noticed how elegant her feet were.

"Nicholas," she said.

He blinked and glanced up.

"Time for you to take something off," she purred.

Deciding that two could play at both games, he undid the buttons at his throat with elaborate casualness. After tugging his shirttails loose, he pulled his shirt over his head, making sure that his muscles flexed impressively. He emerged from the linen folds to find Clare watching him, eyes wide. Though he wore an undershirt, it was a sleeveless singlet and cut well below collar level so it showed a great deal of his bronze skin.

She swallowed hard and wrenched her gaze back to the table, but she was off her game and didn't manage to pot even one ball.

Blithe with anticipation, he cleared the table in less than a minute. "The other garter is next, I assume?"

She gave him a teasing smile. "So it is." She perched on the edge of the chair and lifted her skirt so she could repeat her performance, but this time the garter didn't cooperate. After a minute of fussing, she glanced up with a frown. "The ribbon has knotted and I can't get it undone. Will you help?"

He felt like a trout who was being tickled by a master. Any moment he was going to end up gasping on the stream bank, but he didn't care. He knelt in front of her chair and set her bare foot on his thigh. Then he slowly skimmed his hands up the contours of her leg until he reached the garter above her knee.

The ribbon was well and truly knotted, and his fingers felt equally knotted as he fumbled to untie it. Her inner thigh was warm and silky smooth, and she trembled when he touched the pale skin. So did he.

By the time he managed to undo the knot, her skirts had inched halfway up her thigh and they were both breathing unevenly. He unwound the ribbon from her leg, then handed it to her. "Here you are."

"Let me tie it with the other," she said huskily. He lifted his arm and she tied the garter around his wrist.

Their gazes caught and held. She had a sultry, deliciously

available expression, and he wondered if this would be the right time to collect his kiss for the day.

She spared him the decision by leaning forward and pressing her lips to his in a hot, open-mouthed kiss. She tasted like sweet, wild honey.

He had been sitting on his heels, but he straightened up, which brought him forward between her legs. Her skirts crushed between them as he wrapped his arms around her waist. She smoothed his hair over and over, leaning into his embrace until suddenly she spilled off the edge of the chair and slid down the front of him. They ended up tangled in each other's arms, both of them laughing at the awkwardness of their position.

As laughter died, he felt the heat of her loins against his. He was about to kiss her again when she glanced up and said, "Are you ready for the next game?"

His hands tightened on her shoulders. "I'm ready for a different game."

"Don't you want to see how this one turns out?" She accompanied her question with the smile that Eve had used to ravish Adam.

He gave a ragged laugh and managed to pry himself away from her. Not only was she allowing her natural sensuality free rein, but she instinctively understood how delay increased the ultimate gratification. He admired her wisdom—but he wouldn't have minded if she had less of it.

After getting to his feet, he helped her up. "I'm ready, if you remember whose turn it is to start."

She gave a gurgle of laughter. "Mine, I think."

The person who started usually won, as Clare did this time. Nicholas's undershirt was the next garment to go.

As he pulled it over his head, her fingers clenched around her cue stick. Gaze fixed to his bare chest, she said, "We can't go on much longer—we're both running out of clothing."

"Getting close," he agreed cheerfully.

It was his turn to start. A bad carom gave the initiative to Clare, but she was also unlucky. The table changed hands twice more before she finally lost.

She gave him a provocative sideways glance. "I'm going

to need help again. As you said, gowns like this can't be taken off without assistance.''

"It will be my pleasure," he said with complete truth.

The back of her gown was secured with a complicated arrangement of hooks and ties. A good thing he'd had experience at helping ladies out of gowns, or the rest of the night might have been wasted while he puzzled it out.

When the fastenings were undone, he gently pushed the gown off her shoulders. The rose fabric rippled as it fell to her elbows, exposing her creamy shoulders. Completely unable to resist, he leaned forward and kissed her nape through delicate tendrils of dark hair.

As she exhaled with a small, breathless shiver, he transferred his attention to the sensitive edge of her ear, then the side of her throat and the smooth curve of her shoulder. At the same time he drew her gown lower, past her waist, over her hips, until it dropped to the floor around her bare feet.

She turned to him, clad only in petticoat, stays, and shift. Her pupils had dilated until her eyes looked almost black. He thought she would move into his arms, but she touched the tip of her tongue to her lower lip, then said, "My turn to go first."

Since her hair was coming down, he removed the rest of the pins before continuing. Shimmering locks cascaded over her shoulders, then swirled and danced around her hips as she picked up her cue stick. She potted five balls in a row, then missed an easy shot on the last one when hair fell across her face.

Nicholas breathed deeply several times to steady himself, then took his turn. More by luck than skill, he won the game. "Do you need help taking off your petticoat?" he asked hopefully.

She laughed and shook her head. "No, but if you win another game, I'll need help with my stays." She undid the tape that secured the petticoat around her waist, then pulled the garment over her head with a lithe wriggle. The lace-trimmed hem fluttered prettily around her.

Beneath the petticoat she wore only a knee-length, faintly translucent shift and short stays. He had trouble wrenching his gaze from her to the table. It occurred to him that every other time he had been with a female so scantily attired he had ended by making love to her. He devoutly hoped that the result wouldn't differ this time.

He managed to sink his first ball. Clare was watching from the other side of the table. As he lined up his second shot, she folded her arms on top of the cushion, then leaned on top of them. Her breasts were as round and perfect as the ivory billiard balls, and they appeared about to bounce onto the table.

Irresistibly distracted, he accidentally stabbed his cue into the baize, completely missing the ball. "You little witch," he said, laughing. "That was a rotten trick."

Unrepentant, she said, "I wouldn't have missed my last stroke if you hadn't let my hair down."

With a smile like a cat in a creampot, she proceeded to pot all her balls, then straightened and waited for him to take off his breeches.

His gaze on hers, he undid the buttons, then peeled the garment off, leaving him wearing only a pair of knee-length linen drawers. The game was very nearly over. But he would be damned if he would let himself lose before she was down to her shift.

She started the next game and sank three balls before the cue ball skidded on a balding patch of baize.

This was Nicholas's chance. Concentrating as he seldom had in his life, he made his first shot, then his second. His aim was a bit off when he went for the third, but the cue ball clipped the object ball well enough to sink it.

Three more to go. He wiped his hands on his discarded shirt, then bent over and potted the fourth. With a final burst of bravado, he managed to sink his last two balls with one stroke.

Trying to control his anticipation, he restlessly rolled her blue balls into various pockets. "Time for the stays, Clarissima."

Hips gently swaying, she walked over to him, then turned her back so he could unlace her. Since her trim figure didn't require a full-length corset, she wore the more comfortable short stays which ended at the waist. Made of quilted white dimity, the stays provided a smooth line under gowns and supported her breasts enticingly.

Though he'd undone his share of stays, his fingers were clumsy as he pulled the laces through the eyelets. It didn't help that her shift was so sheer that he could clearly see the curving lines of her legs and hips.

When the stays were undone, he pulled the narrow straps off her shoulders, then slipped his hands under her arms and cupped her breasts. Under the flimsy fabric of the shift, her nipples instantly hardened. As he stroked the firm nubs with his thumbs, she sucked her breath in. Then, very deliberately, she pressed back so that the contours of her body molded against him.

His control snapped. Catching her around the waist, he swooped her up and set her on the edge of the billiard table so that their faces were level. His kiss was devouring, and she returned it in full measure. Intoxicated, he moved between her legs and caressed the outside of her thighs, drawing the hem of her shift upward.

Then, to his unutterable shock, her hand moved down his torso. He almost shattered when her fingers curved hesitantly around his heated flesh. Blindly he swept her back so that she was lying full-length on the table. As he moved above her, he had no conscious thought beyond removing the frail garments that separated them.

"Enough, Nicholas!" Her voice rose. "Stop right *now*!"

He paused and tried to focus his dazed eyes on her face. Hoarsely he said, "Christ, Clarissima, not this time." His hand crept up her thigh. "Let me just show you . . ."

A tumult of emotions showed in her face, but there was no doubt in her voice. "No more! Today's kissing is over."

He felt paralyzed, unable to proceed, unable to move away. In the taut silence, the striking of the drawing room clock was clearly audible. One, two, three . . .

Twelve. Triumphantly he said, "Midnight. It's another day, Clarissima, and another kiss."

Then he bent and pressed his hungry mouth to her breast.

21

IT HAD taken every shred of Clare's determination to
tell Nicholas to stop, and her resistance crumbled when
his heated mouth made magic on her breast. She arched
against him, no longer able to remember why she had
wanted this to end, for she had no will beyond desire.

He pulled the strap of her shift off her shoulder and began
kissing her other breast, this time on her naked flesh rather
than through sheer fabric. Feverishly she stroked his bare
back, her hand digging into the flexing muscles. His fingers
traced a burning path to the secret place between her thighs.
When he touched her intimately, she moaned and rolled her
head back and forth, for she had no words for the fierceness
of her response.

Deftly he caressed the moist folds, spreading and opening
her. Then she felt a hard, blunt pressure, slow but inexo-
rable. Instinctively she knew that he offered the completion
her body craved, and she moved upward against him, welcoming the weight of his body.

Then pain struck, tearing her so fiercely that desire vanished. Feeling that she was being ripped apart, she pushed
frantically at his shoulders. "Stop!"

He froze, his weight supported above her, his face rav-
aged as he stared at her. The hard shaft that pressed against
her throbbed menacingly as if determined to thrust forward
of its own will.

As pain and panic pushed her beyond thoughts of morality and revenge, she begged, "Please—no more."

For a moment the outcome hovered in the balance. Then,
the tendons in his arms standing out like steel bands, he
lifted himself off her, swearing viciously under his breath.

Relief was instantly followed by shattered confusion. Dear God, how could she have allowed this to happen? She pressed her wrist against her mouth, trying to contain the bitter shame that swept through her. *Sow the wind, and reap the whirlwind.*

Knowing that she was a hair's breadth away from hysteria, she pushed herself to a sitting position and pulled her shift down to cover as much of her body as possible. Nicholas had folded onto the floor, his head bent forward so that his face was invisible. His hands were locked around the opposite wrists and he was shaking as badly as she was.

She looked away, guilt stabbing her as sharply as physical pain had a few moments earlier. Even at her most angry, this was not what she had intended. She had wanted to teach a lesson, not ravage both of them.

After inhaling deeply, Nicholas said with bitter humor, "Your imitation of a pious schoolmistress isn't bad, but you're a damn' sight more convincing as a teasing bitch."

The tears she had tried to contain broke through and she began to weep with gut-wrenching misery. Hating herself, she gasped, "Don't stop there. I'm not only a bitch but a spiritual fraud, a hypocrite. For a few moments I wanted to be a fallen woman, and I couldn't even get that right!" She buried her face in her hands. "I wish to God I had never been born."

After a long silence, he said dryly, "That's a bit extreme. What would your father have done without you?"

"My father hardly knew that I was alive." Her throat closed, as if retaliating for the fact that she had said aloud what she had never admitted to herself.

And Nicholas, damn him, understood the significance of her agonized statement. Voice more controlled, he said, "You didn't feel that he loved you?"

"Oh, he loved me," she said bleakly. "He was a saint— he loved everyone. He had time and compassion and wisdom for everyone who asked. But I couldn't ask, so there was never any for me." She kept her head down, unable to look at Nicholas. "You're the only one who ever asked what it was like to live with a saint, so I'll tell you the truth: it was pure hell. The first thing I learned from my mother was that God's work was more important than the preacher's family, and we must always put that work first. I tried so hard to be what my father expected, to be devout and serene and generous, as good a Christian as he and my mother were. I suppose I believed that if I made my father's life easy enough, eventually he would have more time for me. But he never did.''

Her mouth twisted. ''When you told me how he helped when you came to Aberdare, I was jealous because you had so much more of his time and attention than I did. Not very generous of me, was it?''

''It's very human to want a parent's love. Perhaps we never get over the lack of it.''

''I don't know why I'm telling you this,'' she said miserably, her nails biting into her palms. ''Your family was far worse than mine. At least my father never sold me, or said that he wished another girl was his daughter. And when he remembered, he always thanked me very politely for taking such good care of him.''

''It's simple to hate someone who has openly betrayed you,'' Nicholas observed. ''Perhaps it is more corrosive and painful to resent a selfless saint who has betrayed you in more subtle ways—especially when everyone in your community assumes that you must be selfless and saintly, too.''

He understood too much. Angrily she wiped the tears from her eyes. ''But I'm not a saint. Though I didn't mind giving, I wanted something back, and I've never stopped resenting the fact that I didn't get it. I'm selfish and greedy and I deserved to be driven out of Zion Chapel.''

''Why do you think you're a fraud?''

She stared at her hands, which were knotted together. ''The heart of my religion is direct experience of God. In the early days of English Methodism, John Wesley personally interviewed prospective members of the society to be sure that their experience and belief were genuine. If that had been done to me, I would have failed, for I have never— not once—experienced the sense of divine presence. I've seen it in others—sometimes when I was talking to my father he would stop listening and gaze into the distance, his face glowing as the spirit flowed through him.''

Her voice broke. "I was jealous of that, too. When I was younger, I prayed for hours every day, asking God to let me feel, if only for an instant, that spiritual connection. But even though my mind believed, my heart was empty.

"The horrible irony is that others learned of my prayers and assumed that I was deeply pious. When I declined a leadership role in the chapel, it was thought that I was becomingly modest. I should have told the truth, but it was easier to pretend to be what others thought I was. Acting saintly and selfless made me seem to be a real person. But since I met you, all my pretenses have crumbled away, one by one, and now there's nothing left. I'm not a real person at all."

She didn't know that he had risen and crossed the room until his fingers lightly brushed her tangled hair. "You seem very real to me, Clare, even if you're not the woman you thought you were." His fingers slipped around her head and caressed the taut nape of her neck. "It will take time for you to learn who you really are. The old has to be destroyed before there is room for the new, and it's a painful process. Though in the long run you'll be happier, I'm sorry for my part in bringing you to this. I know it sounds contradictory, but though I've wanted to ruin you, I never wanted to hurt you."

She rested her cheek against his hand, thinking how strange this conversation was. Both of them seemed to have moved beyond anger to bleak resignation. "It's not your fault, Nicholas. There is nothing you have done to me that is as bad as what I have done to myself. And I'm thoroughly ashamed of what I tried to do to you." She attempted to smile. "Now I understand why God reserved vengeance for Himself. When a mortal attempts revenge, it goes wrong too easily."

"Things often go wrong between men and women," he said wryly. "It's amazing the human race manages to survive. Mating seems much easier for beasts that don't think."

Perhaps that was her problem—she thought too much. She sighed. "I don't know why I've blurted out all the worst things about myself. Expiation for my bad behavior, I suppose."

His fingers tightened around hers. "I'm rather flattered that you have chosen me to be honest with. Stop castigating yourself, Clare—your sins are minor, a product of confusion rather than malice."

"A woman my age should not be so confused."

He moved away for a moment, then returned and draped his coat around her shoulders. "Go to bed. I'll take care of things here. No one will know what . . . almost happened."

Even now, that mattered to her. With his help, she climbed off the table. She still could not bring herself to look in his face, but she was glad to see that he had put his pantaloons back on. The more barriers between them, the better.

She slipped out the door and made her barefoot way through the sleeping house. The moon was nearing full, and it cast enough light for her to find her path.

It wasn't until she reached her own room that she realized she was bleeding. A bubble of hysterical laughter rose in her throat. Did that mean she was no longer a virgin? Could one be partially virgin? Nicholas would know, but she couldn't imagine asking him about such an intimate topic, even though he was the one responsible for her semi-virginal state.

As she fashioned a pad to absorb the blood, she thought that it would be ironic if she was now officially ruined without having enjoyed any of the benefits. She wrapped a blanket around herself and curled up on the windowseat, too tense to go to bed.

Reluctantly, as if testing a sore tooth, she thought back to those mad moments when she had been blind to everything but passion. She shivered as the memory of desire swept through her, warming the secret places he had brought to aching life.

For the first time, she truly understood how passion could blind someone to honor, decency, and common sense. It hadn't even occurred to her how ludicrous, how *vulgar*, it was to be deflowered on a billiard table. If it had not been for the sudden, unexpected pain, she and Nicholas would be lovers now.

Though oblique references by married women had hinted

that losing a maidenhead hurt, Clare had had the impression
that the discomfort was minor and would quickly pass. Obviously women must differ in the amount of pain they experienced. Should she be glad that it was hard for her
because pain saved her from the ultimate folly? Or should
she be sorry? She would probably be much happier if she
had irrevocably turned away from virtue; certainly she
would be less confused.

Now that both passion and pain had cooled, Clare wondered if she had planned her little revenge with the secret
hope that Nicholas would overwhelm her with his intoxicating masculinity. If he had succeeded, now she would be
sleeping in his bed, warm and protected in his arms. A
sinner, but a happy one.

She looked up at the cool face of the moon, which floated
dispassionately above the teeming hive of London. In western mythology, the moon was always female; Diana, goddess of the moon, had been aggressively virginal. What
would the goddess have made of Nicholas? Clare smiled
ruefully. Diana would probably have thrown away her bow
and arrows and pulled him down into a mossy forest bed.

She drew the blanket more tightly around herself, thinking how much she missed the solid certainty of her old life.
Though she had occasionally had secret doubts, she had
been able to ignore them most of the time. Then she had
become involved with Nicholas and certainty had dissolved
like a house of sand, leaving her in a state of constant,
uncomfortable flux.

Yet, though she had finally admitted that she was a fraud-
ulent and inadequate Christian, she could not jettison morality entirely. In her heart, she still believed that it would
be wrong to become Nicholas's mistress. If she gave herself
to him simply to satisfy lust, she would despise herself as
soon as desire was satisfied. And from a strictly practical
point of view, she would be a fool to trust herself to a man
who would neither love nor marry her.

The mistress issue was probably moot now. Though
Nicholas had been surprisingly kind to her after the night's
fiasco, she couldn't imagine that he would want to have her
around any longer. So perhaps that meant that Clare would

be successful in achieving one of her earlier goals: getting him to send her away.

Success, in this case, would not make her happy.

With a sigh, she uncurled herself from the windowseat and went to her bed. She couldn't change the disastrous events of the evening, and it was far too soon for her to understand what kind of woman she would be now that she no longer had her facade to hide behind. Instead, she must bend her weary mind to the question of how to face Nicholas in the morning.

Business took Nicholas from the house early, for which he was grateful. It was hard to believe how short a time had passed since Clare had stormed into his life; they seemed to be compressing years' worth of complications into as many weeks. Their relationship had changed the night before, and he had no idea what would come next. He desired her more than ever, yet her near-breakdown had been as harrowing for him as for her.

When his business was completed, he briefly considered stopping by a very expensive, very discreet establishment where the girls were beautiful, warm, and willing. He dismissed the thought immediately; coupling with a stranger would not eliminate his desire for Clare, and would surely leave him more lonely than satisfied.

His house was near Hyde Park and Clare often walked at this hour, so he decided to drive home that way. Since the day was raw, the park was relatively empty, and soon he spotted Clare and the dutiful maid who followed her.

He gave his reins to his groom with orders to go home, then quietly dismissed the maid with a gesture of his hand. When he fell into step beside Clare, she gave him an un-surprised glance. She wore her plainest clothing and there were shadows under her eyes, but she had regained her usual composure.

"You've the most remarkable talent for appearing and disappearing," she observed. "Rather like a cat."

He tucked her hand under his elbow and they strolled toward the small lake called the Serpentine. "I'm glad that you're talking to me today."

She sighed and looked away. "I have no cause to be angry with you. Everything that has happened to me can be traced to my own willfulness and bad judgment."

"You may not feel that you're a very good Christian, but you've certainly mastered guilt."

Her head came around and she gave him an indignant glance. "I prefer that to having no conscience, like some I could name."

He patted her fingers where they rested on his arm. "Good. I like it much better when you're snapping at me. More normal."

A reluctant smile tugged at her lips. "If normal means a desire to box your ears, I'm in prime condition."

"The first rule of Gypsy fighting is never to box the ears of someone who is eight inches taller than you."

"I'll bear that in mind."

They reached the edge of the lake, where ducks squabbled noisily and two small boys were launching toy sailboats under the watchful eyes of a nursemaid. As they began circling the water, Nicholas nodded toward the boats. "Lucien says plans are under way to hold victory celebrations here in June. The Prince Regent will probably restage the Battle of Trafalgar on the Serpentine."

"Are you serious?"

"God's own truth," he assured her. "Plus fireworks, parades, and a jolly, vulgar fair for the groundlings. If you'd like to see the spectacle, I'll bring you back to London then."

"I can't look two months ahead—I can barely imagine how to get through the next day." She looked up, her deep blue eyes haunted. "We can't go on as we have. Surely you can see that."

His mouth tightened. "Why not?"

"We've been playing a dangerous game of seduction and teasing, pushing closer and closer to each other's limits," she said bluntly. "Between my hysteria and your frustration, we'll destroy each other if we don't stop."

"Perhaps you're right," he said with deep reluctance. "What do you propose instead?"

"Surely it would be easiest for both of us if I went home to Penreith."

A wave of anxiety swept through him. "What I said before still stands," he said harshly. "Leave before the three months are over and I'll drop my plans for the valley."

She stopped walking and stared at him. "I simply don't understand why you care that much about my presence or absence. By this time, I would think that you would want to pursue matters at the mine if only to vex Lord Michael."

He didn't understand himself, but he knew damned well that he didn't want her to go. He started to lift his hand, instinctively wanting to persuade her with touch. She tensed in a subtle but unmistakable withdrawal.

His stomach knotted and he dropped his hand. If she started to fear him, he would be unable to bear it. He could think of only one acceptable solution, though he hated the thought. "I'll waive my daily kiss. That should make it possible for us to be together without losing our sanity. Wasn't chaste abstinence what you originally suggested as a stake when we started playing billiards last night?"

Her brows drew together. "Now I understand you even less. You flatly refused to consider giving up your kisses last night."

"That was then. This is now." He took her arm and started her walking again, relaxing since it seemed that he would carry his point. "It should be obvious that I enjoy your company. When we return to Aberdare, maybe I'll look into getting a dog, but for the time being, you'll have to do."

She smiled, her expression easing. "Since you put it in such flattering terms, how can I refuse?"

He was glad to see her smile. But as they walked back to Aberdare House, he glumly faced the fact that he had only two months to convince her to stay with him, and he could no longer use passion to persuade her.

The Duke of Candover returned home to find his houseguest on the verge of leaving. Concealing his uneasiness, Rafe said, "Have I neglected you too much, Michael?"

Face expressionless, his friend said, "Not at all. However, I can't afford to waste any more time lying around like an invalid—I've too much to do. There's nothing wrong with me—I've had worse knocks on the head by walking into doors.'' Remembering his manners, he added, ''Thank you for putting me up.''

''Why not give up your rooms and stay here?'' Rafe suggested. ''It's such a bloody great barn that I'd enjoy the company.''

''I'll be leaving London. I've neglected my business interests for too long—it's time I visited them in person.''

Rafe felt the back of his neck prickle. ''Does that include your mine in Penreith?''

Michael accepted his hat from the butler and put it on, the brim casting a shadow over his eyes. ''As a matter of fact, it does.''

The duke felt like swearing. ''One war has just ended. I hope you're not going to start another one.''

''No one loves peace more than a retired soldier,'' Michael said, his expression cool and unreadable. ''I'll let you know when I return to London.''

He turned and walked out the front door without looking back.

22

For THE Morrises, Sunday was a day for the family as well as the Lord. Usually that included a walk after the midday meal. Sometimes Marged came, but more often she stayed home, saying frankly that she liked a bit of quiet now and then. For his part, Owen enjoyed the time alone with his children. If a man didn't make the effort, it would be easy to miss the growing years.

It was a very Welsh sort of day, with showers and sunshine taking turns. At the urging of Owen's older son, Trevor, they took a different track into the hills. Few people came this way, for it ran by Lord Michael Kenyon's estate, Bryn Manor, where visitors were not welcome. Surrounded by a stone wall, the estate was very different from Aberdare, which was criss-crossed by public pathways. However, Owen knew that as long as they stayed off Kenyon property there would be no problem, and the track was a lovely one on a spring day.

Megan, very much the little lady, walked with her father while the boys raced back and forth like a pack of puppies. It did Owen's heart good to see little Huw larking about with his own boys. Since leaving the mine, the child seemed to have grown three inches, as well as putting on weight and achieving healthy color. According to Marged, he was an apt pupil, approaching every new lesson with the same hunger that he showed at the kitchen table.

As the trail wound upward, Owen asked Megan, "Your birthday will be here soon. Is there something special you would like?"

She glanced at him askance. "A kitten."

He raised his brows. "We already have a cat."

"But I want a *kitten*," she explained. "Of my *own*."

He hid a smile. "Kittens turn into cats," he warned her, "and if you get one, you'd have to take care of it yourself. Still, you'll be ten—almost grown up. If you're sure that's what you want, I'll talk to your mother. If she objects—"

Megan cut him off with an unladylike crow of pleasure. "Mama said to talk to you, and if you didn't object, it would be all right. Ethelwyn's cat just had kittens. In a fortnight, they'll be ready to leave their mother."

Owen grinned. He'd never had a chance. Not that he could deny Megan anything, since she looked so much like her mother.

Contentment was shattered when Trevor bolted out of the woods. "Dada, come quickly, it's Huw," he panted. "He wandered off to pick daffodils for Mama, then came racing back like the devil was after him. I asked him what was wrong, but he just cries and won't answer."

Owen increased the length of his strides. A few minutes of walking through the trees brought them to the other two children. Huw was sobbing frantically, daffodils clutched incongruously to his chest. Patting him ineffectually on the shoulder was Owen's younger son David, who greeted his father with relief.

Owen scooped Huw up in his arms and made soothing noises. For all his new growth, he was still only a tiny lad. When the child's tears had abated, he asked, "What's wrong, boyo?"

Huw rubbed a grubby fist into his eyes. "I . . . I saw the gates of hell, Uncle Owen."

In spite of patient questioning, Owen was unable to get a more coherent explanation. At length he said, "Trevor, take David and Megan home now. Huw can show me what he saw."

Trevor obediently led his younger siblings back to the trail. Huw looked unhappy, but when Owen took his hand he set off willingly enough. They went deeper into the woods until they reached a crumbling stone wall. Huw let go of Owen's hand and scrambled through a gap in the stonework.

Owen frowned. "This is private land, the Kenyon estate. You shouldn't have gone in here."

"I saw daffodils and wanted to pick some to take back to Aunt Marged," Huw said guiltily. "It's not far."

Knowing it would be better for Huw to face his fear rather than have nightmares, Owen squeezed his way through the narrow gap in the wall. On the other side was a ridge, with a drift of brilliant daffodils blooming near the top. Though the hillside was heavily wooded, the branches were still bare so it was possible to see smoke rising from the other side of the ridge.

Expression anxious, Huw looked over his shoulder and touched a finger to his lips. Then he crouched over and made his way stealthily to the crest of the ridge, which overlooked a small hollow. As they settled behind a sheltering shrub, Owen put his arm around Huw and looked down to see what had frightened the boy.

"The gates of hell" proved to be a shabby hut built into the hillside. A trick of the sunlight made the drifting smoke glow infernally, which explained why Huw had misinterpreted the sight. "See, lad, how the sun shines through the smoke from behind?" Owen said. "It's only a woodsman's hut."

Though Huw didn't reply, he relaxed a little. Yet instead of leaving, Owen regarded the hut curiously. Odd to have so large a fire on a warm spring day.

As they watched, the smoke trickled to a halt, and a few minutes later the door swung open. As two dark-clothed men came out, Huw hid his face against Owen. "Demons," he whispered.

The men were George Madoc and Huw's father, Nye Wilkins. Owen's gaze sharpened. If Huw had gotten an unexpected glimpse of his terrifying parent, it might have contributed to the boy's belief that he had seen the nether regions.

Madoc closed and locked the door and the two men began walking away, in the opposite direction from their hidden watchers. While he waited for them to disappear from view, Owen considered what he had seen. As Lord Michael Kenyon's manager, Madoc had a perfect right to be here; Madoc's own house was on Kenyon property, nearer the village. But his presence at a crude, hidden hut was strange. And why was Nye Wilkins here? At the mine he was something of Madoc's pet, but this was Sunday. It seemed unlikely that the men would see each other socially; Madoc was too conscious of his superior status.

When the men were safely out of sight, Owen told Huw, "Wait here. I want to take a closer look."

After making his way quietly down to the hut, Owen peered into one of the small windows. The interior was dominated by a large oven that reminded him of a pottery kiln he'd seen near Swansea. But he couldn't imagine George Madoc being interested in pottery. He studied the tools and implements set on a crude table. Some he recognized, some he didn't.

He was thoughtful as he and Huw walked back to the village. Perhaps his imagination was running away with him and nothing of significance was taking place. Nonetheless, when Nicholas Davies returned from London, Owen would tell him about the mysterious hut.

Clare learned that living without kisses was much simpler and more comfortable than living on the edge of danger. It was also, alas, much less enjoyable. She missed not only the physical contact itself, but the easy familiarity that had gone with it. Now Nicholas never touched her except in formal ways, such as helping her in and out of a carriage. Though they still conversed easily, part of him had withdrawn. On the return to Aberdare, he rode his horse rather than sitting in the coach with Clare and Polly. That reduced the stress of proximity, but made the journey seem much longer than the trip to London.

Clare felt a strange mix of emotions as she returned to the valley. It was home, the most familiar place in the world. Yet she felt that she was a different woman from the one who had left. She had changed, and home would never be quite the same.

The first thing she did after arriving at Aberdare was to meet with Rhys Williams. After describing what she had ordered for the house and when her purchases could be expected to arrive, she asked bluntly, "Have any of the servants left because they won't stay in the house with a depraved, immoral female?''

After a moment's hesitation, the butler answered with equal bluntness. ''Two—Tegwen Elias and Bronwyn Jones. Bronwyn didn't want to go, but her mother insisted.''

It could have been worse; morality was a serious business in the valley. Clare said, ''Will there be more problems?''

''I don't think so. I could easily have hired two more maids, but thought you'd rather do it yourself when you returned.'' He gave a satiric smile. ''Jobs are hard to come by. There aren't many people who will walk away from a good one because of a bit of gossip. I wouldn't myself.''

So pragmatism was on her side. She thought about asking him if he had a personal opinion about her morals, or lack thereof, but decided that she would rather not know.

The day after returning home she was busy evaluating what had been done in her absence. Rhys Williams and the servants had done a splendid job on the public rooms, which were now clean, bright, and no longer cluttered by too much ugly furniture. With the addition of the paper, paints, and fabrics she had ordered in London, the house would soon be as lovely as it deserved to be.

Yet even though her household tasks were going well, her anxiety rose as the day progressed. Her class meeting was that evening, and she was not sure what kind of reception she would receive. At dinner Nicholas noticed her mood and asked if something was wrong. When she explained, he remarked, ''I'd volunteer to go with you, but I'm sure that would add to your problems. I don't suppose you'd consider not going.''

She shook her head. ''That would be cowardly. Worse, it might appear that I think I'm too good for my old friends now that I'm hobnobbing with the nobility.'' Her face tightened. ''If they ask me to leave, at least I'll know where I stand.''

After dinner, Clare went upstairs and donned one of her own, pre-London dresses, which she could put on without help. The class members were her closest friends and the people most likely to believe in her. Yet in her heart, she felt that she deserved to be expelled from the meeting.

Though she might, technically, still be a virgin, there was no question that she had been guilty of immoral misconduct. And worst of all, she wasn't sorry. Confused and unhappy, but not truly sorry.

She drove her cart to the Morrises's cottage, arriving just before the meeting was due to start. When she walked in, the room fell silent and eleven pairs of eyes stared at her. Marged broke the silence by coming over and giving her a hug. "Clare, it's glad I am to see you. Can you come by the school soon? The children miss you." She smiled. "They're also desperately anxious to visit Lord Aberdare's penguins."

Clare was glad for her friend's support, but that did not automatically mean the rest of the class would regard her with favor. She glanced around the room, offering a tentative smile. Several of the other members smiled back and young Hugh Lloyd winked. Her gaze went last to Edith Wickes, who was most likely to condemn her. Clare asked, "Am I still welcome here?"

Edith clucked her tongue. "You've shown very poor judgment, child. Half the valley is convinced that you're a trollop."

"I am not Lord Aberdare's mistress," Clare said, profoundly grateful that she could say that with truth.

"Well, I should hope not," Edith said briskly. "But there are those who would rather think ill, such as Mrs. Elias." She sniffed. "When the Lord comes to separate the sheep from the goats on Judgment Day, he won't find much good wool on her. She said you wouldn't deign to come to class now that you're working at the big house, but I knew better."

Wanting to sing with relief, Clare leaned over and embraced Edith. "Bless you for having faith in me. I can't say that my conduct has been above reproach, but I haven't done anything dreadful, either. How has the Sunday school teaching gone?"

In his capacity of class leader, Owen said with gentle reproof, "Save the talk for later, ladies—it's time we began the meeting. Let us sing a song unto the Lord."

Gratefully Clare relaxed into the familiar ritual of hymns,

prayers, and discussion. When her turn came to talk, she said briefly that London was full of both excitement and temptations, and it was good to be home.

When the meeting was over, everyone stayed on for tea, cakes, and the chance to hear Clare talk of her trip. After she had regaled them with tales of the Tower, mechanical monsters, and her visit to the Foundry, which had been John Wesley's home chapel, she rose regretfully. "Time I was leaving."

As the group broke up, Owen said, "I'll escort you back to Aberdare, Clare. I don't want you going so far alone."

She gave him a curious glance, for the valley had always been very safe, but agreed readily. As they rode back to Aberdare in her cart, he explained that his primary aim was to talk to Nicholas. Nothing important, mind, but perhaps his lordship would be interested.

Hearing the front door open, Nicholas came to the hall from the library, as if he'd been awaiting Clare's return. Seeing Owen, he offered a wide smile and a hearty handshake. "This is a coincidence, for I have some questions I hope you can answer."

"I have a few questions of my own," Owen replied.

"Should I be present or absent?" Clare inquired.

"Present," Nicholas answered as he ushered the others into the library. "Owen, you first."

As Owen settled into one of the deep, leather-upholstered chairs, he said, "This may mean nothing, but a few days ago I saw something a bit odd." He went on to describe the hut he and Huw had found on the Kenyon estate.

When he had finished, Nicholas said, "Interesting. Do you have any opinions about what, if anything, it might mean?"

"If I had to guess, I'd say the hut was being used to process high-grade metal ore," Owen said slowly. "Possibly gold, but more likely silver."

"Is that possible?" Nicholas said with surprise. "I know that occasionally gold and silver have been found in Wales, but never very much, and never in this area."

"Sometimes very pure silver is found in clumps called wire silver," Owen explained. "Once I saw a specimen that had been found near Ebbw Vale. Amazing stuff—so pure that it could be melted down and cast into ingots with no more than a very hot oven, like the one in the hut. I don't think wire silver would be found in a coal bed, but remember that closed shaft where I said the coal seam ran out when the rock changed? It's possible that the different rock might have silver in it.''

Nicholas's brows knit together as he thought. "So perhaps Wilkins discovered silver and went privately to Madoc. If the metal is in small deposits and very pure, it could be brought out of the mine without the other men noticing. The Kenyon estate is a perfect spot to melt it down secretly, since Lord Michael isn't in residence and Madoc is overseeing the property."

"Why would Wilkins have gone to Madoc rather than keep a valuable find for himself?" Clare asked.

"Nye Wilkins isn't clever enough to process or sell the silver without an experienced partner like Madoc," Owen replied. "If our guesses are right, they could be making a nice bit of extra money between them."

"This is exactly what we've been looking for!" Clare almost bounced from her chair in excitement. "Lord Michael's lease covers coal only, not all mineral rights. If Madoc and Wilkins are taking silver or any other valuable ore from the mine, you have grounds to break the lease. Even if Lord Michael is ignorant of what his employees are doing, surely his company would be legally liable for taking anything that belongs to you."

There was a suspended moment. Then Nicholas gave a whoop, leaped from his chair, and swept Clare up for a kiss. Barely in time, he remembered to keep it quick and light.

Turning to Owen, he said, "I saw Lord Michael Kenyon in London. He's been with the army in the Peninsula, which is why he's neglected his business. Since he flatly refused to make any changes, we've been trying to think of a way to break the lease. And now, by God, we've got it, thanks to you and Huw."

Owen smiled. "You were right the first time—it's by God. It would be hard to believe that it was accident that Huw found his way to the hut, then took me there."

Declining to digress into theology, Nicholas said, "So far this is all speculation—what we need is first-hand evidence. Could you take me into the pit again? If the two of us can testify that we've seen illegal mining, I can go to court and close down the existing operation, then start my own."

Owen frowned. "Going down pit won't be easy. After Madoc forbade you the premises, he gave orders to notify him instantly if you come onto the property. The banksman who manages the main shaft is a decent fellow, but he'd never go against Madoc."

"What about going down at night? Once we're underground, it won't matter what time of day it is."

"After your first visit, Madoc had a fence built around the minehead, and at night there's a watchdog and a guard. We might be able to get past them, but it would be impossible to operate the whim gin without being noticed. We all think Madoc's a bit mad to go to such efforts to keep you away." Owen shrugged. "Of course, we've always thought him a bit mad."

Clare said, "What you've described eliminates the main entrance, but what about the old Bychan shaft? The one that's used mostly for ventilation now."

Owen's eyes widened. "What a memory you have, lass. I'd almost forgotten the Bychan myself."

"Would it be usable?" Nicholas asked.

"It should be," Owen said thoughtfully. "It's very narrow, but there's a bucket that can raise or lower one man at a time. The bucket is operated by a man and a pony, so we'll only need one other man to help. Not only that, the shaft goes down near the closed tunnel so you won't have to travel far underground and risk being seen. It could be done."

"Shall we plan on doing it four days from now? That will give me time to have my Swansea man of business look into the legal aspects," Nicholas said. "Also, before we go into the mine I want to visit that hut so we can examine it more carefully. If silver is being melted, there should be traces around the oven or on the equipment. More evidence."

Owen nodded. "Four days it is. That will also give me

time to check that the rope and bucket are in good working order.'' His expression turned grim. ''The sooner something is done, the better. In the last fortnight, the gas problems have been getting worse, and there have been three tunnel collapses because of poor timbering. No one has died since the day you went down, but I feel in my bones that something terrible is waiting to happen.''

''A week from now, the mine will be in my hands and I can make the needed improvements,'' Nicholas said confidently. His Gypsy instinct told him that they had found the way to wrest control away from Lord Michael. And if Michael didn't like that, it was too damned bad.

23

GEORGE MADOC had no time to prepare himself for the visit of his employer. Lord Michael Kenyon simply strode into the office without allowing the clerk to announce him.

Madoc would not have recognized the gaunt, hard-eyed newcomer as the fashionable young lord who had hired him four years earlier. Yet when the stranger spoke, the deep voice was unmistakable. "Sorry to walk in on you without warning, Madoc, but I decided to come to Penreith on impulse."

Madoc scrambled to his feet and shook the offered hand. "Lord Michael, what a surprise," he stammered. "I didn't know you were in Britain."

"I was sent back on convalescent leave a couple of months ago. With the war over, I'm selling my commission, so I'll be taking a more active role in managing my business interests." Not waiting to be asked, Lord Michael took a seat. "To begin with, I want to see the account books for the last four years."

"Have you complaints about my management?" Madoc said stiffly, trying to sound indignant rather than worried.

"Not at all—you've produced very respectable profits. I merely want to familiarize myself with the operation again." His lordship gave a faint, humorless smile. "After years in the army, I need to relearn the ways of civilian life."

"Of course." Madoc thought rapidly. "The earlier ledgers are at my house. I'll collect them and send everything to you at once. Are you staying at the inn?"

"No, I'll be at Bryn Manor. I'm on my way there now, but thought I'd stop and see you first."

"You've come back to stay?"

Kenyon shrugged. "I don't know how long I'll be here. I'm in no hurry to leave—Wales is pleasant in the spring."

"Would you like a cup of tea, or maybe something stronger?"

"No need." Lord Michael got to his feet again and began pacing restlessly around the spacious office. "Has Lord Aberdare caused you any trouble?"

"A bit," Madoc said, startled. "How did you know that?"

"I saw him in London and he gave me a lecture on mine safety," Kenyon said dryly. "We disagreed—with some violence."

Madoc snorted. "The earl doesn't seem to realize that mining has always been a dangerous business."

"Exactly what I told him." His lordship turned, his expression harsh. "Has he trespassed on my property?"

"Once. I ordered him to leave and put guards on to watch the mine at night. He hasn't been back."

"Excellent. If Aberdare comes here again, I expect you to take all necessary measures to keep him out."

A faint idea glimmering, Madoc said, "To be honest, even though he was making a nuisance of himself, I had some misgivings about denying the earl entrance because he's a friend of yours."

"Was. That is no longer the case," Lord Michael said in a voice as chilling as the winter wind. "Aberdare has done enough damage. I will not allow him to disrupt my business as well. Inform me immediately if he tries to make trouble again."

"Very good, sir. I'll send the ledgers tomorrow morning."

With a curt nod of his head, Lord Michael left the office, closing the door behind him.

Madoc sank into his chair, then took a flask of whiskey from a desk drawer and poured himself a generous measure with shaking hands. Lord Michael Kenyon had always been disconcertingly shrewd, but now he was downright menacing. Why couldn't the bastard have gotten himself killed on the Peninsula?

Madoc congratulated himself on having the good sense to keep the false ledgers up to date. He'd go over them tonight to make sure, but there shouldn't be anything to alert his bloody lordship. After all, the mine was making a decent profit. Not as much as it should, but there was nothing in the account books to reveal the amount of money Madoc had skimmed off.

Nonetheless, Lord Michael's return was a disaster. When he first bought the mine and had been enthusiastically involved, the man had had a nasty habit of turning up where least expected, and he had been regrettably observant. He might notice a discrepancy between the amount of money allegedly spent on timbers and the actual condition of the mine tunnels. He might also stumble across signs of Madoc's profitable little side venture. That would have to be halted for the time being.

As the whiskey steadied his hands, he leaned back in his chair with a scowl. The son of a Swansea shopkeeper, he'd worked hard for everything he had. For four years he'd managed the mine with as much care as if it were his own, and he'd be damned if he would meekly take orders from an overbred aristocrat.

Unfortunately that overbred aristocrat did own the company. Madoc would have to play the obedient servant for the time being. With luck, Kenyon would soon become bored and leave the valley, and things would return to normal. But if he didn't . . .

Madoc didn't bother to complete the thought, but as he refilled his whiskey glass, he began considering what he might do to improve his position. His first idea had the virtue of simplicity, though only a middling chance of success. If it failed, he would try a more complicated scheme that would require him to enlist other men. That was always a risk; however, if it became necessary, he knew where to find ruffians who would do whatever he ordered and hold their tongues afterward.

As he finished his whiskey, an unpleasant smile spread across his face. Though his first reaction to Lord Michael's return had been anger, the more he thought, the more clearly he saw that this was the chance to get what he deserved. He was cleverer than Aberdare or Michael Kenyon, and he had worked harder. Because those two were weak fools, the time had come for George Madoc to make himself the most powerful man in the valley.

Seeing the very small Olwen Lloyd in pursuit of a nervous penguin, Clare put a restraining hand on the child's arm. "Don't frighten the poor fellow, Olwen. Think how upsetting it must be to have so many strangers visiting him and his friends."

Actually, the penguins were bearing up to the invasion very well. When the bird in question saw that the child wasn't following, it stopped waddling away and began pecking unconcernedly in the grass. Olwen bent over and picked up a white feather that had fallen out, then eyed the penguin with calculation. "I won't hurt him, Miss Morgan," she promised.

Noticing that Olwen was already clutching a fistful of black and white feathers, Clare asked, "Are you taking those home to show your little brother?"

The child said solemnly, "If I get enough feathers, maybe I can make my own penguin."

Clare smiled. "Perhaps a penguin doll, but only a mama and papa penguin can make a real penguin baby."

Olwen sniffed. "We'll see."

As she went off to collect more feathers, Clare laughed, then surveyed the crowd of energetic children with satisfaction. The penguin picnic was a great success.

The day after her class meeting, she had talked to Marged about taking the children to see the creatures. Her friend had pointed out that it was almost May Day, and what better way to celebrate spring than with a picnic?

Organizing the outing had not been difficult, which was fortunate since they only had two days in which to do it. Three Aberdare wagons had been filled with straw and driven to the school. There they had taken on loads of giggling children, along with several mothers whose job it was to prevent overexcited youngsters from tumbling off. Then the wagons had lumbered back to Aberdare, across the estate, and up the track to the penguin pond.

Even the notoriously unreliable weather had cooperated and the day was sunny and warm. Not that rain would have caused a postponement; the Welsh are a hardy race, even the children. Still, blue skies and mild breezes were preferable.

Rather than ride in a wagon, Clare was on Rhonda, the gentle Welsh pony. Nicholas was also on horseback. She had been surprised when he volunteered to come on the expedition, but he had said, a twinkle in his eyes, that he wanted to protect the penguins from being loved to death.

Whatever his reasons, he was enjoying himself as much as the youngsters. As Clare watched him, she realized that he had the ability to live in the moment that was characteristic of the very young. Rarely did that trait survive into adulthood. She envied him, for she could not remember ever feeling the kind of uncomplicated pleasure she saw in his face as he fed the ecstatic penguins from a barrel of fish that he had brought.

She had known a different kind of joy, in his arms. . . .

As he expertly hauled a sodden child from the pond, she turned away, her face burning. Though they were living together like brother and sister, her unruly memory would not let her forget how they had been earlier.

It was better this way, she told herself forcefully. Before her mind could offer rude disagreement, she joined the other women, who were starting to dispense the mutton pies and currant cakes that had been provided by the Aberdare cook. Luckily the food baskets had been well-filled, for the penguins received more than their share of crumbs and cakes.

The sky was clouding over, so when everyone had eaten it was time to go home. Nicholas lifted the smallest children onto the wagons, where most of them curled up in the straw and napped like well-fed puppies. When everyone was accounted for, he signaled the drivers to start and the wagons rumbled from the clearing.

Nicholas and Clare were the last to leave. Because his black stallion was too high-spirited to be safe around curious children, he was riding a placid chestnut hunter. "That was great fun. We'll have to do it again."

She smiled as she started Rhonda after the wagons. "I'm

glad you feel that way, because you don't really have a choice. When the children go home and tell their families about this, social pressure will force you to schedule a fete that the whole village can attend. A Saturday afternoon would be best.''

He laughed. ''Very well. How about Midsummer Day? If the whole village is coming, it would probably be best to have the picnic in a lower clearing and restrict the penguin viewing to smaller groups. I don't want the greedy creatures to decide to give up fish in favor of currant cakes.''

They rode in companionable silence. Ahead, Marged's voice lifted in a song, and soon the air filled with the fluting voices of those children who were still awake. For Clare, it was one of those perfect moments when the cup of life was full to the brim.

They were a third of the way down the mountain when Nicholas said casually, ''Perhaps you haven't heard, but yesterday Michael Kenyon returned to the valley. They say he's staying at Bryn Manor and looking into matters at the mine.''

Clare's head whipped around. ''He's here?''

''So they say.'' He smiled a little. ''Don't look so horrified, Clarissima. Bryn Manor is the only house Michael owns, and it's perfectly natural that he live in it.''

''It's not natural if he's decided to pursue his quarrel with you here.'' Uneasily she scanned the hills around them. ''He's a dangerous man, Nicholas.''

''Yes, but also an intelligent one. He's hardly likely to murder me when he's the first person who would be suspected,'' Nicholas said reasonably. ''My guess is that when he cooled down after our duel, he remembered what I said about the mine and decided to investigate.''

Unconvinced, Clare murmured, ''I hope you're right.''

Ahead of them, there were several seconds of silence as one song ended and another one was chosen. The sky was now thoroughly gray and a rumble of distant thunder sounded. An instant later, thunder cracked again, much closer. Clare's pony shied and Nicholas's hunter reared into the air with a squeal.

Nicholas swore furiously as he fought to retain his seat.

After wrestling his mount under control, he leaned over and slapped Rhonda on the flank. "Get around that bend ahead," he barked. "Now!"

The pony bolted, the hunter right behind. Clare almost fell off, but after a few heart-stopping moments, she managed to regain her balance. They flew down the hill until the track curved around an upthrust of rocks.

Nicholas called, "You can slow down now. We should be safe here."

Clare reined in her mount and glanced over at Nicholas. Before she could ask what had prompted their flight, she saw blood flowing down the hunter's neck. "Merciful heaven, that was a rifle shot, not thunder!" she gasped. "Are you all right?"

"I'm fine. Caesar was creased, but the bullet missed me." He bent his head and examined the chestnut's wound. "Only a graze. There will be a scar, but no real harm was done."

"No harm done?" Clare cried. "You could have been killed!"

"It wouldn't be the first time a poacher accidentally shot someone. We were lucky." He stroked the chestnut's sweat-streaked neck, murmuring unintelligible words of comfort.

Clare felt like hitting him for his obtuseness. "Do you seriously think it's a coincidence that Lord Michael returns to Penreith and a day later someone tries to shoot you?"

Nicholas regarded her calmly. "This *is* a coincidence, Clare. How would Michael know where to find me today?"

"Everyone in the valley knew about today's expeditions," she said with exasperation.

Tacitly conceding the point, Nicholas said, "If Michael wanted to shoot me, he wouldn't do it where a stray bullet might hit a woman or a wagonful of children." He pressed his handkerchief to the chestnut's neck to stop the bleeding. As in London, he added, "Nor would he miss."

Knowing that hysteria would not further her case, Clare said carefully, "Wouldn't it be safer to assume that the rifleman was Lord Michael? Taking a few precautions could save your life."

"What would you have me do?" Nicholas signaled his horse forward in an easy walk. "I could make a good guess about where that shot came from, but whoever fired it is long gone by now. If I went to a magistrate and accused Michael of attempted murder, I'd be thrown out because I haven't a shred of evidence. Even if that bullet was intended for me, I'm not going to spend the rest of my life cowering indoors and avoiding windows for fear of being shot—I'd rather be dead.''

He slanted a glance at her. "I'm not saying this to keep you from worrying, Clare—I honestly believe that was an accidental shot by a poacher. If Michael comes after me, it will be face to face, not like this."

"How long are you going to make excuses for him?" she said helplessly. "Though I admire your loyalty, I don't understand how you can be so sure about what Michael will or will not do. You haven't seen him for years, and he has changed greatly in that time."

Nicholas rode silently for a time. Finally he said, "No human is entirely predictable, but it's possible to know a person well enough to understand the range and limits of what they might do. Michael is one of the handful of people I know that well. It doesn't surprise me that he is angry, bitter, and destructive—the seeds of that have always been in him. Yet at the same time, honor is as much a part of him as his blood and bone. Yes, he is dangerous. But I will never believe that he is vicious."

"Yesterday you visited the hut on the Kenyon estate and found evidence that silver has been processed there," she said. "Tomorrow you and Owen are going down pit to look for proof of illegal mining. If and when you find it, do you think Lord Michael will stand idly by while you destroy his company?"

He regarded her coolly. "I don't particularly want to destroy his business. All he has to do is improve the safety and he can keep it. But if he chooses to be difficult . . ." Nicholas shrugged. "So be it."

Recognizing her own words on his lips, she said dourly, "I'm not asking you to spend the rest of your life cowering indoors, but could you at least keep a watchful eye?"

"Don't worry—while in London, I revised my will. If something happens to me, you'll become administrator of a trust fund with enough money to do what is necessary to keep Penreith prosperous. A nice stipend for you is included, to compensate for your time and effort.'' He gave her an ironic smile. ''You really ought to be praying that Michael does kill me, because you and the village will both benefit by my death.''

This time she did hit him, or at least tried, swinging at his face with a wild, open-palmed slap.

He caught her hand easily and held it immobile in the air as he reined in his horse. As her pony obediently halted, he asked, ''What was that for?''

''How dare you tell me to pray for your death.'' Tears were sliding down her cheeks. ''Some things shouldn't be joked about.''

''Life is a joke, Clarissima.'' He touched his lips to her fingertips, then released her hand. ''And laughter is the only way to survive it. Don't waste your time worrying about me.''

''I have no choice,'' she whispered. ''And you know it.''

His face tightened and he turned away, setting the chestnut into motion again.

As they rode silently down the track, she knew that he understood what he saw in her eyes. But he was no more capable of acknowledging it than she was.

24

NICHOLAS AWOKE to a world shrouded in fog. He smiled with satisfaction; perfect weather for a clandestine visit to the pit.

After dressing in worn miner's clothing, he went downstairs for a quick breakfast. Clare was already up, and she regarded him gravely as she rose to pour coffee. "Be careful, please."

"I will be." He gulped down the scalding coffee, then covered a slab of bread with marmalade. "By this evening, success will be in our hands." Munching on the bread, he left the house and made his way to the stables.

The swirling mists made the journey to Penreith hauntingly beautiful. Nicholas was almost humming with excitement as he picked his way down the familiar road. Odd to think how he had at first resisted Clare's efforts to draw him into the affairs of the village; he felt more alive than he had in years. Now, if only he could draw Clare into an affair, too. . . .

The thought deflated him a little. This damned brother and sister business was increasingly difficult to maintain. There was something irresistibly erotic about Clare's blend of primness and passion, and images of her haunted him day and night. He'd never be able to look at a billiard table calmly again.

His levity faded quickly. The present situation was almost intolerable; the future was worse, for she had every intention of leaving when the three months were up. No doubt there was a solution to his dilemma, but damned if he knew what it was.

It was a relief to arrive at their rendezvous, a clump of

trees not far from the mine. Owen was already waiting, along with an older man with a wooden leg. After Nicholas dismounted, Owen performed the introductions. "This is Jamie Harkin. He'll operate the rope and bucket."

Silently they set out for their destination, Nicholas leading his horse. The usual clamor of the nearby mine was distorted by the mist. They were in the bottom of the valley here and the fog lay thickly, forcing them to go slowly or risk losing their bearings. Nicholas didn't mind. The Bychan shaft was close enough to the main pit that someone might have noticed suspicious activity, but today the fog covered their activities.

When they reached the shaft, Nicholas hitched his horse to the wheel that operated the bucket. He'd picked a strong, tranquil bay gelding for the occasion. Owen checked the pulley and rope, then nodded. "I'll go first. Jamie, we'll signal you by pulling this line, which rings a small bell."

After demonstrating the signal, he lit a candle and stepped into the bucket. Harkin set the gelding into motion and Owen dropped out of sight down the narrow shaft, accompanied by the sound of the creaking wheel. When the bell rang, Jamie reversed the direction of the wheel, raising the bucket to the surface.

Then it was Nicholas's turn. His candle was already lit, so he stepped in and nodded for Jamie to begin. As he descended, he decided that traveling in a bucket was somewhat better than perching on a loop of rope, as he had done on his first trip down pit. However, the Bychan shaft was so narrow that he felt he was falling down a rabbit hole. Air swooshed noisily past and the bucket swayed and banged against the sides of the shaft. Just before he reached bottom, his candle blew out. Luckily Owen was waiting with his own candle glowing.

Nicholas climbed out of the bucket and relit his candle from the other man's. "Which way?"

"Along here." Owen set off to the right. "It's not far, but I'm taking a roundabout route so we're less likely to be seen." It was one of the oldest sections of the mine, and support timbers were few and far between. As he followed the other man, Nicholas remembered his first trip down pit,

and the delightful complications of being trapped in the
flood with Clare. She had made major advances in kissing
that day. . . .

Rigorously he controlled his thoughts. He had already
learned that a mine was no place for wandering attention.

They passed one of the adits that drained water from the
mine, then concealed themselves in an abandoned passage
while half a dozen boys pushed empty corves along the main
tunnel. After the rattle of wheels had faded, they continued.

When they passed a tunnel where the metallic banging of
picks could be heard, Owen said with a frown, "That's
where the lads were taking the corves. Some fellows have
decided to work a new face along there. I don't like it—
there's too much gas in this part of the mine, which is why
it hasn't been worked in years. But there's a good vein down
that tunnel, so there are some willing to take the risk. Particularly since Madoc lowered the payment rates recently,
and a man has to cut more coal in order to make the same
money as before."

A few minutes later, they reached the passage that had
the timber nailed across it. Owen dropped down and crawled
under, Nicholas following. He observed with interest that
the dust on the tunnel floor had been disturbed recently, and
often.

He kept one eye on the walls and saw the stone change
color as they reached the end of the shaft. Owen began
skimming the walls with his palms. "If we can find what I
suspect is here . . ."

Doing the same, Nicholas asked, "What are we looking
for?"

"Now and then we come across air pockets in the stone.
They're called voogs, and can be any size from a walnut to
a large room. It's the sort of place where wire silver might
be found. Wilkins was one of the hewers when this vein was
being worked. My guess is that he broke through into a
sizable voog hole and kept his mouth shut when he realized
what he had found. Since the vein had played out and work
stopped, nobody noticed."

Nicholas's patting hand abruptly disappeared into a gap

around knee level. He knelt for a closer examination and found a shaft about two feet high. "This might be it."

As Owen joined him, Nicholas dropped onto his belly and wriggled into the hole. "Let's see where this goes."

The cavity curved to the left, then opened into a larger space. He raised the candle, then gasped in surprise as the light reflected from a thousand glittering surfaces. The voog was an irregular oblong chamber roughly eight feet square and six feet high. What made it extraordinary were the masses of sparkling crystals that jutted from the walls. Moving cautiously so as not to brain himself on a clump of quartz, he got to his feet and called, "Come on in. This place is incredible."

A moment later Owen joined him. After getting to his feet, he studied his surroundings with awe. "A crystal cave. The ancient ones believed such places were magic, and maybe they were right. I've seen small crystal caves, but never one so large."

Nicholas pointed to a cluster of smashed quartz. "Is this what we're looking for?"

Owen brushed aside shards of broken crystal and brought his candle closer. As he did, light flashed from a brilliant silver splinter. He pointed to a tiny thread of metal at the heart of the shattered area. "This is it," he said triumphantly. "That's a thread that broke off when a clump of wire silver was chiseled out. Let's see how many other broken areas there are."

They began a systematic survey and found almost forty places that had been chiseled. Several showed traces of wire silver that had been left behind. They also found 'another low passage. Owen said, "After Wilkins had taken all the silver here, he probably tapped around, hoping to find a voog next to this one."

Owen led the way through the gap into a smaller voog that also contained quartz formations, though not as many. It must have been newly discovered, for there were few chiseled areas.

As Nicholas raised his candle and studied the ceiling, a shimmer of light caught his eyes. He looked more closely and saw a knot of silver threads wrapped irregularly around a spur of quartz. "Eureka," he said softly. "An intact formation."

Owen came and looked over his shoulder. "Almost too pretty to break, isn't it?"

"Almost, but we should take it back as a sample. When we go to the law, this will help us make our case to a magistrate who has never seen any wire silver."

Owen had brought several small tools, and he began chiseling at the quartz. "Takes time to cut them out," he said conversationally. "Plus most of the formations are probably buried among the crystals and not so easy to find as this one. My guess is that Wilkins has been working here for months, a few hours at a time so nobody would notice what he was up to."

He freed the whole formation, quartz and all, then handed it to Nicholas. "This belongs to you."

The sparkling specimen was about the size of an apple, only much heavier. To protect the delicate crystal and silver spikes, Nicholas wrapped a handkerchief around the sample, then dropped it into one of the deep pockets of his jacket. "When we get out of here, I want to take you into Swansea so we can both swear affidavits before a magistrate. My solicitor is ready to ask for an injunction. By tomorrow, the mine should be closed."

Owen's brow furrowed. "I didn't help you so miners would be put out to starve."

"Of course not," Nicholas assured him. "I'll take all the men on at the same salaries. They can work at the slate quarry and start building the tramway. No one will lose by this."

Owen gave a nod of approval, then dropped down and crawled from the voog. Nicholas followed automatically, his mind busy with plans. They made their way back to the main passage and began retracing their steps.

As they passed the tunnel that led to the new face, they heard men moving toward them. Owen said, "I've always had a knack for detecting gas, and it's heavier now than it was earlier. If it were any worse, we'd have to put out our candles and find our way back in the dark. One of the lads must have noticed and persuaded the others to leave, thank heaven.''

''Either that, or one of the lads sent the others out so he could try the old technique of lying down, igniting the gas, and letting it race over him.''

"It's done sometimes, but I hope they won't try it here.'' In the flickering candlelight, Owen's expression was concerned. "Because of Madoc's skinflint ways, the shoring here is the worst in the pit—most of the timber has been removed and reused in newer tunnels. Wouldn't take much to cause a collapse. There's also a danger of triggering dust explosions.'' He grimaced. "Even dusty air can explode under the right—or wrong—conditions.''

Nicholas told himself that experienced miners would not do anything that was clearly dangerous, but he found himself walking faster. In his experience, every group had its share of fools. He breathed a quiet sigh of relief when they reached the open area where the bucket waited.

An explosion boomed from the passages behind them. As they both froze, a distant man screamed in agony and a hideous rumble thundered through the tunnels. Another explosion shook the earth, this one closer. Face ashen, Owen exclaimed, "God help us, the whole place is coming down!''

Nicholas stared at the waiting bucket, his mind racing as he tried to imagine a way that it could lift both of them at once. It took only an instant to realize that was impossible. He grabbed Owen's arm and shoved him toward the bucket. "You first, you've got a family.''

Owen hesitated for an instant, then jerked away, "No!''

Nicholas started to say that the explosion probably wouldn't reach this far, but he never had a chance. Rather than waste time talking, Owen drew back a work-hardened fist and smashed it into Nicholas's jaw.

The unexpected blow caught him completely unprepared. Though Nicholas didn't quite lose consciousness, his vision faded and his knees began to buckle. He tried to protest as Owen shoved him into the bucket and wrapped his hands around one of the lift lines, but to no avail.

When he was safely stowed, Owen yanked on the signal

rope. The bell rang faintly above and Nicholas began rising toward the surface, swearing furiously at his helplessness. Below him the sounds of disaster were drawing nearer. Wind sucked through the shaft, making the bucket rock wildly against the walls.

As soon as he reached the surface, Nicholas dived out, shouting, "Send this damned thing down again! There's been an explosion and we have to get Owen out!"

Jamie Harkin obeyed instantly. Frantic to speed the process up, Nicholas went to the horse's head and used every bit of Romany magic he knew to persuade the beast to go faster.

But it was already too late. Beneath them the earth roared and clouds of suffocating smoke spewed upward, black against the pale fog.

The force of the blast blew the bucket up the shaft and into the air like a rocket. After ripping loose from its supporting ropes, the bucket crashed to the ground fifty feet away. As Nicholas watched in horror, the shaft collapsed inward, cutting off the billowing of smoke.

The catastrophe everyone had predicted had finally struck the Penreith mine.

25

THE EXPLOSION was heard throughout the valley, and able-bodied men for miles around converged on the mine to help with rescue operations. Since the Bychan shaft was irrevocably closed, Nicholas ran to the main premises and joined the first group of rescuers to go below ground. Though a couple of men recognized him with surprised glances, no one questioned his right to be there. In the pit, he was not an earl but another pair of needed hands.

In a rage of energy, he shifted broken stones for hours, until his hands were raw and his muscles trembled with exhaustion. Once he crawled into a precariously balanced tumble of debris and managed to free a youth who was still alive. More often, the men uncovered were beyond help.

After uncounted hours of labor, a new man coming on took his arm and led him back to the lift, saying that he needed rest or he'd be more harm than help. When Nicholas reached the surface, he found that the fog had burned off and the sun was setting, flooding the valley with a blaze of blood-red light. Somewhere nearby an authoritative voice was barking orders, but he was too tired to pay attention to the words.

As he squinted against the glare, another good Samaritan pointed him toward a table where sandwiches and hot tea were being served. The thought of food turned his stomach, but he accepted a mug of steaming tea that someone pressed into his hand. It was heavily sugared, and the heat and sweetness cleared his head a little. Though he had numerous scrapes and bruises, he felt no pain. He felt nothing at all.

The premises teemed with people. Though some moved purposefully, more were family members hoping for news

of the missing miners. Some wept while others waited fa-
talistically. Nicholas would never forget their faces for as
long as he lived.

He was unsurprised to see Clare. An island of calm
strength in the midst of chaos, she seemed to be in charge
of providing food for the workers. Though she was fifty
yards away, she must have sensed his glance, for she looked
up. For a moment their gazes held as a complex current of
grief and compassion flowed between them. Abruptly he
turned away, knowing that in his present state she might
slide through his barriers. If that happened, he would break
down entirely.

Reluctant but unable to stop himself, he walked over to
the results of carnage—two rows of bodies that had been
laid on the ground and covered with empty coal sacks. He
counted twenty-eight. As he watched, another victim was
laid to rest at the end of a row. The body was badly burned,
but a frantic woman knelt and looked at a ring, then burst
into wails of grief. As the body was covered, an older man
led her away, tears streaming down his own face.

Sickened, he turned away, and found himself face to face
with Marged Morris. At sixteen she had been the prettiest
girl in the valley, and she had grown up to be a lovely
woman. Now her face was haggard and she looked twice
her age. She whispered, "Owen is missing. Is . . . is there
any chance for him?"

Nicholas would rather have died in the mine than have to
answer her question. Yet answer he must, for only he knew
where Owen had been at the time of the explosion. "I don't
think so, Marged," he said painfully. "The Bychan shaft is
blocked and the tunnels beneath it must have collapsed at
the same time." His throat closed. After swallowing hard,
he finished, "The engineer doesn't expect any survivors
from that part of the mine."

For a moment she simply stared at him, and he wondered
if she understood. Then he saw that she was shaking all
over, as if she had a violent chill.

Unable to bear the expression in her eyes, he drew her
into his arms, as much to comfort himself as her. She clung
to him like a drowning woman, sobs racking her slim body.

Anguished tears in his eyes, he said hoarsely, "You and the children will never lack for anything, Marged. I swear it." Even as he spoke, he knew how paltry a substitute money would be for a missing husband and father.

Face bleak, Clare was approaching. He sent her a glance of desperate appeal over Marged's head. Understanding, she went to her friend and said gently, "If there is good news, you'll be notified immediately. But now I'll take you home. The children need you."

Slowly Marged straightened and dragged the back of her hand across her eyes. "Of course, I must go to the children. And I must t-tell Owen's mother," she said dully. For a moment rage flashed across her face. "I'll never let my sons work here. Never!" With Clare holding her arm, she turned and walked away.

Nicholas watched the two women until they disappeared into the milling crowd. It was almost dark and torches were being lit. The flickering light made the mine premises look like a lurid medieval painting of hell.

Heart like lead, he crossed to the main shaft and joined a group of other men who were returning to the pit after a break. Covered with black coal dust, they were almost indistinguishable from each other. Nicholas knew he must look the same.

As he waited to descend, a familiar voice snapped, "What the devil are you doing here, Aberdare? Get off my property!"

Nicholas turned and saw Michael Kenyon bearing down on him. Vaguely he realized that it had been Michael's voice he had heard giving orders, organizing the rescue work with the efficiency and coolness he had learned under fire.

"Save your tantrums until this is over," Nicholas said wearily. "Until then, you need all the help you can get."

When the other man's mouth opened for a retort, Nicholas forestalled him with a raised hand. "Michael—shut the hell up."

Spots of angry color showed on Michael's cheeks, but he argued no more. Lips compressed to a thin line, he pivoted and walked away.

And Nicholas returned to the mine.

* * *

After taking Marged home, Clare didn't see Nicholas again until two days after the explosion. That was when Lewis the Cart, who did most of the delivery work around Penrcith, delivered the unconscious earl. When Rhys Williams summoned Clare outside, she was shocked to see Nicholas's condition. Not only was he ragged and filthy, but streaks of blood marked his hands and clothing.

Seeing her concern, Lewis said reassuringly, "He's not hurt, Miss Morgan, only fagged out." He gave an approving nod. "The earl may be a Gypsy, but he's a right 'un, he is. Not afraid to get his hands dirty. Didn't sleep for two days, they say, but mortal flesh has to rest eventually."

Williams and a footman lifted Nicholas from the straw-filled cart. Seeing Clare's expression, the butler said, "Don't worry, miss. We'll take good care of him."

Knowing she would only be in the way, she turned back to the carter. "Do they have final casualty figures, Mr. Lewis?"

He grimaced. "Thirty-two dead, dozens injured, five still missing. Hardly a family in the village that hasn't been affected. They don't expect to find anyone else alive. A crew will keep looking for bodies, but tomorrow regular work will start again in the parts of the pit that weren't affected."

Life had to go on, Clare supposed sourly; no doubt Madoc and Lord Michael didn't want to lose any more of their precious profits by delaying. "Thank you for bringing Lord Aberdare home." She hesitated, wondering whether he was expecting a more tangible reward.

Guessing her thoughts, Lewis said, "No need, Miss Morgan. Lord Michael Kenyon took care of me. He's another tough one, he is, but fair. Went down pit himself several times." His voice dropped confidentially. "The men are hoping he'll manage the mine himself now. George Madoc would never have spent so much time on rescue work."

So perhaps Lord Michael did have some redeeming qualities. After bidding the carter farewell, Clare went indoors and hovered indecisively in the hall, wondering what to do. She had also worked long hours since the explosion. Besides making the arrangements to feed the rescue workers and performing basic nursing chores, she had gone to the homes of bereaved friends to offer both comfort and practical aid.

Exhaustion had overcome her earlier in the day. After three hours of sleep, she had been preparing to return to the village, but from what Mr. Lewis said, the immediate crisis was over. Though there were certainly things she could do, her help was no longer vital, especially since she was so groggy that she couldn't think straight.

With a sigh, she climbed the stairs and went back to bed.

When Clare woke again, it was dark. Though she felt drained, her mind was clear as she faced the painful knowledge that she would never see Owen again. Her own sense of loss increased the heartache she felt for Marged and the children.

The night echoed her mood, for a storm was rising, the wind whistling around the house and rattling branches against the window. Music blended so subtly with the wind and her sorrow that it took time for her to recognize that the elegiac tune wasn't in her head. It was like her first night at Aberdare, but this time she knew the source. Nicholas had woken from his sleep and was playing a dirge for the dead.

Unable to bear her aloneness, she got up, put on her slippers, and splashed cold water on her face. She still wore her crumpled day gown, for she had not undressed earlier. Rather than put her hair up again, she tied it back with a ribbon and went in search of Nicholas. It was very late, and she guessed that everyone else in the household was long asleep.

She found him in the dimly lit library, softly singing an ancient lament. Bathed and dressed in his usual black and white, he looked almost normal, except for a bruise on his jaw and the blood his raw fingers left on the wire strings of the harp. He glanced up when she entered the room, his eyes opaque. Then he bent to his instrument again. Though the words and tune were Welsh, a plangent Gypsy sorrow wound through the music.

Wordlessly she crossed the room and added more coal to the fire. Then she sat in a wing chair and rested her head against the back, letting the music flow through her. It helped to be in the same room with him.

The last chord filled the room, dissolved and died. In the silence that followed, a distant crack of thunder sounded. As if that was a signal, Nicholas said in a strained voice, "I should have done more. You told me how dangerous the mine was, but I didn't take your warnings seriously. To me, the whole business was only another game."

Surprised by his self-reproach, she said, "You talked to Lord Michael and you were doing your best to break the lease. What else could you have done without legal authority?"

"I could have done more." He set down the harp and rose to his feet, then began prowling about the shadowed room. "It's my fault Owen is dead."

"Don't blame yourself," she said softly. "Everyone who worked at his coal face died."

"But Owen wasn't at that face, he was with me. He should be alive now." Stopping by a window, Nicholas opened the curtains and lifted the sash, then inhaled deeply, as if trying to draw the storm into himself. "We were at the foot of the Bychan shaft, ready to leave, when the first explosion went off and the tunnels began collapsing. The bucket could only hold one man."

His fingers tightened on the sill. "Because of his family, I told him to go first. Rather than argue, he walloped me in the jaw and shoved me into the bucket. Another minute or two and he could have escaped, but there wasn't enough time. Not enough time . . ." As his voice trailed away, the first raindrops spattered against the glass and sprayed through the open window.

He swung around, his expression showing the same wild fury she had seen when he had slashed his wife's portrait. But this was worse, for his rage was for himself. "If my life was worth a hundred gold guineas, Owen's was beyond price," he said savagely. "Owen knew how to build, how to sing, how to laugh. He loved and was loved. *Goddamn it, why him and not me?*"

Her nails bit into the arms of her chair. In his position, she would feel exactly the same; death would be easier than living at the cost of a friend's life. Wanting to ease his torment, she said, "If he sacrificed himself for you, it was because of the power you have to make changes. Because of you, many lives might be spared in the future."

"That's not good enough!" With sudden, shocking violence, Nicholas scooped up his harp and hurled it across the room with all his strength. The graceful instrument crashed into the wall with a grotesque shriek of wounded strings, then fell to the floor in pieces, leaving a note of painful dissonance quivering in the air. Lightning crackled through the night sky, illuminating Nicholas and the broken harp with eerie brilliance.

As thunder echoed across the valley, she cried, "Stop blaming yourself! You're not God!"

"From what I can see, even God isn't God," he said bitterly. "I've read the book of Job, and the Deity does not show to advantage."

Clare knew that she should reprove him for sacrilege, but she couldn't; it was hard to believe in divine justice when good people had died tragically.

Nicholas's restless pacing brought him to the fireplace. Bracing his hands on the mantel, he stared into the embers. "If I had acted sooner—if I had spent as much time thinking about men's lives as I did about getting you into bed—this wouldn't have happened. Owen would be alive, and the others as well." He drew a shuddering breath. "Two of the victims were children no older than Huw Wilkins."

"If you must blame someone, Madoc is the obvious choice. Or Lord Michael, who had the authority but gave it away to a greedy fool."

Unpersuaded, he said, "The game is over, Clare." He turned to her, his face implacable. "I'm releasing you from our bargain. Go home to Penreith. I'll fulfill my end of the agreement and do everything you wanted for the valley. But I'll do it alone, without injuring you any more than I have already."

She stared at him, face paling, unable to believe that he would dismiss her so arbitrarily.

His voice rose. "You heard me—get out! You don't ever have to endure my selfish, profane company again."

To ease his agonizing guilt, he needed to punish himself, she realized. And he was going to do it by sending her away at the very moment when he needed her most.

Numb to the point of paralysis, she stared at him helplessly. The thunderstorm that was sweeping across the valley was matched by the emotional storm that raged in this quiet, dim library. And she was equally powerless before both tempests.

Lightning flashed again, and in that instant of soul-piercing light she experienced an inward wrenching, a splintering of fears and doubts. Yet the result was not fragmentation, but breathtaking wholeness.

All of her life she had yearned for spiritual connection, and for human love. Lacking both, she had despised herself for being too weak and small-souled to deserve either.

Yet between one heartbeat and the next, her world changed, like the tumbling patterns of a kaleidoscope. Though she had never before felt the divine love or inner guidance that were the bedrock of her religion, she now knew absolute certainty. She loved Nicholas; she always had. That soul-searing truth brought her entire life into focus.

And she knew in the marrow of her bones that she must stay.

She closed the distance between them and took his battered hands between hers. "You said from the beginning that only willing women interested you, Nicholas." She kissed his bloody fingertips, then drew their clasped hands to her heart. Looking up into his face, she said softly, "I'm willing now."

As thunder rumbled again, his body went rigid. "Pity is a poor excuse for willingness, Clare."

"I'm not offering pity." Slowly, holding his gaze with hers, she released him and began unbuttoning the throat of his shirt. When it was loose, she slid her hands under the fabric and gently massaged the knotted muscles of his shoulders. "I'm offering friendship."

He closed his eyes and drew a shuddering breath. "I should refuse, but I can't." He opened his eyes again, his voice dropping to a whisper. "God help me, I can't."

She stood on her toes and pressed her lips to his, wanting to take his pain into herself and transform it with the force of her love. This time there would be no turning back.

With a groan, he pulled her against him so tightly she could scarcely breathe. His hands worked with raw desperation, as if he could not get enough of her.

Sinking to his knees, he buried his face between her breasts, his ragged breath warm against her. She stroked the silky tangle of his hair as he spread his hands and drew them the length of her body, shaping the curves of her hips and thighs. Then he tugged her down so that she was knee to knee with him on the plush Oriental carpet, the fire warming her left side. Outdoors, the rain increased its force, battering the windows as if seeking to destroy their private refuge.

His mouth met hers, devouring, intoxicating, as if he was trying to absorb her very essence into himself. His deft fingers worked behind her back to unfasten the tape and button that secured her dress. He moved his hands between them and undid the drawstring of her shift, then dragged both garments down so he could cup her bare breasts.

She sucked her breath in sharply as the rasp of his palms sent tendrils of flame spiraling through her. The weeks of teasing kisses and sensual games had sensitized her, laying the foundation for this firestorm of passion. Needing to feel his flesh against hers, she dragged his shirttails from his breeches and slid her hands beneath the fine linen. Her fingers skimmed over his chest, brushing across the dark hair that patterned his torso. When she touched his nipple, inspiration struck. She raised his shirt, then leaned forward and kissed the soft nub until it hardened against her tongue.

He gasped, his head thrown back and the pulse beating visibly in his throat. Transferring her attention to the other nipple, she delicately teased it with her teeth.

He made a choked sound deep in his throat, then yanked the shirt over his head and tossed it aside. The reddish glow of the coal fire danced across the contours of his muscular torso as he reached for her and drew her full-length onto the carpet.

A maelstrom of sensations flooded her mind. His kiss,

demanding and possessive; the pressure of hard muscles against her sensitive nipples; the prickle of carpet fibers and the dry heat of the fire. Then, searingly, his hungry mouth on her naked breast. Her frantic fingers dug into his shoulders. She wanted to feel his heat and strength everywhere at once, most of all in the throbbing place deep inside her.

He swept her skirts up to her belly, then began stroking her inner thighs, his sure hand moved higher and higher until he touched the moist, hidden folds of flesh. She gave a little cry of shock at the sensations that blazed through her, white heat that matched the lightning bolts that flared across the sky.

Her body took on a life of its own, rubbing involuntarily against his hand. She almost wept when he paused. There was a rasp of fabric, the rattle of a falling button that was ripped off by his rough impatience.

She tensed when he moved over her, expecting pain and steeling herself not to show it. But this time there was only an instant of discomfort, followed by a smooth, powerful penetration that filled her heart as surely as her body.

Bracing his hands on either side of her head, he thrust fiercely into her, the roll of his hips setting a rhythm that she recognized, though she had never known it before. This was passion without subtlety: a primal, desperate need for union that swept them both into the heart of the storm.

The tempest lashed the house with full force and thunder was everywhere, around her, within her, transforming her with its irresistible power. As she convulsed around him, she no longer knew where she ended and he began, for they were one, stronger together than either could ever be alone.

He drove forward one last time, crying out as he shuddered deep inside her. Lightning crackled directly over the house, filling the library with shimmering blue-white light and shaking the windows with thunder. Another bolt flashed again, limning the planes of his face with unearthly light.

He was unbearably, shatteringly beautiful, and whether he was a demon earl or fallen angel, prince of light or prince of darkness, she neither knew or cared. All that mattered was that she loved him, and this sharing of flesh and spirit was the truest act she had ever done.

26

PASSION SATED, they lay quietly in each other's arms before the fire. The worst of the storm passed and thunder was only a distant rumble far down the valley. Clare stroked Nicholas's head where it rested on her breast. She had never felt happier, or more complete, in her life.

Strange that profane love had healed her spiritual weaknesses. Or perhaps it wasn't strange at all. Feeling unloved by her earthly father, her needy spirit had been unable to accept divine love; she had been hollow inside.

Admitting her love for Nicholas had opened the gates to her heart. She had always known, in her mind, that her father loved her the best he knew how. It had been her life's great sorrow that what she needed was different from what he was able to give. Now, finally, she was able to accept her father as he had been, and to love him without resentment.

She felt reborn, alive as never before in her life. By attempting to transform Nicholas's pain, she had also transformed herself. She wanted to laugh aloud for the sheer joy of it.

She also wondered, without anxiety, what would happen next. The fact that she loved him did not mean that he would ever love her back. Her stroking hand stilled. She would miss him dreadfully when their singular relationship ended. But she would survive, for her heart was finally whole.

The fire was almost dead and a cold draft gusted through the open window. Even Nicholas was not enough to keep her warm, and she began to shiver. With a soft exhalation, he pushed himself to a sitting position and looked down at her. Though his face was somber and rather distant, the wild anguish was gone.

She opened her mouth to speak, but he touched a finger to her lips, hushing her. After tugging her garments loosely into place, he got to his feet and adjusted his own clothing.

With swift, economical movements, he closed the window and the draperies, turned out the single guttering lamp, and collected his crumpled shirt. Then he knelt and scooped her into his arms and carried her from the library, leaving no trace of what had happened between them.

Her head pillowed drowsily on his shoulder, she was content to let him take her to her room. After laying her on her bed, he stripped off her clothing before tucking her under the covers. Though modesty was foolish after what had just passed between them, she was glad they were in near-total darkness.

She expected him to leave, but to her surprise she heard the sounds of the key turning in the lock and clothing being removed. Then he joined her in the bed and pulled her into his arms. She found that, while she might be modest about being looked at, she was quite shameless about twining her bare body around his.

Conscience clear and spirit at peace, she slept.

Clare woke at the sound of someone wrestling with the doorknob. It was early morning, time for Polly to bring in her tea, and for a moment she couldn't understand why the door was locked. Then memories of the night before flooded her mind.

Polly, clever girl, gave up and went away. Thank heaven she wasn't local. She was also discreet; if she guessed that Clare had not slept alone, she would hold her tongue.

Clare reached out an arm and discovered that she was alone in the bed. But if Nicholas had left, why was the door still locked? She sat up and looked around.

He stood by the window, arms folded across his chest as he gazed into the valley. He was gloriously naked, his skin glowing like warm bronze in the pale dawn light.

Hearing her movements, he turned his head and their glances met. He wore an expression she had never seen before: not the despairing guilt of the night before, nor the wild fury he had sometimes displayed. Certainly not the playful openness she loved. Instead he looked—determined? Resigned? He seemed almost a stranger, and one who was a little frightening.

Hesitantly she asked, "How do you feel this morning?"

He shrugged. "No less guilty, but much less crazed. I'll survive." His gaze drifted over her. "You seem remarkably calm for a ruined preacher's daughter."

Realizing that, except for her long hair, she was as bare as a baby, she quickly pulled the sheet over her breasts.

"It's a bit late for modesty."

Defiantly she let the sheet drop to her waist and tossed her hair back over her shoulders.

Some of his composure dropped away and his breathing quickened. With visible effort, he raised his eyes to her face. "Obviously we'll have to get married, and the sooner the better. I'll send to London for a special license today."

Calm vanished and her mouth dropped open. "Marriage? What on earth are you talking about?"

"I should think it would be obvious," he replied coolly. "Legal matrimony. Husband and wife. Till death us do part."

Though her spirit might be reborn, her mind was still capable of utter confusion. "W-what?" she stammered. "You swore that you would never take another wife. Why on earth would you want to marry me?"

"For a very basic reason—you might be carrying my child."

Ruthlessly she suppressed the spurt of joy the thought gave her. "You told me once that there are ways to prevent that."

"There are, but I wasn't thinking about them last night," he said dryly.

"I suppose it's possible I might have conceived," she admitted, "but the odds are that I didn't. Surely it would be wiser to wait and see rather than do something rash that you'll soon regret."

"It might be weeks before you would know for sure." His brows rose. "Do you want to have a 'seven month baby,' with everyone in Penreith knowing that you had to get married? As a virgin, your conscience was clear, which gave you the strength to face the condemnation of those who believed the worst. That is no longer true—I've made you vulnerable, and there is only one way I can remedy that.''

She fell silent. Though she was not ashamed of solacing him with her body, she loathed the idea of gossips condemning her act of love as cheap and wicked. Finally she asked, ''Why were you so set against marriage?''

His lips tightened and he looked out the window so that she saw only his dark profile. ''The great passion of the old earl's life was the succession to Aberdare. Refusing to sire a legitimate heir was my way of thwarting him. Since he is beyond caring whether there will be a sixth Earl of Aberdare, it was a childish kind of revenge, but the only one within my power.''

He turned toward her again. Since he was silhouetted against the morning sun, she could not read his expression. ''My responsibility to you must supercede my meaningless revenge against my grandfather. Though my conscience wasn't troubled at the prospect of ruining your reputation and taking your virginity, accidentally impregnating you would be unacceptable. Hence, marriage.''

There was nothing on earth she wanted more than to be Nicholas's wife, but before this morning, the idea had been literally unthinkable. She wondered if his decision to marry her was a way of expiating the guilt he felt over Owen's death. ''Ever since we struck our bargain, you've been doing your best to seduce me,'' she said. ''I'm having trouble understanding how your success could produce such a sudden change of heart.''

His glance was satirical. ''I didn't seduce you—quite the contrary.''

Her face burned. ''I wasn't trying to trap you into marriage.''

''I know that, Clare,'' he said quietly. ''You gave me a great gift, from the most generous of motives. But accepting it imposed certain obligations, and I always honor my obligations.''

She suppressed an involuntary shiver. "That's a cold basis for marriage."

"Oh, it's not the only one." A familiar light gleamed in his eyes, warming his icy detachment. "For example, now that I've finally had my wicked way with you, I want to do it again. Often."

As she hesitated, he said, "I see you need persuasion."

In two long strides, he was on the bed. Before she had time to catch her breath, she was flat on her back and he was kissing her, one hand twined in her hair and the other caressing her breast.

Her husky gasp must have sounded like surrender, for he lifted his head and murmured, "Do you have any special requests for the wedding? A small one would be best, I think, but the thing should be done properly."

She struggled for common sense, not easy when he was doing such marvelous things to her eager body. "I . . . I haven't said that I'll marry you."

His face was scant inches from hers, and she saw his eyes grow even blacker. "Why not?" he demanded, harshness in his voice. "You don't seem to dislike my lovemaking. Of course, there are women who will sleep with men that they would never receive socially."

"Don't be ridiculous," she said acerbically. "You've gotten it backwards. Earls don't marry village schoolmistresses."

"Just as the sons of earls don't marry Gypsy girls? Your father was a vicar, an educated son of the gentry, and your mother of respectable yeoman stock. There are many who would think those better bloodlines than mine." His expression lightened. "You really must marry me, Clare. You owe it to our unborn child to give it a name."

A choke of laughter escaped her. "I'm by no means convinced of the existence of this unborn child."

"You should be." He skimmed his palm lightly down her belly, then began toying with the soft curls between her thighs. "We're about to double the chances of its conception."

"Stop it!" She slapped away his hand. "I can't think when you're doing that."

Undeterred, he replaced his hand and continued what he had been doing. "It doesn't take much thought to say yes."

She grabbed his hand and immobilized it. Dead serious, she said, "I can accept the fact that you would be marrying me without love, but not that you might come to hate me for trapping you in a marriage that you didn't want."

"I could never hate you, Clare," he said with equal seriousness. "I am going into this with my eyes open—I won't punish you for a situation that was of my creation."

She hesitated, hating the necessity of her next question. "There's something else."

He raised his brows encouragingly.

Her gaze slid away from his. "It has been said that you were not faithful to your first wife. Is that true?"

His face shuttered. "It is."

"I understand that aristocrats feel differently about such things, but I am no aristocrat," she said with difficulty. "I . . . I couldn't bear it if you had other women."

The silence stretched. His face was unfathomable, and when he finally spoke it was in a voice of cool neutrality. "I'll propose another bargain. I shall be faithful to you as long as you are faithful to me. But if you should ever visit another man's bed, I promise you that I shall also look elsewhere."

Dizzying relief flooded through her. "If you agree to that bargain, you are destined to have a long, dull life, my lord, for I will never turn to another man."

"Dull? With you? I don't think so." His expression eased. "Does this mean you accept my proposal?"

She closed her eyes, wanting to clear her mind so that she could hear her inner voice. Instantly a tide of certainty began rising in her, as it had the night before. This was right—what she was born to do. Since she did not think he would welcome an outright declaration of love, she opened her eyes and contented herself with saying, "Yes, Nicholas. With all my heart and soul."

He rolled from the bed, went to her desk, and rummaged in the drawer. When he came back, she saw that he was carrying her penknife. As she watched in mystification, he raised his hand and pierced his wrist with the sharp, narrow blade. A deep crimson drop formed on his dark skin, quickly followed by another. Then he lifted her hand.

Guessing what was coming, she managed not to flinch when he made a similar incision on her wrist. Holding his wrist to hers so that the blood flowed together, he said quietly, "Blood to blood. The deed is done, wife."

She stared at their joined wrists, feeling a deep, primal sense of connection. Blood to blood, till death did them part. "This is a Romany rite?"

"One of many. The Rom are a varied lot." He smiled. "Typically the wedding feast ends with a mock abduction. It's considered bad form for the bride to look too willing to leave her family. Since you were coerced into coming to Aberdare, we can count that as the abduction." He raised her wrist to his mouth and licked the blood away, his tongue soothing the sting of the cut. "Shall we proceed with the consummation?"

She lifted her arms in welcome, her waist-length hair spilling around her in a provocative mantle. "With great delight, husband."

As he kissed her, he thought fleetingly of how unexpected life was. Three days ago the mine had been running normally, Owen Morris had been alive, and marriage had been out of the question. Now everything had changed, drawing a sharp line between Nicholas's past and a future he had never imagined. For better and worse, he had made a binding commitment to the woman in his arms. His life of restless freedom had been supplanted by the prospect of a more conventional existence of family and home. Yet as he tasted the rich depths of Clare's mouth, it was hard to regret his new course.

This time he would not be swift and heedless, as he had been the night before. Desperately needing her warmth and understanding, he had taken her with violent urgency. Thank God she had no longer been technically a virgin, or he would have hurt her badly. She would have accepted the pain philosophically, but he would have hated himself after his wild despair had passed. This time he would use all the skill at his command to show her what passion could be.

She was bewitchingly lovely, not with the lushness that

too easily became excess, but with a slim roundness that he found irresistible. As he bore her back against the pillows, he whispered, "Lie back and enjoy, Clarissima. Last night was a synopsis. Now it's time for the unabridged version."

Obediently she relaxed, her long hair swirling over the pillow in entrancing patterns. He kissed every luscious curve and hollow until she sighed with astonished pleasure. When she was moist and ready, he positioned himself between her legs so that his hard arousal lay on the tiny nub that was the center of female sensation. He doubted that she knew it existed, but before he was done today, she would.

As he suckled her breast, his heated flesh slid voluptuously against her. The sensual friction caused her eyes to fly open, dazed and deeply blue. "N . . . now?" she quavered.

"Not yet." While continuing to woo her with hands and lips and tongue, he began rocking his hips with blatant carnality. She whimpered, a raspy, drawn-out sound that echoed the rhythm of his movements. Then she squirmed against him, instinctively seeking. He gasped, the hot rush of his breath flowing around her taut nipple.

Bracing himself on his arms, he began making longer strokes, caressing her with the full length of his shaft, from base to head and back again. Her hands clamped on his arms, the nails biting deep, and her mouth opened to draw great, gusty pants of air. He brought her to the brink of culmination and tantalizingly held her there until her torso filmed with moisture and her head twisted back and forth frantically.

He intended to ease the pace a little, but in the white heat of pleasure he pulled back so far that his position shifted. Suddenly he was pressing into yielding, seductive flesh. He held still, muscles shaking, trying to make himself retreat, but she pressed her pelvis upward and he was lost. When he slipped into her body, it clasped him like hot, wet silk.

At first he moved slowly, until he was sure how deeply her body would receive him. Then he began thrusting with a steadily escalating tempo, withdrawing painfully far before surging back with exquisite gladness.

When she cried out, he instantly enfolded her, burying

his face in the curve of her shoulder. Her hands bit into his hips as turbulence rocked her, and he groaned, his ecstasy flowing seamlessly from hers. The hidden depths of her body were the sweetest he had ever known.

They lay together in a tangle of sweaty limbs and intimate scents, both of them trembling with reaction. When breathing had returned to a semblance of normal, she murmured, "I think I understand why organized religion disapproves of sexual congress. This could make someone forget about God, for it is hard to imagine that heaven can offer anything more."

He laughed a little. "That sounds like blasphemy."

"Very likely it is." Her fingers curved around the nape of his neck. "I'm beginning to understand why you were so keen on seduction. Passion is rather wonderful, isn't it?"

"Yes—though not always this wonderful." His hand rested on the gentle swell of her belly and he wondered if a new life was blossoming inside. "The first time you came to Aberdare, I knew that you would make an extraordinarily gifted bedmate."

It was her turn to laugh. "I thought you were mostly interested in getting rid of me."

"That too," he agreed.

She lifted his arm and kissed the small cut that he had made with the penknife. "Even though the legal ceremony is still to come, I feel very married."

"Good, because I have every intention of joining you every night from now on." Remembering the real world, he sat up with a sigh. "However, for the sake of the tattered remnants of your reputation, I'll come and go discreetly. It's still early enough that we probably haven't attracted the notice of anyone beyond my valet and your maid, and silence is part of their business."

She gave him a rueful smile. "Thank you. No doubt it's feeble of me to care what others think, but I do."

"Since we're going to be living in the valley for the rest of our lives, discretion is not out of place." He bent and kissed her, then straightened, resisting the urge to climb back in the bed. "I'll send a note to Lucien this morning and ask him to go to Doctor's Commons for a special license. He's rather good at arranging such things. We should be able to have the ceremony in about a week.''

She nodded, her gaze following Nicholas as he pulled on his clothing and slipped from the room. Everything had been so sudden that she still didn't quite believe it. Yet though he had offered marriage reluctantly, he did not seem unhappy. She vowed to do everything in her power to keep him from regret.

Since the earthly part of her life was prospering, Clare decided that it was time to attend to the spiritual. She got out of bed and pulled on a robe, then knelt in the sunshine that streamed through the window. Her hands loosely clasped in her lap, she cleared her mind.

Like a stream of living fire, transcendent faith filled her heart. This was the divine peace and joy her father had known daily, and dedicated his life to sharing. As her meditation deepened, she felt a brief, fragile sense of her father's presence. With wonder, she understood that he had known of her weakness and prayed for her salvation. Now he had come to share in her awakening.

Her father's presence faded after a few minutes. She smiled a little. Even now, on the other side, he was busy helping those less fortunate, but she no longer resented that.

Tears of awe and humility stung her eyes, and she gave a prayer of thanks. Now that the light had been kindled within her, she knew that it would never be extinguished.

And it was love that had shown her the way.

27

CLARE WAS so deep in her meditation that it was a shock to rise and discover that Polly had come and left a pot of tea and a steaming pitcher of water. Remembering how much there was to be done, she washed and dressed quickly, then went downstairs for breakfast. First, however, she made a detour to the library.

Resisting the temptation to stare at the carpet where they had made love, she knelt by the wreckage of Nicholas's harp. She was studying it when he entered the library himself.

Glancing up, she said hesitantly, "Many of the pegs snapped, and the bow has separated from the box, but it looks as if the pieces can be joined again."

He went down on one knee and lifted the pieces. "You're right," he said when he had finished his own examination. "There is no damage that can't be repaired." He stroked the satiny willow-wood. "I'm glad. Tam was a great artist—it was sacrilege to try to destroy his work."

"Luckily the harp is very solidly made. It put a sizable dent in the wall." She sat back on her heels. "Last night, when you hurled it away, I felt as if you were also trying to destroy the music in you. I hope you weren't successful." She ended with a faint, questioning lilt.

"I suppose that was my intent, though I wasn't thinking that clearly." He plucked one string that was still taut, and a melancholy note sounded. "Perhaps I should write a song about the mine explosion. Commemorating the honored dead is an ancient Celtic tradition."

She laid her hand over his. "Please do that, and sing it

at the next local eisteddfod. It would mean a great deal to everyone in the valley.''

His face tightened, and she guessed that he was thinking that it would have meant more if he had been able to effect changes at the mine earlier. Though his grief and guilt were under control this morning, they had not gone away. She guessed that he would never be entirely free of them.

The stillness was broken when Williams entered, a panting young boy at his side. Recognizing Trevor Morris, Marged's oldest, Clare got to her feet. ''Does your mother need me, Trevor?'' she asked. ''I was about to go down to the village.''

He shook his head. ''No, Miss Morgan, it's wonderful news. My da is alive! They found him this morning. Mama sent me tell you as soon as they brought him home.''

Clare's heartfelt, ''Thank God,'' was drowned by Nicholas's exuberant, ''Hallellujah!''

It seemed almost too good to be true, but the proof was in Trevor's shining face. Nicholas's face reflected the same joy, and she knew that this news would heal him as nothing else.

Nicholas said, ''Williams, order the curricle. Trevor can tell us the story while we ride into the village.''

Within five minutes, they were racing toward Penreith at a speed that would have frightened Clare if the driver had been anyone less skillful than Nicholas. Squeezed between them, Trevor explained, ''The explosion blew Da into one of the older tunnels and broke his leg. He was unconscious for a long time. When he woke up, he remembered he was near one of the adits.''

Sparing a quick glance from the road, Nicholas said, ''One of the old drainage tunnels?''

The boy nodded. ''He had to dig his way through a roof collapse to reach it. When he got to the adit, he found that the explosion had dropped the water level, so there was air. He crawled out last night, and this morning a shepherd found him.''

''A miracle,'' Clare said quietly.

''That's what my mother says.''

There was silence for a time. Then Nicholas asked, "How will the families of the men who died manage?"

"There are two friendly societies," Clare replied. "People put in a bit each week, so there's money to help those who fall on hard times."

"So many deaths will put a strain on the societies," he said. "Do you think that anyone's stubborn Welsh pride would be offended if I made contributions?"

"I'm sure no one will object."

When they reached the Morrises' cottage, Nicholas asked Trevor to walk the curricle back and forth to cool the horses, a task the boy accepted with alacrity.

The cottage door was opened by Marged. The circles under her eyes were insignificant next to the joy of her smile. Clare went straight into her friend's arms and they had a good cry together. When they were coherent again, they all went inside, where Marged insisted on serving them tea and currant buns.

Voice low so as not to wake Owen, Marged repeated what Trevor had said. "And there's more good news," she added. "Two more men were found alive in an air pocket." She gave the names; Clare had taught children of both men.

Marged continued, "They say there are going to be changes at the pit. Apparently Lord Michael Kenyon wasn't satisfied with what he's found, and he's taking over direct management."

Nicholas's gaze sharpened. "What about Madoc?"

Marged smiled with deep satisfaction. "His lordship hasn't said a word against Madoc in public, but that doesn't disguise the fact that for all practical purposes, Madoc has become an overseer, only there to carry out the owner's orders. They say Madoc's furious, but he daren't complain or he might lose his fancy salary and house."

After swallowing a bite of currant bun, she said, "His lordship has put all the men to improving the shoring in the shafts that survived. They say he's also ordering a new Watts steam pump and a winding engine, so that the men won't have to ride up and down on that dreadful rope like a bunch of grapes."

"Thank heaven!" Clare said fervently. "It sounds as if

everything necessary will be done. With luck, the mine will never have such a disaster again.''

''Michael seems to be picking up where he left off four years ago,'' Nicholas agreed. Looking at his hostess, he said, ''Marged, if Owen is awake, might I talk to him?''

''I'll go see.'' She went to check on her husband, then returned and said, ''He's awake, and he'd like to see you.''

''I suppose it would be too much for him to see me as well,'' Clare said. ''Marged, will you join me in offering a prayer of thanks?''

Marged cocked her head curiously. ''I never thought you resembled your father, but for a moment, you looked just like him. Thank you for reminding me that it's time for a prayer. I've been at sixes and sevens ever since they brought Owen home.''

As the two women knelt together, Nicholas went upstairs. Owen and Marged shared a tiny room at the front of the house, not much larger than the double bed that dominated the space. Owen was pale and his left leg was splinted, but his expression was peaceful. Wordlessly he raised his hand.

Nicholas clasped it hard and sank onto his knees by the bed. ''Thank God you're all right,'' he said intensely. ''It's hard to believe that you survived such a blast, then three days of being trapped below ground.''

''I guess it wasn't my time,'' Owen said, his voice a little hoarse. ''A miracle I wasn't killed outright, and another miracle that I was close enough to the adit to work my way out.''

''You deserve some of the credit as well,'' Nicholas said. ''Finding your way out of a maze of tunnels, in total darkness, with a broken leg, was an amazing feat.''

''I was highly motivated.''

Nicholas studied the other man's face. ''Why did you make me go first? You have a family and are needed far more than I am.''

Owen smiled faintly. ''I knew that if I died, I'd go straight to heaven, but I had serious doubts about you.''

For a moment Nicholas wondered if the other man was joking. When he realized that Owen was perfectly serious, Nicholas began to laugh helplessly, resting his head against the oak frame of the bed. Yet even in the midst of his laughter, he knew that he had seen an awesome demonstration of faith, one that would affect him profoundly for the rest of his life. Unable to speak of that, he said only, "You were absolutely right. If heaven and hell exist, I'd now be frying like an egg."

"Very likely." There was a hint of twinkle in Owen's eyes. "Now you'll have more time to change your ways. Not that you're truly wicked, but I doubt you've ever given serious thought to the state of your soul."

"Right again. Clare will undoubtedly have a positive effect in that area." After a moment's pause, he added, "We're to be married in a week. You're the first to know."

"Fancy that, our Clare a countess," Owen said with pleasure. "You couldn't make a better choice—you need a woman with her feet firmly planted on the ground."

Seeing that the other man was tiring, Nicholas stood. "If you're on your feet by then, perhaps you'll be able to give Clare away. I think she'd like that."

"On crutches?" Owen said doubtfully.

"We'd be happy to have you there in a bath chair." Feeling as if a boulder had dropped from his heart, Nicholas went downstairs again. More people were arriving, so he and Clare bid Marged farewell and left to make room for other well-wishers.

As they returned to Aberdare, Clare said, "If you had known that Owen was alive, last night wouldn't have happened, and today you wouldn't be facing a life sentence of marriage."

He shrugged. "Perhaps it was meant to be. It's done, so there's no point in brooding." His mouth quirked up. "As you may have guessed, there's a broad streak of fatalism in the Rom."

"As long as you are . . . content."

He gave her a quick glance, wondering if she regretted the prospect of marrying him, but her expression was serene. "Apparently Michael took what I said in London seriously. Now that he has seen the situation for himself and taken steps to rectify it, there is no need to break the lease."

"I must admit I'm impressed. Apparently when he re-

trieved his temper, he turned into a reasonable man,'' Clare
said. "Now you'll have more time for the slate quarry."

"Would you like to spend your honeymoon riding to the
Penrhyn quarries? Just the two of us, mountains, daffodils,
romantic nights beneath the stars . . .''

Her brows rose. "And when it rains?"

"Cozy but less romantic nights in travelers' huts in the
mountains.''

"Sounds lovely." She gave him a smile that made him
want to tether the horses and drag her off into the bushes.

After mature consideration, he did exactly that.

The next week was a whirl of activity. The wedding didn't
require much planning, for they had decided on a small
ceremony at Aberdare. However, there was much to be done
in the village among the families of men who had died in
the mine. Clare went to a dozen funerals, held weeping
women in her arms, and helped widows plan for the future.
As word of her engagement spread, there were some who
regarded her with disapproval or resentment, but her marriage was minor news compared to the explosion. She
thought it ironic that the village's concern over the disaster
made her own situation easier.

More troubling was Nicholas's attitude. He was charming
and considerate, and clearly he delighted in her body. Yet
she felt that in most ways they were less intimate as lovers
than they had been as adversaries. It was as if he was com-
pensating for their increased physical closeness by stepping
back emotionally. Though his withdrawal did not shake her
belief that it was right to marry, it grieved her greatly. She
could only hope that the dailiness of marriage would dissolve his reserve.

On the fifth day after her engagement, she returned to
Aberdare in late afternoon and was met by Williams. "The
Earl of Strathmore is in the drawing room. He arrived two
hours ago."

"Oh, dear," Clare said ruefully as she removed her bonnet. "And Nicholas hasn't returned from Swansea yet?"

"No, miss."

She entered the drawing room and found the earl comfortably ensconced with a book and a tea tray. "Lucien, what a surprise. Nicholas didn't tell me that he was expecting you."

Lucien rose and took her hands, then kissed her lightly on the cheek. "He wasn't—I decided to deliver the special license in person. He should have known that I wouldn't want to miss his wedding. Every groom needs a friend by his side. To his regret, Rafe can't come. Tied up in the Lords—some bill that he's been working on is coming up for a vote. He did, however, order me to kiss the bride on his behalf." He brushed her other cheek with his lips.

"I'm not quite a bride yet."

"Then I'll have to kiss you again on your wedding day," he said placidly. "Twice, unless Nicholas objects."

"I'm sorry you've had to wait so long."

"It's what an uninvited guest deserves."

"Would you like to go for a walk in the garden?" she suggested. "It's a perfect May day."

"If I recall Wales correctly, we'd better get outside quickly, or it might be raining when we get there."

She made a face. "Sad but true."

The sunshine was still there when they emerged onto the flagstone patio. A peacock strutted up and fanned his tail, the sun shimmering magically on the blue-green patterns of the feathers. "Handsome creatures," Lucien remarked, "but staggeringly stupid. A clear example of the curse of beauty."

Clare laughed. "You and your other Fallen Angel friends are beautiful, and none of you seem stupid."

He took her hand and tucked it in the crook of his elbow, amusement gleaming in his green-gold eyes. "True, but we didn't become friends because of appearances."

"Is there any particular reason why you banded together and have stayed friends for so long? Beyond the obvious fact of enjoying each other's company, I mean."

"Most groups of boys consist of a leader and a number of followers," he said reflectively. "Perhaps we became friends because none of us enjoyed being led."

"I would have supposed that you were all natural leaders.

Each of you could have ruled a circle of adoring syco-
phants.''

"But we didn't choose to. Rafe despises toadeaters, and
as the heir to a dukedom, he attracted them like a horse
attracts flies. You know Nicholas—trying to get him to do
something he doesn't want is like trying to order the wind,
yet he has no desire for power over others. Too much the
Gypsy, perhaps. Michael, I think, preferred to test himself
against his equals rather than settle for the easy domination
of weaker characters.''

"And what about you?" she asked, intrigued by his anal-
ysis.

"Me? Like Nicholas, I dislike taking orders, but I don't
particularly enjoy the visibility that goes with leadership.''

"Born to be a spymaster, in fact.''

"Afraid so.'' He looked doubtfully at the peacock, which
was strutting before an unimpressed peahen. "Do lower
your voice. Those peafowl might be French agents.''

She laughed as they went down the steps to the gravel
path. "Nicholas may be hard to order, but his sense of responsibility can lead him to do things that he might prefer
to avoid.''

Lucien gave her a shrewd glance. "Are you concerned
that he is marrying you from a sense of responsibility?''

"A little.'' Unable to resist this chance to discuss her
concerns, she said carefully, "When he and I struck our
original bargain, I was a stranger and it was easy for him
to threaten to ruin me. But as he came to know me as an
individual, I think he started to feel guilty, and his proposal
was the result. Previously he had been quite adamant about
not wanting a wife. I hope that he doesn't come to regret
our marriage.''

"While he takes responsibility seriously, it wouldn't get
him to the altar if he didn't want to go,'' Lucien replied.
"I don't believe I have ever known Nicholas to do something that he truly did not wish to do. As the old earl learned
to his cost. That's why they were usually at loggerheads.''

The gardens were improving rapidly now that the old gardener had three husky young assistants. Risking the gardener's ire, Clare stooped to pick a scarlet tulip. "What was

Nicholas's grandfather like? I was never in a position to know him."

"A difficult man. His attitude to Nicholas was very complex, but warmth was never part of it. They would have gotten on better if Nicholas had groveled. Instead, though Nicholas was always courteous, he had a way of being . . . not quite there."

"I know exactly what you mean," she said, thinking how he had been for the last few days. "It's rather maddening."

"Certainly it maddened his grandfather."

Their wanderings had brought them to the rockery. As they followed the twisting path, a peahen began to shriek from her perch in a nearby tree. Clare regarded the bird with disfavor. "At least the males are decorative, but the way the females screech tempts me to experiment with peahen fricassee. To the extent that I ever thought of it, I assumed that peafowl were elegant and aristocratic, but it turns out they're only noisy, glorified pheasants. It's been a sad disillusionment."

"So much for the glamor of the nobility." Lucien's mouth quirked up. "For some reason, talk of peacocks reminds me of Nicholas's first wife."

Clare toyed with her tulip. "What did you think of her?"

"I suppose I shouldn't say, but I will. It's useful for a second wife to have some understanding of the woman who went before." He thought a moment. "She was very beautiful, of course, and very aware of it. She had great vivacity as well, yet I never really liked her. There was an essential coldness in her nature that repelled me." He gave Clare an amused glance. "That's a minority opinion. Most men would have gladly thrown themselves down like carpets so she could walk on them, if that was what the Incomparable Caroline wanted."

"I don't think I would enjoy walking on a carpet of human bodies," Clare said dryly. "Not at all comfortable."

"Which is why you and Nicholas will probably deal very well together. Though he admired her considerable charms, he wasn't good carpet material."

Clare wondered if that was the source of the problems in the marriage. "He loved her enough to make her his wife."

''That wasn't love—it was an arranged marriage, you know.'' Lucien's brow furrowed. ''Or perhaps you didn't know. It was the old earl's idea, of course—he wanted to see the succession secured before his death. Nicholas was doubtful, but he agreed to meet Lady Caroline, and was pleasantly surprised. He had been afraid that his grandfather had chosen some horse-faced female with good bloodlines and no conversation. But the old earl was clever enough to know that if the girl was unattractive, Nicholas would never cooperate. As it was, Nicholas agreed to the match readily enough.''

''Were there problems in the marriage from the first?''

''As arranged marriages went, it appeared more auspicious than most. Nicholas seemed satisfied with his bargain. But after a few months . . .'' Lucien shrugged. ''Something went wrong, I have no idea what. Nicholas sent Caroline to Aberdare and stayed in London alone.''

''And drowned himself in debauchery,'' Clare said helpfully, since her companion didn't seem inclined to elaborate.

''I'm afraid so,'' he agreed. ''Not that I have anything against debauchery, but he didn't seem to be enjoying it much. Though I saw him occasionally in London, he didn't confide in me. Then came that dreadful business here at Aberdare, and he left the country. You probably know more about that than I.''

''Thank you for speaking so freely. I want to understand as much about Nicholas as I can.'' She picked a white tulip to go with the scarlet. ''Sometimes I feel as if he is a play, and I came in on the second act and must deduce what has gone before.''

Lucien smiled. ''That is the nature of all human friendships, and what makes them interesting.''

''Speaking of friendships, did you know that Lord Michael is living in his house on the other side of the valley?''

Lucien's head whipped around, and he regarded her with sharp concern. ''I hadn't heard that. Has there been trouble?''

Clare was vividly reminded that under his light manner, Lucien was a formidable man. Wanting to share her concern, she said, "The day after Lord Michael returned to Penreith, a rifle bullet almost struck Nicholas when we were riding. I was afraid that Michael had fired it, but Nicholas insisted that it must have been a poacher."

"Have there been any similar incidents?"

"Not that I know of. Lord Michael has been busy." Clare described the explosion at the mine and the steps his lordship was taking to improve conditions.

Lucien's expression eased. When she was finished, he said, "It sounds as if Michael is recovering his natural equilibrium. Obviously he came here because of his business interests, not because of some ill-founded hostility toward Nicholas."

"I hope so. I didn't enjoy wondering if he was going to put a hole in Nicholas." She bit her lower lip. "Since this seems to be my day for impertinent questions, I might as well ask what his good points are. He must have some, or he wouldn't have such admirable friends."

"Courage, intelligence, honesty," Lucien said promptly. "One always knew where one stood with Michael. When in good spirits, which was usually, he was a witty, thoroughly enjoyable companion. He was also absolutely loyal to his friends."

"He hasn't been to Nicholas," she pointed out.

"Yes, and I wish I knew why," Lucien said. "Still, it sounds as if his state of mind is improving."

"I hope so, since we seem destined to be neighbors. Will you call on him while you're here in the valley?"

"I think I shall. With luck, he'll have forgiven me for seconding Nicholas in that duel." Lucien smiled. "Speaking of Nicholas, here he comes now."

As the two men shook hands, Clare remembered how Lord Michael had appeared at the Duke of Candover's ball. Though she wanted to believe he was no longer a threat, it was hard to believe that such hostility had completely vanished. She prayed that she was wrong.

That night it was very late when Nicholas came to Clare's bed. Thinking that he and his friend would talk until dawn, she had fallen asleep, but she woke when the mattress sagged under his weight. Sleepily teasing, she murmured, "Who's there?"

She heard a sharp intake of breath, and the temperature of the room seemed to drop twenty degrees. "Who the hell were you expecting?" Nicholas said in freezing accents.

She came fully awake in an instant. "That was a joke, Nicholas. Obviously a bad one."

"Very."

She leaned forward and put her arms around his rigid shoulders. Quietly she said, "It doesn't take a genius to guess that Caroline was unfaithful to you. I suspect that was at the root of your own adultery. But I'm not like her, even if my sense of humor is sometimes inappropriate. To me, the idea that I could even think of making love with another man is ludicrous." Feeling him soften, she added, "Considering what an amazingly difficult time you had getting me into your bed, what makes you think any other man would be successful?"

He put his hand over hers. "Only someone essentially innocent could offer such flawed reasoning, but having made my share of stupid jokes, I'm in no position to throw stones." A hard edge came into his voice. "You guessed rightly—my noble first wife was a slut. It isn't something I care to dwell on."

"I can think of better things to dwell on," she agreed. Her hand glided lightly down his torso until she found what she sought. "For example . . ."

He sucked his breath in. "You're a remarkably quick learner. It's time to skip to an advanced lesson." With a flurry of cat-quick movements, he flipped her over and followed her down, doing things that astonished her.

There was a possessive fury to his lovemaking that night, as if he was seeking to brand her as his own. She accepted him gladly, eager to erase all memory of her unthinking remark. For a handful of moments, the distance she had sensed in him was burned away by the fires of passion and they were fully intimate, body and soul.

That sense faded later, but if it could happen once, it could happen again. Clare fell asleep in his arms, as happy as she had ever been in her life. But before sliding into slumber, she found herself hoping that the hell of fire and brimstone truly existed. And that Caroline Davies, duke's daughter and faithless wife, was burning in it.

Michael Kenyon was working in his study when his man-servant, acting as butler as well as valet, came to announce that the Earl of Strathmore was paying a call. Michael hesitated, struck by a sharp longing to see his old friend. More than that, he longed for life to be as simple as it once had been, when he and Luce and Rafe and Nicholas had breezed into each other's lodgings with the casual ease of brothers. . . .

But life hadn't been that simple in years, and in London, Lucien had aligned himself with Aberdare. "Tell Lord Strathmore that I'm not receiving."

A hint of disapproval showed in the servant's eyes, but he said only, "Very good, my lord," and left the room.

Michael tried to return to work, but it was impossible to concentrate on his accounts. Irritated, he shoved the ledger aside and strode over to the window to stare broodingly out over the valley. When he saw Lucien riding away, his mouth tightened. Luce must have come for Aberdare's wedding, news of which was all over the valley. Apparently Aberdare was marrying his mistress, the small female who had been with him in London. Michael recalled her as being reasonably attractive, and she had seemed sensible, apart from her willingness to bed Aberdare, but she was a far cry from her predecessor.

His stomach twisted and his gaze went to the mine, which was dimly visible in the distance. He'd come to Penreith with a purpose, and because of the disaster at the pit he was no closer to accomplishing it than the day he had arrived. Every waking moment had been filled with activity, first directing rescue work, then putting together plans to implement the improvements that should have been done years ago. It was bitterly galling to acknowledge that Aberdare had spoken the truth about the mine when they had met in London.

Probably Aberdare was also correct that Madoc had been embezzling, though Michael hadn't yet found the proof. The figures in the account books added up, but they didn't quite make sense. He was disinclined to pursue the matter at the moment; if Madoc had been greedy, it was Michael who had given him the opportunity. And the fellow was extremely useful.

Besides, Michael had far more important things on his mind; feverish activity was no excuse for cowardice. Soon he must resolve the horrifying dilemma that had brought him back to Penreith. And no matter how painful it proved to be, justice must be done.

28

CLARE BECAME the Countess of Aberdare with
miraculous smoothness. She wore an elegantly simple
cream-colored gown and carried a bouquet of bright spring
flowers. Marged stood up with her and Owen gave her away,
crutches and all.

She had also invited the other members of her class meeting, all of whom attended, brimming with good wishes and
bright-eyed curiosity. Nicholas was at his most charming,
and even Edith Wickes seemed persuaded that he had re-
nounced his evil ways in favor of the love of a good woman.

Clare sailed through the ceremony and the wedding
breakfast with an amazing absence of nerves. Perhaps that
was because she had felt married ever since her blood had
flowed with that of Nicholas. Even the Methodists con-
sumed champagne after Nicholas persuasively explained that
it was no more intoxicating than common ale. As a result,
good cheer abounded on all sides.

Needing to return to London, Lucien left immediately
after the wedding breakfast, which lasted into the early afternoon. Clare gave him a heartfelt hug, glad that he had
made the long trip to Wales. She suspected that much of the
reason he had come was to show that Nicholas's well-born
friends supported a marriage that most of society would
consider a sad mésalliance.

After the rest of the guests left, singing with true Welsh
vigor and tuneful Welsh voices, Nicholas took Clare's hand
and towed her playfully through the house. "I've something
to show you. It was installed yesterday, when you were out."

When he led her into the billiard room, her eyes widened.
"The table has the new slate top?" She ran her palms over

the green surface and found not a single bump or lump. "Smooth as a baize-covered mirror. This could start a new fashion."

"I anticipate selling much slate for the purpose, all at a premium price." He put his hands on the end of the table and gave it a hard shove, with absolutely no effect. "An advantage I hadn't thought of is that it's so heavy that it takes ten men and a boy to move it. No more accidental jostling that ruins shots. The carpenter had to reinforce the legs and the frame to support the weight of the slate."

"Shall we test it with a game of wedding-day billiards?" She grinned. "You should be able to win. Since I've had two glasses of champagne, even my leather-tipped cue won't make my strokes accurate."

"Billiards has so many marvelous double-entendres—strokes, balls, pockets, even leather-tipped cues. . . ." He gave her a wicked smile. "I had a game in mind, but it wasn't billiards."

"Nicholas, it's mid-afternoon!" Half-laughing and half-serious, she skipped around to the other side of the table. "What if someone comes in?"

"The staff are all enjoying champagne in the servants' hall." He moved toward her purposefully. "And have you forgotten that it was afternoon the day we drove back from Penreith? And in the hayloft three days ago. And . . ."

"But those times it just happened, it wasn't premeditated like this." Her voice was prim, but she leaned over and rested her arms on the table rail so he could see her decolletage.

His brows took on a diabolical arch. "You're claiming those occasions aren't premeditated? Then why did you follow me up the ladder to the hayloft and put your hand on my—?"

Laughing, she cut him off. "Please, my lord! Must you remind me of how weak-willed I am?"

"I prefer to think of what a splendidly obliging wife you are." He began to circle the table, like a cat stalking a mouse. "I need to erase the memory of that last game in London, or I might never play billiards again."

Her eyes began to sparkle. Perhaps it had been three or

four glasses of champagne, not two. "In that case," she purred, "we should reproduce the general conditions of the game, while changing the conclusion."

Gracefully she sat on the edge of a chair, drew up her hem, and kicked off her kidskin slipper. Then she lifted her foot and languidly peeled off a stocking, careful to let him catch a fleeting glimpse of inner thigh. It was much like what she had done in London, but this time the game would end differently. A slow burn of desire curled through her at the knowledge. She tossed the stocking at Nicholas. "Your turn, my lord husband."

He caught the sheer silk with one hand and inhaled the scent. "An intoxicating fragrance of lilacs and Clare." His dark eyes watching her with hypnotic intensity, he peeled off his coat with a ripple of muscular shoulders.

Then it was her turn again. Garment by garment, they slowly unclothed themselves, not touching except with heated gazes. It was like an exotic dance, both sensual and ragingly erotic.

When the time came to remove her stays, she glided up to him, then turned so that he could release her. For a man who always moved with absolute mastery, he suffered an amazing attack of clumsiness, his hands drifting to curves that were nowhere near the laces.

He dropped the quilted dimity to the floor and pulled her against him, caressing her breasts with luxuriant thoroughness. Sighing with delight, she leaned back, tempted to stay in his embrace. It was obvious from the hard ridge of flesh that pressed into her buttocks that he was fully aroused, as was she. But she summoned her schoolmistress discipline and slid teasingly away again, for delay would only fan the flames higher.

He removed his drawers, revealing himself in all his rampant masculinity. The last item left was her shift. Drawing out the moment, she untied the drawstring, then pulled it provocatively over her head, shimmying her whole body as she did.

He stepped toward her eagerly, but she held up a hand, stopping him. She levered herself up to the rail on the end of the table and perched there, legs loosely crossed. Then she pulled the pins from her hair and shook it free so that it cascaded over her back and breasts like dark silk.

The effect was explosive. Like a tempest, Nicholas swept her back onto the green baize, and they completed what had been so painfully unfinished in London. In the last week their bodies had become exquisitely attuned to each other, and their joining was tender and playful and wild.

After, as they lay in each other's arms, wantonly fulfilled, he murmured, "There is much to be said for premarital consummation. It makes the wedding day far more enjoyable."

"That is a truly subversive thought, exactly the sort of thing that gets a man a rakish reputation." She laughed softly. "You were right at the beginning, when you said that if I lost, we would both win."

He stroked his fingers into her tangled hair. "I think it was a draw, due to your clever management. We both won without either of us having to lose."

Except Nicholas, who had lost his bachelorhood, but since he didn't seem troubled by that she would not remind him. "The new table has a wonderful playing surface," she said lazily, "but I think it needs to be heavier—surely our activity must have moved it two or three feet across the floor." Her voice became schoolmistressy. "Also, baize cannot disguise the fact that slate is cooler against one's bare person than the wood was."

Effortlessly he lifted her on top of him. "Is it sufficiently warm if you lie on this bare person?"

"Mmm, yes." Once again their lovemaking had contained a hint of that ultimate intimacy, and her heart was so full that she could no longer keep silent. Looking down into his black eyes, she said a little wistfully, "Can you bear it if I say that I love you? I have since the first time I saw you, I think. I was five or six years old. It was spring, and you came to the cottage looking for my father. You rode bareback on a piebald pony and were the most fascinating being I had ever seen. You didn't even notice my existence."

He became very still, his gaze searching hers. "Really?"

"Really. I watched you whenever I could, remembered every word you ever spoke to me."

"Some of them were probably rude."

"Yes. Shall I recite them for you?"

"I'd rather you didn't." He linked his arms around her naked waist and studied her warily. "If you were in love with me, you certainly didn't act like it when you came up here to bully me into helping with your projects."

"I never thought of it as love—how could there be anything between the heir to an earldom and the penniless daughter of a dissenting preacher? I might as well have wished to have the moon in my pocket. But you were always there, in my mind. In my heart, though I didn't admit it to myself."

He was silent, his hands restlessly kneading her lower back and buttocks. Again she sensed withdrawal, and knew that her love was a burden he did not want to bear.

She rested her head on his shoulder, her hair spilling across his chest. "I'm sorry," she said, quietly aching. "I shouldn't have told you. It sounds as if I was being dreadfully calculating. But I wasn't."

"You're right, you shouldn't have told me." There was a dark edge to his voice. "I distrust people who say they love me. The words are invariably used as a weapon. Those I trust most are those who have made the least show of their devotion."

She supposed that he meant friends like Lucien and Rafe. Who were the ones who had openly declared their love? His mother? His grandfather? His wife?

His betrayers.

"Forget I spoke," she said lightly. "I married you to give our hypothetical unborn child a name, to have a partner for billiards, and because a husband is a very cozy thing to have during a Welsh winter. No trust is required."

He smiled, but it didn't reach his eyes. "For what it's worth, I trust you as much as I trust anyone." Catching her face between his hands, he kissed her with a strange kind of yearning, as if he both wanted and feared her love. But when he spoke again, it was only of the mundane. "I hope that the weather stays fine like this tomorrow for the trip to Penrhyn."

Weather was such a useful, *safe*, subject.

* * *

Cold eyes watched through the field glasses as the Earl of Aberdare and his brand-new countess rode away from Aberdare, casually clothed, their horses carrying full saddlebags. The watcher gave a grim smile of satisfaction at the sight. Once he had decided what must be done, everything had fallen into place perfectly. Aberdare made no secret of his plans to ride to northwest Wales, or his route. A few casual words spoken by servants, and soon the whole valley knew where Aberdare was going, and when, and why.

It would have been harder near Penreith, but once Aberdare was in the wild hill country, it would be dead easy to set the ambush. All of the arrangements had been made—the plan set, the route chosen, the men hired. Within forty-eight hours, his problems would be solved—and justice would be served.

The first night of their honeymoon was clear and they slept beneath the stars just as Nicholas had promised. After making love, Clare cuddled in his arms while he pointed out different constellations and related the Romany legends of how they had been placed in the sky.

As she drifted off to sleep, he wondered how he had come to be so lucky. She was everything Caroline was not—warm, witty, down to earth, perceptive and loyal; she filled spaces that had been empty in his life since he was a child. A little too perceptive, perhaps; he hadn't realized how much he had revealed to her until she had made her uncomfortably accurate guess about Caroline. Luckily the worst of that would never be known.

He supposed, Clare being the woman she was, that love and loyalty went together. He could bear the knowledge that she loved him as long as she was discreet on the subject. It was far safer not to say too much, or expect too much.

He rolled onto his side and gathered her close, then tucked the blanket around her chin. The night was alive with wind and soft sounds, a true Romany bedchamber. Someday he'd have to take her on a visit to meet his mother's people. He grinned, wondering how far she would get in reforming Romany ways or trying to teach reading to Romany children. Even Clare would fail there. Be a good way to keep the minx humble.

Heart at peace, he slept.

Clare had known she would enjoy this journey simply because she would be with Nicholas, and for a few days they would have no tasks beyond riding and reveling in each other. Nonetheless, she was surprised at how very much she was enjoying herself. In the day and a half they had been traveling, he had opened up, become relaxed in a way she hadn't seen before. The open air must bring out the Gypsy in him.

As she gave him a doting glance, she noticed a dark coiled shape showing below the cloak that was lashed on top of his saddlebags. "Why did you bring a whip when we have no carriage?"

"Gypsy habit, mostly. A whip has many uses. For example . . ." He detached the whip, then cracked it sharply. The tip wrapped around a branch high above their heads. When he tugged on the handle, the limb bowed down within his reach. "If there were ripe apples there, we would be able to feast."

She laughed. "I never thought about it, but I can see that a traveling life has a special body of knowledge all its own."

He coiled and replaced the whip, then indicated a bird in a nearby tree. "There are Gypsies near."

She studied the slender black and white bird. "To me that looks like a pied wagtail, not a Gypsy."

"It's also called the *Romani chiriklo*, the Gypsy bird," he explained. "If you see one, there are Rom in the vicinity."

She glanced around, but they were high in the hill country, with no signs of human existence except the narrow road. "They conceal themselves well."

"Watch and we'll see."

About half a mile farther, he gestured at a tree. "See the gray rag tied to that branch?" When she nodded, he explained, "That's a trail mark, for one kumpania to tell others that it has passed. A mark is called a *patrin*, which means leaf, but it can take many forms—piles of twigs, or stones, or rags, like that one. See how it is tied above the eye level of the average rider? If you don't know to look, it would be easily missed.''

Intrigued, she said, ''So your kin leave messages for each other. How clever. Do you know the people who left this one?''

''Probably—I've visited every kumpania that travels regularly in Wales.'' He studied the rag. ''In fact, I can narrow it down to one of about five groups. There's a Romany campsite a few miles farther along this road. Would you like to visit if they are there?''

''I'd love to,'' she replied.

But the weather was against them. There had been fitful showers all morning, and as the afternoon advanced a steady, drenching rain began to fall. Clare did not complain—to live in Wales was to know about wetness—but it did take some of the enjoyment out of the day.

As she tugged her cloak around her, Nicholas said, ''There's a travelers' hut not far ahead. Shall we stop for the night?''

''With pleasure,'' she said fervently.

The frame hut was a little off the road, almost hidden in a grove of tall trees. Two stories high and solidly built, it even had a shed on one side to shelter horses. As they dismounted, Nicholas said, ''Go inside and get warmed up. I don't want you to take a chill on your honeymoon.'' He gave a playful leer. ''If you're going to be confined to your bed, it should be for a more interesting reason.''

Clare laughed and went into the hut, which was simply furnished with a table and several chairs. A couple of minutes later, Nicholas brought in the saddlebags and an armload of dry firewood that had been stored in the shed. Then he went out again to bed down the horses. He took such good care of her, she thought fondly. It was a pleasure to be pampered.

Once the fire was crackling, she explored. It didn't take long because the upstairs was a single spacious room exactly like the one below, only without furniture. A faint layer of dust covered all surfaces, but under that everything was reasonably clean. She was descending the steep steps when Nicholas came in again. "I didn't expect this," she remarked. "Are there many such huts in the mountains?"

"None quite like this one." He stripped off his soaked hat and coat. "In the middle of the last century, a prosperous wool merchant was caught up here by a blizzard, and would have died if a shepherd hadn't taken him in. In gratitude, the merchant established an endowment with the nearest parish to build and maintain a shelter for travelers. Being a man of delicacy, he specified a second room, in the event that ladies were ever trapped here amidst crude males."

"But I *like* being trapped here with a crude male."

"Not all females have your good sense." He wrestled off his riding boots. "So the hut was built, and every spring the parish sends someone up to repair the ravages of winter. Not much else is required, because people who know about the hut use it carefully. For example, before we leave in the morning, I'll collect enough wood to replace what we burn. By the time the next traveler comes, it will be dry and ready."

"Fascinating, though the shepherd who saved the merchant might have preferred a fast ten quid paid directly to him." She knelt and put more wood on the fire. "Do the Rom stay here?"

"Good Lord, never. No self-respecting Rom would stay inside when there's open air available. They hunger for the wind." His gaze rested on her thoughtfully. "You, however, would do well to get out of those wet clothes." He started across the room. "Let me help you take them off."

She had a pretty fair idea where his help would lead, and she was right. Quite delightfully so.

Afterward, they dozed lazily before the fire before rising and donning dry clothing. Clare prepared a simple supper of ham, potatoes, and onions, which was accompanied by an expensive bottle of claret which Nicholas had brought in the spirit of honeymoon. They spent the evening sprawled lazily in front of the fire, chatting and sipping tea. As they finally rolled up in their blankets, she murmured, "Let's take a trip like this every spring. No one else but us."

"I'd like that." He kissed her lightly. "Don't ever be-

come too much of a countess. I like you exactly as you
are.''

She smiled up at him. ''If you're the Gypsy Earl, does
that mean that I am now a Gypsy Countess?''

''I suppose it does. That makes you a *rawnie*, a great
lady. But then, you always were.'' He tucked her back
against his chest, his arm folding her close. ''Sleep well,
Clarissima.''

Members of the small band grumbled about the rain, but
the leader shut them up, reminding them how well they
would be paid for that night's work. He was irritated himself, though, for he hadn't expected his quarry to be sheltered in a building.

As they waited for the early hours of the morning, passing
around a bottle of whiskey to warm their bones, he considered the best way to accomplish his task. It would be sim-
plest to storm the hut, but likely the door was latched, and
breaking it down would take away the element of surprise.
It was also likely that the quarry was carrying a pistol, and
he looked like a man who could be dangerous.

Leaving his men, the leader quietly scouted the area
around the hut. The construction was rugged, the windows
small and set too high to climb through easily. Deciding to
have a look in the shed, he slowly opened the door. One of
the horses whickered, but not loudly enough to disturb the
people sleeping inside. Against the wall of the hut was a
dark mass that proved to be dry firewood. He gave an ugly
smile, for now he knew the best way to flush his prey.

He'd burn them out.

29

NICHOLAS CAME awake suddenly and completely. For a moment he lay still, wondering what had alerted the part of his brain that never slept.

The smoke. There was far too much for their small, banked fire. He sat up and scanned the room and saw a faint, wavering glow in the window opposite the fireplace. The rain had stopped, and in the silence he heard a faint, menacing crackle.

Beside him Clare still slept. He shook her shoulder. "Wake up, there's a fire outside."

When her eyes were open, he rose and swiftly pulled on breeches, boots, and a shirt. But he was not unduly worried; the door was only a few feet away, so there was no chance that they would be trapped inside.

Clare got to her feet, blinking sleepily. For once ignoring her delightful nakedness, he tossed over the nightgown she hadn't gotten around to wearing. "Pull that on so we can go outside and see what's burning. With luck the fire can be put out easily, but I don't want to take any chances."

She nodded and obeyed, putting on her own boots and lifting her cloak as she headed for the door. Nicholas picked up his saddlebags, which contained everything they had of value, and followed right behind her.

Yet he couldn't shake the itchy feeling that something was wrong. Sparks from the chimney could have ignited a fire, but it was damned odd, given the damp condition of the forest. And why were the flames on the side of the hut opposite the shed? He didn't recall seeing anything flammable there.

As Clare unlatched the door and started to swing it open,

he realized that crackling sounds were coming from both sides of the hut. Warning alarms went off in his head. If the shed was burning, why weren't the horses screaming? And how could accidental fires start in two different places?

Looking over Clare's shoulder, he saw a flash of movement twenty or thirty feet from the door. The lifting and pointing of a long, straight object.

A rifle.

Horror ripped through him. Dropping the saddlebags, he caught Clare around the waist and dragged her to the floor. At the same instant the rifle fired. A bullet blasted over their heads and smashed into the back wall. Acting on pure instinct, he wrapped his arms around Clare and rolled away from the open doorway. When they were out of the line of fire, he reached back and slammed the door shut. Within seconds, three other bullets hammered into the heavy wood.

"Dear God," Clare gasped. "What's happening?"

"Someone wants to kill us," he said grimly. "Or more likely wants to kill me, and doesn't care if you die at the same time."

He sprang to his feet and fastened the door's simple hook latch, though it would give only the barest protection. He had brought a pistol, so he dug it out of his luggage and loaded it. Then he peered out the window in the front side of the hut. The area was lit by flickering flames from both ends of the building. Judging by the amount of light and smoke, the shed was burning merrily and well on its way to complete destruction.

Five armed men were standing at the outer limits of the light. Beyond them, he saw their two horses, which must have been removed from the shed before the fire was set. As he watched, one of the men began moving cautiously toward the door, his rifle raised and ready.

Nicholas smashed the glass of the window with the barrel of his pistol and snapped off a shot. The man shrieked and spun around before crashing to the ground. Nicholas swiftly reloaded and fired again, but the other attackers were beyond the effective range of the pistol and he did no damage.

A voice barked an order and one of the men started circling around the hut toward the rear. Nicholas swore under his breath; any chance they might have had to escape out the back window was now gone.

Voice tight but composed, Clare said, "The hut is on fire, isn't it?"

"Yes, and there are at least four men out there, armed and ready to shoot if we come out." Rapidly he scanned the possibilities. "Since it's probably me they're after, they might let you go if I give myself up to them."

"No!" The smoke was thickening fast, stinging the eyes and clogging the lungs. In her vehemence, Clare inhaled too much and began coughing. When she could speak again, she said, "They can't leave me alive as a witness to your murder. If we surrendered, they would probably rape me, then kill me anyhow. If I'm going to die, it will be at your side."

"I'd rather not die at all." A possibility flashed through his mind. He uncocked his pistol and thrust it in the waist of his breeches, then snatched up his whip. "Upstairs. Move!"

"Wait." She yanked a shift from her baggage, ripped it in half, and dipped the pieces in the pot of water that had been set aside for morning. "Put this over your mouth."

Crouching to get under the worst of the fumes, they raced up the steps. The smoke worsened rapidly as they climbed, and the upper room would have been lethal without the damp rags. The heat was already uncomfortably high; within minutes, the whole structure would be engulfed in flames.

"No escape here," Clare said coolly. "A short marriage, but a good one. We never even had a fight." She coughed, then sagged against the wall, her face a pale blur in the thickening smoke. With a smile of unearthly sweetness, she said, "Forgive me for saying this, but I love you, Nicholas. I regret nothing, except . . . except that we didn't have more time."

Her words were like knives in his heart. Their lives could not end like this—he would not permit it.

He peered out one of the end windows, but couldn't see the armed man who had circled the house. Good; that meant the fellow couldn't see him, either. The window was a casement, so he undid the latch and swung it open. Flames were licking up the outside wall only a few feet below him, and he began coughing as more smoke poured in from outside.

After quickly calculating distances and deciding it was possible, he beckoned to Clare. "We have a chance," he said urgently. "Grab the edge of the back roof and climb on top. Don't be afraid—I won't let you fall."

She nodded with grim understanding. He climbed into the window and straddled the frame, fighting the heat and smoke to maintain consciousness. Clare crawled across his lap, then stood on the frame so her body was outside the window. He steadied her as she reached up and caught the edge of the roof, then boosted her from below until she managed to scramble up safely.

Praying that the smoke was concealing their exit from watching eyes, he wrapped the whip around his waist, then stood on the sill and reached for the roof himself. He caught the edge easily and was lifting himself upward when his fingers began slipping on the wet slate.

He was an instant away from plunging into the flames below when Clare's hand caught his, stabilizing his slide. Swinging like an acrobat, he managed to get his left leg over the edge of the roof. From there, it took only a moment to pull himself onto the slanting surface. The roof was a patchwork of garish light and stark shadows. He saw that Clare had anchored herself with one hand on the ridgepole before helping him. Thank God for a woman with brains.

So far, the billowing smoke and increasing noise of the two fires had concealed them from the attackers, but their refuge was perilous. The first floor of the hut was already burning and it was only a matter of time until the whole building was engulfed. Crouching, he helped Clare to the other end of the roof, keeping a hand on the ridgepole in case one of them slipped.

As they skidded across the slippery slate, he hoped to God that the nearest tree would be suitable. It was: a tall, thick elm that was within whip range of the hut, though only just.

The next part was the most dangerous because he would have to straighten up. If he was seen, he would be an easy target for a rifle. But there was no help for it. He unwound the whip from his waist and stood, bracing one foot on the ridgepole for balance. Then he lashed out at the one dimly seen branch that looked close enough, and strong enough, to support them.

The thong curled neatly around the branch. He tugged experimentally, but the hold didn't feel secure. Fighting down his raging impatience, he worked the whip loose and drew it back again. Perhaps it was his imagination, but the slate seemed to be getting hotter. Time seemed unnaturally distorted. How long had it been since he had awakened—five minutes? Three?

What mattered was how much time they had left. Stretching out as far as he could, he snapped the whip again. This time when he tested it, the hold seemed stronger. It had better be, for there wasn't time for another cast. He extended his free hand toward Clare. "Come here."

She crawled to his side and stood up. He took one instant to press his mouth to hers in a kiss that was meant to say what he could never have put into words. Then he wrapped his arm around her waist. "Hang on tight, my dear."

Her arms went around him, slim but strong. An instant later, they were swinging across emptiness, supported only by the dark, supple leather. He felt a shift, a loosening of the whip's hold on the branch. If they fell to the ground, the fall might not be fatal, but the attackers would be on them in seconds.

The arc of the swing took them downward until they slammed into the tree trunk. Clare gasped as air was knocked from her lungs. He tried to absorb the shock with bent legs, but even so, the force of the impact almost caused him to drop her. For an instant they hung free, the weight of them both dragging on his strained right arm.

The thong began to uncoil under the weight. They were on the verge of falling from the tree when he kicked out and managed to get his foot on a limb. It wasn't much support, but it was enough, and a moment later they were safely balanced on a thick branch.

He worked the handle of the whip until the thong dropped free. As he coiled it again, the roof collapsed with a hideous roar. A pillar of flames and sparks shot skyward and a wave of searing heat struck them. In the lurid light, he saw the silhouette of the roughly dressed man who had been waiting with rifle ready in case they had tried to escape from the back window. Though no more than thirty feet away, the attacker had not seen them in the smoke and darkness. As Nicholas watched, the man lowered the gun and made his way around the blazing hut, from which no one would now emerge alive.

They were high enough that Nicholas could see the attackers who waited in front on the far side of the fire. One of the men had a tall, rangy figure that was vaguely familiar. His mouth tightened to a bitter line. Glancing down, he saw that Clare was looking in the same direction, her face coldly furious.

Now was the time to escape, while the attackers watched the fire in primitive fascination. He touched Clare on the shoulder and they began to work their way downward. The lowest branch was still well above the ground, so once again the whip was pressed into service to lower them.

When they were safely down, he coiled the whip, then led Clare straight into the woods, away from the hut and the road. The ground was soggy from the earlier rain, and the air was damply chill. A good thing Clare had escaped with her cloak.

When he judged that they were about a mile from the hut, he stopped for a brief rest. Clare's breathing was ragged, so he drew her into his arms. She was shaking violently, and he guessed that it was not only from cold. "We're safe here," he whispered. "Even if those bastards are thorough enough to wait until the fire dies down and check for bodies in the ashes, that won't happen before dawn at the earliest."

Voice muffled against his shoulder, she said, "You saw him, didn't you?"

He didn't bother to ask for clarification. "I saw a tall man who could have been Michael Kenyon, and I can't think of anyone else who might want to kill me," he said harshly. "But that is a question for later. Now we have to get to safety."

"Are there cottages nearby?"

"No, something better than that." He put his arm around

her shoulders and began walking, drawing on the sense of direction that had been bred into him. "We're going to the Rom."

They walked through the woods for hours, stumbling over rough ground and getting saturated by water that dripped from the trees. Clare gave fervent thanks they had both put on their boots before escaping, or they would be in trouble now. As it was, she was soon exhausted and would have collapsed under a tree if Nicholas hadn't been half-carrying her. He seemed to know exactly where they were going, though to her, all wet trees looked exactly the same. And they didn't feel very nice when one walked into them.

The sky was beginning to lighten when they caught a wispy scent of smoke. "The site is occupied," he said with satisfaction. Only then did Clare realize that he had not been sure if they would find help here.

Suddenly an explosion of barking broke out, and the shadowy forms of half a dozen dogs charged toward them. She froze, wondering if they should run or look for a tree. But as the ferociously baying pack closed in, Nicholas drew his arm back and made a broad throwing motion. Though his hand was empty, the effect was magical. The dogs immediately fell silent and began milling around, following them into the camp.

There was enough light to see that the kumpania consisted of three wagons. Dark shapes under the wagons appeared to be beds, and she guessed that the rain had driven the Rom to take that amount of shelter. Roused by the noise, several men rolled to their feet and approached, posture alert. One carried a coiled whip in his hand.

Nicholas put his arm protectively around Clare and squinted at the nearest man. "Kore, is that you?"

There was a moment of astonished silence. Then a baritone voice roared, "Nikki!"

Suddenly they were surrounded by people jabbering noisily in Romany. Nicholas managed to get silence by lifting his hand. Arm still tightly around Clare, he gave a terse explanation in the same language.

A clucking female with a smooth, handsome face took

Clare's arm. Nicholas said, "Go with Ani, she'll take care of you. I'll join you later."

By this time, Clare was quite willing to put her fate in the hands of someone else. Ani took her to one of the bow-topped wagons and helped her onto the porch-like ledge at the end. When the door opened, Clare saw a row of small heads pop up from under a feather quilt, the black eyes bright with curiosity. Nicholas's eyes, she realized. The children started to chatter questions, but Ani hushed them.

The near end of the wagon was covered with a thin pad. Ani said in lightly accented English, "Sleep here."

Clare took off her wet cloak and struggled out of her boots. Then, muddy hem and all, she lay down. Ani dropped another feather quilt over her, and within three minutes, Clare was asleep.

It was mid-morning when Clare woke with Nicholas's arm across her waist. Like her, he was wearing the clothes he had escaped in, breeches and a shirt that gaped open at the neck. He still slept, his face youthful and heart-stoppingly handsome. Rolling over, she kissed his forehead lightly.

His eyes opened. "How are you feeling?"

"Very well, thank you. A few bruises from walking into trees, but nothing to signify." She suppressed a shiver. "You're a useful man to have around when danger threatens."

His face tightened. "If not for me, your life would never have been at risk."

"We don't know that." She gave him a jaunty smile. "And what a splendid adventure. How many people can boast of such a honeymoon?"

Though he smiled a little at her sally, she felt the bleakness inside him. She wondered how she would feel if one of her oldest friends—Marged, for example—was trying to kill her. The thought produced such a wrench of pain and disbelief that she hastily thrust it away. If she found it so upsetting even in her imagination, how much worse it must be for Nicholas, who wanted to believe in friendship. Deciding to attend to the practical, she asked, "Where do we go from here?"

"The kumpania was heading north, but they're willing to turn around and take us back to Aberdare. It will take about three days at wagon speed."

She thought of her pony and sighed. "I hope whoever ends up with Rhonda takes good care of her."

"When we get home, I'll send a couple of men up here to make inquiries. If someone sells the horses, perhaps I can buy them back. That might also uncover the men who attacked us."

She nodded and went to her next question. "Is there anything I should know about living among the Rom?"

He thought a moment. "Try to observe the cleanliness taboos. At a campsite, water is taken from the stream at different points, with water from the highest, 'cleanest' location being used for drinking and cooking. Washing and bathing water are taken from farther down. Always wash in running water before eating, never put food utensils in impure water, because that makes them *marhime*, polluted, and they would have to be thrown out." He gave her a wry glance. "You won't like this, but women are also considered impure. Never let your skirts brush any man but me, never walk in front of a man, or between two men, or in front of the horses."

She frowned. "You're right, I don't like it."

"It makes sense for people living in such close quarters," he explained. "It gives women a degree of privacy and protection that would otherwise be impossible, and reduces sexual tension as well. Though Gypsy women have a reputation for sexual allure, in fact promiscuity is almost unknown among the Rom."

"I see. I'll try not to offend anyone."

Drawn by the sound of voices, Ani peered in the wagon. "Breakfast. You go, Nikki, I bring clothes for your wife."

He obediently rose and climbed from the wagon, then helped Ani in. The Romany woman was wearing a loose, low-cut blouse and layers of full, brightly colored skirts. Earrings of dangling gold coins matched the jingling coin necklaces looped around her neck, and a patterned scarf covered her hair.

Clare was outfitted with a similar costume, though without the jewelry. Looking down at the deeply scooped blouse, she remarked, ''Nicholas will love this.''

Ani grinned, her teeth white against her glowing dark skin. ''It is good Nikki has taken a wife. How long since you marry?''

Clare counted mentally. ''Three days.''

''So recently!'' She took Clare's hand and looked at her wrist, then nodded with approval when she saw the small, almost healed cut. ''It is good. We will have a feast to honor the marriage. But now,'' she added practically, ''you must eat.''

They climbed from the wagon, which was made of wood and decorated with bold painting and carving. The rain had cleared, leaving the sky fresh and clear. The men were gathered around the tethered horses in the middle distance. Closer to hand, women moved gracefully around the campsite and a pack of near-naked children raced about, shouting gleefully. A tiny old woman with a face like a wrinkled walnut studied Clare intently, then nodded her head and went back to smoking her pipe.

Near the wagon was a cook fire with a tin pot and a cauldron warming over the coals. As Clare sniffed hopefully, Ani said, ''Wash first.'' She lifted a metal pitcher and indicated that Clare was to wash her hands under the stream of water that Ani poured. As Clare obeyed, she was glad that Nicholas had given her that brief lesson in Romany ways.

Ani served her with a mug of fierce, sweet coffee and a plate of fried onions and sausage. Both were delicious. As Clare ate, she saw that the women were packing things away in preparation for leaving, but without any great sense of urgency.

Nicholas returned with three men, all of them talking earnestly. He had acquired a loose leather vest and a red handkerchief around his throat, and looked entirely at home among his kin. She would never have known him for a British nobleman.

He saw Clare and started toward her, but made a detour when he saw the old woman. "Keja!" he called. She gave a gap-toothed smile and the two began talking in Romany.

As Clare finished her coffee, a boy ran into the camp. "Men are coming this way," he panted. "Carrying rifles."

Clare's heart leaped into her throat. Perhaps they were simply hunters, but it seemed more likely that they were last night's attackers, looking for the prey that had eluded them.

"This way!" Ani made sweeping gestures toward the wagon.

Clare and Nicholas both clambered inside. "Lie down," he said, suiting his actions to his words.

As Clare obeyed, Ani brought an armful of feather quilts that had been airing outside. One by one, she spread them over Clare and Nicholas until they were completely covered by layers of quilts. Then a weight plopped down on top. A weight that wiggled.

Feeling Clare start, Nicholas took her hand in a warm clasp. "Ani has put her four-year-old son on top of the *dunhas*. Even if someone is searching for us, they won't look beyond little Yojo. He's usually quite sticky."

Though she felt half-suffocated, Clare forced herself to lie still, her hand gripping Nicholas's. A few minutes later, she heard a hard voice just outside the wagon, speaking in English. "Have you seen a man and woman, traveling on foot? We're worried. They . . . they have fever and wandered off from our camp."

One of the Rom said, "No Gorgios today but you, sirs."

"Tell your fortune, honored sir?" a female voice said. "A beautiful woman lies in your future, with hands as graceful as birds. Only cross my palm . . ."

Ani chimed in, "No, honored sir, for *dukkerin*, I am the best. I have the true Gypsy sight."

Next a child's voice, "A penny for the guy, good sirs!"

A shrill chorus of children's voices rose. "A penny, sir, or a ha'penny." "A penny, please!" "Penny for the guy, sir."

"For God's sake," the visitor snarled, "Guy Fawkes Day is six months away. Get away from me, you brats."

The door to the wagon opened with a squeal. Clare's fingers clamped so hard on Nicholas's that she must have stopped the blood. A preternatural sense of danger warned her that one of the attackers was looking into the end of the wagon only two feet from their heads.

The child above them suddenly began squirming. "Penny, penny!" Yojo demanded.

Another English voice said, "Anything inside?"

"Just another filthy little brat," the first voice said in disgust. "They must be born knowing how to beg."

The door slammed shut and the voices faded as they walked away. Clare let out the breath she had been holding. Nicholas had known what he was doing when he sought refuge with his kin.

It was a long, stuffy wait beneath the feather beds. Yojo soon wandered off in search of more congenial pursuits, but they stayed where they were until a male voice said, "You can come out now, Nikki. The Gorgios are gone. Maybe you should stay inside wagons when we are on the road, but I think you're safe now."

Nicholas pushed aside the quilts and they both sat up with relief. Squatting outside on the wagon's ledge was Kore, a handsome, stocky man who was Ani's husband and the leader of the group. Nicholas asked, "Was the green-eyed man I described one of the Gorgio?"

Kore shook his head. "There were four men, but not the one you spoke of." He lifted a stone jug. "The boys are back from searching the ground around the burned hut. Not much was found. Your things were all destroyed and the horses taken. Nearby was this empty jug of whiskey, and this." He handed over a flat silver case.

Clare's heart twisted when she saw that it was a card case, the kind a gentleman carried. His face like stone, Nicholas opened it. The cards inside were damp but perfectly legible.

Lord Michael Kenyon.

Seeing Nicholas's expression, Kore politely turned away and jumped from the wagon.

Clare whispered, "I'm sorry, Nicholas."

His hand clenched to a fist, snapping the case shut. "But it makes no sense," he said, stark pain in his voice. "Even assuming that Michael has gone mad and decided to hunt me down, why here in the mountains? Why hire men to help him do what he is quite capable of doing himself? And if he was looking for me, he would have known that a Gypsy kumpania would have to be searched more thoroughly.''

"But he wasn't with the men—he may have wanted to be sure that no suspicion could fall on him," she said quietly. "This far from Penreith, our deaths might have been thought accidental. If there *was* an investigation, bandits would have been blamed when it was seen that several men were involved." She hesitated, then added, "It may not make sense, but it's likely that he isn't fully rational."

It was all perfectly plausible. Yet as she took Nicholas's hand, she wished with all her heart that it wasn't.

30

THOUGH CLARE was within sixty miles of her home, traveling with the Gypsies was like visiting a foreign country. Many of their customs were British, and all spoke at least some English and Welsh as well as Romany. Yet in other ways, they were totally alien. As Nicholas's wife, she was able to see them as few Gorgios ever did, for they accepted her with charming casualness, as if she were a kitten that had wandered in. Though she could not approve of some of their attitudes, neither could she resist their warmth and immense vitality.

Seeing the Rom gave her a better understanding of Nicholas. Their ability to live in the moment, as if there were no past or future; their cheerful fatalism; the graceful freedom of their movements—all of those traits were part of her husband's heritage from the Rom.

Yet though he blended in easily and was very popular, gradually she realized that he was not truly a member of the group; there were parts of his mind and spirit that had grown beyond the narrow world of the Rom. She wondered if he would have been happier if he had never left the Gypsies. Perhaps someday she would ask him, but not now. When they reached Aberdare, Michael would have to be dealt with, and she felt the grief of that inside Nicholas.

On their final night, the promised feast was held, with lavish amounts of food and drink and laughter. The centerpiece was a suckling pig stuffed with apples and roasted over the open fire. As Clare finished her portion, daintily nibbling the roast meat from a bone in her hands, she remarked, ''I hope this piglet was honestly come by, but I'm afraid to ask.''

Nicholas grinned. This evening he had buried his concerns and was enjoying himself with Gypsy gusto. "It's legitimate. By luck, I happened to have a guinea in my breeches when we escaped. I gave it to Kore as my contribution to our expenses. I saw him pay for this little porker myself."

Ani approached the log where they sat. "Since this is a feast in honor of your marriage, we will have a little ritual, yes? Not the abduction, nor the lament, but a little something to symbolize your union."

Clare said doubtfully, "I don't know your customs."

"This will be simple," Ani said briskly. "You will have no trouble. I will ask Milosh to take up his fiddle now. Later, Nikki, you will play the harp for us."

As Ani bustled away, Clare said, bemused, "Lament?"

"Usually the bride sings a song to her mother, bewailing the fact that she has been sold into marriage and wishing she were dead," Nicholas explained.

Clare stared at him. "Not very festive."

"It's considered very moving. That and the ritual abduction paint an interesting picture of Romany history."

She licked the last traces of grease from her fingers. "Where did the Rom come from originally?"

He took a swig of wine from a jug before answering, drinking Gypsy style, with the container slung over his shoulder and his finger linked through a loop on the jug's neck. The effect was very dashing. "Since Gypsies have no written language, no one really knows. An Oxford linguist who has studied the language told me that his guess was that the Rom began their wanderings in Asia. Northern India, perhaps."

Thinking of what she had read of India, she studied the dark-skinned people around her and decided that the linguist's theory sounded plausible. "Are there no oral tales of Romany history?"

"Many, most of which contradict each other." He chuckled. "There's an old saying: ask the same question to twenty Gypsies and you'll get twenty different answers. On the other hand, if you ask one Gypsy the same question twenty times, you will still get twenty different answers."

Clare laughed. "You're telling me that consistency is not considered a virtue to the Rom."

"And all of them, from the youngest to the oldest, can lie beautifully and fluently when necessary." He took another swig from the bottle, then handed it to the next man in the circle. "Or they may lie from an excess of creativity, or for amusement. A crafty man is admired here, just as an upright man is honored among the Welsh."

On the far side of the campfire, Milosh struck up a tune on the fiddle, another man accompanying him with a tambourine. Conversation died and people began clapping hands, emphasizing the old beat of the music. Her lush body swaying, Ani walked over and presented Clare with a crimson scarf. "You and Nikki dance together while holding the ends," she explained. "To show that you are now joined."

Though Clare's dancing skills were almost nonexistent, she was willing to try. As she got to her feet, Nicholas suggested, "Let down your hair."

Obediently she took off her head scarf and raked her fingers through the thick tresses so that they fell into a dark, shimmering mantle. Then she and Nicholas took opposite ends of the scarf, and they moved into the center of the circle. "Behave like a flirtatious maiden," he said with his Demon Earl smile. "Be the teasing minx I know you can be."

She thought about that as they began circling slowly, the scarf taut between them. How had she felt when falling under Nicholas's spell? Terrified of his sexual magnetism, yet utterly unable to resist it. Looking deep into his eyes, she let the potent memories flow through her.

She began by lowering her eyes in a pantomime of shyness, then letting her low-cut blouse slip seductively off one shoulder as she turned away. Lithe and powerful, Nicholas responded as pure male animal in pursuit of his mate, tugging on the scarf to draw her back.

She glided close, then slid away when he reached for her. When he followed, she darted beneath his arm, her hair lashing across his face, both defense and enticement. He allowed her to retreat, then whipped her close again. Modestly she covered her face with her free hand, yet when she spun away her skirt swirled provocatively high. He followed with the proud arrogance of a stallion, wordlessly promising conquest and fulfillment. As the music beat faster and faster, they whirled across the circle like beings possessed, their movements a fiery prelude to the inevitable end of their dance.

With one last wild flourish, the fiddle stopped, leaving pulse-pounding silence. Nicholas swept Clare into his embrace, bending her back over his arm.

As she pitched backwards, she experienced an instant of reflexive panic. It vanished as quickly as it had come, for she knew in every cell of her body that Nicholas would never let her fall. As her hair splashed across the grass, he gave her a kiss that claimed her as his own. The Rom roared and stamped their feet with approval.

Gently he brought her up again, his gaze a caress. "One last ritual, Clarissima. We must jump over the branch of flowering broom that Ani just laid down."

Hand in hand they raced across the clearing and leaped over the broom. Under the cover of the ensuing applause, she hissed, "Jumping the broomstick is an old Welsh country tradition that has probably been around since the Druids."

He laughed. "The Rom are very eclectic. They'll adopt any custom that pleases them."

The fiddle struck up again, and this time everyone joined in the dancing, from old Keja to all children who could walk. Circles formed, then split into smaller groups. The musicians took turns so no one would miss a chance to dance. For Clare, it was a revelation. This was not dancing as mere amusement or sinful temptation; this was dance as the breath of life.

And Nicholas was the most ardent of all. When he caught her hands and swung her about, she felt his energy pulsing through her like a river of fire. She responded with all of the passion that had so recently blossomed within her. Before she had been the maiden; now she danced as the temptress, a woman proud of her femininity and utterly confident of her ability to please her man.

Later, after the exhausted children had been put to bed

and even the adults were too tired for another tune, Kore brought out a small Welsh harp and handed it to Nicholas.

Gently he strummed the instrument, tuning the strings while he considered what to play. He chose a long Romany ballad that seemed to be woven from the haunting joys and sorrows of his wandering race. Clare sat beside him, her eyes closed as she absorbed the beauty of his deep, rich voice. At the end, he sang a verse that he must have translated to English for her sake.

Worldly goods possess and destroy you,
Love must be free as the blowing wind.
Capture the wind between four walls and it dies.
Open tents, open hearts,
Let the wind blow . . .

The poignancy of it caught her heart. Though she doubted that he meant the words as a message to her, she sensed that the way to hold Nicholas was never to try. *Love must be free as the blowing wind. . . .*

Then they retired to their bed, which they had laid some distance from the others. Sandwiched between the soft warmth of two dunhas and roofed only by stars, he made fierce, possessive love to her. Desire had been intensified by their mating dance, and now it was raised to fever pitch by the silence with which they came together.

Wishing that words of love were not forbidden, Clare let her body speak for her. Later, when he slept, his head upon her breast, she caressed his thick black hair, filled with wonder at the man she had married. A Gypsy, a Welshman, a nobleman, a bard—he was all of those things, and more. And she knew that she would love him until she died.

The next morning Clare felt a little fragile. She had been most immoderate the evening before: eaten too much, drunk too much wine, danced too long, and had had wildly intemperate sexual congress with her husband. More than once, in fact. John Wesley might not have approved. However, now that Clare had developed her own inner guidance, she checked directly with the Divine and concluded that He didn't mind at all, for love was the wellspring of her passion. Nonetheless, the slight headache was a useful reminder that moderation still had a place in her life.

As the kumpania was breaking camp, old Keja walked up and announced, "I must talk with you. This morning you ride in my wagon."

Clare was happy to accept. Though she had scarcely exchanged a word with Keja, she had often felt the old woman's gaze on her. They had the wagon to themselves, Keja having used her influence to procure privacy.

For a long time Keja simply stared at Clare, puffing on her pipe. Abruptly she said, "I am cousin of the father of Marta, Nikki's mother."

Clare's interest quickened. If so, Keja was one of Nicholas's closest relatives. Wanting to take advantage of this opportunity, she asked, "Why did Marta sell her son? That knowledge has been a wound in Nicholas's heart."

"Marta was dying of lung sickness," Keja said with equal bluntness. "She should have left Nikki with us, but she had made a vow to her husband to see that their son learned the ways of the Gorgios." The old woman grimaced. "Because it was what Kenrick had wanted, and she knew that soon she would no longer be able to care for Nikki herself, Marta took him to his grandparents, who were his closest blood kin."

"The fact that she sold him for a hundred guineas makes it hard for me to believe that she was acting selflessly," Clare said, her voice hard. "How could any woman sell her child?"

"The old Gorgio offered the money of his own will," Keja said with disgust. "Marta almost spat in his face, but she was Rom—if the Gorgio wanted to be a fool, she would let him."

Thinking of what she had learned about the Rom, Clare said hesitantly, "In other words, the two transactions were separate—she took Nicholas to his grandfather for Kenrick's sake, and in her mind, the money really had nothing to do with Nikki."

Keja gave a gap-toothed smile, her head bobbing. "For a Gorgio, you have good understanding. I show you the proof that Marta did not sell her son for gold." She opened a chest and delved in, withdrawing a heavy leather pouch. Handing it to Clare, she said, "She left this with me to give to Nikki when the time was right."

Clare opened the pouch, then sucked in her breath at the sight of the gold coins.

Keja said, "It is all there, except for a guinea or two that Marta used to buy food on her way back to the Rom. Mine was the nearest kumpania, so she stayed with us."

"What happened to Marta?"

Keja puffed her pipe hard, smoke wreathing her head. "Marta died with the winter, in my arms. The gold I have kept for Nikki all these years."

Bewildered, Clare asked, "Why was he never told that his mother gave him up because she was dying? The knowledge would have made a great difference to him. And why didn't you give him the gold earlier? You've seen him often over the years."

"Marta made me swear an oath to tell only Nicholas's wife, for a woman would understand that a mother must do the best she can for her child," Keja said softly.

"But Nicholas had a wife before me."

Keja looked as if she would have spat if she had been outdoors. "Bah, he bedded that one, but she was not his true wife. You are the one Marta foresaw. She had the gift, and she said that a woman would come who would heal her Nikki's heart."

Clare stared at the golden coins, tears stinging her eyes. Had Marta really foreseen Clare? She had been young when she died, perhaps younger than Clare was now.

Would Marta have left Nicholas with his grandfather if she had known how cold and abusive the old man was? Perhaps she had assumed that Kenrick's mother would care for Nicholas. But the old earl's first wife had already fallen into the long twilight that had clouded her mind for the last years of her life, leaving her unable to love her grandson.

"Poor Marta," Clare said with deep empathy. "It must have been terribly difficult for her to choose between her own people and her promise to her dead husband. And even more difficult to give up her son to a stranger. I hope she is resting in peace."

"She is," Keja said matter-of-factly. "She is with Kenrick. Now that you have come to take care of Nikki, she will no longer worry for her son."

Clare felt the hair on the back of her neck prickle. As a Christian she believed that spirit was immortal. She also knew that there were rare individuals who manifested "gifts of the spirit"—the ability to know things beyond the visible realm. It was said that John Wesley's own mother and sisters had been so gifted. Nonetheless, it was eerie to hear someone speak of the supernatural with such calm acceptance. She was learning more from the Rom than she had expected.

"I love Nicholas, and I will always do my best for him," she said quietly. Remembering the form for Gypsy oaths, she added, "May you burn candles for me if I fail in this."

"Bater," Keja said gravely. "May it be so."

The wagon rumbled to a stop and Nicholas called, "Clare, we're home."

She closed the leather pouch and deposited it in an inner pocket. Since Nicholas had more pressing concerns at the moment, she would wait before telling him Marta's story. But she would not wait long; though he might find it painful to have the old scars probed, she hoped that ultimately the knowledge would take away his feeling that his mother had betrayed him.

She kissed her companion's leather cheek. "Thank you for trusting me, Keja." Then she climbed from the wagon.

The kumpania stood in front of Aberdare. Williams was on the steps. Apparently he had come out to shoo the Gypsies away, then been bemused to see his employer emerge from a wagon.

There followed an orgy of farewells. Clare hugged Ani particularly hard. "You'll come back?"

The other woman chuckled. "Oh, yes. Like the wind, we come, we go, and we come again."

After waving good-bye, Clare and Nicholas climbed the stairs to the house, his arm around her waist. Expression as bland as butter, Williams held the door open for them. Clare found herself very aware of the lowness of her blouse and the shortness of her skirts. But she held her head high and swept past the butler as calmly as if she had been respectably dressed.

By tacit agreement, they went directly to their bedchamber. Clare pulled off her boots and wiggled her toes with pleasure. "I'm going to ring for a bath. Though I really enjoyed your kinfolk, there was a sad shortage of hot water."

He smiled, but there was an abstracted expression in his eyes. Dropping her levity, Clare said, "Nicholas, what are you going to do about Lord Michael?"

He sighed. "Lay evidence before a magistrate. Michael will be arrested right away, I imagine. If he can't come up with some damned good explanations, he is going to be in serious trouble."

"He's a wealthy and powerful man. Will that protect him?"

Nicholas's eyes narrowed. "I am the Earl of Aberdare, and my wealth and power exceed his. If he is behind the attempt on our lives, he will not escape justice."

It was the first time she had seen a resemblance to his formidable grandfather. Relieved that he was willing to use his influence to protect himself, she said, "I'm glad that you're leaving justice to the law rather than taking it into your own hands."

"I don't believe in duels. They're a barbaric remnant of the Middle Ages." He took off his Romany vest and scarf. "Your class meeting is tonight. Are you going?"

She had forgotten herself. "Yes, unless you'd rather I stayed with you this evening."

"No, go to your meeting. I want to start working on that song to commemorate the mine explosion. I had some ideas over the last few days. But since we'll be spending the evening apart, I think I'll monopolize your time for the rest of the afternoon." He ran his gaze over her with blatant carnality. "Order the bath. Interesting things can be done in a tub."

Blushing, she did as he asked while he withdrew to his dressing room. But instead of disrobing, he slipped out of the other door, went down to his desk in the library, and jotted a hasty note. After sealing it, he rang for the butler.

When Williams appeared, Nicholas handed over the missive. "Have this taken to Lord Michael Kenyon. Most likely he's at the mine at this hour. If not, I want the messenger to track him down and wait for an answer. And don't tell anyone about this—especially not Lady Aberdare."

"Very good, my lord."

With that attended to, Nicholas made his way back to his dressing room. Nothing could be done for several hours, so he was going to use the time in the best possible way.

31

RECOGNIZING THE seal, Michael Kenyon's mouth tightened as he slit open the note. The words were terse and to the point:

Michael: I must speak with you alone. I suggest 7:00 this evening. The ruins at Caerbach are convenient and neutral, but I will meet you at any time and place of your choosing as long as it is soon. Aberdare.

"Bloody hell!" Michael snarled after reading the familiar handwriting. Crumpling the note in his hand, he pitched it furiously across his office. "Damn Aberdare!"

The messenger said politely, "Is that your reply, my lord?"

Michael's anger burned away quickly, leaving ashes. He dipped a pen into his inkstand, then scrawled: *7:00 tonight, at Caerbach, alone. Kenyon.*

He sanded and sealed the note and gave it to the messenger. The man bowed, then left.

Michael stared blankly across his office, feeling the inner tightness that always came before battle. The day of reckoning had come. Deep in his bones, he had known that he would not be able to avoid this confrontation, though God knew he had tried.

He looked at the stack of work on his desk, then shoved it aside. It was impossible to care about projected delivery dates for his new equipment. Wearily he rose, lifted his hat, and strode out of his office. Pausing at Madoc's desk, which was just outside, he said, "I'm leaving for the day. Was there anything you needed to discuss with me?"

Madoc leaned back in his massive chair and linked his fingers across his midriff. "No, everything is fine."

With a faint nod of relief, Kenyon left.

Madoc made a pretense of returning to his work, but inwardly he was thinking about the interesting little episode with the Aberdare messenger. He waited until ten minutes had passed and he had seen Kenyon ride away. Then he went into his employer's office—the office that had been his own for four years. Since no other employees were near, he didn't bother to conceal the bitterness of his expression.

Many records were kept in Kenyon's office, so no one would have thought twice at seeing Madoc inside. That had proved very convenient on several occasions.

After Kenyon's oath, there had been a sound of paper being crumpled and thrown. Madoc scanned the floor and quickly located the wadded note in one corner of the office. Smoothing it out, he read it once, then again, unable to believe his luck. This would be perfect, absolutely perfect.

God was definitely on his side.

As usual, Nicholas had been right: very interesting things could be done while bathing. The process left Clare spotless and purring. She and Nicholas dozed afterward, then rose and shared a light meal. When she finished eating, she gave him a light kiss. "I'll see you after the meeting. Are you the sort of artist who doesn't like to show work in progress, or might I hear the early results of your composing tonight?"

"I prefer to wait until I have the piece roughly worked out." His gaze held her for a moment. Then he gave her a gentle pat on the backside. "Off with you, or you'll be late."

After donning her bonnet, she went out the side entrance to the stables, where her pony cart was waiting. She had driven around the front of the house before she recalled that she had intended to take some books to Owen. It would be weeks before he could return to work, and he wanted to use the time well. Though she had sent some volumes home with him the day of the wedding, he might be ready for more.

She halted the cart in front of the house and looped the reins around one of the granite urns. Skipping into the

house, she went right to the library. No sign of Nicholas;
he must have withdrawn to the music room.

She had selected the books and was on the way out when
a brilliant flash of light drew her eye to Nicholas's desk.
Curiously she went to investigate, and found that the slanting rays of the sun were reflecting off a chunk of quartz and
twisted silver. She lifted it and turned it over in her hands.
So this was the famous specimen of wire silver that had
been collected with such risk, and which in the end had not
been needed. With everything that had happened in the last
fortnight, she hadn't seen it before. Well, it made a decent
paperweight.

She was about to set it down when she saw the note that
had been resting underneath. The paper unfolded, revealing
slashing black handwriting. *7:00 tonight, at Caerbach,
alone. Kenyon.*

Dread struck with paralyzing force. No . . . dear God,
no. . . .

Dumping her books on the desk, she snatched up the note.
As she read it again, fury blazed through her. Damn Nicholas! After swearing that he would do nothing foolish, he
was stepping right into the lion's den. A formal duel would
require seconds, so perhaps Nicholas only wanted to talk,
but how could he be so stupid as to trust Lord Michael after
all that had happened? And how could she have been so
naive as to believe Nicholas's assurances?

Only the night before he had mentioned that Gypsies lied
fluently when necessary, and obviously that was a skill he
had retained. He must have sent a message to Lord Michael
before making love to her, and received the answer before
they had dined. The damned, treacherous, pig-headed . . .

Imprecations boiling through her mind, she raced through
the house and out to the stables again. Seeing the head
groom, she gasped, "Has Lord Aberdare gone out?"

"About five minutes ago, my lady."

"Saddle a horse for me," she ordered. Remembering that
Rhonda was gone, she added, "A gentle, biddable one. And
use a regular saddle, not a sidesaddle."

He gave her modest day dress a doubtful glance, but went
off obediently. Fuming, she paced in front of the stables,

vaguely aware that she had never allowed herself to feel such rage in her life; the passion that Nicholas had unleashed in her was emerging in unexpected ways. Of course, never in her life had she felt such fear. Every nuance of their lovemaking that afternoon returned to her. Looking back, she realized that it had been unusually intense; had he been saying good-bye in case something went wrong? Her stomach knotted at the thought.

Briefly she considered taking the groom with her, but after a moment's reflection she decided against it. This was not the sort of conflict that could be resolved by armed retainers, like bands of medieval knights. A single female would have a better chance of preventing violence between the two men. They had both been raised as proper English gentlemen, and she would use that fact ruthlessly.

The groom brought a chestnut mare to the mounting block and Clare swung into the saddle. Her skirt bunched around her knees, baring her calves, but propriety was the last thing on her mind. She did remember her pony, so as she gathered the reins she said, "Please bring my cart from the front of the house. I won't be needing it."

Then she galloped out of the stableyard. Thank God she had done so much riding over the last weeks, and thank Nicholas for the fact that all of his mounts were beautifully trained.

Caerbach was a small ruined fortress that stood on common grazing land about halfway between Aberdare and Bryn Manor. Originally it had been an outpost of the main castle of Aberdare. It would not take long to reach it.

How soon until she was close enough to hear a gunshot? As she pounded along the track, she prayed with the greatest fervor of her life.

Caerbach stood on top of a hill and had once commanded a wide view of the valley. Over the centuries the woods had encroached and the cut stone had been taken for use elsewhere, leaving a scattering of rocks and partial walls set in the center of a sunny clearing. For children it was a delightful place to play hide-and-seek; for adults, it offered undisputed privacy.

Nicholas kept an alert eye on the trees as he rode through the woods, but was unsurprised to find that Michael was already in the clearing, lounging against one of the low walls with his arms folded across his chest. His casual posture did not match his taut face.

As Nicholas dismounted, Michael growled, ''You're late.''

''I see you still have your watch set fast.'' Nicholas tethered his horse outside the ruins. ''You never could stand the thought of being even a minute late.''

''Don't waste my time with vapid reminiscences. Why the hell did you ask me here?''

Unhurriedly Nicholas picked his way among the stones, the coils of his whip gently slapping his leg underneath his coat. Though he had chosen not to bring a pistol to this meeting, he hadn't wanted to be entirely defenseless. He stopped opposite Michael, fifteen feet of clear ground separating them. ''A couple of reasons. The most important is to get to the bottom of why you decided to hate me. Since you haven't taken against Rafe and Lucien, I presume there must be something specific about me.''

Tight-lipped, Michael said, ''You presume correctly.''

When no further comment came, Nicholas said encouragingly, ''The only motive I can think of is sheer bad sportsmanship. Youth is competitive, and you and I often went against each other. It was usually a pretty even match. I never much minded when I lost, but you hated losing. Is that the problem—that I won too often and defeat has been festering for years?''

''Don't be absurd,'' Michael snapped. ''Schoolboy competition has nothing to do with this.''

Nicholas refused to get irritated; it had never been easy to extract information from Michael. ''What did I do that is so dreadful that you can't bring yourself to speak of it?''

A muscle in Michael's jaw twitched. ''Once I say it, the die will be cast. I . . . . I'll have no choice but to kill you.''

And he didn't really want to, Nicholas was interested to see. ''I didn't come here to die, Michael, though if I have to fight you, I will.'' He put one hand on his hip, brushing back his coat to expose the whip in case Michael hadn't noticed it. "But before we get to that, I must find out if you were responsible for the recent attempts to kill me." He felt a brief flare of the anger that he had been keeping under rigid control. "The one thing I find truly unforgivable is that Clare's life has been endangered. That is also why I questioned whether you're behind it. Have you become so mad that you would kill an innocent woman to get at me?"

"I have no idea what you're talking about."

"The day after you returned to Penreith, I was riding with Clare and a party of children when a bullet grazed my horse. Clare was sure that you had fired at me, but I thought it was a poacher. You're too good a shot to miss."

"You're right—if I had wanted to shoot you in the back, I would have done it." Michael frowned. "It must have been one of your other enemies."

"I can't think of anyone else who wants to kill me, so I'll stay with the poacher for the time being." Nicholas's voice hardened. "However, it's impossible to explain away the five men that ambushed Clare and me at a traveler's hut in the mountains. They set it afire at midnight, then waited outside with rifles to shoot us when we tried to escape."

Michael's eyes widened with what seemed like genuine surprise. "You both got out unharmed?"

"No thanks to you." Nicholas dug into his pocket for the silver card case, then flipped it across the clearing. Michael instinctively reached under his coat. The movement confirmed Nicholas's suspicion proving that the other man had come armed.

When he saw that Nicholas was not throwing anything dangerous, Michael swiftly changed his action to a one-handed catch. Recognizing the flat silver box, he said, "Where did you get my card case?" He lifted his head, his eyes molten with anger. "Have you been trespassing on my property again?"

"It was found outside the hut where the ambush took place," Nicholas retorted. "In a court of law, that might be enough to hang you. Yet in spite of the evidence, I have trouble believing you would be so cowardly, or that you would hire bandits to help you." Remembering the bullet that had almost struck Clare and the terrifying escape that

followed put cracks in Nicholas's composure. "Well? What
have you got to say for yourself?"

"I don't have to answer to you, Aberdare, but for what
it's worth, you judged correctly. I did my best to break your
neck in London, and I've been planning on challenging you
again, to a real duel this time. But I had nothing to do with
any ambushes." Michael held up the card case. "This went
missing several days ago. I don't know exactly when or
where, because I often forget to carry it." He dropped the
case into a pocket. "So much for evidence of my treachery.
You obviously have more enemies than you thought."

Seeing that the other man didn't see the implications,
Nicholas said with exasperation, "You damned fool, don't
you see what this means? If you're telling the truth, someone is trying to kill me and pin the blame on you. If that
doesn't worry you, it should."

Michael looked startled. "That makes no sense."

"Have you got a better theory?"

The silence was broken by the sound of pounding hooves.
Nicholas turned and saw Clare cantering through the trees,
hair and skirts flying, fear on her face. She relaxed when
she saw that he was all right, but her gaze was anxious as
it went to Michael. Feeling a flicker of humor, Nicholas
said, "I trust that you recall meeting Clare in London."

Michael scowled. "Can't you control your wife, Aberdare?"

"It's easy to see that you've never been married," Nicholas said dryly. "But he's right, Clare. Your interference is
neither necessary nor desirable."

Scowling as if they were both recalcitrant schoolboys, she
swung from her horse, showing an amount of leg that made
Nicholas want to wrap his coat around her. "Men always
say things like that when they are about to behave stupidly.
I hope that if I'm here, you won't murder each other."

"I don't think murder is imminent," Nicholas said. "The
interesting topic on the table is who tried to kill us. Michael
disclaims any involvement in either the shooting incident or
the attack at the hut."

"And you believe him?" Her brows arched skeptically.
"If not Lord Michael, then who?"

A new voice cut across the clearing. "You're about to find out, Lady Aberdare." All three of them swiveled around to see George Madoc step from behind one of the higher walls, eyes like ice and a rifle steady in his hands. Glancing at Clare, he said, "I didn't plan on you being here, but I can't say that it much bothers me to kill you along with the others. You always were a damned trouble-maker."

Michael made a sharp movement, and Madoc swung the rifle toward him. "Don't try anything, Kenyon, or I'll shoot you where you stand."

Madoc gave a nod of satisfaction when Michael stilled. "I like to see you obeying orders instead of giving them. Lift your hands into the air, all three of you. Did you know that Nye Wilkins was a sharpshooter when he was in the army? A dead shot. He's kept in touch with some of his old friends, too. I was surprised when I heard that you managed to get away from them, Aberdare—you're cleverer than I thought. Of course, Gypsies are known for slyness."

As Clare and the others raised their hands, Wilkins stepped forward and trained his rifle on Nicholas. The miner had a rangy build that resembled that of Lord Michael; Clare guessed that he had been the one she and Nicholas had seen outside the hut the night they were attacked.

Michael's eyes narrowed to dangerous slits. "I assume that you stole the card case from my office."

"Aye, just as I found Aberdare's note today." Madoc's pale eyes gleamed nastily. "You never took me seriously, did you? I was only a lowborn hireling. You probably don't think I know how to use this gun, but I'm a damned good shot. I practiced by hunting on your land while you were off hunting Frenchies. I almost killed Aberdare at a range that even an army sharpshooter would have had trouble with." He gave a coarse laugh. "I'm cleverer than you, and tougher than you, and now I'm going to take what's mine."

"Which is?" Michael asked.

"The pit. I've worked and sweated over it for years, and by any fair standard it should belong to me." His eyes flashed with his sense of injustice. "I'm the one responsible for making it so profitable. Even after sending you a plausible amount of money, there was plenty left over for me. And you were too stupid to notice that I was cheating you.''

''Wrong.'' Michael's steady gaze was like that of a tiger waiting to pounce. ''I knew you were embezzling, it simply wasn't important to learn the details until I had corrected the other problems caused by your mismanagement.''

A vicious expression crossed Madoc's face. Clare tensed, wondering if Michael was deliberately trying to provoke him.

Perhaps wondering the same thing, Nicholas's cool voice said, ''This is all very interesting, but where do I come in? We had one brief run-in when I visited the mine, but it hardly seems enough for you to mark Clare and me for murder.''

''I despise you both. Even though you're tainted with Gypsy blood, you're an earl. And what is that pious bitch but a jumped-up village girl? Neither of you have my intelligence or ambition, yet through no effort of your own, you're wallowing in wealth,'' Madoc said with a sneer. ''But you're right that I don't hate you as I do Kenyon. That's why I decided to give you a quick death, leaving evidence that Kenyon was responsible.''

He gave an ugly smile. ''I was looking forward to seeing the noble Lord Michael Kenyon being tried and executed for murder. Hanging is said to be painful, but not half so painful as the public humiliation would be. You've tried so hard to prove yourself, and all of it would have ended on the scaffold.''

From the tightness of Michael's face, Clare guessed that Madoc understood his victim well, but when Michael replied, his voice was ironic. ''Sorry you'll be deprived of your amusement.''

Madoc shrugged. ''Part of intelligence is being flexible. Since I failed at killing Aberdare and blaming it on you, now I'll simply shoot you both. Since your hatred of Aberdare is well-known, it will be thought that you shot each other and her prim ladyship got caught in the crossfire. A pity, but no more than one might expect from a Gypsy and a half-mad soldier.''

His expression was mocking. ''And when the dust settles, a

very nicely forged amendment to your last will and testament will be found. As a reward for my 'faithful service,' you're leaving me the mining company, Bryn Manor, and five thousand pounds as well. I knew better than to try for your whole fortune—that would have made your family suspicious. No, I'll settle for the pit, the estate, and a bit of cash. With you two dead, I'll be the most powerful man in the valley.''

He was almighty proud of his cleverness, and Clare wondered if there was some way to use that against him. Already his need to boast had caused him to string this hideous scene out; a wiser man would have shot them out of hand. And he was making the same mistake he had accused Michael of—underestimating his opponents.

She glanced at Wilkins, and her faint hope faded. Whatever Madoc's weaknesses, Wilkins did not look like a man who would be distracted from his lethal duty. Terror threatened to engulf her. She believed in life immortal, and that her soul was now in decent shape. Yet though she did not fear death, she didn't want to die yet; not when she and Nicholas had just found each other.

''Thank you for answering my questions,'' Nicholas said with mocking politeness. ''I'd hate to die in ignorance.'' He looked at Michael, his gaze intent. ''You should have worked faster, Michael. Now you've missed your chance to kill me.''

Perhaps it was Clare's imagination, but it seemed as if a silent message passed between the two men. Her heart skipped nervously; though Nicholas and Michael were both formidable, they were also unarmed. What could they do against two rifles when they were both weaponless?

Insight struck her with brutal clarity: there was no point in meekly waiting to be slaughtered. Nicholas and Michael would have known that from the start. At any moment they would attempt suicidal assaults on the gunmen, for a faint hope was better than none, and there was more dignity in dying fighting.

Her mind began to race. There were three of them and only two single-shot rifles. Once the weapons were dis-

charged, the struggle would be hand to hand, and if it came
to that, she would put her money on the Fallen Angels.

Since she was a woman, the gunmen were paying the
least attention to her. She was the closest to Wilkins; if she
attacked the sharpshooter, it would take him a moment to
turn his gun on her, and the ensuing disturbance might give
Nicholas and Michael the critical seconds they needed.

Madoc's gloating voice interrupted her racing thoughts.
"Say your prayers, if you think it will do any good. Wilkins,
you take Aberdare and his wife. Kenyon is mine."

Before Clare could put her feeble plan into action, Nicholas said, "Wait. No doubt you think I'm a damned senti-
mental fool, but I'd like to kiss my wife good-bye."

Madoc studied Clare with interest, as if seeing her for
the first time. "You know, you've turned into quite a hot
little wench. They say that all preacher's daughters are sluts
at heart—you'd have to be, to spread your legs for a Gypsy.
Wilkins, don't shoot her yet. We might as well have a spot
of entertainment after we kill the men." He nodded at Nicholas. "Go ahead, kiss her. Make it good so she's warmed
up for us."

Lethal rage flared in Nicholas's eyes. Clare's heart almost
stopped; if he flung himself at Madoc now, he was doomed.
She bit her lip to keep herself from crying out, her eyes
making an agonized plea for him to wait.

He drew a shuddering breath and managed to master his
fury, then closed the distance between them. His low voice
only emphasizing his intensity, he said, "I love you, Clare.
I should have said so sooner."

His words startled her so much that she almost missed
what he whispered when he bent to kiss her. "When I push
you to the ground, roll behind that stone wall, then run for
your life."

Their minds had been working on similar lines, she saw.
By coming to kiss her, he was now closer to Wilkins, and
their embrace might provide the kind of distraction that she
had been considering. Knowing that a move on her part
might disrupt his plan, she nodded agreement, though she
had no intention of running. Aloud she said, "I love you,
Nicholas. And if you're not going to heaven, I'll go wher-

ever you do." Her voice wavered. "May you burn candles for me if I fail in this."

She saw unbearable pain in his face, and knew that it was mirrored in hers. Whatever scheme he had in mind, the odds were against them and this might indeed be their last kiss.

They came together like a storm, a lifetime of emotion flaring between them. It seemed impossible that in a minute she might be dead, her body torn and bleeding. And Nicholas . . .

Her fingers bit into his arms. She forced herself to loosen her grip, so that when he pushed her she would not slow him down.

Even through her desperate yearning, she sensed the avid interest of the gunmen. Their slackening of alertness was the opportunity Michael had been waiting for. He hurled himself to one side, away from Madoc's gun.

At the same instant, Nicholas shoved Clare away, shouting, "Now!" As she tumbled to the ground, he leaped in the opposite direction, toward Wilkins.

Caught off-guard, the gunman lost a few precious seconds trying to target his quarry. Before he could, Nicholas's whip magically appeared in his hand and he slashed out violently.

His bold rush brought him close enough to get the tip of the lash around Wilkins's rifle. The whip dragged the barrel down, spoiling the miner's aim. Savagely Wilkins jerked his weapon, trying to wrest it free so he could shoot.

Clare saw that Michael was not unarmed, he had a pistol. He and Madoc took aim at each other and fired simultaneously, the reports shattering the woodland silence.

Madoc's shout was cut off by a gurgle of blood when the bullet ripped through his throat. Michael went down, rolling across the ground. Though Clare did not see a wound, she guessed that he had been hit, perhaps mortally.

But there was no time to tend Michael, for a violent tug-of-war was raging between Nicholas and Wilkins. As Nicholas tried to wrench the rifle away, the gunman held on with furious determination. Clare scrambled to her feet and darted toward the two men.

With only the smooth barrel to cling to, the whip abruptly

slithered loose, throwing Nicholas off-balance. He staggered and fell to one knee. Wilkins stepped back, out of range of the lash, and took aim, an unholy light in his eyes. Nicholas tried to dodge, but his awkward position made it impossible for him to move quickly enough to avoid Wilkins's shot.

Driven by heart-stopping panic, Clare dived forward in a desperate attempt to block the bullet. Her palm struck the barrel at the same instant that the rifle exploded with ear-shattering power. A blow numbed the left side of her body and spun her around as she fell to the grassy turf. She lay still, too stunned to move.

Nicholas shouted, "Clare!" His expression frantic, he dropped to his knees and lifted her upper body onto his lap.

Clare looked past his shoulder and saw that a swearing Wilkins was reloading with unbelievable speed. As the gunman raised his weapon, she tried to warn Nicholas of his danger, but she couldn't seem to speak.

Another shot exploded, this time a lighter, sharper crack than the rifle. Scarlet blossomed on Wilkins's chest and he spun around and fell, his rifle spinning through the air before it, too, struck the ground.

Clare turned her head and saw Michael lying flat on his belly, the pistol firm between his hands and a wisp of smoke trickling upward from the barrel. He was not only alive, but he had saved Nicholas's life, she thought with mild wonder. Truly the Lord worked in mysterious ways.

Clare felt dazed, not quite able to grasp that a skirmish that was over in seconds had left two men dead. Michael seemed uninjured, for he got to his feet easily, but she was too numb to know whether she was seriously wounded or merely stunned.

As Nicholas ripped open Clare's left sleeve, pain shafted through her and she whimpered. After a quick examination, he said soothingly, "The bullet went through your upper arm. It must hurt like bloody hell, but it missed the bone. You'll be all right, Clare. Even the bleeding isn't too bad." He yanked off his cravat and bound her arm tightly.

Her numbness began to wear off. As Nicholas said, her arm hurt terribly—anyone who talked of "only a flesh wound'' had never had one—but it was no worse than when she had broken her ankle.

Cautiously she sat up, and Nicholas moved her back a few feet so that she could sit supported by the wall. After settling her, he said violently, "Why the *hell* did you do something so stupid? You could have been killed!"

She gave him an unsteady smile. "Why didn't you do something to protect yourself when Wilkins was reloading?"

"I knew that Michael would take care of him. And when I knew that you had been hit . . ." His voice broke off.

"You risked your life for mine, love. Can't I do the same for you?" Clare said with a gentle smile.

His face worked as he tried to control his chaotic emotions.

Before Nicholas could speak, Michael said, "Lady Aberdare is all right?"

Nicholas inhaled, his expression smoothing out. "Yes, thanks to you." He touched Clare's hair with fingers that still trembled slightly.

"Stand up and move away from your wife, Aberdare," Michael said harshly. "It's time to settle what brought us here, and I don't want her to get hurt."

The note in the other man's voice cut through Nicholas's preoccupation. He looked up, suddenly wary.

Michael was standing silhouetted against the setting sun, his pistol locked in his hands.

And the gun was pointing straight at Nicholas's heart.

32

HIS GAZE on the pistol, Nicholas stood and stepped away from Clare. "So we're back to that," he said conversationally. "You never did say why you want me dead."

Michael moved closer. With the sun no longer behind him, Nicholas could see the wild despair in his green eyes. Whatever madness Michael carried had been triggered by the violence that had almost engulfed them all.

White-faced, Clare struggled to her feet and leaned against the stone wall. "If you kill Nicholas, you'll have to kill me too, Lord Michael," she said fiercely. "Do you think I'll keep silent if you murder my husband?"

"Of course not. You'll see me hanged, and justly so. That doesn't matter." He stepped over to the whip. Keeping his gaze on Nicholas, he stooped and tossed it out of reach. "Perhaps I'll save the hangman the trouble of executing me, because I can't imagine living with myself after this."

"Then don't do it!" she cried. "What has Nicholas done to warrant death at your hands?"

"I promised that justice would be done, never thinking that I would be called on to fulfill my vow," Michael said bleakly. "When the time came, I turned coward. I spent four years in the army, hoping that a bullet would spare me from having to do this. Yet fate preserved me and brought me here." Pain crossed his face. "I can no longer fight fate."

"To whom did you make your vow?" Nicholas asked softly. "My grandfather? He hated me and did his best to alienate my friends, but I never thought he would try to have me killed."

"Not your grandfather. Caroline."

There was a moment of frozen silence. Then rage exploded through Nicholas. "Christ, so you were one of her lovers! I should have guessed. The evidence was all there, but I didn't want to believe it." His voice cracked. "I wasn't *able* to believe it, not of you."

"We loved each other from the first time we met, at your wedding, when it was already too late," Michael said, his face stark with guilt. "Because you were my friend, I fought against my feelings, and so did she. But . . . but we could not stay apart."

"So you became another victim of Caroline's lies," Nicholas said with furious disgust.

"Don't speak of her that way!" Michael's fingers whitened on the butt of the pistol. "She would never have been unfaithful if you had not mistreated her so wickedly." His words poured out as if they had been festering. "She told me all about you—your cruelty, the revolting things you forced her to do. At first I had trouble believing it. Yet how much does a man know about how his friends treat women?"

"And how much does a man know about how a woman treats other men?" Nicholas said caustically.

Before he could continue, Michael cut him off. "After I saw the bruises on her body and she had cried in my arms, I came to believe. Caroline was terrified of you. She said that if she died mysteriously, you would be to blame, and that I must avenge her. I gave her my word, never thinking that I would have to carry it out. Even though you had treated her monstrously, I never believed you capable of murder."

"If Caroline had bruises, it was because she liked her sex rough—as her lover, you must have noticed that," Nicholas snapped. "And she died in a coach accident because she insisted that the driver go too fast. I had nothing to do with it."

"Perhaps you caused the accident, perhaps not. It doesn't matter. If she hadn't feared you, she would not have fled Aberdare when you were caught in the act of bedding your grandfather's wife! You are as responsible as if you shot her in the heart." Michael wiped the sweat from his face with a trembling hand. "Did you know that she was pregnant when she died? She was carrying my child, and she was running away to me. I had begged her to leave you earlier, but she refused from some mistaken sense of honor."

"Caroline didn't know the meaning of honor." Nicholas's mouth twisted. "But maybe you did father her child. Certainly it wasn't me—I hadn't touched Caroline in months. You weren't the only candidate for the honor, though."

"Don't slander a woman who can't defend herself!"

The hysterical edge in Michael's voice forced Nicholas to rein in his anger. Though he had never truly believed that his old friend wanted to kill him, the fact that Caroline was involved changed everything. Now Michael was holding a gun, and if he snapped, Nicholas was a dead man.

He would have to reveal the whole ugly story; there was no other choice. Unable to suppress his furious bitterness, Nicholas said, "*Caroline was my grandfather's mistress.*"

There was a moment of horrified silence, and he heard Clare gasp. Then Michael shouted, "You're lying!"

As Michael's finger tightened on the trigger, Clare cried out desperately, "No! I beg you, don't do this."

The urgency of her plea caused Michael to hesitate, his face reflecting the struggle raging inside him.

Swiftly Nicholas said, "Damn it, Michael, we've known each other for twenty years, and for most of that time we were closer than brothers. Don't you owe me a chance to be heard?"

The wildness faded a little, though Michael didn't lower the pistol. "Go ahead then, but don't expect to change my mind."

Nicholas drew a deep breath, knowing that he must be both calm and convincing. "As you know, my grandfather arranged the marriage to secure the succession. Once I met Caroline, I agreed to the match quite willingly. But the marriage was a lie from the start. When I made my offer, she tearfully confessed that she was not a virgin—that an older man, a friend of the family, had seduced her when she was fifteen years old. She wept very prettily, and was so convincing that I would have called her seducer out if she hadn't said the man was already dead.

"I was willing to overlook what had happened, yet after we married, I began to wonder if she had told me the truth—she was remarkably skilled for a girl who claimed to be the next thing to a virgin. At the very least, she had had a serious affair. I didn't like the idea that she had lied, but women have never had the freedom to sin that men have. I decided that Caroline thought that she had to conceal the truth in order to make a respectable marriage."

The planes of his face went taut when he thought of his gullibility. "I wanted to make excuses for her. She said that she loved me, you see, and she was so responsive that it was easy to believe her. And I . . . I don't know if I loved her, but I wanted to." Nicholas started to say more, then cut himself off; he would rather be shot than reveal more of himself.

Returning to the safer topic of his wife's behavior, he said, "I thought we had a good marriage until the night I went to her bed and found love bites on her breasts. She made no attempt to deny her infidelity. Instead, she laughed and said that she didn't expect fidelity of me, and I shouldn't expect it of her. She claimed to know how to prevent conception, and gave me her word that she would not bear a child that was not mine."

Once again he felt the disgust that had swept through him when he realized that the marriage he had begun to need was a travesty. "I flatly refused to accept those conditions. Thinking she could change my mind, she tried to seduce me. When I refused, she became furious, saying that no man had ever left her, and swearing that she would make me regret it. And she did. Christ, she did." He caught Michael's gaze with his own. "That little scene took place in April of 1809. Would it be fair to say that her love for you overcame her moral scruples about adultery within a few weeks of that night?"

The grayness of Michael's face was answer enough.

Nicholas took an unobtrusive step closer to Michael before continuing. "I packed her off to Aberdare and stayed in London myself. In retrospect, I should have been suspicious of how tamely she went, but I was too confused to think clearly. After a spell of trying to find the meaning of life in bottles and boudoirs, I decided that it was time to go to Aberdare and talk to Caroline. I thought that she might have had a change of heart and we could try to cobble the marriage together again.

"Instead, it was a classic theatrical farce: the foolish husband returning home unexpectedly and finding his wife in bed with another man. And the other man was my grandfather."

It was betrayal beyond his worst nightmares, and even now his stomach knotted with remembered horror. "They both laughed at me while the old earl happily explained how clever he had been. Very like Madoc, now that I think about it. From the beginning, my grandfather had despised my Gypsy blood and schemed for a way to get around it. He was hampered by the long illness of his first wife, but as soon as she died, he married again. However, Emily failed to conceive, in spite of his best efforts."

"You're lying," Michael said tightly. "Why should your grandfather go to such efforts to have another son when you would inherit anyhow?"

"You underestimate his ingenuity," Nicholas said dryly. "He prepared a set of obviously false documents about the marriage of my parents and my own birth. If he had managed to sire another son, he would have destroyed the real papers and taken the false ones to a lawyer, saying sorrowfully that his desire for an heir had encouraged him to believe that I was legitimate, but he could deceive himself no longer. I would have been disinherited and thrown out like the piece of rubbish he always thought I was."

Clare made a soft exclamation. "Those were the duplicate documents I discovered in the family Bible—the ones you burned."

He glanced at her. "You understand now why I was angry?" Turning to Michael again, he went on, "But he didn't manage to impregnate Emily, so he had to find another way to cut me out. He had always been a lusty old bull, though he was discreet about his affairs—he didn't want to jeopardize his reputation for piety. Since Caroline was already his mistress, he came up with the notion of marrying her to me. She probably agreed because the sheer decadence of the arrangement titillated her. Bloody hell, she might have suggested it herself.

"The reason my grandfather was so willing to explain all this to me was because Caroline had just told him she was pregnant. He was triumphant, absolutely convinced that it was his child and male, so my Gypsy blood would disappear from the Davies line. Though he couldn't stop me from inheriting, when I died I would be succeeded by my grandfather's son. Charming little scheme, wasn't it?" Nicholas's voice became sardonic. "He went on to say how clever Caroline was, and how she had taken precautions to insure that she would not become pregnant by me. My guess is that since he failed with Emily, the child was probably yours, not that it matters.

"If ever I was to commit murder, it would have been that night. But I didn't lay a hand on either of them. Instead, I said that I was going to take Emily to London. Then she and I would institute the two ugliest divorce suits in British history so that my grandfather and Caroline would be revealed for what they were. I had inherited money from my grandmother, so I was in a financial position to do it."

His hands clenched. "Perhaps I could be accused of causing my grandfather's death. Adultery, betrayal, and incest didn't bother him, but apparently the threat of exposure triggered a heart seizure almost as soon as I left the room to go to Emily. He died in his own bedchamber. I think Caroline helped him there to conceal their misconduct. Then she took her jewels and abandoned her lover and went tearing off into the storm to you, as you were clearly the best choice left.

"Even in death, her luck held. When my grandfather's valet came to inform Emily that her husband was dying, he found us together, Emily in her nightgown. So she and I got the accusation of adultery, and Caroline died with the reputation of the saintly, injured wife."

"You're lying," Michael said again, his face ashen. "You're making this up to conceal your own crimes."

Clare spoke up, her voice soft. "Lord Michael, I am Nich-

olas's wife now. Our courtship was a difficult one, and
many men might have been driven to violence. But not
Nicholas. I, who know him better than anyone, swear that
he could never abuse a woman the way Caroline claimed.''

As Michael wavered, Nicholas began walking toward him,
one step at a time. ''In all the years we've known each
other, did I ever lie to you?'' He stopped moving and held
his breath when wildness flared in the green eyes again.

''Not that I know of,'' Michael said hoarsely, ''but I saw
you lie to others. You would spin outrageous tales about
being an Indian prince, or a Turkish warrior, or God knows
what else. Later we would laugh about how convincing you
were. You were so persuasive that one of the most avari-
cious courtesans in London bedded you for free because she
thought you were royalty. Why should I believe you now?''

''Those were innocent games. I don't lie to friends.''
Nicholas began moving slowly forward again. ''Christ, if I
were lying, do you think I would make up a tale so utterly
humiliating? To be cuckolded by my own grandfather! Not
only is the very idea obscene, it makes me look like a weak
fool. I preferred to be thought a monster whose wicked selfishness had destroyed his own family.''

A last step brought him face to face with the other man.
''When I left Britain, I didn't think I would ever come back.
But running away didn't take away my pain, any more than
returning to the army took away yours. Murder won't help,
either.'' He held out his hand. ''Give me the pistol.''

Michael took a step back and the gun sagged toward the
ground. His face was a deathly gray and he was shaking,
like a man being torn apart from within.

Quietly Nicholas took the weapon from the other man's
unresisting hand. After unloading it, he tossed it aside.

Michael crumpled in on himself, folding to the ground
and burying his face in his hands. ''I knew that what I was
doing was utterly wrong,'' he said with anguish. ''Yet I
couldn't keep away from her, even though it meant betray-
ing everything I believed.''

Clare crossed the grass and knelt beside him. ''To love
and be loved is the most powerful of human needs,'' she
said with deep compassion. ''The fact that Caroline was

unworthy of your love was tragedy, not a crime." Gently she took his hands in hers. "It was a terrible thing to be caught between two loyalties, but that's over now. Don't torture yourself any longer."

"What I did was unforgivable," he said dully.

"Nothing is unforgivable if there is true repentance."

She spoke with a power that reminded Nicholas of her father. Her kindness and warm certainty were balm to the soul, and he felt his own bitterness begin to dissolve. What was done, was done; he must not let anger poison his life with Clare.

For Michael it was harder. He raised his head, tears marking his gaunt cheeks. "In London I called you a whore, and I came within a hair's breadth of killing your husband. Can you forgive that? I can't."

"But you didn't do it." Clare brushed his hair back as if he were one of her schoolchildren. "Deeds are what matter. No matter how hard you tried, you couldn't force yourself to commit that ultimate betrayal of your friendship." She cast an appealing glance up at Nicholas, silently asking him to help.

Nicholas's fists tightened. It hurt, badly, to know that one of his closest friends had been Caroline's lover. It had been easier to accept madness than betrayal. Yet as he studied Michael's tormented face, he felt unexpected pity. Though Caroline had put Nicholas through hell, he had never had to suffer the bitter self-reproach that was shattering Michael.

He sighed and knelt beside the other man. "Caroline was the most convincing liar I've ever met, and she made fools of all of us. I never loved her as you did, yet even so, she almost destroyed me. She did her best to wreck our friendship, too, because she knew how much it meant to me. Will you let her have that success beyond the grave?" Clare still held Michael's hand, so Nicholas laid his own on top of both. "I've missed you, Michael. We've all missed you. It's time to come home."

Michael made a choked sound. Then his hand turned and grasped Nicholas's with desperate strength.

The three sat like that for a long time. Nicholas sent his mind back, past violence and betrayal, to the best memories of his long friendship with Michael. As a foreign-looking schoolboy who didn't fit into the smug world of Eton, Nicholas had needed his friends badly. Michael had been a rock—utterly loyal, and utterly reliable. As dusk enfolded them, the warmth of those memories dissolved Nicholas's anger; he hoped that some of the warmth of that shared past was reaching the other man.

Finally Michael took a deep breath and lifted his head. "Nicholas, can you forgive what I've done?" he said with stark, painful humility. "If the positions were reversed and you had been involved with my wife, I don't know if I could."

"We're different in many ways—that's part of the point of friendship. Besides, though you considered killing me, you didn't. Instead, you saved my life, and that of Clare. For that, I can forgive anything." Nicholas held out his hand. "Pax?"

After a moment of hesitation, Michael shook it, his grip ferociously tight, as if he were grasping a lifeline that had dropped into hell. "Pax. And . . . thank you, Nicholas. You're a better man than I."

"I doubt it, but I do know that it's easier to forgive when one has a full heart." His gaze touched Clare.

Movements stiff, Michael got to his feet. In a heartbreaking attempt at humor, he said, "What does one do after making a supreme fool of oneself?"

Nicholas stood and helped Clare up. "One gets on with life. Show me a man who has never made a fool of himself and I'll show you someone who is supremely boring."

"In that case, I should be the most interesting man in Britain," Michael said wearily.

Since the evening was getting cool, Nicholas retrieved his coat and draped it around Clare's shoulders. She accepted it gratefully, though she winced as the weight of the fabric brushed her injured arm. Glancing at Michael, she said, "Come to Aberdare tonight, so you don't have to be alone."

Michael hesitated a moment, then shook his head. "Thank you, Lady Aberdare, but I think I need some aloneness now."

"Call me Clare, please—we've gone beyond formality."

Brows knit, she studied his face. "Will you dine with us tomorrow? I'd like to meet you under normal conditions instead of drenched in high melodrama."

Seeing Michael's uncertainty, Nicholas said, "Please come. It's a happy house now." He put a light hand on Clare's shoulder.

"If you're sure." Michael rubbed his temple tiredly. "You two go home now. I'll inform the authorities and take care of the bodies, since I'm experienced at cleaning up after battles." His voice grew a little stronger at the prospect of useful activity. "I imagine the magistrate will want to talk to you, but not until tomorrow."

"Will you take care of Clare's horse? I want to carry her with me," Nicholas said.

Michael nodded. "Of course. I'll bring it tomorrow."

Nicholas helped Clare onto his mount, then swung up behind her and turned home. He suspected that she might have found it easier to ride alone, but he had a primitive need to have her close, and she must have felt the same. The warm, yielding weight of her body helped dispel the terror he had felt when he had feared he would lose her.

They were almost home before he spoke. "Now you know the whole sordid story."

Her head moved against his shoulder as she nodded. "It's ironic. For all your grandfather's pride in his exalted ancestry, you were wiser, more civilized, more generous. What a pity that he couldn't see you for the extraordinary man you are."

"I don't know if I'm extraordinary, but it's true that he never saw me. I was an unfortunate necessity, a compilation of the worst qualities of my wayward father and my impossible Gypsy mother. As I said once before, as an heir he considered me better than nothing—but only just."

"How did you survive such hatred?"

Nicholas shrugged. "Once I realized that his contempt had nothing to do with me, I let it blow by like the wind. Most of the time I managed to be happy in spite of him."

Her arms tightened. "Michael is easier to understand— he *had* to believe in Caroline. To betray a friend was despicable—to acknowledge that he had done so for a woman who was utterly unworthy would have been intolerable.''

"Though he would have scoffed at the idea, he needed love a great deal, and that made him vulnerable to Caroline's wiles," Nicholas said. "Poor devil. It's amazing he survived her."

"He's a strong man," Clare said, "and someday he'll be happy again. But I can't understand Caroline at all." Her fingers caressed the small of his back. "How could a woman want other lovers when she had you!"

He laughed a little. "You're wonderfully comforting." He glanced down at the dark head nestled against his shoulder. "You've changed in the last fortnight. You seem more serene. I'd like to think it's a result of my irresistible charm, but I suspect there's more to it."

"There is." She hesitated. "It's hard to explain, but when I admitted to myself that I loved you, it resolved my spiritual failings as well. I finally feel the sense of inner connection that I longed for, and love was the key."

His arm tightened around her. "I'm so glad," he said softly. "Someday, I want to hear more about that."

But not yet, for they had reached Aberdare. Leaving his horse to a groom, Nicholas carried Clare into the house and right up to their room. She protested, "I'm not hurt that badly."

"I'm not taking any chances." After laying her on the bed, he cleaned her wound with brandy, then applied an herbal poultice. "A Gypsy remedy," he explained as he bandaged her arm again. "I keep a variety of them around. This one will prevent infection, and one of the ingredients reduces pain as well. Tomorrow we'll get a doctor out here to check you over."

"You know the most useful things." She made a mental note to get the recipes for his remedies later. "It already hurts less."

"Now you should get some rest."

"Not yet. Since this seems to be the day for exposing old secrets, there's one more." She sat up and took his hand, then repeated the story of Marta, and why she had given away her son.

As he listened, Nicholas became very still and his face shuttered, so Clare could not read his reaction. When she finished speaking, she went to her dresser and got the leather pouch Keja had given her. Then she returned to stand by him.

"Your grandfather and Caroline betrayed you, but not Marta," Clare said quietly. "According to Keja, Marta wanted me to be the one to explain, because another woman would know that a mother would always do the best she could for her child. Marta loved you, and she left you everything she had of value." She opened the pouch and poured the contents across the counterpane.

Bouncing among the guineas was an ornate gold band that Clare had not noticed before. Nicholas lifted the ring and turned it in his fingers. "My mother's wedding band." His hand tightened around it. "I wish to God I had known she was ill."

"Would you have let her leave you if you had known?"

He thought, then shook his head. "No, we were very close, which was why it was so devastating to think she could sell me. But if she was dying, my place was with her."

"She might have feared that you would contract her disease. Also, if you had been with her when she died, would the Rom have taken you to your father's family?"

This time there was no hesitation in his reply. "Never. They would consider it indecent to turn a Romany child over to a Gorgio, even a half-blood like me."

"So in order to fulfill her promise to your father, she had no other choice but to act as she did."

He tried to smile. "My mother was right to know that another woman would understand. Or rather, that you would understand and be able to explain it to me." He closed his eyes and a pulse beat visibly in his throat.

She drew him into her arms, his head resting against her breasts as he absorbed the facts that changed his past. Finally he murmured, "It's strange—whenever I thought of my mother, it hurt. It still hurts, but in an entirely different way."

"Better or worse?"

He sighed. "Better, I suppose. Though I'm mourning her death, I can believe in my childhood again."

She stroked his hair. "Are you sorry that she didn't leave you with the Rom?"

There was a long silence before he said slowly, "I might have been happier. Certainly my life would have been simpler. Yet, it's like Adam eating the apple—once there is knowledge of a wider world, it's impossible to imagine going back." He raised his head and caught her gaze with his. "And if I had stayed with the Rom, I never would have met you."

Suddenly shy, she said, "Did you mean what you said earlier, before you kissed me? Or was that only part of your attempt to distract Madoc?"

His face eased. "I meant it." He pulled her down so that she was sitting on the bed next to him. "It's remarkable how the prospect of death focuses the mind. Almost as soon as you came to Aberdare, I was determined not to allow you to leave. That's why I threatened to withdraw my aid whenever you talked of going away—it was the only tactic I had to persuade you to stay. My desire to thwart my grandfather's wishes was so strong that the obvious way of keeping you never occurred to me."

"You mean by marriage?"

He unpinned her hair and buried his fingers in the loose tresses. "Exactly. Notice how quickly I insisted on a wedding after we became lovers? I didn't dare wait, because if we learned that you weren't with child, I wouldn't have had the excuse to marry you. Apparently my devious mind had already concluded that you would never become my mistress, so I needed an excuse to honorably reverse my vow not to marry."

As delight bubbled through her, she began to laugh. "You did accept the idea of marriage with amazing ease."

"Not the idea of marriage—the idea of *you*." He tipped her face up, his eyes dark and soft as black velvet. "I think I always knew that if I won your loyalty, you would never betray me. And I was right, wasn't I? Today you risked your life for mine." His mouth quirked wryly. "I guess I've been looking for that kind of loyalty all my life. But don't ever let me catch you doing that again. If Wilkins's bullet had hit a couple of inches lower . . ." He shuddered.

"But it didn't." She touched his cheek "Actually, you've had quite a good day. We're both alive, you're finally free of your grandfather and Caroline, and you've regained your mother and Michael."

He looked startled. "When you put it that way, it's been a magnificent day."

"I think I can think of a way to make it ever better." She regarded him thoughtfully. "My arm scarcely hurts at all."

He began laughing. "Do you mean what I think you do, you shameless wench?"

"Yes," she said, unrepentant. "I want to feel you inside me, my love. After coming so near to death, I want to celebrate life."

He bent his head and kissed her, his mouth warm with tenderness. "I love you, my dear schoolmistress. In fact, I would be delighted to experience another lesson in love right now. You're sure your arm isn't too sore?"

Laughing, she leaned back on the bed, pulling him down with her. "If you kiss me again, I won't notice it at all."

He made love to her gently, as if she were the most precious being on earth. As her lover, he had ravished her senses. This time he ravished her soul, for he held nothing back. And neither did she. Spirit to spirit and flesh to flesh, together they found the closeness she had dreamed of, and the reality exceeded her hopes as the sun exceeds a candle.

The Fallen Angel had come home.

Epilogue

August 1814

IT WAS the grandest celebration in the history of the Penreith mine. In fact, it might have been the grandest occasion any mine had ever seen. As Clare and Nicholas rode smoothly down in the new steam lift, along with a dozen other guests, they heard music floating up the shaft, carrying over the sound of the new Watts pumping engine.

It had been Michael's idea to celebrate the pit improvements with an underground reception to which everyone in the valley was invited. The large gallery at the base of the lift was brilliant with flowers and candles, and the crowd was overflowing into nearby tunnels. People were already busy at the refreshment tables, with children swarming five deep around the sweets.

As the musicians struck up a country tune, couples began to dance. Clare noticed that some of them were Methodists; it was hard to think of dancing in a coal mine as sin. Inevitably other guests started to sing lustily. The echoes of voices from stone walls made Clare think of the choir she had heard in Westminster Abbey, and the comparison did not reflect badly on the Welsh.

As they climbed from the lift, Michael came to greet them, a smile on his face. He had put on weight and looked so healthy and relaxed that it was hard to remember the tormented man he had been three months earlier. "What do you think of the pit now?"

"The place looks amazingly civilized," Nicholas replied. "But what will you do with yourself now that everything is running so smoothly?"

"Don't worry—I'll think of something."

Clare said, "Have Rafe and Lucien arrived yet?"

"They reached Bryn Manor late last night." Michael chuckled. "Today, Lucien had to be forcibly dissuaded from taking apart the steam pump to see how it worked."

Clare grinned. In the months since Michael had ended his feud with Nicholas, she had seen the charm and strength of character that had won him such admirable friends. Though she knew that his four years of hell must have left scars, he was determinedly getting on with the business of living. She sensed that his friendship with Nicholas had been tempered by his long ordeal and had emerged stronger than it had been in the past.

She scanned the chamber and saw Lucien deep in conversation with the mine engineer. Closer to hand, Rafe was listening attentively to an earnest five-year-old girl.

"There's Rafe—leave it to him to find the prettiest blonde here." Nicholas glanced at Clare. "Do you want to say hello?"

"In a minute. I want to speak to Marged first."

"Don't go too far away," he ordered.

She smiled demurely. "No, my lord and master."

He gave her a highly indecent pat in a place where no one could see, then went off to talk to his friends. Clare found Marged placidly cleaning up the mess Huw had made when he ate too much marzipan and became ill.

Her task completed, Marged straightened and gave Clare a hug. "Who would have ever believed the old pit could be such fun? Mind, I'm glad Owen accepted Nicholas's offer to be foreman at the slate quarry. There are less opportunities for disaster." She glanced around the stone chamber to where Nicholas, Michael, Lucien, and Rafe had drawn together. "They're still the four best-looking men I've ever seen," she said thoughtfully. "Except for Owen, of course."

They talked for a few minutes, until a gaggle of children came up and carried Marged off. Clare watched them go a little wistfully. There were times when she missed being a full-time teacher, but she didn't seem to have any trouble keeping busy. And now that she had Nicholas's deep purse to plunder, she was able to help people on a broader scale. There were no more hungry children in Penreith, and the valley was becoming the prosperous, happy place she had dreamed of.

She drifted across the chamber toward Nicholas, stopping to talk with friends along the way. Whatever resentment had been engendered by her marrying above herself seemed to have gone away, since she and her husband were clearly part of the community.

Even though she approached Nicholas from behind, he sensed her presence. Without looking, he reached back and pulled her in front of him, then linked his arms around her waist. She relaxed against him, feeling as if she had come home. Tonight, she thought dreamily, she would tell Nicholas that she was almost sure that the next Gypsy Earl was on the way.

Lucien and Rafe greeted Clare warmly before returning to their fanciful discussion. Rafe declared, "Everyone needs to believe in something. I, for one, believe that since life is invariably fatal, one should at least live it with style."

Lucien offered, "Though I have great respect for honesty, I believe that deviousness is an underrated talent."

"I believe in honor," Michael said promptly, "and the relaxing power of a good cigar."

Clare's eyes gleamed. "I believe that women are the equal of men."

The Fallen Angels looked alarmed. "She's dangerous, Nicholas. You'd better keep her happy," Rafe said.

Nicholas laughed. "I intend to. And as to what I believe in . . ." He thought a moment. "I believe in penguins . . ."

"Not an easy thing to believe in even when one has seen the beasts," Lucien interjected.

Nicholas grinned. ". . . and friendship." His arms tightened around Clare's waist. "And most of all, I believe in love."

Author's Note

For those who love historical trivia as much as I do:

The first slate-topped billiard table was manufactured by John Thurston in London in 1826. For decades, slate from South Wales was the preferred material. No doubt Thurston got the idea from Clare and Nicholas.

The leather cue tip was invented by a French infantry captain called Mingaud, somewhere between 1807 and 1820. He was in jail at the time, which gave him plenty of time to practice. In fact, when his sentence was up, he asked to stay in the slammer for another month while he practiced his technique. Permission was granted. (Some people will do anything for a free table.) On his release, he promptly turned professional and became the world's first exhibition billiard player, amazing everyone with his skill.

At the time *Thunder and Roses* is set, the British coal industry was on the brink of the great expansion that created the famous Welsh mining communities. In 1815, the Davy safety lamp was invented; it protected miners from the explosive effects of firedamp, which was a mixture of air and methane. The Methodist societies, with their spiritual passion and concern for segments of society neglected by the established church, were a powerful moral influence among the miners.

The oddest bits of mining lore in the book are the ones that really happened: blind miners, wire silver, and the miner who sacrificed himself because he knew that he would go to heaven, but he was worried about the soul of his colleague. (It happened in Cornwall, and the miner miraculously lived to explain why.)

I'd like to give special thanks to Carol Hanlon and Dean Stucker, geologist and mining engineer respectively, for helping me with mining sequences.

As for the penguins—well, why not?

Don't go to bed without Romance!

💙 Contemporaries
💙 Historicals
💙 Suspense
💙 Futuristic

🖎 Book Reviews
🖎 Ratings
🖎 Forthcoming Titles
🖎 Author Profiles

Read **Romantic Times**
your guide to the next two months' best books.
100 page bi-monthly magazine • 6 Issues $14.95

Send your order to: Romantic Times,
163 Joralemon St., Brooklyn Hts., NY 11201

I enclose $_____ in ☐ check ☐ money order

Card #_____ Exp. Date_____

Signature_____

Name_____

Address_____

City_____ State_____ Zip_____

Please allow at least 8 weeks for delivery.
Offer subject to change or withdrawal without notice.

*B*UY TWO TOPAZ BOOKS AND GET ONE FREE ROMANCE NOVEL!

With just two purchases of Topaz books, you'll be able to receive one romance novel free from the list below. Just send us two proofs of purchase* along with the coupon below, and the romance of your choice will be on its way to you! (subject to availability)

Check title you wish to receive:

☐ *TOUCHED BY MAGIC*
Patricia Rice
0-451-40298-7/$4.99

☐ *THE SILVERY MOON*
Edith Layton
0-451-40285-5/$4.99

☐ *WINTER ROSES*
Anita Mills
0-451-40292-8/$4.99

☐ *THE GILDED CAGE*
Edith Layton
0-451-40264-2/$4.99

☐ *DANGEROUS MASQUERADE*
April Kihlstrom
0-451-17080-6/$3.99

☐ *THE DASHING MISS FAIRCHILD*
Emily Hendrickson
0-451-17127-6/$3.99

☐ *THE HIGHLY RESPECTABLE WIDOW*
Melinda McRae
0-451-17126-8/$3.99

☐ *REBEL DREAMS*
Patricia Rice
0-451-40272-3/$4.99

☐ *THE RECKLESS WAGER*
April Kihlstrom
0-451-17090-3/$3.99

☐ *LORD KANE'S KEEPSAKE*
Sandra Heath
0-451-17226-4/$3.99

☐ *THE CONTENTIOUS COUNTESS*
Irene Saunders
0-451-17276-0/$3.99

*Send in coupons, proof of purchase (register receipt & photocopy of UPC code from books) plus $1.50 postage and handling to:

TOPAZ 🔽 GIVEAWAY
Penguin USA, 375 Hudson Street, New York, NY 10014

NAME_____

ADDRESS_____ APT. #_____

CITY_____STATE_____ZIP_____